D0787438

ALOHA, MOZART

WAIMEA WILLIAMS

LUMINIS BOOKS

LUMINIS BOOKS
Published by Luminis Books
1950 East Greyhound Pass, #18, PMB 280,
Carmel, Indiana, 46033, U.S.A.
Copyright © Waimea Williams, 2013

Certain Hawaiian words such as *lei, hula, luau,* etc. have entered the world vocabulary and are not
italicized in this book or given now standard punctuation. Less familiar words are punctuated and
translated according to current use. Common place names such as Hawaii, Kauai, Oahu, and
Waikiki are left in their familiar form.

Cover design for *Aloha, Mozart* by Carol Colbath.

Hardcover ISBN: 978-1-935462-66-8
Paperback ISBN: 978-1-935462-63-7

Printed in the United States of America

10 9 8 7 6 5 4 3 2 1

Advance praise for *Aloha, Mozart:*

"Few know the secrets of Salzburg in 1968: the glamorous, high-stakes world of young competitors for renown in classical music. The most wonderful reward of the novel is the immersion it provides in a beautiful old culture, the cuisine and the architecture and the customs and the high art, as well as the corruption, of a great civilization."
—Louis B. Jones, author of *Ordinary Money, Particles and Luck, California's Over,* and *Radiance*

"With this poetic debut novel—set in 20th century Hawai'i, Manhattan, and Salzburg—Waimea Williams delivers the bittersweet story of Maile Manoa. Gorgeously conceived and enacted and textured, this richly pleated story unfolds with dark and thrilling suspense."
—Al Young, California poet laureate, author of more than 25 books; poems and novels

"*Aloha, Mozart* really got under my skin; the knowing narrative voice, the quiet passion and intensity of the story, the sensuality with which Williams evokes place. I came away feeling it took me to places I'd never been, but recognized completely. The only thing this wonderful novel lacks is a soundtrack."
—Cai Emmons, author of *The Stylist* and *His Mother's Son*

To teachers, for passing on knowledge that must be learned early in life and at the start of a career.

Acknowledgments

It's been a very long road. Gratitude for taking the trip with me goes…

To my agent April Eberhardt, who manages to be both gracious and tenacious.
To Luminis Books for treating a first novel with care and providing a chance to be heard.
To the Ragdale Foundation for its generosity.
To the Squaw Valley Community of Writers, for years of support and kindness. Mahalo nui loa.
To Richard Ford, Robert Stone, Oakley Hall, and Ann Close, for encouragement when I was green.
To the Breadloaf and Napa Valley conferences for scholarships.
To Roger Jellinek for over a decade of support and friendship.
To Joy Johannessen, a brilliant editor who asked all the right questions.
To teachers and musicians in Hawaii and Salzburg, gone now and yet not:
Shigeru Hotoke, Patsy Saiki, Hanna Ludwig, Paul Schilhawsky, Robert Kuppelwieser, Erik Werba, Kumu John Keolamaka'āinana Lake.
To the Austrian government for giving support to a foreign student.
To Donna Levin of San Francisco for years of sharing her devotion to novels and fiction.
To present day friends outside the field of writing who remain sources of inspiration:
Mahea Kauka Wong, Kaponoi'ai Molitau, Mahi'ai Cummings.

Aloha mai no, aloha aku. Love given is love returned.
Aia no ka mea e mele ana. Let the singer select the song.
—*'Ōlelo No'eau, Hawaiian Proverbs,* M.K. Pukui

Nichts ist gefährligher als eine schöne Melodie. Nothing is more dangerous than a beautiful melody.
—Frederich Nietzsche, *Der Fall Wagner*

1

MAILE MANOA'S SINGING came from the ocean, people said, from the mountains, from flowers. It floated on the wind like a message sent to each listener, a voice of ancient beauty, ancient power. Some claimed that dogs and horses stopped eating to listen to her, chickens in the yard, even sharks out beyond the reef. She knew all the verses to more than a hundred songs and hymns, and could pull a melody out of the air, pitch perfect, rhythm perfect, as if capturing a spirit and releasing it to share. Impressive for a girl of eleven, but she didn't consider herself special. Singing was simply something she did.

One afternoon Maile's sixth-grade teacher at Lihue Grammar School pulled a black disk from an album of records in brown paper sleeves. "Art and music illuminate the world," he told the class. "This is music none of you have heard, from my own collection. It was composed by a man named Verdi."

The class quieted in expectation. Records were made on the mainland and came to Hawaii by ship, a journey of two thousand five hundred miles. On the outer island of Kauai, the only records in the school library were recitations of the multiplication tables for students who needed help with arithmetic.

The teacher set the disk to spinning on a small phonograph and lowered the arm. "Now," he said, "imagine you are in ancient Egypt. On the banks of a river. It's nighttime." The needle made contact. From the speaker came scraping orchestral sounds, a whirring of flute tones, then a voice, slow, strong, high-pitched: "Oooo pa-treee-aa mee-a . . . "

The students stiffened in surprise. Maile sat forward. Her long black braid swung over one shoulder, and tiny hairs at the back of her neck stood up. The sounds ground onward, on instruments she couldn't name, in a melody that kept getting longer, more complicated, unlike any of the songs she knew. Some lady screaming, she thought. Why put that on a record?

The teacher watched his pupils wincing and frowning. He raised the phonograph arm and regarded them with a stare of patient disappointment. This music, he explained, came from a great country in Europe, Italy, which they had just studied, and which also had great art, all those scenes from the Bible, remember? Yes, they could locate Rome on the wall map, and they recalled the paintings of Abraham's Sacrifice and the Slaughter of the Innocents. They remembered pyramids, pharaohs, and mummies, but could make no connection to the music their teacher had tried to give them. Finally he excused them a few minutes early. They picked up their books in silence and bolted out to the playground to wait for the last bell.

The twenty students in Maile's class were a typical outer-island combination of Japanese, Filipinos, mixed-blood Hawaiians, and a few Caucasian children of plantation owners. Their school was bordered on three sides by fields of high green sugarcane topped by thick clusters of white tassels. To the south the sugar mill's smokestack poked into the blue sky. A stream of soot flakes drifted down onto the playground as the students traded jeers and hoots at a safe distance from their teacher: "Oooo pa-tree-a!" Anyone with Caucasian ancestors was singled out to explain the weird music, the more white blood the better. The son of a plantation owner said his ancestors were American, not Italian. The daughter of an Irish rancher sided with him. Maile was Hawaiian-Chinese-German, and a girl of Japanese ancestry asked her, "You got *haole* blood, you know wat's 'at music, e?"

"S'posed to be singing," Maile said.

"Not!" a Filipino boy shouted, and the challenge was passed to other students who were part Portuguese, Spanish, Scottish. All refused any connection to the teacher's music.

What bothered Maile most was the unfamiliarity of the sounds. Everyone she knew played some kind of instrument. Every town on the island was full of musicians. Guitars and ukuleles were common, although sharkskin temple drums had disappeared long ago, and violins were unknown. From Nāwiliwili to Hā'ena, upright pianos in assembly halls were in constant use, no matter how rusted and warped. A string bass could always be borrowed or made from a bucket and a length of clothesline. Few families owned a radio or record player, although people heard music all week: "My Country 'Tis of Thee" at school, backyard Waikiki hula after work, Japanese farm ditties, jump rope chants, blunt Protestant hymns on Sunday in English and Hawaiian. Nothing was even close to this Vur-dee.

The bell rang and the students scattered off the playground. Maile headed toward Kanemā'ulu village, crossing the bridge over the railroad yard at the sugar mill. Under the trestle a train from the cane fields chuffa-chuffa-chuffed toward the unloading dock. On the outside wall of the mill the exposed hooks of the cane-washing machinery clattered in an exciting rhythm. From inside came the creak and screech of the massive cane crushers. Maile listened to the cacophony and heard underneath it the opening melody on the record, the high, powerful voice. Italy and Egypt.

Other than schoolbooks, Maile's only link to the world beyond Kauai was her grandmother's radio. The Korean War was nearly over, but Tūtū still listened faithfully for news of local soldiers. Reception was often spotty, though at times the radio could pick up Honolulu stations from a hundred miles away across the rough Ka'ie'iewaho channel. Programs originated in distant New York, the Empire State, where people were Americans. Before Maile was born, the radio had come by freighter from San Francisco all the way to Nāwiliwili harbor. Since then it had stood in the front room of her grandmother's small house, an object of veneration and suspicion, cared for like an infant, fed with electricity, its case dusted regularly and polished with *kukui* nut oil.

When Maile got home, Tūtū was outside grating coconut meat and chatting with neighbors. She wouldn't turn on the radio for another two hours, and then only for twenty minutes of local news, because on Wednesdays the next show was *Fibber McGee and Molly*, a mainland comedy no one understood.

Maile fed the rabbits and the ducks. Inside the house she cut lengths of string to mend a scoop net for shrimp. With slow precision she completed a page of arithmetic homework. She was *hānai*, by tradition adopted at birth by Tūtū so her grandmother wouldn't be lonely when Maile's parents moved to Honolulu to find jobs that paid cash money. She hadn't seen her family since, because only plantation own-

3

ers could afford traveling to other islands to visit relatives. The Manoa clan did not write letters or make phone calls, except at Christmas or to report a death. There were now nine children, but Maile didn't really miss the parents and siblings she had never known. She was the one who waded onto the reef to catch Tūtū's favorite squid, who sat next to her in church with the adults, who found her eyeglasses when they went missing, and was rewarded with a warm embrace and a hand that smoothed her hair. Having Tūtū to herself felt better than sharing a mother and father with a crowd of brothers and sisters, like most children had to do.

From out in the yard came squawking: Paka-paka-paaaaa! Pak, pak!

The old rooster Maile was supposed to catch, kill, pluck, and clean for dinner. Tough meat needed to stew until dark. She groaned and headed for the kitchen to heat water for scalding feathers. From nearby came another sound, the soft haaa . . . haaa of her grandmother's broom sweeping fish scales from the packed clay by the back door. Together the sighing and stabbing tones made a tantalizing combination: chicken and broom, each with a pattern predictable enough almost to form a melody. The schoolteacher's strange music stirred under her skin. Why would anyone go to the trouble of making a record unless it meant something to a lot of people?

With the stealth of a river crab, Maile turned away from the stove. She was not allowed to enter the front room until five o'clock, when Tūtū sat down for the news, and only after washing her hands and feet of the red dust that drifted in from the cane fields. The room and the radio were otherwise taboo. Tūtū's Hawaiian-language Bible was *kapu* too, along with touching the chiefly birthstones at Wailua river, going near a burial cave, or talking loudly at an ancient temple. The limitless power of *kapu* also meant never sassing a teacher and always sharing food. Life on Kauai had one basic rule: Everything wrong came from greed and me-only, and everything right began with respect and sharing. Long ago Maile had accepted that "I want" came last. Still, she knew by now that the world was not simply separated into good and bad. There were always shadings, although balance had to be maintained. Mostly good with a little bad was okay, was the way life worked.

Paka-paka-paaak! Haaa . . . haaa . . .

She crept into the front room. In the far corner the radio stood on its thin wooden legs. Five times in the past two years she had secretly listened to strange songs, turned down very low. Wanting music was an itch inside her head, a place she couldn't reach. Besides, Tūtū's super-strict rule was for little kids, not a sixth grader. She glanced around, then gave the radio's brown knob a turn that produced a neat click. Its green eye pulsed with the silent rhythm of warming up. She bit her lips in concentration and advanced the dial past soft, crackling static, like schools of reef fish escaping a barracuda. Faint ukulele music faded in and out against a gentle whoop-whoop of background noise. She dialed on. Once there had been circus music, another time a melody played on what sounded like tiny bells.

A man's voice shot from the speaker: " . . . an unbelieeevable catch as the runner sliiiides into third, first out of the '53 Series!" She snapped off the radio. Rapid footsteps came through the kitchen. Tūtū entered the front room, broom in hand, her eyes lit with anger. "What you listen?" she demanded. "Tcha!"

Maile imagined leaping out the window, but that was too stupid for someone her age, and she considered excuses, bargaining, then slumped and turned around. "You old enough to know, *e?*" her grandmother said. Maile eyed Tūtū's bare feet, her curled broom with fish scales glinting in its bristles, her sun-bleached blue mu'umu'u, her thick hands, long arms, and wide shoulders, her smooth-skinned face with black eyes like oiled pebbles. The heap of white hair that made her taller than most men.

A prolonged squawk came from the yard: Paka-paka-pak! Maile flinched.

Tūtū assigned her extra chores for the rest of the week. "Go catch 'at sassy bird," she added, and gave her a swat with the broom like a reminder that naughty girls deserved spankings.

To save face, Maile sauntered outdoors, but knew that by nightfall everybody would be talking. She was not Tūtū's little sweetie, had to sort fish guts for days while her friends splashed in the surf. Because of the radio. Because she still had to obey little-kid rules.

Glumly Maile eyed the old rooster. It skittered under a low *noni* branch as if sensing its fate. "Ooo," she cooed to it, "pa-tree-ah . . ." She inched toward the *noni* tree, repeating the phrase. For a moment the bird stood hypnotized. Then it zigzagged through a tomato patch and flapped down to safety in a gulch full of *keawe* thorns. Now grabbing the rooster meant getting scratched bloody, or catching it with the repaired shrimp net, which would tear again. But if she could just reach a piano, she could pick out the entire song. Maybe even fill in some of the instrument parts in the background. The melody coursed in her head, a stream rushing down a steep hill.

She hurried through an avocado grove toward the church parish hall, but adults stood out front with brushes and cans of paint, covering black streaks of mold with a fresh coat of white. They would tell her to help them. She hung back out of sight and felt the melody slipping away. What came next, after the tune got complicated? —meee-aahh, something, something.

The minister and his wife were also painting the hall. There was a piano at their house, although used only for wedding and funeral receptions, which made it doubly *kapu* to children of any age. Maile was sure it would be safe if she just barely touched the keys. Nobody would hear that from a distance. She ran to the minister's house and called out, *"Hui!"* Only a saggy-eyed mongrel let out a mild snort of greeting.

Inside, she went to the front room and slid open the piano lid. In soft repetition she plinked a middle key, *O pa-tri-a*, then one note down, *mi-a*, one more note down, *da, da-da-da-da*, and another note down: *da*. To her delight the scrap of melody developed. Gradually she attached six more notes to it, reconstructing the song tone for tone. In her excitement and concentration she didn't notice that the dog had come inside, that people were entering the room behind her, the minister with paint on his hands, mothers and fathers, Tūtū, all of them silent.

MAILE HAD TO kill, pluck, and clean forty chickens for the luau that Sunday celebrating the first birthday of the minister's baby boy. She started at dawn. By noon she was too tired to complain, or even cry about not being asked to sing for the event. Tūtū helped by carrying the stinking remains to the garbage pit, but she didn't speak until after lunch, as Maile continued ripping out feathers. Life, Tūtū said, was *lōkahi*, balance, and for Maile that meant Hawaiian values, German-American good manners, and Chinese patience. Like everyone in her family, Maile possessed three spirits—ancestral, upper, and lower—in addition to the *mana* that came before birth and persisted after death. The clan was proud of being Hawaiian, and that heritage accounted for almost half her blood, but the other ancestors had to be honored as well.

As Tūtū talked, Maile nodded to avoid being scolded for resisting an old lesson. Her Hawaiian grandfather, dead for two years now, had been a strict Christian who forbade all talk of ancestors because they had been pagans; the old days and ways were junk. You stay with Jesus, he'd insisted to Maile, you watch out for the black devil on your left shoulder and respect the angel on your right. She yanked out pinfeathers with a pair of pliers and wondered why being any amount of Hawaiian was a matter of Kauai pride. Hawaiians had less of everything than the American descendants of missionaries and traders who owned the plantations.

"All gods and ancestors, they get respect," Tūtū said.

Again Maile nodded, although what she heard made little sense. Caucasians on Kauai were obvious outsiders who didn't share their land, yet they were magically smart and successful, blessed by God. Chinese were smart too, but they could be real stingy. Where did she fit in with her pieces of this and that? All *haole* or all Asian: not so good. All Hawaiian: good, as long as you weren't flat-out stupid, which could happen. Best was Hawaiian with a salting of *haole* and *Pake*. Yes, Tūtū, Maile promised, she would respect her ideal mixed heritage, but all she wanted was not to get caught next time she was tempted to break baby rules.

Two days after the luau Maile discovered that a neighbor's heavyweight fishing line could make spectacular bah-wing bah-woing noises. Its spirit begged to be let out for a run. Furtively she took the fishing line from a shed and strung long strands between trees for greater effect, being careful because the thick nylon was expensive. She sat down to wait for a breeze. On her left shoulder the devil she pictured as a cranky black chick began to hop up and down until its feathers stood straight out. A sudden wind rose, catching the lines and filling the air with fantastic sounds that made her head feel like a kite soaring up into a storm, music gone wild. An instant later the lines snapped and swirled into a giant knot, tangled beyond saving.

The following week Maile borrowed a fine ukulele without asking, no crime until she accidentally sat on it. The violations continued, serious and not so, each having to do with music. Some folks excused them because the girl had a singer's gift to reach people and trees and animals, even rocks and water. Others were less forgiving. Tūtū relaxed her rules, tightened them again, and was finally called to a meeting at the minister's house.

BY THE TIME the *sampan* left Nāwiliwili harbor, Maile was crying for her school friends, the minister's dog, the radio. Her best muʻumuʻu with the starched sleeve ruffles had already wilted. Beside her on the deck lay a heap of bananas, mangoes, dried fish, and jars of guava jam for her family in Honolulu.

From the dock Tūtū called out, "Jesus bless you, sweetie!" Maile wiped her eyes and scowled. Tūtū couldn't carry the fifty-pound bag of rice from the store anymore, and Maile could, but it had still been decided that the girl was too rascally for her own good. *Was spoil rotten, 'at's wat.* She needed her brothers and sisters. Tūtū accepted the decision with regret and made a phone call to Oahu that cost a whole dollar twenty cents. An exchange of children would take place.

As the *sampan* turned toward the ocean channel and picked up speed, the wind whipped Maile's hair across her face. "Remember where you born," she heard Tūtū shout. "Kauai folks, they different!" She shouted more in Hawaiian, something about *minamina*, regret, and *aloha pau 'ole*, unending love, her words lost in the slap-slap of choppy waves. Maile sobbed, no longer a temporary only child with a grandmother all to herself. She couldn't understand why music wasn't always a good thing, why it was also trouble, why everything in the entire world was always half of a pair—right and wrong, good and evil, *kapu* and okay.

Beyond the breakwater, the *sampan* passed the last high green cliffs that formed a protective crescent around the harbor. People standing on the dock shrank to the size of pebbles on a beach, then to grains of sand that disappeared among the pilings. Maile turned to stare at the open sea. Within her the lower spirit she called *pili* shivered with dread. She had seen only a few old photos of her parents. There was one phone call a year at Christmas, shouting "Hello" and "Howzit" to children and adults she couldn't picture. On the other side of the channel lay Honolulu, a city full of stacked-up buildings and swarms of cars that all went too fast. As soon as she landed she would be run down by drivers who didn't even know her name. The boat split a wave, and spray shot up, drenching her. She gasped and crouched behind the fish storage chest, hugging her knees as she waited for the hours to pass.

Half a day later at Kewalo Basin, several dozen relatives crowded onto the landing to greet the *sampan* from Kauai. The Manoa clan cried and sang for the nine-year-old son who was leaving, and kissed and hugged the almost-grown daughter who had arrived. Family members told Maile their names as they laughed and joked and wiped away tears. Children, elders, and adults carrying babies and Tūtū's gifts filed onto a city bus. Borrowed for two hours, an older boy told Maile, "It's special for us." She had never ridden a bus and tripped getting on. He snickered. An aunt swatted him.

The bus driver said to Maile, "I'm your father. You can call me Makua." He kissed her and gave her a *pīkake* lei, flowers usually reserved for adults. Maile beamed. The dainty jasmine buds took hours to pick and string. She was pulled away to sit in back with the children and teenagers, and they rode off singing songs about the beauties of Kauai's valleys and mountains, "Hanohano Hanalei," and "Nani Wale Lihue." Maile craned to look at the driver. "Makua," she knew, was short for *makuakane*, "father," like a Hawaiian version of Dad. So modern-sounding. She wondered where her mother was, and inhaled the intense fragrance of *pīkake*. New sounds assaulted her: the huffing of the bus, an airplane droning overhead, the whoosh of passing cars. Fast, so fast!

Partway through the city, Makua stopped at a large building and said, "Come, Maile." She got off with him and they were joined by everyone else who wasn't holding an infant. It happened only last night, he explained; her mother was in the hospital and needed an operation. Half the relatives took the stairs to the third floor. Maile rode an elevator for the first time, more curious than worried, and she entered a ward as large as the Lihue Grammar School cafeteria. With her family she stood around a bed to gaze down at a sleeping woman with brown skin and black hair. For a moment they watched the white sheet pulse with the slight, gentle motion of her breathing.

"*Pīkake*," the woman murmured, and opened her eyes. "I smell *pīkake*."

Maile stood paralyzed with importance, prepared to say hello, to take off the lei and give it to her mother, but a nurse came over and ordered the visitors to leave: This patient needed rest. No one was allowed a kiss or a final word, and they all trooped back to the bus.

At home more relatives waited. For Maile the weekend dissolved into a swarm of people who cooked, ate, sang and danced, told funny or boring stories, slept, played cards, washed dishes, and started over. The party flowed out into the road, where passersby joined in. "*E*, girl got a voice," people exclaimed when Maile sang for them. "*Hana hou*, one more time!" She was startled to meet a group of aunts who worked as musicians, something she felt sure that Tūtū did not know. On Kauai singing for money was a disgrace. If God gave you a good voice, the only thing to do was share it.

ON MONDAY, MAKUA went off to work. Ma stayed in the hospital. With school closed for the summer, Maile was just one of eight brothers and sisters still living at home, aged two to fifteen. None of them spent much time with Makua or knew much about either of their parents. Because, she soon realized, from sunup to sundown everybody was too busy: peeling, scraping, sorting and cleaning fruit, rice, fish, washing dishes, diapers, clothes, watching babies, little kids, old folks.

Each morning it was get up, grab a clean blouse before a sister put it on, pick bananas for breakfast, feed the baby first, you heard me, and go chase 'at mean dog come in again, *e?* Family members went to church, although Maile was surprised when several uncles lounged at home on Sundays and nothing was said. No one talked much about Jesus. After a month she felt that having a black chick and a white one on her shoulders was something only a first grader would believe.

The family lived in the Papakōlea neighborhood of winding streets spread out along the hot slopes of Punchbowl Crater, two miles by foot from downtown Honolulu. The area unsettled Maile, a packed community of unpainted houses on both sides of badly paved roads, home to clusters of mixed-race families. The Manoa clan occupied a one-story four-room house with additions built onto three sides. A constant stream of relatives from elsewhere on Oahu came to borrow a sewing machine, return a loaned guitar, make vats of mango jam. Aunties were in every room. Older sisters with boyfriends sat outside on a sprung couch, and silent teenagers repaired a junked car until long past midnight.

Maile ached for Tūtū. She wanted her own bed, not shared with little sisters, wanted a house for just two people, quiet enough to hear a breeze coming down from the mountains and rustling the leaves of all the different kinds of trees it passed through before reaching the *noni* branches where the chickens hid. Life at the edge of Honolulu felt like being part of a vast, ticking machine that could never be fully explored. Her relatives did not point out what was *kapu*. They didn't discuss *mana*. She was drawn to the huddles of older girls talking about their monthly *ma'i*, trading tips and secrets, although she wasn't yet a woman and had nothing to share. Sometimes at night when the house was quiet she hummed *O patria mia* and thought about the word "opera" and the name Verdi. During the day she was alert for similar music anywhere in Honolulu, but heard none.

FROM HER FIRST days in Papakōlea, Maile idolized her fourteen-year-old sister Jade, who considered herself more Chinese than Hawaiian or *haole*. Jade's only explanation was, "I pull my Oriental side." This impressed Maile, but Jade rejected her younger sister as a pest, and refused to explain the Chinese book and sticks she used to tell the future. Siblings closer to Maile's age deserted her to go off with neighborhood friends. In her loneliness she charmed babies with imitations of a machete whacking into a stem of bananas, an overripe papaya plunging to the ground, a lizard's peep-peepity-peep song as it flickered into a wall crack.

Her brother Hermann, thirteen, noticed and followed her around, demanding, "Think you special, e? Watchu know bout downtown, country doodoo-head?" He set chewing gum traps and slipped cockroaches into her hair. She chased him up a mango tree. He pelted her with rotten fruit and mocked her outer-island pidgin and her Standard English carefully learned in school. She sharpened a thumbnail to pinch him until his skin bled, furious and shamed because she couldn't talk like Honolulu kids: "E, we go spark cheerleaders," or "You chocho lips, no more da kine." She had never seen the football stadium, or tasted saimin soup with green onions and pink pork, or been downtown where everyone wore shoes. The only good thing about her new life was that the radio in the kitchen stayed on all day.

Among reports on sugar and pineapple production, news of ships and storms, from time to time Maile heard snatches of music from distant places: cowboy songs, jitterbug, jingles for selling soup and soap. One morning there was a chorus of people singing one word at high volume, "Hallelujah," over and over, voices rushing onward in complex rhythms, halting to sway down into a softer, slower mood, as if passing from a storm-swollen river to a quiet pool. An aunt paused in the kitchen, listened for a moment, then said with a sigh, "Fancy church music. Some mainland church." Not-our-kind-of-music, Maile knew, something as unattainable as the lives she saw in movies. There was an unknown world outside the crowded house, and she wanted to grab it with both hands, but she had no idea where to begin.

IN LATE AUGUST the entire household was roused just after dawn. Children were hustled into proper clothes and given fierce warnings to behave. Ma was finally leaving the hospital. Makua took off work to fetch her in his truck, and an hour later he carried his wife and the mother of their nine children inside to a room set up with only one bed. Siblings fought to be allowed to take in flowers and special treats that weren't eaten, to tell Ma stories and ask questions that weren't answered. As the girl who had never known her mother, Maile was easily elbowed aside. The older women regretted the absence of the one son living with Tūtū. Cancer, they whispered, the doctors cut off both Ma's *chi-chis* but it spread anyway. Got her eggs. Then, you know, no hope.

The dying took just a day. When the feet were cold, and the legs and torso, and the neck and face, and there was no sign of breath, the family elders began wailing, *"Auwe, auwe, ua hala!"* Their ancient howls embarrassed the teenagers and frightened the babies. At midmorning Ma's few possessions were distributed: an ivory-handled hairbrush, a thin gold bracelet with black enamel, worn by court members during the monarchy period; for Jade, a deep green pendant on a gold chain.

Maile received a small leather pouch with a silver quarter, on one side the Hawaiian coat of arms, on the other King Kalākaua's profile and the date 1883. She stared at it in confused disappointment. Makua told her that the coin had been his wedding gift to Ma, the only thing left from his grandfather, the German. "Now 'at quarter's worth real money," he added with tears in his eyes, "so you keep 'im safe, e?" Maile nodded, crushed not to have something as personal as the brush, which had strands of her mother's hair threaded in its bristles. She hid the pouch in a dresser, under the roach paper in the bottom drawer, which was hard to open and for that reason unused.

During the week, relatives from all over Oahu gathered, but Tūtū did not come from Kauai. The only music everyone wanted to hear was Maile singing "Aloha 'Oe," over and over, as though the melody that vanished so quickly into the air around them could be held on to. She sang as often as asked, sensing the brief power it gave her over Honolulu people, but she felt only shallow grief for Ma. Her own breasts had begun to grow, which made her worry that she would also get sick, and get cut.

On the last funeral evening, after the babies were asleep and the last food was packed up for the last relatives to take home, Maile was nowhere to be found. Auntie Lani became concerned. "That girl," she told Makua, "first no more Tūtū, now she loses Ma. And our kids, they rough on her, you know."

As Tūtū's oldest child, Lani was allowed to boss her younger brother Makua. She did not abuse the privilege because she and three sisters worked in Waikiki until midnight and needed a place in the city to sleep. In contrast to Tūtū's enduring good looks, by middle age Lani's features and figure had spread and sagged. She harnessed her vast bosom into a black brassiere that children stared at when they saw it hanging on the clothesline. Her eyelids drooped at the corners, her naturally broad nose had flattened more with each decade, and her wide mouth opened enormously when she sang. Each night after work the four aunties slept in until rampaging children made Lani rear up in bed to disperse them with a shout. Then she wound her waist-length gray hair into a topknot, lit a cigarette, coughed, and went out back to wash.

Makua stared at his sister with a look of sleepwalking exhaustion. "Jus give 'er time," he mumbled, and wandered out front to help his brothers stack folding chairs borrowed from the church. An hour later Lani demanded to know if Makua was waiting for the police to call saying they had the girl. His drained expression didn't change, but with his sister he searched every room, then the dark backyard, where they found a ladder leaning against the house. Makua climbed up and saw Maile sitting alone on the roof.

"Watchin' stars," she replied when asked, " 'at's all." What she was unable to put into words was that the spirits she felt in her gut had expanded until she was overwhelmed: the dim ancestors, the upper spirit that remembered everything, and the rascal *pili* that remembered nothing but was always ready to go. Three souls, Tūtū had said. Everybody got.

Auntie Lani wouldn't stand for leaving Maile on the roof. "Fall asleep up top 'n roll off?" She traded places with Makua on the ladder and coaxed her niece to come down. Inside the house she stretched Maile out on an empty couch for a massage and told her that she was now part of the aunties' vocal group, Voices from the Reef. No back talk. Learn Waikiki songs. Get ready for your try-out day and turn pro.

"Wad-evah," Maile murmured.

14

2

MAILE LEARNED THE standard entertainer's repertoire of seventy songs from her aunties, but she could only tag along with them after school, too young to work in Waikiki. She didn't like the music at Robert Louis Stevenson Intermediate: Souza marches played by the band at assemblies, holiday tunes played on harmonicas. *O patria mia* and "Hallelujah" nagged her, so unlike pretty Hawaiian songs. Sometimes the phrases ran through her mind, alternating with all the verses of "The Cockeyed Mayor of Kaunakakai," memorized for the Voices from the Reef. She searched for a common ground, a connecting force of music, but found none.

Once, during an English test, she was stopped by the first question: *With two sentences, demonstrate the active and passive forms of the verb "to knock."* She had never understood why the last word was spelled like that, or how a language could be so twisted around with sounds that snapped and clicked and hissed off the tongue. The classroom was quiet with concentration, and in the stillness two sharply accented tones entered her mind: *tok-tok*. Not music, something much older, from her spirits. *Tok-tok*, distinct and unmistakable, a sound from a particular place, a hand slapping a dried gourd. First heard when she was about four years old, hiding behind a coconut tree on a deserted, rocky shoreline. Too young to join in, she had watched a group of hula students going down to a blowhole where a lizard goddess was trapped under the stones. Sometimes when a cresting wave struck the coast, the goddess cried out with a jet of seawater, but only if a certain dance was offered.

The girls had lined up in silence. Their teacher knelt beside them with her tan gourd, shaped like the breasts and belly of a pregnant woman. In the calm, hot afternoon air, rain clouds overhead turned a darker and darker blue. The ocean below rolled in wide, heavy waves topped by a ruffled edge of white, looking calm but ready to respond if called in the right way. The platform of rocks baked under a bright afternoon sun that left ghost rims of salt around every tiny pool. Seaweed at the girls' feet gave off a fresh green smell. The water glittered. No breeze stirred. Then *tok-tok!* on the gourd. A sound that had shot out in all directions, going into Maile's bones, rapping on her spine.

The teacher chanted, and the girls moved to her strong voice and the slapped rhythm, *E mai, e mai, eia makou . . .* Come, come, we are here. A wave flowed forward. The blowhole groaned, then hissed, louder and louder, until a geyser shot up through a lava tube and howled into the air. Water spattered down on the rocks, burst into steam, foamed into crevices. The girls continued dancing as the misty steam drifted inland. Under all the competing sounds Maile had heard only *tok-tok, tok-tok,* even after the dance changed to a lesson, the teacher demonstrating hand movements, the girls repeating them in silence. She still heard it after they finished and stood trading jokes. Heard it as she'd run home, *tok-tok* hidden in a rustling cane field, in the whine of a dog, in grease popping on a skillet as Tūtū fried squid for dinner.

Maile handed in her English test and crept off to recess, not knowing who she was. One of a thousand students at Stevenson, she couldn't hide in their midst because she walked and talked more slowly than city girls, wore plain homemade dresses, had one pair of sandals for school. Every day she grieved for her lost life with Tūtū. She didn't miss cleaning chickens, but she longed to go squidding and shrimping, and hear stories about sharks and horses. Honolulu didn't have either. Her family brushed aside questions about three souls with a nervous laugh, saying, *"E,* old-timey stuff."

As the year passed, Maile's connection to Kauai withered and her memories wore ever thinner. After a while the ache she felt was replaced by a dull sense that nothing would change, at least not until she got her monthly *ma'i,* which would make her an official woman, in charge of her own life.

THE VOICES FROM the Reef worked in the noisy dining room of a hotel for vacationing military families, four hefty middle-aged women providing background music and comic hula routines. Through the seventh and eighth grades Maile spent afternoons in the aunties' car in the hotel parking lot, studying Standard English in hopes of sounding less like she came from an outer island. The word "best" replaced "more better," and her spelling improved: "bath," not "baff," and "bathe," not "bave." She learned to keep proper English and pidgin separate so that Jade couldn't accuse her of trying to be *haole*, and teachers didn't embarrass her with corrections in class. In late afternoon she listened to the car radio, got dinner from the hotel kitchen, slept, and rode home with the Voices at midnight.

Waikiki had glamour—a new word—and tourists on vacation did a lot of kissing. After dark Maile often saw couples in the parking lot with their hands under each other's clothes, the woman's digging into the man's shorts, his quick fingers unbuttoning her blouse. They were always white people with sunburns. Hawaiians didn't stay at hotels or buy souvenirs in the shops. They drove cabs and carried luggage for *haole* tourists, they cooked, waited tables, hauled garbage, and made lame jokes about being a dumb *moke*. In Honolulu, Maile now understood, being Hawaiian was not a matter of pride—that was outer-island, rural, Kauai. Here it meant working as a hostess or beach boy and being glad to earn a buck seventy-five an hour. It meant telling people you were also German and Chinese, and feeling good about being German, or any kind of *haole* but Portuguese, because they worked in the cane fields. Germans had always been too smart for that.

For Maile the best thing about being around adults so much was that it made her feel grown up. One morning she got proof: while she was dressing for school, her bare breasts brushed against a rack of freshly ironed blouses, and the starched cotton made her nipples harden. Chicken skin swarmed over her arms, tiny bumps that spread up to her neck and down her back. Images from hula songs she had never quite understood came to mind: a squid leg teasing the lips of a cowrie shell, raindrops making a *pīkake* bud open up. She knew about sex. It had rules and certain *kapu*, although on Kauai little kids who stumbled upon adults having sex were waved off with a laugh, a curtain drawn or a door closed as the groans of pleasure continued. Lovemaking meant the man got stiff and the woman got excited and they wrestled like champions, no matter how fat, old, or funny-looking, and then each grinned as if they had caught a big fish.

All through breakfast and walking to school, Maile thought about sex. By the time she reached the dried-out grass around the flagpole, she could think of nothing else. For the past semester she had noticed ninth-grade boys watching her in a shy and hungry way, yet at thirteen she still didn't have her monthly *maʻi*. With faked indifference she had told her sisters and classmates, "*E*, yeah, got," but she knew that thirteen was late, way late. Since sixth grade she had been waiting to join the girls who left childhood behind to become women, news announced in solemn whispers during recess or with shrieks in the lavatory as another life changed in an instant. Now she figured that if she just did it with a boy, that would force her *maʻi* to come.

During history and civics she stared back at each boy who offered her love eyes. At lunchtime three of them jostled to eat with her. She chose a surfer and they touched hands under the table, his pointer finger going dig-dig-dig into her palm. After school she dawdled so that she could walk home alone. She pressed her schoolbooks to her chest, and a delicious shiver went from her breasts to her cowrie shell, two tingling lines into one. At the base of Punchbowl she sneaked a look at the boy, who was trailing several yards behind. He had beautiful dark eyes and a bowed forearm from when a wave grabbed his board and flung it, breaking a bone that healed in a curve.

She led him into an abandoned garden where a pink bougainvillea bush as high and wide as a car concealed them. He said he loved her. They kissed, crookedly, then mashed their mouths together, better than biting into a ripe slippery mango. She stepped back and posed like a movie actress, hands behind her head, elbows out. He yanked down his trousers. His *ule* stuck straight out like a man's. She fell back against a tree trunk, jammed the hem of her skirt into the waistband, and pulled off her panties. They did it standing up, sat down wet and dripping, and did it again face to face with her legs locked around his back. They panted in exhaustion, crying tears of excitement, and did it a third time, Maile lying down with the boy on top because they agreed that was how Hollywood stars had sex.

Finally they lay side by side, gulping in huge breaths of air. The boy scratched his stomach and said he felt as if he'd had all the candy in the world to eat. Maile wiped herself with a bunch of grass, not minding that her cowrie shell hurt. Blood streaked her thighs and now she was a woman.

MAILE'S TRY-OUT DAY as a paid singer came two weeks after she turned fourteen. By then three boyfriends had not worked out, a secret she managed to keep from her family. A worse secret was that she still did not have her *ma'i,* but now she had a chance to enter the world of adults and become a woman in a different way. For the past year the Voices had been coaching her to sing under all sorts of conditions without freezing up. Our girl can pass for sixteen, the aunties agreed, she's tall and gorgeous like in movies. The expanding clan needed money for all the usual reasons, but the risky plan would succeed only if Maile kept cool head, main thing.

That afternoon the Voices drove down to Waikiki earlier than usual. Auntie Lani parked her rusted old Chevrolet at Queen's Surf, where it wouldn't be noticed, and led the way back to the Moana Hotel. At the end of a long stretch of sand, the entrance to the famous resort was marked by a white-columned porch. Above it rose five stories of rooms with white-arched balconies and white awnings. Tourists strolled up from the beach for cocktail hour. Cool breezes stirred along the shore with the first suggestion of evening.

The Voices carried ukuleles and wore their best yellow satin mu'umu'u. Maile had on a red hibiscus-print sarong, knotted tightly to show off her full breasts and small waist. Her blazing red lipstick matched equally bright hibiscus buds pinned in a fan over the left ear. Her hip-length black hair hung down her back in a swath that swayed lightly as she walked. She had never been to the top-notch end of Waikiki. As they approached the hotel she stared at the front steps, where a pile of leather luggage gleamed like freshly polished shoes. To the left and right was a row of rocking chairs with cushions.

"Don't look so big-eye, make like eeea-sy," Auntie Lani said, and hustled Maile away to a side door. They all hurried through a hall full of laundry carts heaped with tablecloths, down another hallway where women were folding towels, turned a corner and stepped outdoors.

In the middle of the Banyan Courtyard, an enormous tree forty feet high and sixty feet wide shaded a long mahogany bar that faced the beach. At the water's edge, spent waves gently spread out and withdrew. Brown-skinned bartenders sliced pineapples into drink-sized spears. Brown-skinned busboys wiped dozens of little round tables and emptied abalone-shell ashtrays. On a small stage between the bar and the beach, *haole* men set up microphones for a weekly radio show broadcast to homes from San Francisco to New York. Sometimes, Auntie Lani had been told, the master of ceremonies came early to check the equipment. If not today, they would return each day until he did.

A stocky red-haired man in swim trunks and a pink aloha shirt walked briskly past the bar out onto the sand. He stood with foam lapping his feet. "Got that bass link?" he shouted to a man putting on earphones.

"Move," Auntie Lani told her sisters.

They advanced, tuning as they went. Directly ahead, Maile saw a frightening array of broadcasting equipment, black boxes and shiny chrome, cords winding up the trunk of a palm tree. Locals didn't mess with mainlanders who owned expensive things. Seconds ago she had been convinced that she was beautiful and talented, but even being here was *kapu*. No chance the Voices would work for this fancy-kind. They'd be thrown out, fined by police, never hired again as musicians in Waikiki, forced to get jobs making beds in some cheap hotel.

The aunties began a soft vamp, *dum-da-dum, da, dum-da-dum.*

"Him," Auntie Lani said quietly. The redhead bent to dangle a microphone over the sloshing water. Maile stood empty-handed in front of the Voices, their special singer. The man took no notice of them. Bristly orange chest hair poked from the neck of his shirt. His pink face and arms were covered with freckles that ran together in blotches, like a mango ruined by fruit flies. He was maybe five foot five, way short, and he flunked all Maile's tests for good looks. Just give us a job, she thought, you big-time, you Hollywood.

20

The aunties hummed in a rich harmony. Maile took a deep breath, picked up the cue, and sang in a pure, straight-on soprano, "Sweet Lei-la-nee, hev-ven-lee—"

"The hell?" the man muttered. He turned on them as if attacked. "That's my theme song!" Maile choked off the last note. The aunties' strumming stopped. "You can't sing that," he shouted, "hear me?"

They had studied his five o'clock show on their car radio, in the parking lot at the military hotel, and had chosen the piece to grab his attention. But no one could *kapu* a song. They looked at each other wide-eyed.

"Well," he said in a milder tone, "I gotta admit." He grinned and walked over to them. "You work here? Don't think I seen you around. Take it from the top."

During his show that evening, Maile and the aunties waited for an hour in a side room. Afterwards Danny O'Doyle tried her out on a range of songs in a variety of styles. Okay, he said at last, one song a week on the show, fifty bucks, Voices from the Reef not included. If things worked out, in six months Maile could become his "Polynesian Princess of the Airwaves." Auntie Lani accepted as her guardian and chaperone.

On the way to their regular hotel job, the aunties talked over each other in high excitement. Fifty dollars was more than Makua brought home every week after twenty years of driving a bus. The family always pooled their salaries, and this year with all the extra they could buy graduation presents for Kalei and Jackie. Get a new radiator for the Chevrolet. Fill up the gas tank.

Maile sat in back, silent, until Auntie Lani asked what was chewing her guts. She replied that Tūtū considered singing for money shameful. What if her distant grandmother found out?

"Nemmind," Auntie Lani said, "old-fashion, da kine. How we can eat, drive, buy kids' school stuff?" Maile had to admit that made sense, but something she couldn't put a name to slipped away from her, another piece of Kauai. She'd had to leave there because of music, because of *O patria mia*, but that kind of music didn't belong in Waikiki either. The only trace of it in Honolulu had been the "Halleujah" song on the radio, so it must be something that didn't matter much.

FOR MAILE'S FIRST broadcast, Makua assembled the clan at home in Papakōlea to listen to a tourist show they usually ignored. Jade's boyfriend worked at the Moana setting out and collecting beach chairs, but except for the Voices, no one in the family had been to the hotel.

At the Banyan Courtyard, bartenders lined up drink glasses and the cocktail crowd gathered. The aunties were allowed to watch from a side hall. Maile stood with them and trembled at the thought of singing for a million listeners. At the same time, after a month of rehearsals she felt so well prepared that nothing could go wrong unless a tidal wave rolled in. She had sung her song so often it didn't feel like music anymore. Every phrase was timed to the second, which meant not stretching a single note with extra feeling and messing up the schedule.

The tables under the wide shading tree filled all the way to the back. Danny O'Doyle came over to Maile and whispered, "I want you perfect. Canned pineapple in syrup. Picture all the rough skin peeled off, fruit sliced up nice and neat." He looked at his watch, walked off onto the beach, and waded into the foam. At exactly five-thirty he dangled a microphone over the water, held up a hand to his technicians, counted off three seconds of sighing surf, then spoke his opening lines: "And nooow . . . as the sun slooowly sinks in the west . . . " Eleven seconds. In the courtyard the clinking of glasses faded into silence.

On cue Maile stepped up onto the platform—two seconds—and a vast invisible audience expanded in her mind like a liquid map opening across the Pacific to America. Her intro began, eight seconds, music with Danny O'Doyle's kind of precision, music to fit his word syrup, smooth and full of sugar. No performer was allowed to change a syllable of his show, he'd told Maile, because mainlanders wanted Danny O'Doyle's version of paradise and he had the formula down pat.

The microphone head inches from her mouth looked like a little silver coconut. She slid her voice into "Sweet Leilani," and imagined people at radios in Los Angeles, Saint Louis, Boston, little bits of her souls spread out over them like thin mist. "I dream of paradise . . . " Was her *mana* shrinking or growing? Was this how it felt to sing for money? " . . . dream come true . . . " Maybe it wasn't that bad. Maybe it was all *lōkahi*. She didn't miss a beat, a rest, a cue, and remembered to bow: down and hold two seconds, up and hold one, then get off the stage.

THE SCHOOL COUNSELOR smiled with friendly professionalism and introduced himself to Maile's father as they sat down. "Edgar Perkins, fresh from Indiana. Quite an island you got here. I like it." He eyed the large brown-skinned man with thick black hair.

In return Makua gave him a wary look. Not even local *haole*, he thought. In years of raising children he had been called in after school when his boys did something that bordered on getting arrested, but he'd never had those problems with his girls.

Perkins scanned the Parent Information file on his desk and tried to form a picture of the family. Maile's father had dropped out of University of Hawaii after one year. Worked as a movie extra in 1938, then became a lifelong bus driver.

Carefully Perkins read aloud, "Bernhard Lanihuli Manoa," and started to comment on such an interesting name, but instead said, "Look. The reason you're here is none of my business, because it's not happening on school grounds. Ordinarily I'd ask your wife to come in, but I'm told she passed away not long ago." He paused for a moment of silence. "The thing is, there's a rumor among the boys here—going on some months now—that Maile's good for sex with no baby trouble because she can't hold the seed. She's had five or six boyfriends." Perkins lowered his voice. "Girls her age get pregnant on the first try. I'd take her to a doctor. And talk to her, find out what's going on."

Makua left the counselor's office feeling more worried than embarrassed. Maile, the daughter he hardly knew, could really sing, was taking a chorus class and loved it. She read music as easy as reading the newspaper. Hermann and Jade still picked on her; no big deal. Kids hit thirteen or so and started running around, but running wild was different. Boys didn't get raped and thrown out of a car. But she can't hold the seed?

At home Jade told him that Maile was at chorus practice until suppertime. "S'posed to be," she added with a bored smirk. "Girl's growing up, *e?*" Makua disregarded the hint, took the rubbish barrel out front for pickup, repaired a fishing reel, and pruned the backyard mango tree. As darkness fell he imagined Maile walking home uphill around the side of Punchbowl: with girlfriends, or alone, or with a boy. She would avoid the thorny *keawe* trees, pass a ginger grove thick as baled rubbish, then come to a tall clump of bougainvillea that had plenty of space behind it.

It made such perfect sense that Makua felt as if he'd entered her mind. He drove his truck uphill and down again until he saw a cloud of pink flowers at the side of the road that stood out like colored smoke. A young man slouched in front of it, puffing on a cigarette, cockily tipping up his chin to exhale. Makua stopped, got out, and whipped off his belt. The teenager spotted him and ran, shouting, *'Pau ar-ready!'* Another teenager bolted from behind the bougainvillea, grabbing at his trousers and dodging the leather strap that swung through the air like a striking eel.

In the abandoned garden Makua found Maile frantically buttoning her blouse. He let her tug down her skirt, then gripped her shoulders and shook her until she wobbled head to foot. For good measure he whacked his belt across her bare legs. She didn't cry out, and refused to speak to him. They rode home in burning silence. Her rejection was so strong that Makua's anger turned to fear that he would lose her and never get her back. At the house she started to leap from the truck and he said, "Wait, sweetie."

His voice was so soft that she sat still. Quietly he told her that at fourteen she was already grown, with her new job, and that she had too many boys who were already men. No woman could handle too many men, and no man could handle too many women. From now on her life could go up, or straight down. His own life had been good until Ma died, then it went down, all down, until he heard Maile singing on the radio. Even though they hadn't said her name, on that day life went back up for him.

Maile stared ahead at the sprawling house on the little parcel of land, home to more than a dozen people already leaning on her two hundred dollars a month. Doing it with six boys had not made her officially grown up. A big part of her was stalled in childhood.

Someday, Makua assured her, they would say her name on the radio, because she was a singer, born for that, not for running wild. Their full name, Mānoa nā Ānuenue, meant many rainbows, the ancient sign of chiefs. On the *haole* side, Makua said, his grandfather Hermann Braumeister had come to Honolulu in 1885, planted his seed, and disappeared a year later, leaving behind only the memory of his name. Ma's grandfather Hee Ming had stayed and died of plague back then, along with most of his relatives, but his name survived in the memory of the next generation. So Maile had all that, and didn't she feel lucky?

The backs of her legs no longer stung. Makua rarely sat to talk with any of his children, and his words felt like love. "Tell me about Ma," she said, hoping for a story, to share with her sisters or keep to herself as a treasured intimacy.

Makua reached across and grabbed the door handle on her side, his heavy arm a barrier that held her in place. "What I heard," he demanded, "boys want you 'cause you can't hold the seed?" She struggled like a child, trying to pry his fingers apart and loosen his grip, but failed and sat in wordless fury with her fists clenched. He waited, both of them fuming, his arm cramping. Finally she admitted her secret: no *ma'i*, no matter how much she went with boys. She'd been sure that was the way to make it come. But don't tell! Nobody knows.

"Fourteen's way late," Makua said. "Can be you got woman sickness same as Ma. Go with Lani tomorrow." He relaxed his arm. "Find out what's wrong. Skip school."

Maile recalled her mother lying in the back room, thin and silent, her eyes stark with pain. She had never imagined worse trouble than breaking a *kapu*, but here in Honolulu things could go badly wrong for no reason at all. She got out of the truck, feeling heavy with dread, went into the kitchen, and began chopping onions to disguise her teary eyes.

EARLY NEXT MORNING Auntie Lani took Maile to an elderly relative of Ma's who lived in back of a Chinatown herbal shop. The alert old woman had a tiny knot of white hair at the base of her skinny neck and wore dull black silk pajamas and flat black shoes, like an immigrant of fifty years ago. Maile saw no connection to herself or to Jade. The three of them drank tea and recited the Lord's Prayer in English and in Hawaiian, then the healer chanted a blessing in Chinese, strange, high-pitched sounds that made Maile even more uncomfortable.

No, she replied when asked, no pain in her eggs. No swollen belly like blood backed up. No problem going lavatory, nothing growing in the wrong place. The healer spent an hour slowly examining Maile through her school clothes. She grunted with approval at her womanly breasts, at the hair under her arms and between her legs. She pulled down Maile's panties to poke a long, skinny finger deep into her *pua*, rotated the finger thoughtfully, then handed over a bowl and ordered, *"Mimi."* In a lather of embarrassment Maile squatted over the bowl. The healer studied Maile's urine, smelled it, swirled it, smelled it, swirled it again. Auntie Lani sat tensely silent. Maile went from feeling humiliated to bored to worried all over again.

Finally the healer said that Maile was a rare kind of woman who could never have children: she lacked the connection pipes between the eggs and the womb. Because of that she would never get her *ma'i*. At Queen's Hospital, doctors could operate modern-style, but they would find the same thing. Auntie Lani sucked in a huge breath and expelled it in a howling sob.

"I'm sick?" Maile asked. "I gone die like Ma?" No, not sick, she was told, and she would die because everybody died, but not the way Ma died, because when Ma was born, she had all her parts.

On the ride home Auntie Lani snuffled and wiped her eyes. Maile felt like she'd been shoved forward into life, given no choice, the way she'd felt standing on the deck of the *sampan* as it passed the green cliffs of Kauai. Her worst fear was being called a freak who could not have a child. When she married, close relatives would have to give her one of their own babies if she asked for it, and then another baby when the first one was a few years old. Hawaiian tradition demanded such generosity to relieve the curse of loneliness. She pictured herself holding an infant boy while a little girl clung to her skirt, gifts from siblings who already had children. They were filled with the pride of young parents keeping little ones safe from hot stoves, knives, passing cars, allowing toddlers to run crazy while teaching them manners. But soon word would get around the family that Maile was cursed, the only one who "couldn't have," as they said, being nice because the word "barren" meant earth eroded to clay where nothing grew.

In panic she shouted, "You keep you mouth shut!" Auntie Lani pulled off the road and stared at her. "Nobody finds out I got no *ma'i*" Maile said, "My business! Nobody calls me freak, feels all sorry."

Auntie Lani insisted that she was just special. Maile didn't believe it and made her promise on God and Pele that her secret was *kapu*. Makua would be told not to worry, his girl was okay. They drove on home in the edgy mood of having to trust each other without further discussion. Maile vowed to bury her secret where not even *pili* could find it, and go in search of more music: born to sing, like Makua had said.

At school she advanced to performing Gilbert and Sullivan solos for holiday assemblies, difficult pieces that were fun but frustrating because they meant nothing. In the public library she listened to records of choral works from famous operas, Italian blacksmiths, Spanish prisoners, German hunters. The name Verdi was there, one among many, but the choruses were just scraps of stories, tantalizing and incomplete. Instead of dating, she befriended *mahu* boys who grew their fingernails long and gossiped about Waikiki and advised her on hairstyles and makeup. On Friday evenings, the Papakōlea family gathered to rip open salary envelopes, put the money in a calabash, and pay the most pressing bills.

AFTER TWO YEARS with Mr. O'Doyle, Maile got a five-dollar raise. On the way home she made a mental shopping list—diapers, bleach, crayons—but once inside the house, she hid the bill in the dresser drawer along with the Kalākaua coin in the leather pouch. Week after week her little hoard grew, the worst kind of crime: selfishness. If discovered, she could not have said why she was doing it. She now sang for *haole* weddings, ten dollars for "Oh, Promise Me," with whispered phrases that brought tears to the eyes of ladies wearing hats. If she was paid in singles, one rolled-up dollar went into the bottom drawer.

The weddings led to a solo at a large church in a part of the city Maile had never seen; *Panis Angelicus*, sacred music from Europe. The simplicity and slow beauty of the melody line made her fearless rather than nervous. She sensed a musical connection to *O patria mia*, to chorus class, to the records in the school library, to the idea of opera. When the church music director motioned with a gentle dip of his wrist, her cue, she sang the odd text that meant "bread of heaven," and in the high, wide interior she felt all her spirits flow out from her lips, mouth, and throat to touch the back wall and echo delicately. No microphone, no cuteness, no sarong, no smile. It was singing for Akua Jesus, like dancing for a goddess.

Soon she worked at churches all over Honolulu, hunting for music, skipping those that relied on the same plodding hymns week after week. One choir director recommended her to a voice teacher, but Maile couldn't afford lessons, and wondered why she needed them; music was just memorize, get the feeling, hit the right notes and rhythm. Her singing made people instantly listen, which gave her a sense of increasing power, even if it lasted only until her final note. She was a fishing net, flung out to gather them in.

A CATHOLIC HIGH school announced work on *The Magic Flute*, an opera to be presented with piano, a violin, a cello, and students supervised by nuns. Maile was equally curious about Mozart and the strange sacred women, who wore only black and white, and she volunteered to make costumes during rehearsals. Each day after school, at the back of the Mystic Rose assembly hall, Maile covered a cardboard outfit in tinfoil: knight's armor for an unnamed prisoner in an unnamed castle. Beside a small stage, Sister Bridget played the piano from a score with abridged sections clipped together by clothespins. Maile listened past the struggling singers and heard how the music connected to a story, a theme. Characters and tunes developed, an important clue, she felt, to something big; a ship rather than a canoe, an opera rather than a holiday medley.

One afternoon she took her scissors and a leg of the costume, and moved closer to the piano. Ahead of her, six students in a line began a solemn chorus of warning. The melody had a deep richness and the cellist's bow sang on the strings, moving to the right, to the left, urging the music to descend the scale. The voices and instruments shifted as one with the strength of a rising wave. Maile followed the printed notes of the score in amazement that they could be so transformed— black dots into human feelings. *Pili* pulsed in her chest, her gut. She started to cut the cardboard without looking and the cold blade of the scissors pressed against her thumb. She froze, certain that music had sent her a message: it possessed greater *mana* than she had ever imagined.

At home Maile shrugged off questions about the opera and did not insist that Hermann pronounce "Mozart" correctly. She went to the remaining rehearsals, and to three performances, and each time waited in tense anticipation for the chorus and the cello to shift the melody. The moment became familiar, a promise of treasures in store.

MR. O'DOYLE PAID Maile three hundred dollars to appear on a locally produced record album as an unnamed lead singer with the Voices from the Reef. She disguised the full payment from them and added ten fives to the rolls of bills lining the dresser drawer like skinny green cigarettes. Her guilty secret: hiding money for no reason when the roof was leaking, the electricity was cut for non-payment, a cousin's outboard motor had broken down. Throughout the remainder of high school she kept saving with the vague intention of rejoining Tūtū on Kauai. They would gather medicine plants in the feathery rain, harvest salt in the stone pans at Hanalei, spend every day on the reef, honor the names of the winds streaking across the water in the season of Lono. But Tūtū was frail now. And there was no *Panis Angelicus* on Kauai. No jobs either. For a hundred years, outer island people had been moving to Honolulu to find work. The day-to-day, week-to-week need for cash always caught up with families, even if they raised chickens, vegetables, and fruit to swap with neighbors who fished.

Maile's first album with the Voices from the Reef was followed by two more, and all sold well. She joined the group of professionals considered successful by local standards, although Waikiki musicians never achieved national prominence. Standards she had sung hundreds of times, like "Hawaiian Wedding Song," were rerecorded by mainland stars and made millions of dollars. Everyone recognized the limits of a singing career in Hawaii.

In 1961, high school graduation was the great event in the lives of teenagers unable to dream of college or good jobs. A third of Maile's class had already dropped out to work, have babies, or join the military. Jade was now assistant hostess at a large Chinese restaurant and the mother of two little girls. Hermann became a father the same week he turned sixteen, and he quit school for a job as a car mechanic. School counselors advised Maile against further study, saying that women who went to college got married anyway and devoted themselves to home life. Classical music conservatories were costly, distant, and part of *haole* culture. She saw herself restricted to hotel floor shows and Hawaiian music fast going out of style in favor of rock 'n roll. The future seemed to be bearing down on her with the force of a storm wind.

ONE AFTERNOON IN August, when all the graduation luau were over, Maile went to the university campus in Manoa to get a catalogue of classes. The lush uplands once reserved for ruling chiefs now held twenty academic buildings and the homes of plantation managers and bankers who could afford views of Diamond Head. She decided that her family name, Manoa of the Rainbows, meant she belonged in this part of Honolulu, but she had no plan other than a fierce desire to get more out of life.

At the registration office she took a catalogue to sit outside under a tree and study the list of courses. Asian Art, no, because it reminded her of Jade; Beginning German, yes, because of Mozart; Classics of European Music, maybe, because there was a lot she still didn't know; Freshman Literature, required; Stagecraft and World Drama, maybe, because opera took place on a stage. She made a mental list of fees, and shivered with fear and importance. Even if she lived at home, the university would cost a thousand dollars a year. She had nearly that much hidden away but dared not spend it and reveal her unforgivable miserliness. And once the thousand dollars was gone, who would pay for the next year, and the next and the next?

The clan met to discuss Maile and the University of Hawaii. It took until late afternoon for everyone to arrive at the house, then for aged relatives from Wai'anae and Waimānalo to be settled and served coffee, for homemade desserts to be consumed and complimented. Twenty-three adults crammed into the front room as babies fell asleep on laps and older children peered in through open doors. An hour later the majority decided that the university was too expensive. Maile had to keep her singing jobs and work full time. The decision caught her by surprise; no recognition of how much she had contributed over the last four years, no offer of half this, half that. What she wanted had been vague, no more than a need to not be locked in place until she was as old as the elders lined up on the sagging couch.

"Talk for me!" she whispered to Makua.

He looked around, uncomfortable at speaking ahead of people in their seventies and eighties, but he murmured to the group that a grown daughter should not be held back. Deliberations continued. After a while Makua reminded everybody that before the war he had gone to college for one year, and still regretted having to leave. He'd never planned on being a bus driver all his life. Auntie Lani spoke with her sisters, then with other women their age. She got them to agree that if Maile wanted to study that bad, it was only—she paused to do the math in her head—ninety-three dollars a month, we can manage, e nei? The objections of Jade and Hermann failed to change the final decision: Maile could study all four years if she continued to work as a singer. She thanked everyone but the thought of doing both filled her with anxiety.

"Girl," Makua said as people got up to leave, "I hope you know wat's wat. At UH they don't like us Hawaiians. Was bad back when, and still yet. You gotta be tough, proud."

"I can handle," Maile replied without thinking.

Makua smiled faint agreement, although his words made her wonder how much worse than high school the university would be. Each year certain teachers had sniped at Hawaiians and Samoans: Go sit in the back row, don't ask questions, don't bother reading that book. You're born stevedores, truck drivers, beach boys, hula girls.

She smiled back at her father. "Nobody can stop me study German, *e?*"

3

MAILE ARRIVED FOR the first day of class wearing a navy blue dress with a white collar. White high heels, navy blue handbag, hair pinned up. She caught sight of one man in a suit who could have been part Hawaiian, but everybody else except for a janitor was Japanese or *haole*. She felt that her clothes were perfect, the only conservative outfit she owned, although students and faculty still regarded her with surprise— a real local-local who could be spotted a block away, the Waikiki entertainer who also sang a little classical music. She headed straight for Beginning German, convinced that Hermann Braumeister, who had fathered children in Honolulu in 1885, gave her a right to be there. She would claim her Caucasian blood in the same way that Jade had decided to be Chinese.

As the students sat down, their professor counted rapidly, *"Eins, zwei, drei, vier, fünf, sechs."* When no more appeared, he said, "Well, it is at least the minimum." He spoke in a precise and foreign way, with what Maile did not realize was a Cambridge accent. On the blackboard he wrote "Avram Chaimowitz" and pronounced his last name slowly.

"By way of introduction," he said, "I am, of course, Jewish. However, in Honolulu that means nothing. I am above all, German. Now, my budding scholars, why in the middle of the Pacific does each of you want to learn this beautiful language?"

To fulfill a requirement, the other students replied, to get a military job, to try something new. "Because I'm part German," Maile answered too loudly, "and because of music."

Professor Chaimowitz waved away the laughter of her classmates. "Culture, dear students," he said, pausing to look at each of them, "is the key. You shall learn that before Hitler appeared, German culture was magnificent. German was the language of poets and philosophers, elegant and uplifting. Unlike its current debasement in American motion pictures, where some brute shouts *'Achtung!'* and the audience guffaws."

Soon Maile entered worlds beyond any she had imagined. The language class offered the exotic temptations of Goethe's *Faust*, the agony of Rilke's panther, but also Professor Chaimowitz's descriptions of his life in Hamburg during the 1930s. After Jews were barred from teaching, he told students, his savings account was seized, his car, his house. He had continued to believe that wisdom and decency would prevail over politics, then new laws restricted Jews from using the same sidewalks as Aryans. It became a game for him to outwit officials and police. One morning he saw a rabbi beaten in a public square, teeth flying across the pavement, the crunch of the skull.

"The same sound," he said, "as a coconut broken open so one can dig out the meat." Still he refused to believe that the country that produced so many of Europe's artists and scientists in the nineteenth century would sink into barbarism. "I was wrong," he told the class. "I left my country of birth by way of humiliating disguises—do not ever ask me about this—and worked cleaning ship hulls. Your islands attracted me because of their reputation for racial tolerance, where people of all origins can live without facing torture or death camps." He assured his students that despite Nazism, his loyalty to what he called "classic German culture" remained firm. Their good test scores showed that they understood the difference. He was proud of them.

Maile had to adjust her view of German history as more than just a progression of musicians and poets. Among themselves the students decided that their professor had a *haole* viewpoint. He didn't understand that for them World War II meant first of all Pearl Harbor and the Japanese-American battalions that had fought in Italy. After that, war meant Korea, and now Vietnam and the monthly newspaper announcements of aircraft carriers arriving and departing. What the German government had done over twenty years ago should be tucked away into history books.

Each morning Maile rose, ate a breakfast papaya over the kitchen sink, rushed off to classes, a brown bag lunch, more classes, then dashed home to change into a sarong and get down to Waikiki. Afterwards she went back to the university to spend hours in the library, and at nine-fifteen she bolted outside to catch the last bus to Papakōlea. Each night she collapsed into bed, got up forcing herself to think in Standard English, and hurried off across Honolulu. Each month Auntie Lani collected the clan's ninety-three dollars and paid it herself in cash at the registrar's office. When the annual fee rose to one thousand eighty-two dollars, she scolded family members who complained.

Maile's exhausting, exhilarating routine continued for four years: Schiller, Brahms, the Salem witch trials, Michelangelo's David, the Inquisition, a small role in a campus production of *Mother Courage*. The tiny Hawaiian Studies department was run by intimidating *haole* professors, and she took no classes from them. Men of all races pursued her, although each lost interest when he discovered she came from that neighborhood full of big families in small houses and rusted cars always being repaired. University students were on their way up in life and didn't want anything dragging them back down. One part-Hawaiian law student didn't care where Maile lived. He visited the house, and pleased Makua and delighted the aunties. After a clan fishing trip, followed by a luau for a new baby, he and Maile made plans to marry the next month. Uncles vied to provide the pig, the bucket of fresh octopus for grilling, the *'opihi* shellfish collected off wave-lashed rocks. One night amidst the excitement of preparations, she told her future husband that she could not have children. He embraced her in silent sympathy. A week later he exited her life with the smooth finality of a mistake erased from a page, there and then gone.

AFTER GRADUATION MAILE continued to sing in Waikiki and at weddings and funerals. She continued to hoard extra money for no purpose she could name. As much as she loved the old Hawaiian songs, years ago she had reached the end of an entertainer's repertoire, and now faced decades of repetition. She haunted a listening booth at the downtown library, putting on the earphones to hear opera recordings made in New York or Vienna, the melodies feeding a hunger to see live performances that were hopelessly out of reach. By the age of twenty-three, she was becalmed in music, although it was all around her.

Annually massed choirs from churches and schools presented a condensed version of Beethoven's *Ninth Symphony*, eight hundred voices in a stadium where wrestling matches took place on Thursday nights. A children's ballet school staged scenes from the *Nutcracker Suite* on the flat roof of the Sears store, watched by an audience in the parking lot. The Honolulu Symphony only performed instrumental works. Except for *The Magic Flute*, she had never seen an opera. In other ways, though, life was changing. Overnight plane flights from the West Coast replaced travel by ship. Magazines from the mainland now arrived only a month out of date. Television sets were common, the shows just one week delayed, and color TV was promised by the end of 1965.

One afternoon Maile arrived as usual at the Moana Hotel half an hour before sundown. Danny O'Doyle stood at the front desk talking intently with several floor managers. In the Banyan Courtyard, waitresses and busboys huddled in conversation. The entire staff was on alert to be particularly courteous to new guests from Argentina, whose journey to Japan had been delayed by typhoons farther north. The group occupied the most expensive suite, a lady and six men sharing two rooms with only four beds. Señora Zoila Mar y Sol spoke half a dozen languages. On the hotel register her profession was listed as "soprano."

Over the following days a constant stream of requests came from the Grand Suite: white truffles, Fleur de Rocailles perfume, Blood of the Bull wine. One evening Maile waited after her performance to watch Señora enter the dining room. The lady wore a chiffon gown the color of sea foam, styled to show off her movie star's lush figure. Tiny diamond suns glittered in her black chignon. Eyes painted like an Egyptian queen's. The men followed her to an orchid-filled table, seated her, then pulled out their chairs in unison to sit down, minor displays of perfection noticed by staff and guests alike. Some frightened housemaids were certain that Señora was the goddess Pele in a new form, eager to curse anyone who displeased her. At times Maile almost believed this herself, but kept seeing a woman of flesh and blood, able to live as she pleased because she was a soprano, not an ordinary singer.

After four days of continuing delay, Señora demanded a high, wide space for work; her voice had to remain in top condition. The hotel manager decided that the outdoor stage was the only possibility. Danny O'Doyle hated classical music and gladly let Maile make the arrangements. She arrived in midafternoon and directed workmen to roll a grand piano into the Banyan Courtyard. Tourists were politely escorted to other lounges. A busboy set pots of orchids around the small stage. Maile stood at one end of the bar, ready to shoo away onlookers; the distinguished guest needed to rehearse, not give a free concert.

At exactly three o'clock Señora appeared on a stairway above the courtyard. Her hair was heaped into an elaborate geisha style, and she wore a pale blue kimono tied with a broad gold sash that glinted in the sunlight. She descended like a gliding bird, followed by six men in tuxedos. Maile felt a rush of embarrassment for them—so overdressed— but she had to admit they looked fantastic.

Señora swept up onto the little stage and faced the ocean with the expression of a goddess surveying the elements. The pianist seated himself as the others arranged themselves behind her. She regarded the calm waves rolling onto shore, then glanced at the tenor. He came forward, the pianist rolled a chord, and the two singers joined in a sudden burst of tones: *"Pre-go, pre-go . . ."*

Maile heard only glorious sound, as solid as a wall but also wonderfully flexible. Soprano and tenor melodies twined around each other and meet briefly in powerful, sensual harmonies. Hotel guests peered from balconies. Waitresses gathered on an adjacent terrace. Maile furiously put a finger to her lips, and waved everybody away.

The singers broke off for a discussion in Spanish. Just as abruptly they started singing again, another explosion of music that wiped out the soft sigh of the ocean, the light rustling of palm fronds overhead. To Maile the voices seemed enormous, no comparison to any church soloist or entertainer she had ever heard. And attitude! Both singers had a fascinating arrogance, as if saying, I am yours, but do not come too close or you will regret it.

At the end of the duet, Señora motioned with a dip of her kimono sleeve. The men filed off the stage to form an audience. She tipped up her chin, the accompanist responded with a light chord, and on a high, whispered note she sang, *"Un— bel di . . . "* The phrase had such drawn-out purity that Maile's spirits trembled with emotion. She knew the melody from a library record, and felt an overwhelming desire to spread her own *mana* into the air, to be transformed into Madame Butterfly, to express her unshakable belief in love, to have such power that listeners believed an Italian story of Japan. Señora's voice conveyed beauty, hope, death. Butterfly described the ship that would never appear, the lover's gentle greeting that would never be spoken, the life that would be cut short. She concluded in defiance, *"T'a spet— to!"*

Spontaneous applause erupted from side lounges; Maile was overcome by inspiration. She stepped in front of the stage and frantically recalled *Messiah* rehearsals, the most impressive music she knew. "Rejoice," she sang boldly, "re-joice," completing the first phrase with all the fancy notes inserted, "re-joi—ce great-ly!"

Señora stared down at her, frowning. In a daze Maile edged back around the orchids. Danny O'Doyle rushed out of a lounge with a drink in hand, face flushed, teeth bared in a scowl. Señora flipped her fingers in his direction, a motion of such authority that he stopped at the edge of the courtyard. She continued to look at Maile, now seeming intrigued rather than insulted. In English she said, "You appear to be a native. Sing me something ancient."

Maile was stunned by the language switch, the invitation. Ancient Hawaiians didn't have melodies, she wanted to say, and considered other excuses, but knew that she had a chance, one. She concentrated on a hula chant, the loudest, strongest sound she could make. Sucking in a huge breath, she focused mind, body, and spirits, and let go with *"E— uli-uli kai,"* dragging out each tone in the shivery style of a kahuna calling up the god of the deep blue sea. *"E—uli-uli!"*

Señora stood with eyebrows raised, unable to conceal surprise. "Your voice is unusual," she said. "You show some promise." She smiled.

A sign of approval, Maile felt, a precious instant of contact that could lead to greater things. "I've been singing for years," she exclaimed. "Everyone knows me in Waikiki! I can give you my records. I can sing arias."

The smile faded. Señora slipped her hands into her kimono sleeves. "The words 'unusual' and 'promise' imply deserved recognition," she said. "That was given to me at about your age. I shall provide you with the name of my first teacher. However." She paused, coldly deliberate. "Do not pursue me with gifts or further requests."

The pianist wrote on a visiting card and handed it to Maile. Señora glided away in a rustle of silk. The men followed her across the courtyard to a private elevator, and one after another they disappeared inside.

Danny O'Doyle stalked up to Maile and tossed his drink into the orchids. "Damn it," he growled, "badgering guests is against policy, and you're my singer, so I look bad. You're fined a hundred bucks. Those people complain, you fork over a month's salary."

Maile glanced at the card, feeling cheated, fobbed off with a distraction while the grand group made their escape. Still, under the printed name was written another name, and an address in New York: Señora's first teacher. For ten years the unnamed Polynesian Princess of the Airwaves had given her family all the extras in life, a used truck, fishing reels, medicine, new underwear for brothers and sisters and aunties and uncles. Maile had sewed, ironed, and cooked, washed dishes, babies, and laundry. Had graduated from the university but still lived at home in a room shared with two teenagers.

She held up the card, saying, "I'm going to New York. To study real music."

Danny O'Doyle shook his head, looking confused, then disbelieving. As she walked off he told her to hold on a minute, wait, just wait, let's talk this over, but she continued across the courtyard, waving to the waitresses and blowing kisses to the busboys.

AT THE PAPAKŌLEA house, the aunties pinned plumeria into their hair before leaving for Waikiki. Relatives of all ages were in the bedrooms, the kitchen, napping, preparing dinner, doing homework. Maile burst in and announced, "It's my turn now!" She showed each family member, even bewildered little children, a name printed on a small white card. To each she said, "I'm gone mainland."

"E, Makua," Auntie Lani called into the backyard.

He put down a blowtorch and pipe he was welding to come inside. No one could believe Maile had quit the job she'd held since the age of fourteen. She struggled to put into words her bright fit of freedom, a soprano who offered ravishing glimpses of the world of opera, who had cast a spell and given her a key. "How come?" they kept asking. "Fo wat?"

"Told Mr. O'Doyle I'm gone," she repeated. *'Pau.* 'At's it. The End, like in movies." She beamed with the assurance of having found the nameless goal that had eluded her for so many years.

The aunties passed out cigarettes and sat down. Makua paced, fending off relatives who pestered him with solutions: Maile-girl could teach school, she could tell Mr. O'Doyle sorry and go back to his show. A toddler waddled in from a back room, his fists full of green paper tubes that stuck out between his fingers. Nobody noticed the little boy until an older sister bent to cuddle him. In a tone of wonder the girl said, "Baby's got money. Look how much."

A trail of tightly rolled cylinders led to a bedroom and a termite-eaten dresser where two other boys were playing with a claw hammer. They had pulled a slat off the bottom drawer, jammed shut for years, as far as anyone knew. The front panel sagged, and five- and ten- and twenty-dollar bills spilled onto the floor. A dozen people crammed into the room to stare. Maile had to force herself to join them, to stare as well, and finally admit her secret. When she tried to leave, they made her stay. Men split the drawer, shook out the contents, swept the hoard into a dustpan, and emptied it again and again into the family calabash.

Makua shouted for someone to start the rice pot for dinner. Auntie Lani sent her sisters off to Waikiki, then she sat with him to smooth the bills and count them into piles: three thousand eight hundred ninety-six dollars. He brought in a tire iron and laid it on the stacks of bills to flatten them. Maile stood alone on the *lanai*, burning with stubbornness and fear that once again music had brought her trouble, this time the worst and most shameful of all. For the rest of her life and after she was dead, the clan would talk about the hidden money until it became the one thing that defined her. She remembered sitting up on the roof years ago, watching the stars, and went into the backyard to .

look for the ladder. It lay half-buried under fallen banana leaves, the rungs damp and rotted.

MOST OF THE money went to pay for roof repair, a month-long job that included replacing rotted beams. Makua put aside six hundred dollars in a paper sack. He asked Auntie Lani how much two years of study in New York would cost, what Maile claimed she needed. Neither had any idea, so they guessed it must be about equal to the saved sum. The next afternoon he took the paper sack downtown, returned with two more Kalākaua coins, and gave them to his daughter to add to the coin in the leather pouch that she had received after Ma's death. "For in case," he told her. Nobody else need know.

That evening at dinner and afterwards on the phone, Makua spread the word that the clan had nine months to raise three thousand dollars. Jade refused outright, saying that Maile had betrayed them. Hermann laughed off the accusation. "Little sister works hard how many years," he said, "now we just get busy, pay back, *e nei?*" Other relatives pleaded illness or only sullenly agreed to help. Auntie Lani organized a Christmas bake sale that raised eighty-two dollars. During January, brothers, uncles, and nephews put together a truck from the parts of four others and sold it to add nine hundred dollars. A repairable fishing boat in Waimānalo brought in eight hundred dollars more. Some grumbled that Maile should stay home, stick to what she knew. Nah, others said, she can make the New York career, like that fellow from Kauai, Johnny Pineapple and his Polynesians, fifteen in a fancy hotel up there.

Makua and Auntie Lani drove the clan as if managing a construction project. Ship and train tickets were bought. Maile was given a stack of travelers' checks, which none of them had heard of before, better than taking cash and running the risk of being robbed. On the first Tuesday in May 1966, everyone in the clan who could get off work went down to the dock.

They came out of ancient obligation, still not understanding why their girl would get on a ship full of *haole* passengers and go so far to learn something she could already do: sing. Elders from Wai'anae wore freshly ironed clothes and *lauhala* hats with fine feather bands. Adult cousins wore hotel uniforms or union T-shirts and dungarees. Jade wore her brocade hostess gown, ready for the early dinner shift, and scolded her little girls for getting their dresses wrinkled. Hermann carried his second son on his shoulders while an older boy stood between his legs. His wife held their youngest, offered to Maile last year, a gift she had declined with thanks although by then without tears.

From above came a blast on the ship's horn. Auntie Lani wept and exclaimed, "Two whole years!" The Voices, uncles, and siblings pressed in with embraces and kisses for each lei they gave Maile: a rope of purple orchids, a fluffy string of yellow plumeria, five strands of *pīkake*, lushly fragrant in the late afternoon heat. More strings of flowers were heaped around her shoulders, rising to her chin, her nose. Jade and others stood back. "Stay here!" Auntie Lani cried. "Get married ar-ready, plenny good husbands around!" Maile glanced away to kill the topic, brought up so often that no one took it seriously anymore.

Tourists streamed toward the ship, conversing tipsily, still dressed in aloha shirts, white trousers, sarongs and sandals, as if their clothes could stave off returning to the continent. At the foot of the gangway the Island Kings Trio vamped into "Keep Your Eyes on the Hands." A line of barefoot women with waist-length black hair, red tops, and green *ti*-leaf skirts swayed out of a warehouse toward the edge of the pier, easing through officers, luggage, porters, crates of watercress and fruit. Stevedores shoved steamer trunks onto a plank stretching into the hold of the ship. The crowd of onlookers gazed up at its white sides, at the braided rope hawsers hung with streamers, at waiters on deck circulating with trays of cocktails.

As the dancers finished, the Manoa clan traded glances, then began to sing, "*Imi au . . . ia 'oe,*" I search for you with love. The solid four-part harmony absorbed the cracked tones of elders and the shrill voices of children, a mournfully sweet melody that engulfed Maile. Tourists turned to stare, looking pleasantly surprised. The song moved past its midpoint, and she felt the end coming on, a page about to be torn from a book. She pictured Tūtū on the dock at Nāwiliwili, calling out and waving, her grandmother dead now two years, never seen again.

Soon Auntie Lani and Makua would be lost to her as surely as a coin dropped into the deep harbor water; yet she had set all this in motion, had demanded it, and now must claim it.

A last call to board came from a loudspeaker. The farewell song dissolved into a flurry of final embraces. A baby wailed. Auntie Lani's lips left a moist streak on Maile's cheek. Makua's chin stubble grazed her forehead. Her *pili* spirit clutched at all of them with greedy fingers, but she pulled away to follow the last passengers mounting the gangway.

FOR DAYS MAILE could not clearly remember leaving, or the trip to the West Coast, or getting on a train bound for New York—hours of staring out at a disturbingly flat landscape, occasionally broken by mountains, going on and on with no glimpse of the ocean. She tried to concentrate on which cities and states she was passing through, but felt only a confusing sense of endlessly moving forward into strange territory.

At her final stop she stepped out into the dark underground heat of Pennsylvania Station, harshly lit by racks of lights. Engine brakes screeched into the surrounding blackness. The dust-filled air stank of oil fumes. Men in suits and fedoras flowed past her toward a distant exit sign, lighting cigarettes and carrying briefcases the way actors did in movies. On the narrow passenger platform she stood like a tree in a flooded river, alone and anonymous.

Terrified, she had a vision of the high green ridges of Kalihi, still visible from the ship a mile out to sea, crested by white strips of mist moving upward into a late afternoon cluster of purpling rain clouds. Slowly she had lifted each lei from the heap on her shoulders, inhaled its fragrance, and flung it overboard, the carnation, the rope of orchids, the frail white ginger, the crinkled yellow plumeria strung by little children, the precious *pīkake*. On the water below they formed a long colored band drawn toward shore, a guarantee of her return, in triumph, two years from now. But now she was on a packed train platform with air as suffocating as a heap of hot sand. Her three spirits were a lump under her ribcage. She dragged her suitcase into a stream of people that never thinned.

Outside the terminal she paused amidst a racket of traffic, groups of men at the curb yelling at yellow cars, a jackhammer ripping into pavement. Across the street a wall of glass panes blazed yellow with reflected suns. High temperatures had softened the tarred cracks in the sidewalk, snagging her high heels. She took a taxi uptown to Washington Heights and a furnished one-room student apartment on 153rd Street, arranged in advance. In a daze of excitement she got a key from the manager, entered the room and sat on the bed until the little square of sky framed by the window faded to night. At last she got up to turn on the light and unpack, and felt a strange, wonderful sensation.

Privacy! For the first time in her life she had a room to herself.

4

ON THE TOP floor of 3660 Broadway at 88th Street, Madame Leah Renska put the last Venus Nipple on her tongue and closed her lips over it. Her students were trained to be exactly on time. This gave her the opportunity between lessons to enjoy *ein kleiner Luxus*, a reminder of a genteel life once lived in Germany. At fifty-seven, she could again indulge herself regularly, although decades ago she had given up on a face and figure that resisted improvement. Her hair had the consistency of steel wool. Her protruding eyes gave her a permanently startled expression, and her nose leaned slightly to the right in a banana curve. Her small mouth was a poor match for her large head, which was an even poorer match for a stubby figure and broad hands with elongated fingers capable of spanning well over an octave on a piano. But the looks that had tortured her in adolescence and denied her a husband as an adult no longer mattered. She had made it out of Europe alive and established herself in Manhattan. She had a beautiful ear for sound.

As the sleek icing melted on Madame's teeth, she heard an unexpected knock on the apartment door. Annoyed, she swallowed her treat and got up to peer through the spy hole. A young woman of a decidedly exotic cast, with thick black hair wound into a topknot, held up a business card with solemn urgency. This was certainly peculiar yet also intriguing. Madame decided to take a chance and opened the door.

The young woman wore a red and white sarong with white high heels. The theatrical effect pleased Madame, but she distrusted it off-stage. The business card was printed with a familiar name, under it Madame's own name and address in black ink. The young woman held out a slip of paper saying, "The doorman asked me to give you this."

Madame read the note and stifled a huff of exasperation: her next student, a brilliant but nerveless tenor, had again excused himself from a lesson. This young woman had managed to slip into his time slot. The name on the business card made Madame suppress a smile: Señora Zoila Mar y Sol—the former Sarah Sonnenberg—was still on world tour to small theaters in remote places. A genuine stage animal who had evidently recommended this young woman. Señora would not do that lightly. Or it might be an elaborate joke. The sarong, *um Gottes Willen,* was certainly an attention snatcher.

"And what is it I can do for you?" Madame asked. "Miss . . . "

Maile faced down the hallway and sang the loudest tone she could manage, a solid high C. Madame stood stiffly, waiting for the reverberations to stop. "Mere boldness is nothing," she said. "Come in."

She intended to spend only enough time with the young woman to determine if all this was in jest, or worthy of consideration. Forty-five minutes later Maile had sung scales that demonstrated an excellent range, and a spirited solo from *The Messiah* that demonstrated an utter lack of coloratura technique. Madame decided that Miss Manoa was a true oddity. Opera singers rarely came from west of the Mississippi, let alone Hawaii—which had a musical heritage Madame didn't care to think about. She also distrusted exoticism, even when backed by what Americans referred to so childishly as "talent." Yet this young soprano not only had the necessary basic gifts, but might possess intelligence as well. She had studied the German language—in Honolulu! And was very attractive; tall and slender as a ballet dancer, with liquid black eyes, highly expressive, a hint of Chinese about the lids. A delicate nose, low and flat, and naturally pouted lips.

Having asked few questions and invited no opinions, Madame mapped out her new student's life. "You shall take one lesson a week, for at least two years. A minimum this long you must study. I shall arrange for you a little access to Juilliard Conservatory. You pay my fee of ten dollars each week in a white envelope. You are always timely and do never ask financial assistance because I give you my lowest fee because you are the unemployed soprano. The room you rent has a piano? Good. You have other clothes? Good. Next Tuesday, then, at this same hour. Perhaps Señora Mar y Sol has made the good guess."

Maile strode up Broadway toward 153rd Street, too elated to take the bus. Her spirits spiraled from throat to pelvis and back again. Street after street she marched uptown, oblivious to the stares her sarong attracted. Two years of study fit her own estimate exactly, as in a

Verdi plot where the heroine's life was ruled by the forces of destiny. Then she would spend six months touring the world's opera houses and six months singing with the Honolulu Symphony, and at Royal Hawaiian Hotel concerts, performing all the local music she could want. Her glorious escape from Danny O'Doyle nine months ago still felt unreal, but she passed the gates of Columbia University, and those were real. The strange American trees she glimpsed along the bank of a wide, dark river were real. And farther on was Harlem, famous for jazz and Negroes who looked great in clothes no *haole* could wear.

By the time Maile reached 153rd Street, her toes ached and her arches throbbed. Trash filled the gutters. A half-dozen dented, stinking garbage cans awaited pickup. Across the street the marquee of a closed movie theater was streaked with rust. Maile's bright mood swept her into the apartment building, up the elevator to the eighth floor, and into the room where she now lived. New York was the most important city in the world, the source of taped radio shows that had reached all the way to Kauai.

OVER THE FOLLOWING weeks Maile's radiant optimism faded as Madame Renska discovered the depth of her ignorance about music. "Vocal, symphony, ballet, you must know all," Madame stated, "even the string quartet. I do not allow the uneducated soprano." She brushed aside Maile's music study at the University of Hawaii, assigned her regular listening sessions in the Juilliard record library, then quizzed her on the differences between French and Italian composers. Every free concert on the West Side had to be attended, early English lute music with tenor, a Finnish choir on tour, a Japanese prodigy playing Paganini.

For better or worse, Maile realized that she had taken a leap into the foreign world of New York, where all languages and races came together. Men flirting with her on the street assumed she was Caribbean, South American, Gypsy. If people asked about her ancestry, they refused to believe she was Hawaiian-Chinese-German, as though she'd attempted to tell a joke that failed. The general rudeness of New Yorkers appalled her, their clothes intimidated her, their food both pleased and repulsed her. What she didn't know about fine art was a constant embarrassment. That began to fade as daily study allowed her the pleasure of developing personal taste. She put aside the dewy-eyed sweetness of Gounod in favor of Verdi, Puccini, and above all Mozart.

Making friends was more difficult. At Juilliard the few Chinese spoke little English, and several Negroes on scholarship never lingered in the building to chat. Caucasian students were brusque and arrogant compared to *haole* in Hawaii, unconcerned with a part-time auditor like Maile. Most students concentrated on fiendishly difficult piano and violin works, and seemed to focus solely on outdoing each other. At recitals she heard performances of explosive beauty from tigerish young musicians who stepped offstage to collapse in exhaustion, or to boil over with fresh competitiveness.

She met few women students, and fewer singers. Her three hours a week at the conservatory were filled with requests to fuck in a back room: Please, baby, gimme relief. She was shocked to find that most Americans considered sex either dirty, or entangled in a weird romanticism of purity and rescue. But musicians and musicmaking were also wildly, unavoidably attractive. She went to a violinist's tiny bare studio in a fifteen-floor walkup, drank sour wine, and ended up under him on his couch. For a month they staged teasing lovers' games, then went back to being acquaintances who exchanged nods in the library.

Week after week Maile drifted along in a loner life that she nevertheless enjoyed. Madame was all business and didn't allow even the usual mild intimacies between student and teacher: no little jokes, no hinting questions about Madame's past. Maile practiced in her apartment, cooked for herself, washed and ironed her own clothes. In one typical week she heard Purcell songs at the Cloisters and a concert version of Mozart's *Abduction* in Queens, with a wobbly-voiced soprano and a spectacular tenor. She learned to rate singers, and understood that not all operatic voices were good.

An elderly widower in Maile's building took to greeting her in German after he saw her carrying a book of Schumann songs. *"Der geniale Komponist!"* he declared, and introduced himself as Herr Melvin Landau. He wore fine three-piece suits and a heavy gold watch that hung loosely on his thin wrist. Twice they shared a pot of tea at the grim cafeteria across the street, exactly half an hour of proper conversation that remained with Maile the rest of the day as a pleasant interval in a disciplined life with few variations. When he mentioned being Jewish, she said that until she attended the University of Hawaii, she had never realized that Jews were a modern people. She had assumed they were confined to biblical times, like the Romans and Hittites.

"*Ach, wohl,*" Herr Landau remarked, smiling, "I am very much here."

MANHATTAN BILLBOARDS ADVERTISED the coming of summer with cheerful beach scenes and smiling couples in cruise wear. Maile found the July heat oppressive. The subways were unbearable, so instead she rode city buses crammed with passengers whose clothes stuck to their chests, arms, and backs. Windows were often jammed shut, but smokers lit cigarettes and filled the interior with a gray cloud. She ached for the Waikiki breezes that flowed through the shoreline palms all year long, threading the air with the faint taste of salt. Even more she missed Auntie Lani's energy and Makua's quiet presence, and she sent them postcards of Manhattan with no expectation of a reply. She ate her first slice of pizza (awful), discovered mangoes in a Jamaican market (great!), but everything from rent to clothes to a packet of tissues bought at a newsstand was ominously expensive. With the approach of autumn she would need a coat, a hat, a scarf, things she had forgotten to budget. "I shall advise on the wardrobe," Madame Renska said toward the end of summer. "Your sense for style must develop." August was so hot that Maile began washing her hair every night. In Washington Heights whole families slept outside on the fire escapes of their buildings, which Madame claimed was a fool's invitation to theft and rape.

Despite soaring temperatures, the Manhattan music community was in a state of high excitement about the new Metropolitan Opera House at Lincoln Center. Maile had difficulty pronouncing the Italian title of the work scheduled for the opening performance: *La Fanciulla del West*. She wished that *Aida* had been chosen instead. The grand aria *O patria mia* remained a personal landmark, first heard in sixth grade and the cause of her exile from Kauai—although no one would ever get that backcountry story out of her.

Advanced music students were allowed into the noon dress rehearsal for the premiere of *The Girl of the Golden West.* Maile joined a crowd that radiated the exhilaration of being present for a historic occasion. Even though she'd studied the libretto beforehand, she couldn't quite follow the action, but for the first time she experienced what it meant for singers to bestride a world stage with full orchestra and chorus. Leontyne Price fascinated her, every tone, every gesture, the delightful and unexpected flashes of wit. The marvelously trained voices projected into a true theater, built for singers, where a fantasy world was created for the sole purpose of enchanting listeners.

After the performance, Maile was swept along with a group of students who piled into a coffee shop to analyze the new building's acoustics. They argued about tempi for chorus versus soloists, and swooned over phrases of perfection. Two hours later, going home by bus, she still felt the excitement, along with something new in the air. It was only five-thirty, but the sky was darkening. A chill swept through the drafty bus doors. Under the seat, the heater blasting at her feet gave little relief. She began shivering: hands, arms, shoulders.

The Negro driver glanced at her in his mirror and said, "Winter's coming, little lady. Next time you're out, now, don't you forget your sweater."

DURING OCTOBER MAILE watched the world blaze with the disturbing beauty of autumn leaves. She feared the increasing cold. Ads she had never seen, for flu medicines and cold remedies, appeared in newspapers, on billboards, in subway stations. On Madame's advice she bought a coat, classily styled camel hair the color of Waikiki beach sand and lined in sheepskin. Its soft luxuries pleased them both, but Maile concealed the fact that it had cost only fifteen dollars at an East Side thrift shop.

As the temperature sank, she bought a fox fur hat, gloves, and a red cashmere scarf from the same shop. For her first Juilliard student recital, she wore them all and walked through Central Park to the performance hall. There she changed into a gown, which she realized too late was not appropriate, but she conquered her nervousness by single-minded concentration on her Schubert song cycle. Easy pieces compared to the aria Madame would not yet allow her to present in public. Herr Landau was ill with stomach flu and unable to attend. Maile's performance was applauded politely by the small audience. Offstage, her accompanist gave her a thumbs-up and dashed away to a lesson. Madame came over to say, "Singing, yes." She paused for a curt nod of approval and stepped back to eye Maile's gown. "Such a satin creation, no." She left to coach a tenor in the newest production at the Met. Maile realized there would be no detailed praise for what she'd sung particularly well, no listing of tiny mistakes, no joyous postmortem in a coffee shop. It was now simply on to the next lesson, the next challenge.

Back at her apartment she found a bill taped to the door: the cost of the space heater she had bought was not included in her rent, which only covered radiator heating, a detail she'd forgotten. Thirty-seven dollars was due immediately at the manager's office. She burst into tears.

AFTER SIX MONTHS in the city Maile's life was still an unbroken round of study. She didn't miss a lesson or a concert, and the treasure of music continued to unfold: Mendelssohn lieder with delicate melodies like sparks rising from a driftwood fire at night, the grand sweep of art songs by Richard Strauss, with his passion for women's voices. She also heard performances by singers past their prime who couldn't hold a pitch, or whose voices were trained but ordinary, or who had a slightly grainy quality that betrayed secret cigarette smoking. Her worst frustration was having expected to be on stage by now, part of an opera production. Instead she sat in the audience at graduate student performances with a score in her lap. She ushered at Carnegie Hall so she could hear a soprano from Berlin. Tickets at the Met were unaffordable, and sold out through next year.

Living thriftily made Maile expert at finding free things to do. In that regard the city was a feast, with a generous heart. At Goethe

House she saw exhibits by Berlin artists and enjoyed surprising people with her earnest German. She got through a solitary Thanksgiving and Christmas by window shopping and attending free concerts in churches decorated with fragrant boughs of pine. At Rockefeller Center she saw the tree lighting, the skaters. Snow was so strangely dazzling that she often stood still among passing pedestrians to watch it fall from the sky, swirled by gusts, or driven sideways by high winds that whistled along the grid of Manhattan streets. But without a crowd of relatives the holidays felt empty. Worse, just to get by she couldn't help spending more money than ever intended. She made a list of unavoidable expenses and figured out that what she had left would only last until next fall—six or eight months short of two years.

The gap between daily necessities and the funds provided by the clan grew ever wider. None of them had traveled or lived elsewhere, or had any idea of expenditures that ordinary New Yorkers took for granted: bus fare, snacks, resoling shoes. Maile imagined Auntie Lani asking, "For real, in cold you need different clothes?" Yes, she even needed different underwear. Staying warm and dry, and not falling ill in a world of ice and slush meant never just throw on a coat, always remember hat, gloves, scarf, umbrella, tissues, ChapStick. Waterproof your boots with mink oil, scrub off the salt rings every night, stuff the damp leather with wads of newspaper.

One day in late February, Maile was picking through a Brahms song when her apartment radiator sputtered, clanked and went silent. The room chilled minute by minute. Outside in the hall the building superintendent went door to door calling out, "Boiler's busted, no heat 'til tonight, boiler's busted . . . " She considered spending the morning in the grimy cafeteria across the street. Everyone else in the building would go there. The food was terrible and the toilets filthy. A surly teenage gang with knives claimed the tables when school let out.

Across the room the apartment's one small window was blotched with sooty ice crystals that clung to the outside. Maile put on her coat against the increasing cold and pulled her suitcase from under the bed. From a pocket she took out the leather pouch, hidden there her first night aboard the ship. "Makua," she said, hoping he might have taken the day off to go spear fishing at Ka'ena Point. Sit on the rocky shore afterwards with his brothers and a cooler of beer. Grill fresh squid. Talk story.

On the windowsill she laid out the three King Kalākaua coins, evidence that her father and Auntie Lani had forgiven her even though she'd broken the greatest *kapu* by selfishly hoarding money. The open suitcase yawned on her bed. In her mind she began packing it: the sarong, white high heels no one wore after Labor Day, her painstakingly assembled winter wardrobe with the fine labels that had fooled Madame. Walking through Central Park in a fox fur hat and camel hair coat, she had looked, she was sure, like a fashion model. At home such *haole* clothes would be useless, would make Jade hoot with jealous laughter.

All too clearly Maile imagined arriving back in Papakōlea with nothing but evidence of her failure. No opera contract, no fame. She returned the coins to the pouch, the pouch to its hiding place, and slid the suitcase under the bed. Taking a score, she went outside to catch a bus to the Lion's Head. For the price of a coffee and Danish she could claim half a small table until noon, shut out the political arguments among Columbia students, and study in warmth.

BY MARCH THE tree branches along Morningside Drive had a faint wash of green. The putty gray sky was almost pale blue. A breeze with a trace of warmth came from the river. Everything Maile saw and felt had such a sense of promise she imagined living in Manhattan for six months of every year. In a larger, nicer apartment, which she would pay for by joining the Met studio on a beginner's contract. Madame had hinted at such a possibility; eight young singers at East Coast conservatories were attracting attention in Manhattan, and Maile Manoa was one of them.

Over the next months she worked part-time at Bergdorf Goodman promoting Tahitian Gardenia perfume. For two hours a day she played with accents and attitudes while selling dreams to women whose sophistication she no longer feared. She visited the Temple of Dendur at the Metropolitan Museum because it was there to be admired. Every payday she bought something small at an exclusive French bakery. She sensed herself claiming the city just a little more, but the sweetness of spring turned to heat that soon frayed peoples' tempers into public bursts of viciousness. Columbia students grew beards, traded their jackets and trousers for jeans, and their manners for aggressive confrontations with strangers. Card tables appeared on the edge of Harlem for voter registration and civil rights petitions, manned by angry young Negroes who insisted on being called "black men." Maile tried to sympathize with their cause but couldn't associate herself with the grim history of slavery.

The route she took to lessons and classes was disrupted by ever larger protests, against the Vietnam War, military spending, Jim Crow laws, and in support of jailed marchers in southern cities she couldn't picture. From inside a bus she watched protesters with Peace Now signs charged by police on horseback. Passengers stared in silence or yelled at the officers to club those bastards.

Madame dismissed the whole problem. "I see all this before in Germany," she said. "I am familiar and can say in America not to worry." She gave no more than this glimpse of her former life. Maile recalled Professor Chaimowitz describing a rabbi beaten to death in public, but if Leah Renska had experienced similarly dramatic events, it was none of Maile's business. Most Juilliard students were puzzled by civil rights, voting rights, states' rights, trifling issues compared to the eternal values of art. If you mastered the Dvorak cello concerto, who cared if you were a hawk or a dove, a Democrat or a Republican?

ONE AFTERNOON MAILE returned to 153rd Street and saw a black coroner's car out front. Inside the building, a policeman stood in the hall writing on a notepad. A sign over the elevator door read CLOSED. A breathless first-floor resident told Maile that Mr. Landau had been knifed, his stomach sliced open. "Likely dead by the time he hit the floor. Blood all over, gold watch gone. Ask me, it's that cafeteria gang, but bound to happen, him going over there, that wrist band flashing like some advertisement."

Upstairs, Maile stared out the window at the black car until it pulled away. She had never known someone who was murdered. A

Jewish gentleman who survived World War II did not deserve such a terrible death in America. Land of the brave, home of the free. Then the sorrow she felt turned into panic at being stuck in this building, forced to use the same entrance the killer had used. Even with her part-time job, her money would be gone by mid-October. The Kalākaua coins were worth about nine hundred dollars, enough to buy her another two months in Manhattan. That would mean staying in the same apartment, and riding the elevator after the blood was mopped up, or going up and down eight flights of poorly lighted stairs.

At the piano she threw open a score to lose herself in music. Her hands shook and her pulse thudded. Finally she found a calming soprano solo in Mozart's *C-Minor Mass*. She focused on the opening phrase so that nothing else existed and played the accompaniment with a light touch. *"Et . . . in—carna—tus est,"* she sang, a slender shaft of sound, the composer at his most graceful. She held her voice back so it fit the piece as cool silver radiance instead of vibrant warmth. The melody's shimmering beauty filled the apartment. *"De spi . . . ritu sancto . . . "* She eased into the difficult interval, letting the tones rise above her to unfold. Mozart himself seemed to be speaking to her from a great distance, across centuries, across a vast ocean.

She played the subtle interlude and imagined the notes as an orchestra, string instruments with a solo flute gently leading the way. In the apartment above, a sudden voice: "C'mon out to the park, it's a breezy ninety dee-grees, we gonna burn, baby, burn!" The nearly deaf veteran who owned the radio didn't react to thumping on the ceiling with a mop handle. The announcer called out hits, runs, strikes. A memory flitted through Maile's mind: years ago, another baseball game on Tūtū's radio. By now she should be auditioning at the Met for an apprentice contract, the only chance to make enough money to stay. As a nonmatriculated student she was ineligible for Juilliard scholarships or loans. As a concert soloist, at best she might squeeze out half a month's rent with pickup jobs, a saint's day mass in Queens, a wedding in Connecticut. Thirty dollars, fifty dollars.

She started over. *"Et . . . incarna—"* Up on Broadway a police siren blared in a competing E-flat. She sang against it, against the radio, and recaptured Mozart, making it all the way through the opening section to, *"Fac—tus est . . . "*

She closed the score. *Mass in C-Minor*, a church job. After the performance, without a doubt, soloists would be asked to donate their fees. Every day in Manhattan musicians performed for free, from the greenest beginners to the greatest artists. On the radio a trio of women sang in tight harmony, "For soup that's mmm-mmm good!"

MAILE GOT OFF the bus at Broadway and 86th to walk the last two blocks to Madame's building. Her stiletto heels clicked on the sidewalk, tak-tak, tak-tak, as irksome as a metronome. She wore an early fall outfit, a risk when the heat hadn't yet lifted, but she planned to ambush Madame. From the beginning her teacher had predicted a promising future, then an unusually good future, finally: a great future. Yet beyond the original two years no deadline was ever set—art could not be rushed. How long did it take to develop as a soprano? No discussion was allowed.

Crossing 88th Street, Maile concentrated on the slow, gliding melody that opened the famous aria from Norma: *Ca—sta di—va,* the first phrase spun out over fourteen notes of silky simplicity. Diva, for divine, for singers who had roses thrown at their feet. She forced herself to enter the building calmly. In the lobby she checked her reflection in a narrow glass mail chute: half a russet pillbox hat, half a plaid shoulder cape in russet and black, a matching mini-skirt. One sleek black shoe. Her hair coiled into a large chignon. Diva-diva. Twenty-six was the right age for a debut.

She rode the elevator to the top floor, rang the bell at 67-A, and adjusted her shoulders for perfect posture. When the door opened, she said, as instructed at her first lesson, "Good afternoon, Madame Renska."

"Feh," her teacher exclaimed, a gasp of pleasure. "Such a lovely ensemble to anticipate the autumn! You are being aware of details like between early and late season." She took Maile's arm and led her inside.

At the piano Maile swung off her shoulder cape and unpinned her hat. Madame's eyebrows were still raised, waiting for a grateful response to a rare compliment. Maile held out the sheet music for Norma. "I have to audition."

Madame gave the pages an affronted glance. "Did I not request Zerlina? We must rehearse your middle-of-range line."

Maile slid the sheet music onto the piano lid.

"Audition?" Madame squinted as though trying to solve a riddle in a foreign language. She turned to a pair of large wall calendars: Juilliard School of Music, Summer Session 1967, and Metropolitan Opera, Fall Season '67, covered with the names of professional singers and students. "I see no audition for Miss Manoa. You are now giving the orders?"

Nervously Maile stared at a bookcase. Madame's one inflexible rule of never mentioning financial problems came from her belief that singers must fight their own battles with the realities of life. It made them better artists. In almost thirty years, Madame claimed, no student had asked for a loan or free lessons. Raising the subject was grounds for immediate dismissal.

The silence between them tightened, as though both were competing for a limited supply of air. Maile dove off a cliff into deep water: "It's the problem we can't discuss." Madame shook her head, but Maile plunged on. "I can only stay 'til October. I can't ask my family for more money."

Madame drew back, silent, then said in a mean little voice that breaking even the most established rule was petty compared to the much greater crime it implied: a brilliant young soprano was simply quitting. Betraying her gift. And because of finances. "Or your sweetheart calls to you?"

"No," Maile said.

"You want babies, babies." She poked at Maile's bosom.

"No! I can't."

"Do you mean to say you are not able?"

Maile nodded fiercely to cut off further questions.

"Well," Madame said, "at least that. Sopranos cannot have babies and husbands. However, after all our work you must know you make excellent progress. I do not praise too much." She stroked her finger-tips across Maile's throat. "Now, pah, you must go home!"

Maile leaned away from her touch. "I've tried so hard. The cost of..."

"I do not relax my standards." A surge of anger colored Madame's cheeks. "If you cannot remain here, go to Europe for further study."

Her words sailed past Maile. Madame could schedule a Metropoli-tan Opera audition with one phone call. "Please." It came out in a wheedling whisper. "An apprentice contract, like you mentioned."

With a forefinger Madame gave the sheet music a contemptuous flick. "You had hopes with this aria?"

"It's memorized. Just listen to the opening." She gripped the piano, ready to beg or cry, but Madame went to a desk. Maile waited for her hands to stray over to the phone, to dial a number that didn't have to be looked up. Opera careers had been launched with a single piece sung for the right director at the right time—in April a mezzo from Florida went straight to debut as Carmen.

Madame flipped through a stack of mail and pulled out a flyer. She wrote down an address. "Meet me here tomorrow. I give you my time for this because of your worth. Now go."

AT THE SOUTH end of Manhattan, Maile went up subway stairs to find herself in the middle of Fulton Fish Market. Men were stacking crates, dumping ice, hosing down display tables. She checked the address Madame had given her, then consulted a city map and walked two blocks east to the John Street Church. Above the open doors hung a hand-painted banner: CULTURAL TALENT SHOWCASE 1 PM TODAY. Baf-fled, she worked her way forward through seafood truckers taking a lunch break on the sidewalk.

Madame sat alone in a back pew. She motioned for Maile to join her. Four other people were seated down front. The mimeographed program was too blurred to read. They listened to African-style drumming and watched a mime troupe demonstrate jungle warfare in Vietnam with cardboard rifles and palm fronds. When the group exited, Madame turned to Maile with a pay-attention look and said, "John Eagleclaw."

A tall brown-skinned man of about thirty, in buckskins and a Cheyenne headdress, stepped in front of the altar. Dutifully Maile focused on him, another unusual performer, still confused as to why they were here. His stark cheekbones and uplifted gaze gave him the look of an idealized Indian in an old Western. After a soft introduction on the organ, he began. "Our Fa—ther . . . who-art-in . . . "

The front row audience sat up. Maile had performed the same piece dozens of times in Honolulu churches, but was unprepared for the gorgeous tone that flowed over the pews like a benign river. Everyone was tensely still, as if also amazed by such a magnificent tenor.

Except for Madame Renska. "There, my dear," she whispered, "is a superb talent who cannot overcome his background. He only studied a little, years ago." Maile eyed her warily. "He is unable to sing a duet, trio, quartet, or follow a conductor's baton. Yet he dreams of a great career as the Caruso of the Indian Nations."

The tenor built toward the conclusion, delivering each note all the way to a profound "Aaa—a-men!" The echo reverberated from the ceiling. People applauded vigorously. Maile sat dazed. Madame nudged her outside and walked ahead to a cab stand.

A minute later they were headed uptown through dense traffic. "You can always go home," Madame said tartly, "and deny your gift. There is no greater shame for an artist." She outlined Maile's future as the Honolulu version of the Cheyenne tenor, performing "The Lord's Prayer" for the rest of her life at weddings and funerals, giving comfort and inspiration on a safe, sentimental level, risking nothing, having no ambition. In short, dying.

Maile protested that she did have ambition.

"Tsk!" Madame Renska clicked her tongue. "How much you must learn. Living in New York has taught you well, yet in America we have only the distant imitation of European music and culture. If you desire success, I shall not be your last teacher. You must know repertoire from the first hand. In places where Mozart lived, for example. Can you describe what separates German opera from Austrian? The difference between one famous conductor and the next? Do you recognize the style of Werner von Wehlen or Gerhardt Trakt? Have you visited the great music festivals?"

She gestured at Maile's chignon and plucked at her suit jacket. "Your appearance is excellent but deceptive. Underneath you are still a country girl. In Germany or Austria or France, voice students can manage with one hundred dollars a month in the not so very large cities." She folded her hands and sat back.

Maile saw the front window of the cab waver as if it were melting. Go home or go to Europe. She imagined arriving at Honolulu airport, stepping into the gentle breeze, met by relatives giving her one lei after another, fragrance for Maile the famous, the good daughter, their singer returned to them. Her mouth went dry.

FOR YEARS MAILE would look back on the next ten days as the time when everything changed in a way that could not be undone. She cried and cried, then consolidated her life so it fit into a trunk, two suitcases, and a shoulder bag. There had been no phone calls from home, no letters, just a birthday card from Auntie Lani, "We love you and we miss you," with twelve signatures. Maile longed to see them all in the backyard, Makua dropping a heap of fish over coals on the oil drum grill, Jade's girls pulling waxed paper off bowls of macaroni salad, Hermann's boys struggling to uncap sodas in crates—how old were they now, two and three, or three and four? She could get on a plane tomorrow. And by the end of the week be jobbing around town singing "Lovely Hula Hands" and substitute-teaching at an elementary school.

She bought a ticket, Rotterdam by ship $200, on an old freighter crowded with European students returning home after summer courses in America. In early September the waters of the North Atlantic were dark even at noon. She searched for the many shades of blue she had known since childhood, but the waves and swells were an unchanging sinister gray. She fought with herself over having sold the Kalākaua coins, her *pili* spirit stirring in aggravation whenever the memory came to mind. Two of the coins were "in case" money, Makua's words, so they were not meant to be kept permanently. But the third, her mother's wedding gift, with its tarnished strip at the back of the king's neck, had lain on the counter of Manhattan Numismatics like an accusation. A coin, Maile had decided, that once belonged to a mother she'd never known, on the occasion of starting the kind of family life she would never have. A bit of monarchy silver passed down from a great-grandfather who had left only a name in Hawaii and disappeared on an unknown ship to an unknown destination. An ancestor ghost of the faintest kind, although he could help her now. She pushed the coin toward the other two.

The European passengers assumed that Miss Maile Manoa was Algerian. On discovering she held an American passport, they couldn't believe she came from Honolulu, a fairyland none of them had visited. One Frenchman suspected her of being a secret Jewess, which made Maile laugh in amazement. At night she drank apricot brandy with Scandinavians, danced hula for them, and twice got into a cot with one man while another watched the door. The gospel of free love spreading across America had stolen aboard the ship.

5

IN ROTTERDAM, CUSTOMS officials announced that ship passengers planning to continue south by train must find alternatives: the tracks were obstructed by a protest over Soviet troop movements in Czechoslovakia. Maile got a sudden, disturbing sense of Russian soldiers not confined to a news article in a Manhattan paper, but it was too late to change her destination: Salzburg, a city just a hundred-fifty miles from Prague. She left her trunk to be sent as rail freight, and arranged to go by Austrian Airlines. The flight would last just an hour, but she had never flown before. Spending extra money for a ticket made her doubly nervous.

Before leaving New York she'd sent a letter: "Dear Makua, This city is too dangerous and expensive for me to stay. I'm moving to Salzburg. That's in Europe. My teacher says I'll be a big success. I'm still coming home by next May. Love, love, and kiss the babies for me." She couldn't tell him that a career in classical music was far more competitive than she'd ever imagined, that opera singers needed patrons and luck, that they often sang in nine different languages, that she wasn't sure of much anymore.

The small plane had Franz Schubert written on its side in curling Gothic script: a plane named for a Romantic composer who had traveled in horse-drawn coaches. *"Austria heisst Österreich,"* she murmured, *"Ich heisse Fräulein Manoa,"* baby German, tourist German, the words as mysterious on her tongue as when she first learned them in Honolulu. Like other women passengers, she wore a traveling outfit that included hat and gloves, but she still attracted glances, and her spirits would not settle down.

There had been a final chilly meeting with Madame at the door of her studio. Maile the rule breaker, demanding to know where she should go in Europe, although not invited inside to sit down for tea. "Paris is a lovely city," Madame had advised briskly, "however the French music is not so worth your life devotion. Italy will train you beautifully, however their laws forbid hiring foreigners. Berlin is a possibility, Vienna. Or provincial Salzburg with its Mozarteum conservatory. I have a contact there. The summer festival is quite grand, otherwise Salzburg is a medieval village. The Fates play tricks to allow Mozart and Hitler to come from the same soil." She had agreed to send a letter of introduction, and then closed the door.

A stewardess offered a dainty cup of coffee but Maile declined, her doubts about Salzburg growing. If Italy and France were out, Germany had eighty-two opera houses, more than any other country in the world. The Bayreuth Festival had been a cultural landmark well before the Nazis and was now fully reclaimed. The German economy was strong again but that meant a more expensive place to live. Austrian students supposedly got along on a hundred dollars a month. Their country was a tenth the size of Germany, the birthplace of Mozart and the waltz, which no one danced anymore. Her future now depended on Madame's recommendation to a teacher in Salzburg who was only a name.

Too soon the little plane began a gradual descent. Maile's chest stirred uncomfortably, and she peered out the window at what looked like a distant bank of fog clinging to the ground. It took on the form of a blue-gray frontier of mountains. Fields of snow glinted on every jagged peak—mountains without the familiar shape of a single volcano, dozens of peaks crowded together, a frightening, magnificent sight. Rainbows of sunlight flashed against the black rock, brilliant reds, yellows, oranges. As the plane turned in a diving arc, an oval of blue and white mountains opened up below like a gigantic crystal bowl, at its center a broad, bright green plain. A fan of blue lakes spread out to the west. The plane glided lower toward a long green river winding past three tree-covered hills, the tallest spiked by a castle, its steep walls topped by the spear points of towers, at its base a maze of twisting streets as dense as a coral reef. Maile stared in edgy enchantment. Buildings and spires crowded together reflected the golden light of a fall afternoon. Everything looked wonderfully old, as old as fairy tales.

On the ground a customs official stepped in front of her and sliced down with one arm. *"Sprechen Sie Deutsch?"* he asked in a pleasant tone.

"Ja!" she exclaimed.

He smiled, took her passport, sighed, and said in English, "The Americans, they are always so very fluent in our language." Then, *"Ach, du Lieber,* born in Honolulu? You are my very first." He asked about her future plans. She replied, and his eyes lost their flirtatious gleam. "Study, sing," he remarked. "How vague." All foreigners were considered tourists, he informed her, and must either stay at an official hotel or register at the police station within twenty-four hours. Failure to do so meant the possibility of deportation.

Sobered, Maile stared at the new entry stamp below the one for Holland. Police. Deportation. But the city of Mozart was just ahead. A cab driver recommended a hotel and asked if she was ready to go. *"Jawohl!"* she said.

A minute later the taxi was rolling along a cobblestone street of shops with arched wooden doors and flower boxes and green shutters. Windows were bordered in curlicues of wrought iron like graceful black ribbons suspended in the air. Bicyclists wove through clusters of women in full-skirted dirndls with puffed sleeves and aprons, men in linen shirts and leather trousers, a boy dressed like his father with an identical pheasant feather on his hat. Maile spotted what looked like an exclusive restaurant, with a wonderful name—*Das Silberne Rehkalb,* Silver Fawn—and wanted to go there for lunch.

Other signs highlighted with gold leaf announced SCHUSTER, GE-MÜSE. Shoemaker, she translated, scouring her memory, Vegetables; delighted to recognize words learned years ago halfway around the world. A large marble fountain had life-sized figures in long robes and at their feet an inscribed date: ANNO 1702. Europe, she wanted to shout, I'm in Europe!

In German the driver said, "The whole world comes to our summer Festival. From Japan, Arabia, Argentina. A shame you missed the performances."

"Ja, das ist wahr," she gasped, just to speak the language, to belong to the scene around them, so pretty, so clean, so unexpected.

The cheapest room at the hotel cost one thousand eight hundred schillings a night: seventy-two U.S. dollars. Maile had been prepared to pay fifteen. The taxi was gone, the only other lodgings were several kilometers outside the city, and she was afraid to spend more money looking around. She agreed to the three-day minimum, thinking of it as a temporary necessity. Apartments were supposed to be laughably inexpensive compared to New York.

In the room she stepped out of her shoes, took off her hat and gloves, then fell back on the bed and lay there stiff as a plank. The toes on her right foot cramped. She shook her ankle. The cramp faded but reappeared behind her knee, and the drone of Manhattan traffic seeped into the room, as if she were still struggling to sing over the whirring, honking blare that reached high up into Madame's studio, penetrated the walls at Juilliard, seeped through her old apartment window. Memories came to her like random snapshots spilling from a shoebox of photos: featured singer on national radio, Easter soloist in Honolulu, first Manoa to get a college degree, middle daughter in a large clan, unable to do the one thing expected of her, produce children. Details collided all the way back to Lihue Grammar School, to sitting in shocked silence after hearing opera for the first time, on a record, in a classroom full of children disturbed by the sounds. *Why is the lady screaming like that?*

She lay staring up at the ceiling, stunned to think of how ignorant she had been. People in Manhattan were raised with classical music. That had to be five times as true in Europe. Austrians grew up attending performances of *The Magic Flute*, knew Mozart by age seven. In the eyes of the world, Hawaiian music meant ukuleles and steel guitars, pretty or funny songs, light entertainment for tourists. The thought of Madame's final coldness felt like a wound. For a year and a half the two of them had worked on arias that brought out the finest points of love, rage, devotion, joy. At their last meeting all that intimacy vanished. Maile wondered if she could ever succeed here, or if she even belonged in a country where Hitler and Mozart had been born just a hundred miles apart.

ON A MAP Maile found the Musik Akademie a short distance from the hotel, across a footbridge over the river and go left half a block. In addition to Madame's letter of recommendation, she had to audition for the new teacher. Until the conservatory's fall session began, applicants could rehearse there. After nearly two weeks of travel she desperately wanted to recover her singing voice.

On Schwarzstrasse a white four-story building had wide steps that led to a broad wooden door. Over it, in large letters chiseled into a white marble tablet: MOZARTEUM. Above that were tall windowed rooms with decorative railings, and four statues on the roof. A wing to the left extended to a porch of white columns in front of the concert hall. All tiny compared to Juilliard, she thought, but more beautiful.

The foyer was empty. At the far end of the main hall, a clerk in a gray suit stacked papers on a countertop. In the basement someone played a kettledrum, boom-boom sounds that droned up through the tiles under Maile's feet. She climbed a zigzag of stairs to a series of doors with neat labels: ÜBUNGSZIMMER, practice room. Each was empty except for a chair and a piano. Cautiously she chose one and sat down.

The first tones she sang were sluggish, barely more than grunts. Do not rush, she reminded herself. Rough sounds could be expected after two weeks of traveling. Madame had said a singer's basic gift never deserted one who was properly trained. Ballet dancers needed their daily warm-ups, and an operatic voice had to be awakened in the same way. Preparing for an audition meant faithfully completing routine exercises, not drinking red wine, not getting so nervous that one's face broke out. After several minutes of low-range humming Maile felt a familiar vibration on her teeth. Her jaw and tongue loosened. With her breath she guided the humming into five low vowels. After another minute the first full tone emerged, "Aaahhh . . . "

Hele on, Maile-girl, she thought, go, go!

She broke off, horrified to realize she was thinking in pidgin, spoken at home by dishwashers and everyone in her family who couldn't manage Standard English. For a moment she forgot where she was. "Salzburg," she whispered, *"Zalzburg,"* pronouncing it as they did. She pictured the church spires she'd seen on the short walk from the hotel, the castle above them. The air and streets here were sparkling clean—like Hawaii rather than Manhattan—yet the encircling mountains were not green all the way to their peaks, and were much higher and fiercer than any she had ever seen. Each time someone spoke, the language hit her like a splash of water. People's everyday clothes resembled costumes in an historical painting. Here she was Fraülein Maile Manoa, and constantly felt off-balance. In fact, she admitted, Miss Manoa from Hawaii was just someone with a dream based on a fantasy about a soprano named Zoila Mar y Sol. The name alone should have been a warning! Because of that fantasy she now sat in a practice room in an unfamiliar country, with no idea of where to go or what to do if the Mozarteum teacher did not accept her. Going home was not possible. Better to climb one of those frightening mountains and just step off.

THIS MORNING'S NUMBER was seventeen, chosen by randomly opening a book of Nietzsche's writings on music and accepting any page number over ten and under twenty-five. Professor Aleksander Jann's fingers had become adept at flipping to the lower figures, so it was necessary to be disciplined and avoid cheating.

Seventeen steps to the back porch to put on a gardening smock and clogs. At the rear of his handsome house was a patch of rich soil where cows once grazed. This fall his rows of yellow and auburn chrysanthemums were planted in a French style of chevrons. Carefully he removed seventeen weeds. He clipped an equal number of flowers for a bouquet to give his wife when she returned from her massage at Kurgarten spa.

On the back porch Professor Jann removed his smock and muddy clogs, and put on slippers. As he passed through the front room on his way to shower, he avoided looking at a particular cabinet. Seventeen minutes later, he sat at a desk in a narrow alcove that functioned as a library. He translated seventeen more lines of a Latin version of *Tristan et Isolde*. And so on through the morning, assigning himself chores or doing things that gave him pleasure until the number of different activities matched the arbitrary number he had started with. He didn't always make it, especially on days when there was no chess game with Baron von Gref to look forward to, or a lesson at the conservatory. He dreaded the approach of old age and the steadily shrinking social life that accompanied the fact of no longer being on stage.

Often, after he completed a dozen or so tasks without cheating or repeating, his thoughts stalled and then revolted. At that point the urge could no longer be resisted. He went straight to the cabinet and took out a glass and the bottle of Chateau Montifaud with a grateful feeling that was as powerful as sex, as love, as music.

This morning, however, he made it to noon, just in time to enjoy luncheon with Dora before going to the Mozarteum. She was his fourth wife, womanly rather than prettily feminine, and she retained the slim figure of a runner who had participated in the 1936 Olympics. A whiff of notoriety still clung to her for having shaken hands with the Negro runner Jesse Owens, an act her husband deeply admired. They had been married for six years and were settled into the pleasures of a mature relationship. He'd promised to retire now that the Mozarteum's summer session had ended, and his last student was under contract in Vienna.

As he and Dora were finishing their meal, the mail arrived with a letter from New York. Dora wanted to take their customary post-luncheon walk, but did not protest when he went alone to the conservatory. He'd intended to clear out his teaching studio but the letter from Leah Renska intrigued him.

Professor Jann hadn't seen her since 1938 when they were both starting out as teachers, and Austria was joined to the German Reich. One day after returning a score to the library, Leah simply vanished. A year later he was relieved to learn she had found work in New York. For nearly three decades their contact remained cordial although infrequent. Professorin Renska retained her ability to "spot a winner," as she put it, and still taught America's finest singers, including several at the Metropolitan Opera. The three tenors she had sent him over the years eventually became well established in Germany.

Yet the fall session was about to begin. The admissions deadline had passed, and a singer from Hawaii was unusual enough to be almost bizarre. Jann opened the windows in his studio to air it out, then read the letter again: Maile Manoa, one of Madame's beginning pupils, a select group with access to The Juilliard School. Three solo recitals there, 1966 and 1967, eleven other recitals elsewhere in Manhattan. Performing arias gratis, he assumed, in college halls and hospital lounges, an admirable American custom. Miss Manoa had a degree in elementary pedagogy from the University of Hawaii, where she had also studied German. He couldn't imagine the language of Heine and Hoffmannsthal being taught in Honolulu. He hadn't even realized that any form of higher education existed in Hawaii. Sugar came from those distant islands, and pineapple in tins. Perhaps this young woman was from a wealthy plantation family able to fund her studies in Europe. It did not seem like a promising background for opera.

Some barriers, Jann felt, were insurmountable. Certain singers came from unusual places, but growing up in the middle of the Pacific surely entailed more risk than advantage when it came to performing sophisticated theater roles. If he trusted Madame's judgment, he didn't quite believe that a Hawaiian could make the leap to the European culture of music. He decided to audition Miss Manoa out of simple curiosity rather than any expectation of being able to forge a career for her. After all, listening to an aria or two did not imply accepting her as a student.

IN THE MOZARTEUM an elderly janitor was waxing the floor to a mirror shine. Three girls with long brown braids sat on the center staircase with notebooks balanced on their knees. A blond man on a bench pulled the mouthpiece from a French horn and examined it with a critical squint.

Over the last two days Maile had eaten regularly, walked for exercise, and focused on her mental routine for auditioning: withdraw, withdraw, withdraw into a knot of energy that would burst to life as music on command. Practicing had progressed from simple scales to great double-octave leaps. An hour ago at half volume she'd sung Aida's lament for her lost homeland, saving her all for the moment that mattered. The final phrase lingered in her mind and gave her a jumpy sense of confidence.

She asked the man with the French horn where Professor Jann's teaching studio was. He flipped the brass mouthpiece into the air and it spun between them before landing back on his palm. "I doubt you will find him there." He pointed to the right. "Jann retired last month."

Alarmed, Maile walked toward a tall white door with an enamel plaque inscribed ALEKSANDER JANN, KS. Inside she heard muffled footsteps. She had not known that Professor Jann was actually Sir Jann. The abbreviation at the end of his name stood for *Kammersänger*, Court Chamber Singer, the Austrian equivalent of a knighthood. A flash of nervousness made her diaphragm contract.

If Ks. didn't accept her, she would not get a residence visa or be allowed to stay in Austria more than thirty days. If no other teacher at the Mozarteum took her, she would have to try Vienna, Berlin, or Paris—on her own—because Madame Renska, for reasons never explained, had severed her other contacts in Europe.

Somewhere outside, a church bell struck the hour. Maile wound herself up to knock on the door, one medium-sized thump. On the other side a deep voice called out, *"Herein."*

Her collarbones bones tingled. She shuffled her music scores, *Aida* on top, *Madama Butterfly* next, then *Norma* and a collection of Wagner. What she knew about Professor Jann came from a thumbnail sketch in the conservatory's little catalogue: renowned basso in the years following World War II, *Boris Godounov, Don Giovanni, Scarpia.* He was performing in fabled opera houses while she was climbing mango trees on her way home from grade school.

Taking a deep breath, she entered and said, *"Grüss Gott, Herr Professor."*

He stood up from a concert grand that stretched from the middle of the room to the windows at the back, a slender and unusually tall man, well over six feet. His thick white hair had a slight wave. His face was dominated by a high forehead, large blue eyes, and lines and dimples that had folded into expressive creases. His elegantly tailored suit looked dismayingly European. The overall effect was of an intimidating maturity. At the base of her tongue Maile tasted a trace of stomach acid, a voice ruiner.

"Shall we try that again?" Professor Jann said in German. "You look scared to death, which is a poor start. A singer's nerves must vitalize, not terrify. It is also surprising since you have come by way of

New York. I expect students from there to 'kick down the door.' Which is a rather good attitude for the theater."

Maile retreated, desperately translating what he'd said. A rather good—what? *Einstellung.* Attitude. Kammersänger Jann had just tossed her out.

In the hall the blond man sat watching her. She gave him a frightened, haughty look and turned away. Tiny fish nibbled at her ribs. She concentrated all her energy on a small white spot, the singer's candle flame, a technique of Madame's. Go, Maile, she told herself. *Holo-holo,* big-time. You look like a diva.

Pulling the door wide, she swept inside, drew a quick circle with her right foot, dipped her left knee, held an imaginary voluminous skirt out to the side with one hand, and with the other offered the music scores. "Maestro?"

Professor Jann smiled and folded his arms. "Your transformation has a touch of wit. You place us in the eighteenth century. Will you sing one of its masterworks?"

Maile straightened up, warmed by his slight approval. "No, Verdi. *Aida.*"

"Close the door, would you, please?" His tone was formal again, less encouraging. He picked up a yellow application form.

She shut the door and pretended to be interested in the long black concert grand. *Aida* was not listed on the form as an audition aria. She wanted to risk it because of the womanly power in *O patria mia,* the exiled princess grieving over her lost country. For lunch she had eaten only toast and tea to avoid a heavy stomach. She smoothed the skirt of her Nile green linen sheath, feeling alert, primed, beyond stage fright.

"Full lyric soprano," Professor Jann read aloud, "with a leaning toward larger roles. Although . . . Verdi? I would be surprised if Madame Renska had suggested *Aida.*"

Maile shrugged, not trusting her German enough to explain that although Madame occasionally allowed students to experiment with arias, *Aida* was her own idea. What else would he consider questionable? She struggled to keep her stomach muscles from turning to gel, and studied a collection of silver-framed photos on the piano: Herr Kammersänger taking curtain calls, being toasted at a banquet, program shots in full makeup. The Mozarteum's catalogue listed other teachers—a pretty Hausfrau who had been a celebrated soubrette, an obscure composer who favored mezzos, a lieder specialist—none of whom could match a knighted artist.

"You will not sing me *Aida*," Jann said. "At twenty-six you are still too young. Let me hear something less demanding. Afterwards we can talk."

For one reason or another he rejected everything else she offered. The book of Wagner received only a doubtful glance. Too young. Less demanding. Her pride smarted. Finally she insisted, "*Norma*. It's the one aria I've practiced the most."

Jann hummed the opening phrase. "That is also a very ambitious piece. Although easier on the voice." He opened the score and sat down at the piano. In an impartial tone he added, "Please ignore me now, except for cues. I am simply your accompanist."

Maile backed into the curve of the grand and slid her right elbow onto the lid, a move so familiar she could have performed it in total darkness. The simmering in her chest returned. She focused on a large antique clock staring at her from across the room.

"The stage is still," Jann said, "cloaked in mist. A moonlit night. You enter through an enormous rock crevice. Your gown is pale. You are a great pagan priestess." He began playing the soft arpeggiated chords of the introduction.

Maile turned slightly so he could see her profile and follow the motion of her breathing. She envisioned a towering split stone, inhaled, and felt her diaphragm slip down like a diver entering the water. Silently she counted the beats preceding her first phrase, then glided through an invisible frame into a parallel world of magic. "*Ca—sta...*"

Jann lifted his fingers from the keys. "Start over."

The sound of his voice jerked her back through the frame into a room with a large clock. Irritably she puffed out her cheeks.

"Breathe again," he said. "You will not reach the end of even the first phrase, let alone the entire piece. This is one of the longest openings ever written."

All right, all right, she thought, I was a tiny bit too breathy. But I would have made it.

He repeated the introduction.

"*Ca—*"

"Too much aspiration on that first syllable. Never rush this." He played.

"*Ca—*"

"Better. Continue."

"*—a—sta . . . di--va.*" She breathed in, relieved, poised for the next phrase.

"Not so much tension." Again he stopped. "You have the whole aria in front of you."

His constant interruptions angered her. All this for two words! The snippet didn't amount to anything resembling music. Madame Renska at her most picky had never dissected a phrase like this—yet Maile sensed that his criticism was reserved for an advanced student who understood painstaking subtleties. Professor Jann seemed to be already teaching. Although he would not accept her on the basis of a few notes.

Once more she began, calmly immersed in the music, and opened her mind to anticipate technical shifts several beats in advance. This time he did not stop her. Her nerve increased, and the entire beginning of the aria felt good, and an exhilarating phrase gave her the courage to sing directly to him: *Tempra tu de' cori ardendi,* Calm the ardent spirits…

He met her eyes until the accompaniment demanded his full attention.

From the midpoint of the aria she moved on toward the climactic A and let it fill the room in a flood of sound: *Ah, riedi ancora qual eri . . .* Return to me! Her lungs inched out a flow of air that spread under starry skies ruled by divine forces. She feathered the last note until it dissolved into a hot, thrilling silence. I did it, she thought. All the way to the end. Priestess and singer.

"Now, your A," Professor Jann said. "That was quite a tone."

Maile stared back and waited for more. Singing demanded immense control, immense sincerity. She had conquered armies and deserved a crown. "One good tone, that's all?"

He stiffened like a man who was not used to rudeness and did not tolerate it. She bit her lips, sensing danger—but opera was driven by passion, and all she wanted was the praise she had earned. Professor gave her a new, keener look and said, "Sing that A again. Top of the aria."

She leaned back and threw the tone at the ceiling. "AaaAAHH—"

He motioned, cutting her off. "Basically the voice is healthy. Marvelously large. Lyric progressing to dramatic, indeed."

Maile felt her lungs and diaphragm relaxing.

"For today only," he said, "I shall continue in English." He went on, speaking in a refined accent that reminded her of Professor Chaimowitz. "You are not expected to immediately understand complex terms in German." He stood and tipped her chin up to examine her profile. "The physiognomy is good. The nose comes off the forehead well. A fine jaw." He walked around her. "A slim figure but a wide torso, which is necessary. The stance when singing must be that of a dockworker. Your tone comes up through the floor. Excellent. However . . . "

He paused, with the hesitant expression of a doctor about to deliver an unwelcome diagnosis. "You lack subtlety of technique. Of feeling. This is critical, especially in Europe, where so much superb singing is heard. Americans have great brassy strength. As with many of your countrymen, you are unaware of vocal shading. Your piano effects go only from single to double, no delicate regression to a whispered tone that still carries. There is a certain brutality to your *forte* production."

Maile's cheeks heated with embarrassment. Brassy strength. Brutality. Like being compared to a lady wrestler.

He gestured at the application form. "I must admit to blatant curiosity in asking you to audition. Hawaii. Good gracious. I am led to believe such an unusual background has not prepared you for the nuances of the opera world. Of Mozart, for example. Or Richard Strauss. On stage a soprano must convey everything from the suave power plays of the Baroque era to the aesthetic instability of the Romantics. Vocal artistry goes far beyond merely producing fine tones." He sat down at the piano again and pinged an E-flat. "Sing me some trills."

Maile faced him, concealing a slump of disappointment. Her beautiful singing was no more than a first step. She matched his tones and worked her way up the scale with full- and half-tone twists, laboring to keep the notes clear and light.

When she finished, Jann handed her a book of Stockhausen pieces. "Sight-read, please. Use *solfeggio*."

She eyed the first composition. Screechy modern music. More than hard. Killer stuff. Killa, killa. *"Mi . . . fi . . . "* she sang, scrambling for each interval. *"So . . . re-si-di, ra!"*

He gave her another book. "Can you accompany yourself?"

Glumly she took his place at the piano. The Schubert song was unfamiliar, but she plowed through it, sight-reading both vocal and piano lines. Madame had accepted her as a student after only half an hour of scales! Her concentration unraveled. She made mistakes she couldn't ignore, then clenched her hands in her lap. Since leaving the stage, supposedly Alexander Jann had taught only eight students, all now established in careers. He accepted one singer at a time. None paid more than the conservatory's annual fee of two hundred dollars. But according to that horn player outside, Herr Professor was retired.

In a quiet voice Jann said, "For a singer to succeed, six things are necessary. Talent. Intelligence. Obsession. Those are obvious. But an artist must understand cruelty as well as joy. Otherwise characterizations have no depth."

Maile nodded, glad to hear him admit this. Madame had claimed to despise cruelty on stage or off, but lived by inflexible rules and was often mercilessly sarcastic.

"A singer must also have connections, or you languish alone with your gift."

Good. Another thing Madame would never discuss.

"Last and most important is being able to embrace success, and at the same time to resist its excesses. A singer who consumes a bottle or a lover between each act becomes a piece of wreckage. Every triumph breeds new doubts. Every fine review creates new judges of one's next performance. Willingness to accept challenges must remain constant. If any one of these six qualities is lacking, you will be only second-rate. Or a comet lasting no more than a few seasons."

He pulled up a chair and sat next to Maile at the piano, his manner still reserved. "Your voice is of such size, you could go to Vienna tomorrow and sing *Aida* in a class-B theater. But no one under thirty-five does justice to the role. Worse, a singer competing on stage against an orchestra of sixty or more instruments before she is ready is like a ten-year-old competing in the Olympics. I am interested solely in students who have the discipline to hold back."

Again Maile nodded.

"Young dramatic-weight voices debut every season. By age thirty-five their vocal cords are often peppered with nodes. Pianists and violinists can be child prodigies, not singers."

Nodes. A word as deadly as cancer.

"If you study with me, you must sing only what I give you. If you audition for some agent with *Aida*, or engage in similar foolishness, we are immediately quits. During next summer's Festival, conductors will be on the lookout for a future soprano at our student recitals. You will probably attract their attention. Just inform me. If you progress well, I shall enter you in the Mozarteum's summer competition. Now, enough lecturing," he added. "Perhaps I don't suit you. Do you have questions?"

Maile felt overwhelmed by his knowledge, directness, courtesy. So different from Madame, who had not been a performer, who was fanatical about etiquette and never invited questions. But a singer staked her future on a teacher, and the wrong one could mean years wasted, or lead to disaster. "How does a bass teach a soprano?"

Jann got to his feet, nodded slightly like a gentleman asking a lady's permission, then took off his suit jacket and strode to the center of the room. He breathed in with sudden force. His shirtfront rose, his waist tightened, and his mouth dropped open in a huge "Rooooaaargh!" that shivered the glass on the clock.

Maile jumped in surprise. The sound dissolved into echo and then silence.

"When I was a student," Jann said, "I often went to the zoo. The lions fascinated me. They have the most incredible diaphragms, and phenomenal sustaining power. I can still hear their wonderful beastliness." He pressed a fist against his stomach. "That gross example of tone is technically the same as this. *Boris Godounov*, Prologue, Coronation scene." Again his shirtfront swelled. He opened his arms to proclaim, *"Skorbit du—sha!!"*

The tones struck Maile like sheets of light. His expression and stance had a czar's radiance, and vaulted her into another world.

As the room absorbed the vibrations, he came to himself again. "A bass teaches a soprano with exactly the same techniques. Many are simple. Only the repertoire differs. Whether singing imitates a scream, a sob, or a whisper, it must be heard by an entire audience. Yet however extreme, theatrical emotions must never harm the voice. Singing is a very natural activity."

Simple. Natural. What he described had the sound of freedom. Not the throat diagrams Maile had dozed over in the Juilliard library, not the charts outlining the path of a conductor's baton. Instead: lions.

"Other questions?"

She wanted him to take her on so badly she could have flung herself at his feet. "No," she murmured. Lessons with him would be virtually free. Rent and food her only expenses in Salzburg. Their mutual silence told her that the audition was over, but he had not signed her application form. He might simply gave it back and thank her for coming, or pass her on to a mediocre teacher with whom she could spend years in graduate student limbo as nothing more than a promising voice. The room around her faded as though someone had dimmed the lights.

Professor Jann stepped forward, put on his jacket, and extended his hand. "With pleasure," he said, "I accept you as my student."

In a daze Maile took the signed form to the registrar, not noticing the horn player or the girls staring at her as she passed them. Outside the conservatory a raging hunger rose from the pit of her stomach. Her voice was, quote, marvelously large. Roo-aar! She imagined a mound of fresh fish and rice that filled a mixing bowl, a platter of grilled meat sticks, and *poi*, she wanted *poi* flavored with salt and seaweed, to scoop up and suck off her fingers. No one had ever understood the size of her appetite after singing.

"Tok-tok!" she called out, and went in search of a restaurant.

6

MAILE RUSHED FROM the Mozarteum's opening ceremony to look at a room for rent. Seventy-two dollars a night at a hotel meant that money was slipping away in handfuls, and another day had passed into twilight. Each morning she followed Madame Renska's advice to dress well and never, ever wear her hair loose. In Austria, braids or flowing tresses were acceptable for girls, but a woman's unbound hair was highly erotic, to be seen only in private by her husband.

All week Maile had expected to find a little room with a bed that folded to the wall, a mini toilet, and a fridge-stove combo the size of her trunk. But except for the river villas of the wealthy, everybody seemed to live above a shop or behind a church, a school, a bakery, a mortuary, in a house full of relatives, with a door to close if you were lucky. That was too much like her family's home in Papakōlea. The latest address, from the conservatory's bulletin board, was in a good location, no price given.

She crossed the river to the Old City, prepared for disappointment. The effort of constantly speaking German exhausted her. Streets were narrow and curved, a spider web rather than a neat grid, everything the opposite of Manhattan. Among Salzburg's grand marble buildings, plazas, cafés, and alleys with courtyards and potted flowers, she had looked at several appealing rooms for a hundred dollars a month. She could afford thirty. The only place for that price was an hour away by bus, in an ugly concrete building next to a Puch motorcycle factory.

Getreidegasse, however, was a straight street with facing rows of four-story stone houses and cobblestone paving laid down before the Crusades. At Number Twenty-five, she tucked up a loose strand of hair and pushed a brass button at the entrance. Inside, a harsh jangling announced her, as if someone had dropped a drawer full of kitchen utensils. Then footsteps, and a woman opened the door. Her hair was arranged in a coronet of gray braids, her broad bosom cinched into a white blouse and navy blue dirndl, set off by a pleated white apron.

Her gaze was neutral: light brown eyes surrounded by velvety white skin. She had a small nose, thin lips, no makeup.

"Das Zimmer?" she asked.

"Ja, die Reklame im Mozarteum," Maile replied. She let herself be examined from head to foot, resisting a rude urge to respond in kind.

They traded names, and Josephina Metzger snapped on a staircase light against the interior gloom, then led the way up a steep staircase to the second floor. As they climbed, Maile got an unexpected view of petticoats hemmed in cabbage-leaf embroidery, thick stockings knotted at the knee, low-heeled shoes with silver buckles.

"I hear," Frau Metzger remarked in a thick Austrian accent, "that Professor Jann's new student is a Hawaii-Mädchen. A great honor for you. He is our best."

Maile murmured agreement, startled that a total stranger knew who she was. Could this woman have some connection to the Mozarteum? To Sir Jann?

Swaying and huffing, Frau Metzger reached a small wooden landing and said in a melancholy tone, "I myself am a widow. My son and his wife emigrated to South Africa six years ago. They are quite happy there." She unlocked a door and gave Maile an awkward glance. "I must confess, a salamander once lived here in a damp window frame." Her shoulders shook, as if a chilly draft had blown across her back. "One tenant was a nun who had broken her vows." She opened the door with a sigh of resignation. "There is no central heating in winter. Tenants these days want modern."

Maile stepped into a large room with walls that had the mellow tint of parchment. Ribs of green Salzburg marble supported the vaulted ceiling and met in the center to form a star. A leaded-glass window let in muted patches of light from the street. Wooden furniture of a rich earth brown was carved with ornate scrolls: a desk, a wardrobe, a Baroque music stand with brass candleholders. An upright piano stood across from a bed. The rent was seven hundred schillings a month, thirty-five dollars.

Pili quivered, greedily alert. Maile murmured that she didn't mind salamanders—never having seen one—and poked at the piano, remarked that it needed tuning, and opened and shut the wardrobe. "I'll take it." She reached for her purse.

"We will talk," Frau Metzger replied. Maile followed her out, eyeing the music stand in the hope that she would get to use it.

Downstairs they sat in a narrow kitchen that faced the entry door. On the table were little bowls of chocolates, hazelnuts, tiny fish-shaped crackers. Frau Metzger glanced at them without invitation, and said, "So then." She asked about Maile's family, her education. Truthfully Maile said that her father worked for the government, but not that he drove a city bus in Honolulu. That her mother had died years ago, but not that she had cleaned houses on a military base and given birth to nine children by the age of thirty. She mentioned her German grandfather, her university degree, and her studies in New York, particularly the works of Mozart and Richard Strauss.

Frau Metzger's face softened and she abandoned her inquisitorial manner. "So, you are a Hawaii-Mädchen but have only part of the brown race. At our summer Festival we also have mixed-race divas, with Gypsy blood, not too much. A little mixture, like yours, is best." She continued in a lighter tone. "Also, you have lived in a very large city, and you dress with style. I appreciate this in foreigners."

Maile was struggling to follow Frau Metzger's German and maintain an interested expression when the words "brown race" jumped out at her. Said with approval, she thought, but Salzburg was one hundred percent *haole*, unlike Manhattan's cosmopolitan population. Here she was in what Madame had described as "a medieval village."

"Clothes I would never wear!" Frau Metzger's eyes lit with an observer's enthusiasm. "People reveal themselves. In the past, you see, we could always spot the Jews because they heaped elegance upon elegance."

Maile recalled the Frenchman on the ship who'd accused her of being a secret Jewess, and she felt ignorant of things that mattered to Europeans.

Frau Metzger named Parisian perfumes, Italian shoemakers, and insisted that because of the summer Festival—which Maile had unfortunately missed—Salzburg was not at all provincial, as too many people claimed. Finally she said with dramatic abruptness, "You may have the room. Do not be concerned about my interrupting your work. I understand artists. They are the pride of Austria."

There was one stipulation. Maile could not move in until her remaining luggage arrived. Otherwise, she might have to borrow little items and forget to return them. Frau Metzger showed her a foreigner's registration form, which would make Maile an official resident in a private home. Later, duly signed and dated, the form must be turned in to the authorities within twenty-four hours. "Oh," Frau Metzger added, "and what precisely is your source of income?"

Maile quashed memories of hoarding rolled-up bills and the clan raising funds for her. "Savings," she replied, and sat back firmly.

Frau Metzger gave her a look of mild surprise that bordered on respect, as if acknowledging a cleverly evasive answer. She smiled and extended her hand.

AFTER MAILE'S FIRST regularly scheduled voice lesson, Professor Jann walked home along the river. Hearing his new student a second time had convinced him that her voice had a thrilling quality, like wonderful raw material. He now understood Leah Renska's recommendation—the kind of pupil who appeared unannounced once in a decade. The lack of a long education in music didn't bother him. So far this odd Miss Manoa had demonstrated a remarkable willingness to leap, to experiment, to question his judgment.

He smiled at the memory of her audition: what a fighter she was! Not trading on her beauty, or playing the coy exotic because of technical failings, or pouting over his unrelenting criticism. Yet her personality seemed to be based solely on a drive to succeed—although not, he felt, because of an overblown ego. She made no mention of her past, her family, who must be supporting her studies. What was the key to her inner self? He was tempted to loan his student fine books, to invite her for tea and listen to records.

Nun wohl. It was still very early in their relationship. And Miss Maile might only seem extraordinary. Too much attention from a teacher at the beginning invariably went wrong. He had never unraveled the mystery of why talent and intelligence and beauty and personality and stamina were so rarely found in any one singer. Nobody outside music understood how easy it was to fail: a lack of nerve and an overweening ego were equally crippling. Some singers with excellent volume and tone could not be trained to sense pitch, or never developed the necessary range for their voice category. Ninety percent of them fell by the wayside. Or simply gave up because they couldn't bear living without a spouse, children, a regular salary and a little garden out back. Simple human needs. He wanted to believe his new soprano was an exception because she came from such a distance, and had conquered obstacles he couldn't imagine. Still, there were no guarantees.

As Jann neared his house, he felt eyes upon him. He looked toward the river in time to see a little old man touch his cap in greeting. The two of them had a history of sorts that went back years, although Jann's status allowed him to ignore the flower seller in a ridiculous green uniform, its silver frogged fastenings and swirls of braid like an old-fashioned theater usher's outfit. A man who in fact lived off gossip he could turn to advantage.

Jann walked on, aware of being under observation because he was teaching at the Mozarteum again. The significance of that would be apparent even to someone far outside the formal realm of music. He felt no cause for immediate concern, but resolved to keep the old man in mind.

IN THE MOZARTEUM'S basement Karl Holzer rehearsed low Ds on his French horn. Above, in the auditorium, he heard the smack of seats folding up and the muffled thump of shoes. He emptied his instrument's spit valve onto the floor and slipped the horn into its case. After his first year at the conservatory, he always skipped the opening ceremony for the fall session. A bureaucrat invariably gave a speech about "Salzburg's greatest son," but never mentioned that the city had in fact treated Mozart with vicious disregard. Or that the school named in his honor had not been founded until fifty years after his death, another hypocrisy as far as Karl was concerned. Peasants like himself were not admitted until 1960. Before that it was talent be damned if you wore hay farmer's clothes and spoke *Gaisbergische* dialect—the invisible policy established by the middle-class snobs who claimed Wölfi for themselves.

Outside, Karl headed to an annual party. An illegal meeting of university students about Prague dissidents had been rescheduled for later tonight. He considered the group poorly organized, but never missed a chance to be part of their Action Plan for the Future. From the river he walked toward an ancient monastery on a hillside ringed by a high wall, beneath it Frauenstrasse and Salzburg's two legal houses of prostitution. At the low end lived a wealthy Canadian or South American assumed to be a spy, political or industrial, posing as an art patron, an almost ordinary combination in postwar Austria. Each fall the man opened his house to music students for an evening. Sometimes he attended in full theater costume; more often he didn't show up at all.

For Karl the party was a yearly chance to eat rich man's food and look over recently arrived foreigners. Fewer than usual had attended the conservatory's summer session—because of student unrest across Europe, he felt—and he looked forward to seeing Jean-Paul Gardes, and the American mezzo, as loud and lusty as a vaudeville singer. Most of all he was intrigued by the new woman from Hawaii. Nobody believed she came from such a mythical place; singers could be tremendous liars, worse than pianists.

At the door to the party house he unpacked his horn, clamped it to his lips and played a gorgeous, spilling phrase from Beethoven's *Seventh*: Dah—da, di-di-di-di, da-da-da-da DAH! Windows flew open in other buildings and people leaned out to yell, *"Polizei!"*

Karl leaped inside the house, where the heat and noise of the crowd closed around him like a goose-down comforter. The main room was lit by flashlights tied to candleholders. Several dozen students attacked the buffet table, or gathered around a low pedestal where a naked couple posed back to back with dueling pistols. "Onegin and Euridice," an onlooker called out. "Too easy!" A young man lay on Arabian carpets, watching his host make an elaborate cat's cradle with gold thread. Foreigners clustered together even if they didn't share a common language. Karl spotted Jean-Paul handing the woman from Hawaii a glass of red as two American choir-directing students joined them. Karl's English was limited to a few phrases from cowboy

films: Saddle up, ride on out, and he hung back, envying the Frenchman, as skinny as a weasel and possessed of a twitchy energy that Karl
associated with jazzmen.

"Newspapers're lousy here," one choir director said to Maile,
"We're days behind New York."

"New York." Jean-Paul raised his glass in salute. "Prro-test!"
The choir director glared. "Shut up, let her speak."

The Frenchman flung an arm around the blond mezzo as she
passed him, and he purred into her hair, "Brrrenda." She shrugged him
off with a shrill giggle. He leaned toward Maile with a somber expression, stroking his black goatee, and said, "The Red Army is back. A
million soldiers just over the Czech border."

"The Red Army what?" she asked.

She sounded alarmed, Karl thought, or perhaps had not understood. He'd heard her speak good enough German for someone not
long in the country, although how had she learned his language? Maybe in Munich or Berlin. He gave her a hypnotic stare of invitation—
come talk to me, lovely creature.

"The Russkis will never dare come here," one choir director said.

"Ahhh," Jean-Paul scoffed, "you naivlings think diplomacy will
stop *les Soviètes*. Every summer they have *les manoeuvres*. Prague Spring
continues!"

Across the room a cello cut in with *O Iris und Osiris*, the grand
hymn to wisdom played allegro molto, and people grabbed partners to
career around shouting, *"Walzer, Walzer!"* They bumped into tables,
tripped over floor cushions, sloshed wine on each other. The choir
directors stamped their feet like square dancers. Karl lost sight of
Maile in the twisting mass of bodies as a screaming flute took over
with "Tambourine Man," then switched to a Mozart minuet, abandoned after three measures because only the naked couple knew the
steps.

Maile ate two portions of roast goose with mushrooms and tiny
potatoes in a rich, dark sauce. She met Brenda and a local student
whose name seemed to be Mah-leez, and saw a tall blond man raising
a French horn to his lips, then lowering it without playing, and knew
that she had seen him before. A Japanese man introduced himself to

her as Kazuo Hitachi. A blast of amplified guitar music from a phonograph swept over them, and instantly everyone was swaying and jerking to the Stones, the few Americans looking sassy and confident, the
Europeans stiff-necked and groaning, "Mahn oh mahn." Maile kicked
off her high heels to laugh and strut, feeling dizzier and dizzier, until
she bumped hips with someone and spun down onto a heap of cushions.

She landed harmlessly on her back. The party's Canadian South
American spy art patron host leaned over her, giving off alcohol
fumes. Stubble rose like burnt grass through a layer of pancake
makeup on his face and neck. Dimly she realized that she was drunk.
She rolled away from him, got to her feet, and felt a wild sense of happiness rushing to the top of her head. At an open window she gulped
fresh air. On the street she noticed a small old man walk past, wearing
a green uniform and carrying a large bouquet of red roses like a character in a play. He disappeared into the blackness farther on. The brief
sight of him left her feeling that she'd chosen the right place to come.

MAILE'S TRUNK ARRIVED from Rotterdam and a railroad porter
wheeled it into town on a handcart, along with her luggage from the
hotel. Frau Metzger made her wait in the little entry hall. Men are not
allowed inside the house, the landlady explained, except for the
transport of heavy objects. Afterwards, Maile could enter her room.

The porter's blue work shirt was darkened by sweat. He rolled up
his sleeves, climbed the stairs with two suitcases, then returned to
wrestle the steamer trunk onto his back. Soon they heard a thud upstairs. *"Nun also,"* he called out, *"fertig."* He came down panting and
holding out a slip of paper.

As Maile took it, a tattoo on the inside of his right arm caught her
eye: a small letter A like an arrowhead, in elaborate Gothic script with
tiny decorative barbs. The porter noticed her looking at it, and he shot
a glance at Frau Metzger, whose stare went from him to Maile to the
tattoo, and for an instant all three of them were focused on the dark
blue mark.

Frau Metzger scowled at the porter. *"Ja, ja,"* he murmured irritably, and jerked down both sleeves.

Maile sensed something forbidden, an open secret shared by the landlady and an anonymous laborer. A tattoo was as personal as a mole. It was also none of her business. She signed the delivery form and paid.

The handcart rattled away and Frau Metzger recited the house rules: no male visitors, ever, and practicing only between the hours of ten and noon, and two to six. With the window closed, please, as specified by law. And pardon me for even mentioning this, but do not hang undergarments to dry in view of the neighbors. "Regis-tra-tion," she said, making a little melody of the word. "Do not forget. Twenty-four hours." She handed over the signed and dated form, and went off to her kitchen.

Maile hurried upstairs. The wooden floorboards under her bare feet were as smooth and soft as old cloth, and made quiet creaking sounds when she moved about. She was curious about the salamander—a curse, a lizard-snake mentioned in a Schubert lied—and she examined the window frame to see if it had left any traces. Not even dust. Was the spirit of the former nun still in the ceiling cracks?

She opened the leaded-glass window and fresh air and bright sunlight poured in. Across the street the canted slate rooftops of the city's houses and churches formed a pathway to the center of Salzburg. There a wall of pale gray-blue marble rose high above all other buildings to the castle of Hohensalzburg. Two thousand feet high and a thousand feet wide. White pennants flew from six towers, fluttering like tiny angel wings. She lived almost in its shadow.

With sudden energy Maile flipped open the suitcases, the trunk, and unpacked dresses, suits, blouses, scarves. Cassell's dictionary went on the desk, music scores on the piano, shoes in the garderobe, a sheaf of concert programs on the bed, a teakettle, a cast-iron pan, a sewing box. *Pili* spread out in the room, taking fond possession of it.

More slowly Maile unfolded her finest gown, black beads on black silk. She was eager to wear it for the right occasion, clothing and costumes being part of an opera singer's grand game of disguise. Like her best suits and dresses, the gown had been rescued from a fancy Manhattan thrift shop. Once, she'd described to Madame making the fitted satin *holoku* her aunts wore to Waikiki for special occasions, a difficult task. "Do not reveal such details about yourself," Madame had said. "Only a servant takes pride in the skills of a seamstress."

At the time it had seemed like snooty advice—typical high *make-make haole*—yet Maile already sensed that in Salzburg a porter was not in the same social class as Frau Metzger, and neither was anywhere near Professor Jann. A soprano was not supposed to mend her own evening wear. What would the gentlemanly Japanese violinist think? No one had to know the origin of her fox toque, her cashmere scarves.

TEN MINUTES LATER, the registration form filled out, all unknown terms checked in Cassell's, Maile set off to make herself an official resident. The twenty-four-hour deadline seemed like a bluff. How could that be accurately reckoned? With a vague sense of where the police station was, she entered a curving maze of side streets that soon ended at a cul-de-sac. A small figure in a bright green and silver uniform hurried away: the little man from last night. A good omen, she thought. People in dirndls and leather *Kniehosen* passed her. She backtracked, got lost, and took out her tourist map. It had been folded and unfolded so often that wrinkles made the center portion difficult to read.

"Suchen Sie die Polizeistation?" a man asked.

Flustered, she realized it was again the little fellow in green. Up close, his looks disturbed her. He had a merry smile, but his sunken eyes were rimmed by dark purple discolorations. His skin resembled crinkly waxed paper. The backs of his hands were transparent, the blue veins like faded tattoos. He reminded her of a concentration camp refugee except for his spotless, theatrical uniform. His too-large cap shaded his forehead and made his macabre gaze all the more chilling. On the cap's patent-leather bill, a line of meticulous silver embroidery spelled out DER ROSENKAVALIER.

Maile let him direct her, thanked him, and made a zig-zag toward Rudolfsplatz and the Old City's one traffic bridge. A stream of dented trucks with Italian license plates roared past on the main route from Hamburg to Rome, leaving a layer of stinking gray exhaust fumes at eye level. On the opposite side stood a row of low cement offices with a large sign, POLIZEIZENTRAL, cheap modern buildings. Maile had been inside a police station only once, to pay a parking fine, five dollars reduced to three because the judge recognized her from a hotel float in the Kamehameha Day parade.

She dodged over the bridge through the traffic, pushed open the scuffed door of *Polizeizentral*, and bumped into a boyish brown-haired officer. *"Grüss Gott, die Dame,"* he said. He touched his cap to her with a grin that revealed a dead front tooth, yellow-brown. Beyond him the wide room was crowded with swarthy men in baggy clothes. Turkish and Greek laborers, the officer told her, applying for temporary immigrant status to haul garbage and sweep the streets. A lady like herself did not have to wait behind them.

He escorted Maile to the head of a long line winding back from an open counter. The men shuffled aside, looking resentful, tired, bored. She avoided their eyes, feeling guilty that a fall outfit and high heels made her a *Dame* who got special treatment.

An officer behind the counter asked, *"Sprechen Sie Deutsch?"* She mumbled that she did. *"Sind Sie Amerikanerin?"* Yes. He sighed as if in mutual sympathy for the tedious business they faced. "Your credentials, please." She handed over her passport, International Health Certificate, driver's license, birth certificate, Mozarteum matriculation, and the signed registration form from her new landlady.

He lined them up. She felt creepily exposed. *"Ha-va-ee,"* he said in surprise, and motioned to officers sitting at desks. Three came forward. Silently they examined everything, then one asked the others if Hawaii was a real place.

"Natürlich," replied the officer at the counter. *"Bei Florida."*

"Nein, im Pazifik," another said. *"Bei Tahiti."*

The first officer asked Maile, *"Ha-va-ee oder Ha-ee-tee?"*

They had Hawaii and Tahiti mixed up with Haiti, she realized—islands thousands of miles apart, in different oceans, as bad as confusing Austria with Australia. She burst into laughter.

Their curious expressions closed down. The counter officer scooped up her papers and retreated to a desk where he and the others whispered to each other with angry little hissing sounds. She bit her lips, looked at her purse, at a lampshade dangling from a long cord, then back at the officers, and tried to telegraph, Please, it just slipped out. I'm sorry.

They unrolled a wall map of the world as cracked as an old window shade. Each in turn scrutinized the Pacific. *"Ach, Sopranistinen,"* one remarked, *"sie ziehen sich so an."* Sopranos dress like that. They took cigarettes from their breast pockets and left.

Maile waited with increasing nervousness as the minutes passed. The room stank of unwashed hair, old shoes. Men muttered in languages she didn't understand. A pulse at her temples throbbed into a headache: doomp . . . doomp. A ragged assault of sounds filled her mind: *Ein Salamander sass, Casta diva,* I Can't Get, *tok-tok.* She reached for memories of calming music: a soft Mozart solo that exhaled melody with the ease of restful breathing: *Et . . . in-carna—tus est . . .* drawn-out tones supported by subdued violins, flutes, harpsichord. What a master he was! Composing sacred music that had all the power and beauty of theater, music of such grace and purity that it went beyond church or opera to some higher goal. Her emotions soared out of the room into the cool air over the river.

A policeman sauntered in through a side door and the immigrant workers stirred with collective weariness. Maile straightened up. One by one the other officers returned. They poked through file folders with a sense of unresolved hostility. Flick flick. A drawer was closed. Another clacked open. The old wall map was rolled up. Snap! Maile wanted to scream.

At last an older official came out of a back office and spread her documents on the counter. He validated them with brisk thumps of a rubber stamp, granting her the usual residence visa. She would have to come back, he said, and do everything again if her address changed or her status changed from student to employee, the process being deregister, transfer, and reregister: *Abmeldung, Ummeldung, Anmeldung.* The terms slid easily off his tongue. After making certain she understood, he added, "To me you are just another foreigner. Like those." He jerked his head at the Turks and Greeks. "With one difference. Americans often have a clownish attitude toward authorities. I dislike this intensely."

She despised him for taking her down a peg but kept a straight face and replied, *"Jawohl, Herr Offizier. Danke schön."* She put away her papers. Walked toward the exit. Refused to acknowledge the stares that burned into her back. Opened the door and went out, thinking, We won the war.

FRAU METZGER REGARDED her new tenant with nosy interest. Maile tried to avoid the landlady, but depended on her daily for information about buying food, locating public toilets, counting the change from a hundred-schilling note. Five hundred grams approximated a pound of bread; cold cuts were sold *per deka*, one tenth of a kilo; an apothecary was roughly equivalent to an American drugstore. Fortunately Maile discovered that she could always end a conversation by saying she had to practice. Frau Metzger gave in at once with an air of respect.

Each time Maile worked in her room, she felt all her souls rolled into one. She belonged to art as surely as if she had sworn a formal oath. Her future was good, even excellent, if she worked very hard. Yet day by day her sense of wholeness eroded until she had to admit that she was a long way from being a fully formed soprano. As much as she wanted to fit in and not be an obvious outsider, she craved the opposite: recognition as a singer who moved listeners to tears, to reflect on love, death, desire. In truth, she was no more anchored in Salzburg than a cowrie shell on a reef, tumbled along with every wave.

By now the clan knew where she was, although Maile felt certain it had shocked them. From halfway around the world she felt their claim on her, the grip of love impossibly knotted into shared responsibilities that kept most of them on the same island. Only she had ever shown an interest in the wider world. The others refused to think farther than Honolulu Harbor. Even if she could sit with Makua in his truck, like old times, nothing would change. Neither he nor anyone else in the family understood her operatic voice. When she'd used it for church solos, the aunties who came to listen always asked, "How come you sing so strong? Make soft, nice, like before."

Now her days were filled with odd, unexpected difficulties. Signs in curlicued Gothic script had to be deciphered letter by letter. The patronizing formality of shop clerks intimidated her. Housewives out on errands walked hand in hand as casually as lovers and kissed each other on the lips when meeting or parting, all strangely thrilling, but mostly strange. She disliked the bold hairiness of their legs and underarms. According to Frau Metzger, each subdistrict of the Salzburg valley had distinctive styles of dress and hairdos: a ridge of braids, or double coils with a middle part, or a knot at the base of the neck was coupled with a particular cut of sleeve, the number of pleats in a skirt. The landlady could spot someone at a distance and say, "Gnigl, they've come to buy Mozart chocolate," or "Berchtesgaden, some latecomers must have autumn squash for sale."

Everyone had their own group, Maile realized, and merely saying hello involved a bewildering range of manners. Little girls curtsied, boys bowed. A man doffed his hat or touched the brim or used a variety of nods and bows. Women were greeted by their husband's titles, Frau Professor, Frau Doktor, Frau Ingenieur. Nobody ran, yelled, or smoked cigarettes in public. Only peasants in the open-air market spat and swore and laughed loudly, scratched their necks, crotches, whatever itched. Well-dressed people did not carry packages but were followed by a delivery boy in a white smock. Above all, clothes seemed to announce who you were and what you did. Dirndls in cheap or more expensive cotton—with long versions in silk and brocade for evening—indicated that one was working class, middle class, or upper class. Traditional silver and garnet jewelry meant upper-working or lower-middle class. Men wore lederhosen shorts, higher-priced knee britches, soft suede jackets and fine wool suits with oak leaves on the lapels and cuffs. Roughly clad farmers were easy to spot.

Maile continued to see the Rosenkavalier out and about in the city. Usually he appeared at dusk, carrying an armload of flowers. She avoided him on Getreidegasse as he went from hotel to hotel and café to café, selling leftover roses that would last a few more hours, moving along the dark streets as lithely as a dancer, his footsteps as neatly executed as a court mazurka. No waiter bothered him. He never pushed himself on a potential client but presented his flowers first to a lady, for viewing, then appealed silently to her escort. His smile was an eerie twitch. He accepted any currency, smoothly approached the next couple, and within minutes he had covered an entire café or wine bar, and he was gone. Local residents out for the evening ignored the doll-like man passing swiftly toward the next lighted cluster of people. He was rumored to know everything that happened in Salzburg after nightfall. Maile felt there was something terrible about his eyes, then scolded herself for thinking he had a sinister nature, for imagining too much.

Finally one evening she asked Frau Metzger about the odd little man in the green uniform. As forthcoming as the landlady was on most topics, her attitude turned curiously stiff. "Ach, him," she said with an annoyed shrug. "A former peasant. Beneath your concern and mine." All she offered was her vision of the "true" Cavalier of Roses, from the Richard Strauss opera that evoked Austro-Hungarian grandeur at its height, the title role played by a slim youth in white satin who bore an aristocratic gift of love, a silver rose on a long silver stem. As a proudly middle-class *Bürgerin*, Frau Metzger asserted that a bumpkin turned street peddler would never dare assume a Mozartian name in the city of Mozart's birth. However, because Strauss's great work was forever associated with Vienna, the self-named flower seller was a proper joke on people from the capital, who looked down their noses at provincial Salzburg. The Rosenkavalier indeed!

7

BY THE TIME Karl came up from the basement practice rooms, the halls were deserted and his stomach growled. He lived at home but spent all his time at the Mozarteum unless an emergency on the farm forced him to skip classes. His talent and emotions were equally committed to piano and French horn, although he knew that making a career meant choosing one instrument or the other. Out front he looked for his bicycle. The only sign of it was a damp track leading away from the rack. Borrowed again, he figured, by the head of the Prague activist group, to check on an empty building behind the Puch factory for their next meeting. They had to be careful: Austria's neutrality meant arrest for any citizens caught meddling in international affairs. He headed for the bus stop, sullenly certain that dinner would be cold when he got to the farm.

At the riverbank a woman on the footbridge stood gazing toward the Old City. The dense line of buildings was tinted with a dusky layer of deep yellow as the mid-fall day prepared to fade into twilight. In pockets where the sun had dimmed, curving Baroque domes and church spires were black silhouettes. Above and beyond them, the walls of the fortified castle rose like a mountainous island. In the distance, the Alps formed a lordly ring.

Some tourist, Karl thought peevishly, in love with our so-called atmosphere. Then the woman brushed back a strand of hair in a gesture he had seen before. The singer from Hawaii. He was used to serious musicians being loners, although he sensed that this woman might actually be without friends. Most Austrians only tolerated familiar glamour—nothing too exotic, *danke*.

Maile walked on into the Old City and the air suddenly turned cool where so many packed buildings cut off the light. No streetlamps shone down. Gray rows of cobblestones winding off through narrow slots between tall houses seemed like pathways in a dense forest. People headed home from work, opening their doors with long ornate keys fished from shopping baskets.

Soon she was lost on twisting, darkening side streets as empty as the warehouse district in Manhattan after sundown. She couldn't decide if Frau Metzger's building was around a corner to the left, or somewhere to the right of the saint's statue in a wall niche.

Someone walked behind her; quiet footsteps, too close. She clamped her music scores to her chest and spun around on the edge of panic. In German a tall blond man asked with a hesitant smile, "Would you care to go for a glass of wine?" He wore a rough suede jacket, linen shirt, leather knee pants. Carried a French horn.

He offered his hand stiffly and said, "Holzer, Karl Holzer." In the fading light she noticed his eyes, pale silver-gray. Unearthly, a color she had never seen before. Snow eyes.

"I found Honolulu on a world map," he said, "twenty thousand kilometers away! You're like Gauguin in reverse, but I can't imagine traveling that far for anything, not even music. That takes guts." He clapped a hand to his stomach. "Sorry! I'm being a peasant." His expression collapsed into rueful embarrassment.

Honolulu, kilometers, Gauguin. She told him her name. He was almost as tall as Professor Jann. The hard leanness of his face was softened by a spray of boyish freckles across his forehead, nose, and cheeks. She felt a sudden eagerness to talk with someone her age, to be with a man.

"Ja," she said, *"ein Glas Wein."*

Side by side, they entered a deserted passageway and fell into the uncomfortable silence of a couple who had agreed to go somewhere but didn't know each other. The upper floors of stone and timber buildings merged into the black sky. The width of the street shrank until she had to walk hip to hip with him, then he stopped at a thick wooden door and pulled on its heavy iron ring. The pleasing aromas of hot food wafted out.

They stepped into a large natural cave with a plank floor and cabinets built into rounded walls. The ceiling was an uneven dome covered by miniature stalactites and chalky white swirls. Candles provided the only light for customers at small tables. At the back stood a row of casks and a butcher block with a ham roasted to crusty perfection, alongside a wheel of black bread two feet wide.

"*Carmen*," Maile said, delighted. "Second act, smuggler's den."

Karl glanced around with a wry expression. "That's Spain. And Bizet was French."

"Never mind, imagine a seacoast in the background. Baskets of oranges. Daggers and fortune-tellers."

"*Ach*, Americans." He snickered. "You have a belief in fantasy we Austrians lost centuries ago. We're all cynics." She frowned, bridling at the criticism. "Don't be offended," he added. "Americans appreciate things we take for granted." He walked off to fetch a carafe of wine, tumblers, and a platter of black bread and ham.

Maile put her scores on a table, brought plates and utensils, and concentrated on getting along with this European. As they sat down, Karl poured the wine, handed her a squat tumbler, and regarded her with serious intent. "If we drink together," he said, "we must address each other as *Du*. You are an honored guest in Austria because of the journey you made to get here."

He raised his glass in silence, a moment of ceremony that touched her. He had the muscular lips of a horn player. His chin was marked by a small cleft, slightly off center. Shaggy blond hair fringed his forehead. His alert expression suggested intelligence, humor.

They drank and she lowered her glass slowly to savor the moment. From now on they would speak to each other with the intimate form of "you," a soft, generous word: *Du. Dooo.* It deepened any relationship. Was used by family members and students, because of what they shared, was found in love poems set to music by Mozart, Schubert.

Karl's look of amusement returned. "*Du, My-lee.* A peculiar name. What does it mean?"

She had been thinking in English and forced a reply in German. "It's a plant. A vine."

"I never heard of someone named for a plant."

A bit defensively she explained, "Not just any plant. At home *maile* grows only in the mountains. It's sacred to the hula goddess."

"The dance, you mean? But a goddess?" His brow furrowed. "Everybody here is named for a saint. We have been Catholics since the third century. So . . . you're a pagan."

"My whole family belongs to the Congregational Church," she snapped. "The only Catholics I know are Filipino. They're new to the islands."

"You're a Protestant, then. I wouldn't announce it here. That's the same as being a pagan." He grinned and forked a slice of bread onto his plate along with a curl of ham. "Our priests will sniff you out as a heretic."

"You asked! I didn't announce it."

"Sorry." His expression wilted into apology. "I've always had trouble with religion." He cut his open-faced sandwich with his knife and fork. "We peasants are supposed to be docile and illiterate but wise— all that nineteenth-century kitsch. Don't believe it."

She smiled, forgiving him, and copied the way he assembled a sandwich not to be eaten by hand. His combination of friendliness and sparring appealed to her; not complicated by too much sensitivity, excitability, ego, all the flaws that haunted so many musicians. Or was he just showing off?

"Peasant kitsch," she repeated. "Didn't Hitler love that?"

Karl swallowed violently and leaned across the table to whisper, "Never say that name in public! People will think you're an Israeli spy." She almost laughed but his stark expression stopped her. "You arrived here by way of New York," he went on, "a city full of Jews. That is a fact, not prejudice. Many Salzburgers think all foreigners are secret Jews who return to snoop for opportunities. We're a neutral country, so spies are commonplace. Another fact."

Maile stared at his chest, and felt her cheeks flush. At other tables a domino was slapped down with a sharp clack. A man let out a luxurious belch. Another lit his pipe and gave her a long stare. She imagined him calling her heretic, secret Jew. History previously tucked away in textbooks stirred with life.

She spread butter on her bread, a dab of horseradish, layered the thinly sliced meat and cut the sandwich into small pieces. The smoked ham was deliciously juicy. The black bread was both crunchy and moist. The wine had a pleasant nip, but she'd killed the conversation. Now Karl would give her the cold shoulder for being so loudmouth, so downright dumb.

He shot a glance at the pipe smoker, then thumped her stack of scores. "When can I hear you sing? Nobody gives up the isles of paradise to develop a minor talent."

She snatched at the safe topic. "Honolulu has no opera house."

"We have a glut of them. They hold up the economy. Otherwise, no military industry, no General Motors, not even a decent soccer team. We're politically impotent, the shrunken remains of an empire, shaped like a little stomach. The national occupation is nostalgia."

She eyed the off-center cleft in his chin, as neat and attractive as a dimple. His silence seemed to solicit a reply and she wanted to match his effortless sarcasm. "Is breast-beating a national trait as well?"

Karl gestured indifferently at the ceiling. "Americans are the world's greatest idealists. They can't believe a place like this is simply practical. *Carmen*. You are too rare to drown in some sweet lie about us."

"Rare. What a romantic word for a cynic."

"I mean don't make stupid mistakes."

She sat back, stung. "So, I'm just a dreamy little girl?"

"No, but for your own protection, you should look deeper." He tapped the spines of her scores. "Music is the only thing in Austria that gets world recognition, and it's justified. It's also the key to everyone's self-esteem. Which makes it dangerous. I can already quote reviews for Vienna's fall season: 'Von Wehlen's masterful grasp of . . . 'His powerful, enduring relationship to . . . ' He's our leading celebrity, born right here, like Mozart. Descended from the prince who halted the Saracen advance at the river."

Maile knew of von Wehlen only as one prominent conductor among many. Karl's point escaped her, but she saw an opportunity to needle him. "You sound jealous."

"Be quiet a moment. I don't expect someone from Hawaii to understand." With the tip of his knife he lined up three crumbs on his plate. "Tiny country. One-sided economy. Ugly history. This makes every taxi driver, ticket taker, and goose woman in Austria a music expert. Middle-class people claim to be the 'bearers of culture' to the rest of the world." He put down the knife. "Critics you can trust regard von Wehlen's renditions of Wagner and Beethoven as superior. His Mozart is undeniably weak. Too forceful and rushed, no delicacy, no wit."

"Doesn't every musician specialize? I can't sing Ravel."

"Ah, you see . . . that's it. Few Austrians will admit von Wehlen has a weakness. His most fanatic loyalists consider any criticism a form of treason."

"That's absurd." *Unsinn*, she thought, good word in German.

"We're a poor country. Von Wehlen is our one international figure. Austria will always crave a replacement for Emperor Franz Josef." Karl formed a triangle with the crumbs. "Herr Maestro controls the so-called Berlin-Vienna-Salzburg axis of music. That makes him untouchable, more important than our president, than the richest winemaker. Everything he performs or produces is a success."

Karl refilled their glasses. Maile sipped from hers, fascinated by his words, slicing to the bone, revealing information no tourist ever heard. He went on, "Most Austrian music expertise is a mask for bitterness. Twenty-three years after the Reich, people are still seething because they were defeated, and the last time they had a feeling of power was under you-know-who. Von Wehlen is a perfect substitute."

"Because he's a musician."

"Even better, one who interprets our holy Mozart."

Karly put their empty plates and glasses into a tin tub at the back of the room. They left, the door closing behind them and the iron ring falling in place with a clang that bounced off the high walls. Maile asked him how local people found their way on dark streets with few lights or signs. "Like this," he said. He reached up to run a finger along a date etched on a marble plaque: 1742, the height of a disastrous flood. Farther on he pointed out a mummified fish, the last sturgeon caught in the Salzach. At an intersection a low stone hay crib inscribed with a crest stood out in the gloom. She was still confused by the turns he took, but soon they arrived at Frau Metzger's building.

"Nun also," Karl said in mild surprise. "My godmother lives here. I've never been invited inside, the Church and all that. Well. Have a

pleasant evening." He walked off with his cased horn bouncing lightly against one leg.

Maile slipped into the chilly entryway, as black as a burial cave. Cheap-apartment fear attacked her and she groped along the wall, slapping the cold plaster until she touched a metal box and snapped on a switch. Wan yellow light spread overhead. A timer began ticking, kik-kik-kik: good for fifteen seconds. She rushed up the stairs, digging for her key, dropped a score halfway to the top, snatched it up and found the key just as the timer stopped and the bulb clicked off. In the blackness she lunged at her door, couldn't locate the lock, then did, then couldn't get it open, fought with it, and finally fell into her room and flipped on a lamp.

Light. She was in Salzburg. Here there was no elevator. No gold watch band.

FRAU METZGER VISITED her husband's grave with a steady appearance of devotion. She still regretted that he had been so old when they married, forty-eight to her eighteen, with the strength of his manliness already waning, so that he could only give her one child. Twelve years later all able-bodied men were called to serve in the Army of the Reich, but not a butcher by then in his sixth decade. Manfred Metzger was assigned a flock of sheep, along with a pistol and orders to shoot anyone caught stealing an animal of any age and in any condition. Both the meat and the wool were military property. He considered himself lucky. Josephina was humiliated; rather than being in uniform at the front, her *Ehemann* was down by the river protecting muttonchops.

The bus ride to the little cemetery outside the city took the entire morning, but Frau Metzger never missed her twice-monthly visit. She had a horror of being gossiped about as a widow who shirked her duties—and to a man who had, after all, left her a house in town and enough money to avoid working for the rest of her life.

At the cemetery gate she crossed herself, did so again at the gravesite, clasped her hands to recite a Hail Mary and a Glory Be, and thumped down a bouquet of daisies. "So, Manfred," she said, her usual greeting. "Where's your pistol now?"

The question she had never dared to ask him in life always made her smile. After the war she'd sold the gun to the Rosenkavalier, and her husband had searched for it until the day he died.

A few sprightly weeds grew around the headstone. She crouched to yank them out, the stems like wire that made green stains and red stripes on her fingers. She decided to leave the real cleaning for All Souls, just two weeks away, when everyone came to scrape lichen off the names of the dead and make each grave as neat as a window box.

"Well, Manfred," she said, straightening up, "my Hawaii-Mädchen has turned out to be a perfect lady. What you think does not matter because this is entirely my business."

She continued, filling him in on the latest: von Wehlen's fall premiere in Vienna this week had been a worldwide triumph; her knees were doing well in the fine autumn weather; their son had not written recently from Cape Town; the house was in good order, roof tiles repaired, a rotted window frame replaced. As usual she quickly ran out of news—talking to her dead husband was never as interesting as her weekly *Kaffeeklatsch* with friends—yet she felt bound to keep Manfred informed.

"The Red Army is in the Czechkei, and a million soldiers are predicted by spring! Father Meyerhof insists nothing will happen, but Frau Guschelbauer says the Cossacks are coming again, just like in '45, and this time they will grab Salzburg by the neck."

The memory made her shiver: the Red Army flooding into Vienna, just five hours away. Soldiers not even human, godless heathens, burning churches, tearing out city water pipes to send back to the Soviet Union, trainloads of pipes, a documented fact. Now, every day, there was a greater and greater threat that the same beasts would swarm down the autobahn to Mozart's city. Not quite yet, winter was on the way and armies didn't like ice, but surely when the first stretch of fine weather came in late March.

She recited a hasty Our Father, the words tumbling out in an automatic, comforting rush: *Vater unser*, God's in his Heaven, all's right with the world. For good measure she made the sign of the cross over the gravestone—may it remain undisturbed—and walked downhill to the bus stop, humming to herself.

AT THE MOZARTEUM'S administration office, Maile received an unexpected message that instantly excited her. The top of the page had the letterhead of the American consulate: "Dear Miss Manoa," she read in English. "We haven't met and I'd like to see someone from Hawaii again. Please come by at your convenience." Signed with an illegible scrawl.

"Salzburg has consulates?" she asked the registrar.

"Fourteen," he replied, "for a population of fifty thousand. The Festival gives us international importance."

"I see," she said. The idea of visiting a consulate by invitation was irresistible. She couldn't imagine who had once known someone else from home. During the midday ban on practicing in homes she casually asked Frau Metzger about the many consulates in Salzburg.

The landlady huffed as though explaining the obvious. Diplomacy had been an Austrian specialty for centuries. The Festival attracted an elite audience from all over the world, and although most Konsulate were active only from June to August, their guest books contained the signatures of Toscanini, the Danish king, Olympic athletes, *Prominenten* who had visited Salzburg since the Festival was established at the hands of none other than Richard Strauss.

Maile went upstairs to eat a sausage and cheese roll. She changed into a fresh suit, neatened her hair, and waited until two o'clock, to be safely past lunchtime, before setting out to pay her visit. Along the Salzach an imposing row of eighteenth- and nineteenth-century villas faced the river, private homes behind thick hedges. Every third or fourth gate had a heavy brass plaque inscribed in two languages. FRANCE FRANKREICH, CCCP UDSSR, incomprehensible lettering for Greece, Thailand. She spotted an American flag at the entrance to a three-story mansion with marble banisters carved into a series of dolphins. Pots of fall chrysanthemums formed an ascending pattern of purple and golden brown.

Pili crouched under Maile's ribs in a fit of nerves. She told herself that no one in Salzburg knew anything about Papakōlea, that she had the finest teacher at the Mozarteum, in the entire country, Sir Jann, who taught only one advanced student at a time.

She stepped into a foyer paneled in mahogany the color of black coffee. A receptionist in a blue suit like a stewardess uniform glanced up from a desk. Maile held out the letter. "Oh, yes," the woman said. "Please sign our guest book."

Maile wrote in her best script, then looked around at rooms opening out from the foyer; garlands of roses carved on the wooden paneling, Alpine landscapes in ornate gold frames. Only a portrait of President Lyndon Johnson with the Stars and Stripes in the background reminded visitors that they were on American territory.

The receptionist handed over a mimeographed page, saying, "Before I forget. This's important for Americans, 'specially with Soviet troops camping on our doorstep. I'll be right back." She went off down a hallway.

Maile studied the paper, entitled, "Just So You Know." The first two paragraphs concerned visas and work restrictions that meant no waitressing, no odd jobs, no selling Tahitian Gardenia perfume. In fact, only music. She turned her attention to the next paragraph.

3) Interference with Austrian internal affairs is strictly forbidden, i.e., no picketing or public speaking on political issues which concern either the United States or Austria. In private conversation, extreme tact is mandatory.

The last word offended her. She wasn't about to lecture fellow students on LBJ and the war.

4) No participation, active or passive, in satirical productions, cabaret and the like. If apprehended in such activity, you have 24 hours to leave the country and a permanent ban on returning.

She looked up, shocked: who made these rules? They were Russian, Communist. Americans were also warned to carry their passports at all times. Police could ask for identification without explanation, and lack of documents could result in arrest and jail. "It's their country," the handout concluded. "Respect how they do things and you'll get along just fine."

When the receptionist returned, Maile followed her down the hall, thinking, Jail. Permanent ban on returning. A U.S. citizen who even watched an antiwar comedy routine in some nightclub could be thrown out of the country.

"The consul will see you now," the receptionist said.

Maile hadn't expected to meet the head man himself, and cautiously entered a room with walls and ceiling tipped in gold-leaf. The large Persian carpet under her feet had red tree branches filled with tiny blue birds. Glass cases displayed swords, dueling pistols, medals, medieval helmets. She thought it was a setting fit for a Renaissance duke, but the man who stood up to greet her looked as shrunken and haunted as an old alcoholic.

"Well," he said. "Hawaii. I'll be damned."

The Honorable Edwin Casey wore a brown suit and maroon tie. He emerged from behind his black marble desk as carefully as a recent invalid. His sparse gray hair was neatly combed, his fine hazel eyes half hidden under trembling lids. "No one from Honolulu's ever lived in Salzburg," he said. "My chauffeur is some distant relative of your landlady's cousin. That's how news gets around when most people don't have phones."

One of his eyelids twitched. He held it down with a pinky finger, an automatic gesture. "Haven't been in the islands since my discharge in '45," he said, "but never forgot the natives, most warmhearted folks on earth. Took us GIs surfing and canoeing. Had us eat with their families. Left me with a permanent soft spot for Hawaii." He winked fiercely and the twitching stopped. "You're here to study music?"

"Yes," Maile said. "Sir," she added, wondering if this strange man just wanted to reminisce.

Casey smiled. "In college I memorized the first five minutes of Beethoven's *Fifth* but tell the truth could never play a single instrument so anybody'd want to listen." From a silver box he took out a cigarette, lit it, and inhaled with a faint groan of relief. "Not much action here during the winter. I'll be mostly in Vienna then come summer that fellow von Wehlen shows up here and I play host for the big shots. I don't sprechen the Deutsch. You?" Maile nodded. "Good," he said. "I'd like to invite you and repay that island hospitality. Maybe you could sing a tune or two." He grinned and showed her to the door.

Outside on the river promenade, Maile imagined a diplomatic reception, a scene from a movie. She pictured herself being escorted inside wearing the black beaded gown. Mr. Casey wanted her to sing. Fantastic! But not until next summer. Would he even remember? Her savings might not last that long. Gone before the Festival even opened.

She headed for her Italian language class, no longer feeling important because she'd signed a guest book like Toscanini. Von Wehlen was just another prominent musician far above her in the professional world. At the reception, if it ever took place, Mr. Casey only needed a translator, one step above a caterer. Nothing about her life had changed. She'd simply traded a routine of hard study in Manhattan for the same routine in cheaper, safer, more beautiful surroundings. Earning money outside of music was illegal. She had to build a career in little Salzburg and would not see Hawaii again anytime soon.

FRAU METZGER PRIMPED her complicated braids, smoothed her autumn dirndl of plum-colored wool, picked up a large willow basket, and went out for her second shopping trip of the day. Getting fresh opinions on anything heard, overheard, announced on the radio, or seen in print was as important as buying fresh rolls. Her earlier rounds to the bakery, the pharmacy, and vegetable market were a routine established before the war.

During the past week, the women she encountered criticized a pregnant Munich Opera diva still singing in her seventh month, and scoffed at the menu for a local aristocrat's banquet. They considered Josephina Metzger daring to have a tenant from Hawaii, *eine echte Exotin*, like an Apache or a maharajah. The men she dealt with discussed Red Army maneuvers just across the Czech border, slowing down now with snow on the way, although no one believed Soviet news bulletins. She heartily agreed that Russians were a Tartar horde ignorant of civilization, closer to wolves than humans. And if America was home to blackamoors who played jazz music, Austrians were fortunate that the U.S.A. Army in nearby Germany had warehouses full of bombs to threaten the U.S.S.R.

At the creamery a friend mentioned seeing Karl with Maile in front of the Mozarteum. Frau Metzger replied in a bored tone that her beautiful tenant talked to ten men every day at the conservatory, and spent entire evenings with talented artists in the Mozarteum's radio room. A minor rumor, she decided. More useful gossip could be counted on to wend its way from butcher to button seller to Frau Metzger's ears. By three in the afternoon, news of her tenant speaking personally to the American consul reached her via the aunt of the diplomat's chauffeur, a spinster who cooked for the priest at the cemetery outside town. Frau Metzger pretended she already knew the facts. She cut short her shopping and went into Skolaren Kirche.

Settled in a front pew with her basket, Frau Metzger ordered her thoughts. All over the city, favors were owed to her, some going back years. As needed, she could collect three chickens from Herr Kohlhaus, plucked and greased for the oven, or five meters of cashmere from Weberei Justus in her choice of color, or an envelope and a stamp from the war veteran whose first name she could never recall. Even the silence she maintained to save a reputation had a price.

At the altar, a boy knelt to dust scrolls carved into the marble base. She watched him absently, sorting out in her mind what she most wanted and needed. The Festival was eight months off. In the meantime, she had to be aware of competition from a certain foul little man, without revealing any knowledge of him, or any interest in the disgusting details about *Prominenten* that he fastened onto like a snail on glass.

AT THE OTHER end of Getreidegasse, the Rosenkavalier was tucked away in the back of the kitchen at the Silver Fawn. Before dinner preparations began, he could count on being undisturbed. He lived off what he called "opportunities," but with the Festival having concluded seven weeks ago, the lean months were upon him. He had calculated that his thriftily parceled-out earnings would only carry him to Twelfth Night. Which meant he had to continue working through winter to avoid cadging hot meals in February, and having his reputation slip.

Out of sight on his cot, he adjusted the lumpy pillow under his head. It had been a profitable summer with the few divas and conductors he served, plus six Czech refugees with Western connections, an unexpected source of income. Now *die Musiker* had returned to Vienna, Berlin, London, New York, and the trickle of Czech asylum seekers would stop with the first snowfall. At least he had a warm place for the winter, behind the main oven in the city's best restaurant—permanent residence because he once disposed of a baby for the owner's daughter. Above him on a spike hung his green and silver hat and uniform. Under the cot was a box for his summer shoes, ice boots, nail clippers, an ear pick, a straight-edge razor and strop. His most valuable possession was a cluster of precisely knotted strings. These replaced a pencil and notebook and concealed his illiteracy. He had devised a system whereby he could finger the strings and recall names, events, and personal details.

In a petulant mood he pulled out the string cluster and worried the knots. The fall crop of Mozarteum students was disappointing: the loud blonde too whorish for society, the Frenchman stingy as a rabbi, the Moor from the Pacific supposed to be quite a singer, but she should be dipped in a vat of bleach. The new knots he'd made for her and Edwin Casey would not be of use for some time, although any career diplomat bore watching. The Oklahoma oilman, advisor to President Johnson, had gotten himself kidnapped in Venezuela. For a year Herr Konsul was held hostage, tortured, then ransomed recently and given the post in Salzburg as a reward. Light duty. No armed rebels.

Idly the Rosenkavalier wondered what kind of torture was used these days. Maybe it hadn't changed that much. Now it was all done in private. Locally, nothing would ever equal the sight of the hanged violinists in back of the Mozarteum. The bodies had stayed there for a week, attracting gawkers. He could still picture the eyes and tongues bulging in death, the stained trousers. But torture and execution were not the same. Some blamed Herr Maestro von Wehlen for involvement in those hangings thirty-three years ago, which was ridiculous, traitorous. The SS had simply caught the Jew musicians fleeing and punished them according to law.

"*Aacch,*" the Rosenkavalier muttered, and rolled up the strings. Whatever good a mere consul and students might do for him in the distant future, it was a comedown after the Festival and getting so close to Herr Maestro's new baritone. With reluctance he made the yearly decision. Until early summer, when tourists and Festival stars began flocking in, he would go out only three nights a week. Keeping his uniform spotless was expensive, but a man dealing in opportunities dared not have even a hint of riffraffery about him.

8

ICY RAIN POURED from a gray oval of clouds covering the Salzburg valley like a lid on an enormous kettle. Women in heavy clothes shopped under slick black umbrellas, men hunched under hat brims that dripped strings of water onto their loden coats. Karl didn't own an umbrella and had gotten drenched going to another meeting about Czech asylum seekers. All the way up Hohensalzburg to hear old news: things are bad in Prague, they'll get worse in spring. He hadn't yet met a refugee.

Too late to get a practice room, he entered the Mozarteum and shook himself like a dog pulled from the river. In the main hall Maile stood with other students waiting for classes to start. He cringed, re-membering their last conversation in Mirabell Garten: during a break in the rain, she eating a little sandwich that fit into her purse while he chewed on a slab of black bread and cheese from his backpack. "New York has true politics," he'd insisted, as if he knew anything about it. "Negro rallies in the streets!" And imagined the huge nation of Ameri-ca in magnificent uproar, unlike tiny Austria, trussed as tightly as a Sunday roast with ancient notions of church and aristocracy.

"The police are vicious," Maile had replied. "It's a dangerous city."

"Did you protest? Get arrested?"

"I hated all that."

"It gave you guts. Women here are afraid to travel great distances on their own. Their only weapons are charm and beauty."

She had laughed, a small annoyed sound. "Who's the romantic now? You don't dream about Fidel, you want to be Fidel."

Karl still hadn't heard her sing except through a door on the day she auditioned. With his father ill since summer, during late afternoon student recitals Karl was invariably at home wrestling fence posts or burying runt piglets, work that threatened his fingers, hands, wrists. Not long ago he and Maile had shared wine with each other as *Du*. Now she seemed freshly distant, facing away from him as Maxi

Chiemseer and Jean-Paul paraded opinions about a Vienna premiere to several violinists. Only Marie-Louise Stäbler had actually seen it; gone by private car while the rest were forced to content themselves with a broadcast in the Mozarteum's radio room. Cautiously Karl eavesdropped.

"Call me Marlise," she reminded Maile, adding, "In a word, the performance was superb."

"Von Wehlen doesn't let his singers breathe," Maxi stated. His thick blond hair and mountain climber's physique were destined for Lohengrin, but his thin tenor made it unlikely he'd get beyond the chorus of the provincial Landestheater down the street. "Herr Maestro is all orchestra."

Marlise dismissed him with a sniff. "*Frankfurter Allegemeine* said that five years ago. Now, the pharynx musculature . . . "

Karl frowned as she seized control of the conversation with a schoolteacher's authority, her thin lips so smug, something he hadn't noticed last June when he took her up to the meadow. Brenda came up through the foyer, shaking out a large lavender umbrella and exclaiming, "Whooee!" Jean-Paul crept toward her on comic tiptoe. "Scram, Frenchie," she said. His reply was drowned by string players quarreling over von Wehlen: he manages his first violinist perfectly, does not, you fool, the opening measures . . . Jean-Paul's voice shot above the others. " . . . of incalculable importance, and we underestimate it at our peril! I name you one man: Che Guevara." His bullying intensity produced silence and he harangued them on the dangers of being confined to their cocoons of opera, concerti. Because of Guevara's assassination, the corpse displayed, governments will fall.

"That rabid Communist," Maxi shouted, "only the cells in Paris mourn!"

Down the hall the registrar stalked out of his office and folded his arms like a librarian enforcing noise regulations. *"Meine Herrschaften das geht schon zu weit!"* Students stared, then groaned and picked up scores, instruments, purses, a half-eaten apple.

Maile watched Kazuo Hitachi pass through the foyer, heading for the upstairs practice rooms. He never took part in raucous debates. She was eager to have even a contrived conversation with him: good day, how nice to see you. Among so many white people, his familiar features made her miss men from home, with their straight black hair, dark eyes, and smooth skin, except for a chest tuft and a dark line from the navel that disappeared under the waistband of swim shorts. Yet she had hesitated too long, and could not now approach Kazuo without hurrying up the stairs in a clumsy attempt to waylay him. And what would she say? His father was Japan's ambassador to Germany. For sure, with the son of a diplomat it was no fool around, no make mistake. Main thing.

PROFESSOR JANN WASN'T certain he had spotted that loathsome little man at the first Mozarteum student recital—a dark figure leaving the back of the balcony quick as a salamander. At the second recital, he got a clear look at the Rosenkavalier and knew that something was in the wind, if not for himself, then for a colleague, because the flower seller was no judge of music. Yet until something surfaced, it did no good to concern himself with the man's rat-like behavior.

In his studio Jann opened *Das Brahms Liederbuch* to the piece Maile had sung at the recital—just one rather than the traditional three. A deliberate choice on his part, a compliment she did not recognize. The apparently simple piece was in fact out of reach for most sopranos. *Dun-kel, wie dun-kel im Wald und im Welt,* a peasant girl about to meet her lover, a romantic figure given a powerful vocal line easily overwhelmed by the equally powerful piano line, thick chords that rolled up from the bass keys. Fräulein Manoa had led with both voice and emotion, not too much at first, keeping the delicate balance between the two, holding it steady through the midsection, increasing slightly, then on to the final, full-throated statement of love, love eternal. *E-wig, e—wig . . . !*

What surprised Jann now was not her command of the music but her confidence on stage. It didn't match a performance record of just a year and a half of recitals in New York. She had a professional edge that he sensed had come from somewhere else—the graceful walk to the piano, the relaxed expression that masked nervousness but had the right touch of emotion to reflect the mood of the piece before it started; the pause before beginning, the single glance at her accompanist. No coughing, throat clearing, artificial poses. What had she done during her years in Hawaii?

Perhaps he was being rudely curious. Or improperly curious, something a teacher had to avoid with such an attractive student. He believed her description of an ambitious daily routine: an hour of vocal exercises first thing in the morning, followed by lieder and memory work; in the afternoon, opera roles with a coach, capped by a full-voice aria; classes in staging and Italian four times a week. If several singers at the Mozarteum were promising, so far none had given evidence of future superiority. At twenty-six a soprano could ripen quickly, sometimes in a matter of months. Fräulein Manoa's volume, range, and vocal coloring were consistent. She might be about to break through to a career. The possibility excited him, but his wife feared the stress it could bring when he should be relaxing into retirement: too much time away from gardening, too much temptation to think hard and assist the process with a glass, or two, of cognac.

He chided himself for masking his own ambition. Over the years he'd learned to perfection how sly and seductive an opera singer's ego could be—and former singers were the least aware of their own vanity. How they all lusted to relive their glory days through someone younger! More to the point would be to make discreet inquiries about finding a patron for Fräulein Manoa—later, when she had proven herself, and if his suspicions that she needed money turned out to be true.

Once he had watched her pick up a discarded bus transfer, examine it, and tuck it in her purse. At noon she sat in Mirabell Garten to eat an apple and cheese. Nothing about her personality suggested miserliness. He assumed that money was simply a constant problem, a usual state of affairs for young musicians, but no voice student ever admitted to being on the begging end of life. Singers had to believe they were aristocrats. Fortunately, a few noble families in Salzburg still felt obliged to support the arts. Baron von Gref was a possibility. He'd been a friend since Jann's days as the leading bass at the Festival. They still played chess once a month, part of an ever-smaller circle of older men who addressed each other as *Du*; the thought of which reminded Jann that once he had also been per *Du* with Werner von Wehlen.

A WEEK AFTER All Saints, a cold snap lengthened into the start of winter, and Karl began wearing his sheepskin jacket and heavy shoes. Outside the Mozarteum, he watched singers bundled against the chill as they walked toward the train station for a state-sponsored weekend of opera in Munich. They would stay at a youth hostel and have back-row or standing-room tickets, culture on the cheap, socialism at its best.

Maile disappeared past the tall ornamental bushes in Mirabell Garten, now clumps of dull gray-green under their winter shrouds of pine branches. Her singing of Brahms at the last recital was still with him: the somber opening as her voice began to rise up the scale, Dark, how dark in the forest and the meadow; the womanly richness of her sound, the hour of solitude, the world is silent. She gave the short piece the gravity of immortal love. He'd noticed that she ate only inexpensive food. Never went to a café. Did not buy a daily paper, or have scores bound in leather, like Marlise, whose name was stamped on the covers in gold. Except for a big-city wardrobe of dresses, hats, and high heels—like a Viennese or a Milanese or a Parisian—Maile seemed to own nothing that suggested a rich family. Which relieved him. He hated luxury, the wealth of the Church, and aristocrats—except for Baron von Gref, although they'd never met.

Since age fourteen Karl had stubbornly hacked out a path of his own—self-taught on six different instruments, playing in beer halls after the harvest was over, repairing the roof at Carl Orff Institute in exchange for lessons, entering the conservatory assured of his potent gift for piano and horn, then four years of punishing work to absorb the finer techniques of scales, embellishments, ensemble pieces. Another three years had put him into a small group of students who professors agreed were destined for outstanding careers.

Karl considered finding Jean-Paul to claim a beer the Frenchman had owed him for weeks. That would mean putting up with whatever maniacal mood the pianist was in.

Going straight home on the bus to the end of the line meant shoring up fences with his father on their steep meadowland. His sister had taken the family bicycle to deliver the last autumn squash to the kitchen at the Silver Fawn. Maile had seen him peddling away on the rusty old Puch a few times, but hadn't teased him about it like local women did. She didn't flirt, either. Did she ever imagine kissing him? Was her maidenhair curly or straight, like Oriental girls were rumored to have? An impulse won out: simply to walk home alone in the invigorating cold, collar up around his ears, fists curled in his pockets.

Approaching the riverbank, soon the train station was behind him, then the railroad bridge, and the tracks leading west and east. He imagined himself a soloist under contract, part of that fabulous group of exiles from all classes of society, their worth determined by excellence alone. His parents rejected such goals; a peasant who got himself educated brought enough problems down on his head. If he became an artist and crossed class lines he was doomed, would never again be satisfied with the life he'd been born into. Artists were surrounded by beautiful women. They made bad marriages. They went mad.

The flat center of the valley led deeper into the countryside—the whine of highway trucks replaced by birdcalls, sheep bleating, the squeals of hungry pigs in a distant pen—but Karl felt no stir of loyalty to the land. He planned to some day return only as an occasional visitor. More than the grimness of physical labor in a harsh climate, he wanted to escape the noon Angelus that made farmers stop for prayers, the mistrust of education and rejection of the new, even something as harmless as banana-flavored candy. The girls he had grown up with all flirted in the same way, and it made him squirm: ritualized pouts, fluttering eyelashes, bosom-heaving sighs, all copied from movie versions of Austro-Hungarian operettas. As adults they picked their teeth or noses during conversations, showed off scabs and scars no matter where they were located, and squatted beside a rural path to relieve themselves while continuing to pass on neighborhood gossip. Yet he'd had no success with town women. They were not interested in his opinions on music as an economic force, a crushing weight, something glorious that must still be regarded with suspicion.

He entered a pear orchard where faded green ribbons hung from a black branch. Tied there in summer by a new bride; green for growth, for babies. Back then he had wished Marlise would do the same for him. Now she snubbed him as if to erase all memory of the sweet grass meadow below Mönchsberg, where she had lain on her back while he lifted her skirts and pulled off her soft white panties. His hard plunge into her maidenly warmth was cut short by a shriek, a sound so terrible he'd withdrawn in fear of injuring her, then had to listen to bitter sobs that he'd taken her purity, she the daughter of an apothecary, the granddaughter of a railroad accountant, while Karl's ancestors were unlettered peasants.

He yanked on a ribbon, snapping the branch, and tossed it aside. All he had to offer Maile was cow shit, hay harvests, two thousand years of tradition. No: he had music. But what if she had a fiancé in New York or Honolulu? Or she might take up with a wealthy student like Kazuo, who could offer a woman an entire world beyond Salzburg.

AFTER THE WEEKEND in Munich, Maile's thoughts were still dominated by impressions of *Don Carlo* and *Lohengrin* at Münchner Opernhaus. Even more memorable was Mozart's *Figaro* at Prinzregenten, a Baroque architectural jewel once reserved for the Bavarian court. The productions at both theaters, supposedly second rank, with secondary casts, were much finer than anything she had seen in New York. Sets, costumes, props, lighting, and supporting roles were so excellent that the Met seemed like a tiny group of star singers backed by little else. America, she now realized, barely registered in the world of real opera. Nothing could equal being in Europe, where music had begun centuries ago and great traditions continued with full government funding. Yet Maile Manoa was still in the audience instead of on stage. Back in Salzburg, Mozart felt more like a legendary, intimidating presence than a man who had worked and eaten and slept just down the street.

Winter descended on the city. Few buildings were equipped with radiators, and Frau Metzger didn't trust Maile to use the large ceramic heating oven properly or thriftily. She came into her tenant's room at dawn and during the day, whether Maile was there or not, to stoke the fire and monitor the coals. Maile knew better than to object.

Being settled and an official resident had solved her immediate problems, but lately she found herself having strange experiences with doors. As she pushed down on a latch and stepped into a shop, everything around her gently vanished and she seemed to be entering her family's home on a slope in a hot, cramped neighborhood below Punchbowl cemetery. Relatives were asleep in the living room, or cooking and chatting in the kitchen. Her brothers and sisters sat on the ripped couch with the newest infants. Boys and girls ran in from baseball practice, paper routes, hula lessons. In the backyard Auntie Lani bathed a half dozen small children with the garden hose, stripping off her mu'umu'u and yelling, "No shame, no shame!" at a neighbor peering at her through the banana trees. Maile caught familiar scents, ripe papaya, a ginger lei, a bucket of diapers soaking in bleach, but she remained an unseen visitor, invisible to everyone. Sentimental tears filled her ghost's eyes. Then the real lives of the Manoa family rose up before her like a surf wave—too many people crammed into too little space in a city where good jobs were always in short supply. A typical mixed-blood clan that was worse off with each new generation, their days dogged by arguments about who let the gas tank go dry, or allowed the hundred-pound bag of rice to molder, or the sewer pipe to rust through; a family that could never afford tickets to see the Rainbow Warriors and had to watch the football championship from someone's rooftop outside the stadium.

Each time the vision slipped away, Maile felt torn. She wanted to go back, but on her own terms. When she'd demanded a chance to study in New York, Auntie Lani had replied, laughing, "E, we never get famous. Too old ar-ready, too fat. You go get famous." At the time it had seemed like good advice: use your gift, work hard-hard-hard; be rewarded; come home.

Maile shadowed Kazuo at the Mozarteum and in town. She watched him going into a book store, exiting the Silver Fawn, visiting his tailor. On her part it was always, *"Guten Tag wünsche ich Ihnen,"* I wish you good day. Then his reply, *"Ach wohl, Fräulein Manoa, ich habe die Ehre,"* Quite, Miss Manoa, the honor is mine. His phrases sounded starched and ironed, pleasingly theatrical, and frustrating.

One icy afternoon in the conservatory's foyer, Maile tried a new approach, sprightly, casual: Hello, what's the latest? That didn't work either, because Kazuo had turned himself into such an Austrian gentleman that she couldn't find a millimeter of common ground unless she played a similar role. In his entire deportment—there was no other word for it—he outdid any local aristocrat she had overheard on the street: "Greet the Lord, Miss Manoa, and may I ask how you are this fine morning? I believe with a little good fortune coming our way, the weather will fulfill its early promise and not become tedious."

All this in perfect German with Frenchified words in the Austrian style, *atmosphère* instead of *Wetter*, *fade* rather than *langweilig*. Kazuo dressed exclusively in custom-made clothes, a gray or brown traditional Austrian suit of cashmere, with green piping, silver stag buttons, and the requisite hat with a boar-bristle brush on the left side. Fall version followed by winter version. A Japanese-Salzburger who after three years at the Mozarteum enjoyed the reputation of an excellent performer and scholar, spoken of respectfully even by teachers. Among all the other students, Kazuo alone could afford a large record collection, fine meals. He ordered Festival tickets months in advance.

Maile approached him once more, attempting to appeal to the sense of homesickness she felt, and was sure he did too. Her offer to share a pot of green tea was politely declined. He had no interest in haiku, sumo wrestling, bon dancing, or any of the other cultural activities she knew a little about from emigrant communities in Honolulu. He was Japan-Japanese, she concluded, a distant relation to the much friendlier Hawaii-Japanese she had grown up with. But her Japanese classmates in high school and college had dated only each other, and the intermarriage rate was one in ten thousand. Which led to another possibility: Kazuo considered her racially inferior.

She had to admit that their gifts for music did not make them equals. Kazuo was not a man she wanted, he was someone she wanted to be, someone not reduced to a student's thrifty little pleasures. Herr Hitachi ate pork tenderloin in champagne sauce at the Silver Fawn. He lived in a house with servants and a wine cellar. According to gossip, von Wehlen's agent had been monitoring his progress for the last two years.

Reluctantly Maile cultivated her social life at the Mozarteum. Students never went to each other's rooms, which were guarded by relatives or landlords determined to prevent hanky-panky. Where did un-married people in their twenties make love? Salzburg lacked Manhat-tan's aggressive sex-as-competition, and she didn't miss that, but hadn't discovered something to replace it. No one at the conservatory owned a television set. Most movies were carefully neutral postwar German comedies or poorly dubbed Hollywood films, decades old. Often the high point of the day was a music broadcast in the radio room, with Maxi singing along with the famous tenor he would never become, Brenda flouncing in late, Marlise taking notes. Karl was often absent because of chores at home.

THE ROSENKAVALIER RECEIVED word that the porter at the train station wanted to see him. Trudging through snow to the *Bahnhof* had no appeal, but he treasured his friendship with the former SS man. Many claimed to have worn the Reich's most impressive uniform, alt-hough few had the blood-type tattoo to prove it. A shame, the Rosenkavalier often thought, that after the war a lack of education had reduced the porter to wearing a laborer's smock.

Train travel at this time of year was light and taxi drivers on the lookout for customers huddled at a standup café. The Rosenkavalier stopped to greet each in the routine hope of collecting useful infor-mation. None offered anything worth remembering with knots on his strings. At a storeroom the porter handed over a small black-framed death notice from a Viennese newspaper. "Gustav Sondergeist," he said, "ten schillings."

At such times the Rosenkavalier regretted being unable to read, alt-hough he recognized the notice for what it was. "A high price," he grumbled, but the porter refused to bargain, saying that a legacy was worth far more than ten schillings. The Rosenkavalier stalled, then feigned reluctant agreement and paid, secretly pleased because the amount would surely be returned fivefold, perhaps more. The two of them shared a celebratory cigarette.

It took the Rosenkavalier two days to accost Dora Jann, once an athlete who thirty years ago appeared scandalously bare-legged to compete before large audiences. She was now in her fifties and no longer a natural blond. That afternoon he caught sight of her shopping with her husband. The next morning she and a lady friend walked their dogs along the Salzach. Several hours later he spotted her alone, entering a spa. He lingered in the heated rear of the building where the trash was collected. At noon she emerged, looking pink-faced and relaxed.

He trailed her to a cluster of pine trees off the promenade, caught up, and said, *"Frau Professorin, bitte sehr."* Before she could reply he slipped her the clipping of the death notice. "Gustav Sondergeist," he added. "You have my sympathy."

Dora Jann blinked in shock. The clipping made no mention of the deceased's career as a leading sports official for the Reich. She still understood that the Rosenkavalier knew too much about things that could never be revealed. Her professional relationship with Sondergeist had become personal after she publicly congratulated another runner at the '36 Olympics, the splendid Schwarzer, whom the Führer himself had refused to acknowledge. Sondergeist shielded her from arrest and certain execution, and in exchange she became his mistress for a decade of living in terror and shame. Germany's defeat freed her from physical obligation, but the former sports official's continuing silence about how she'd spent the war years became a lifelong debt. Now the cost of maintaining that silence was being passed on.

"Is Herr Kammersänger doing well?" the Rosenkavalier inquired. The pink color of Frau Professorin's cheeks had faded. He watched her tear the clipping into scraps and waited in the full assurance that an aging woman who had managed to marry well late in life would not deny him what he asked. "A hundred schillings," he said.

She opened her purse.

"Every month," he added. "In an envelope, if you please. I will seek you out."

As CHRISTMAS EVE approached, Maile saw no animated window scenes, no advertising banners, no tinsel-laden trees. In all of Salzburg there was not a single Santa Claus. Children's Advent calendars had tiny windows to open each day to reveal details of a Nativity scene;

pastry shops sold confections made only once a year, rich hazelnut tarts and crushed almond cookies that melted on the tongue. Government buildings were hung with thick braids of pine branches. Karl was again hired for *Türmbläser*, a tradition so old no one could say if it had begun five hundred years ago, or went back to the introduction of Christianity in the third century. Each Sunday in December, at sundown brass players climbed the towers of four churches to send out call-and-response fanfares.

Maile had missed this before because of class trips to Vienna, but on Christmas Eve she made sure to be in her room and experience at least something of the season. She waited at the cracked-open window, swathed against the cold, her breath forming a thin plume drawn out over the sill. Ahead in the darkness, the city's rooftops and towers were dim outlines against the black sky. She imagined Karl at the top of a tower, huddled next to a cluster of huge bells, his horn wrapped in the heavy wool blanket each musician got in addition to a fee. One year, he'd told her, his horn had cracked nevertheless, and the city replaced it at a cost of ten thousand schillings. Four hundred dollars. Such governmental generosity amazed her, but he considered it an occupational expense.

The street below was quiet, dark bluish-gray on both sides where hard-packed snow lined the fronts of shops. A man and a dog passed by, silent black forms moving with liquid grace. High above the city a distant sound broke the stillness: a tone unfurled, one and then another, long solemn notes from a trumpet and a French horn. Two more instruments joined in to form a quartet, the tone of each layered over the previous tone, building and holding. They formed a simple melody that went out into the night with the force of light advancing, of sound made visible. As the first fanfare began to fade, from a more distant tower came the response, as if to say, I hear, and I pass the message on: a king is coming. And so it went until the call had circulated among four towers and four quartets, and returned to the first, where it was acknowledged with a brief repetition that trailed off into silence.

Maile stayed at the window despite the cold. The air outside still held the sense of an ancient command announcing the arrival of a ruler, of someone with *mana* so great that messengers were sent in advance to proclaim him. Her spirits stirred with a memory: Tūtū describing conch shells blown like thunder at the port of Nāwiliwili when Prince Kūhiō came for an official visit in the 1920s. At the time Tūtū was a young mother, Auntie Lani and Makua little children. "The monarchy gone thirty years by then," Tūtū had said, "but the sky and the winds and the waters, they remembered our ruling chief. Still yet, that sound is there."

The ice-tipped air reached deeper into the room. Maile shivered and shut the window before more heat from the ceramic tiles of the *Kachelofen* seeped out. If the coals in the oven were allowed to die, the room would chill within an hour, and reheating took ten start-up logs and two days.

She hurried down to the street and met Karl at the Dom as he exited the tower. They drank spicy hot wine at an outdoor stand, which she liked so much they shared a second cup. He described other traditions in a remote village high above the Salzburg plain: people who made bark costumes to celebrate winter magic, bear magic, wolf magic. These villagers, primitive by town standards, also carved instruments out of wood—tuba, trumpet, flute, some with crude valves—and played a strange and awful kind of music.

"You're not making this up?" she asked.

"I visited the village some years ago." He hadn't intended to reveal this, but she looked curious, not about to laugh. "Actually," he went on, "those people are distant relatives. Rock-poor, superstitious. I've heard of witches being stoned. Police don't investigate because the roads are impassable in winter, closed for weeks." He felt on thin ice, exposing his humble background, but her interest seemed to be deepening. "Only blood relations matter in places like that," he said. "And hospitality. If you went tomorrow as a traveler, they'd give you everything on their supper table." He turned to her, his emotions beginning to tumble.

She stopped walking to look at him. He seemed hesitant, she thought. His lips were slightly parted. They now stood on a dark, narrow street in an icy stillness that conveyed a sense of owning the night and the city and the world beyond. In the dim light she made out his pale eyes, thick blond fringe, horn player's full lips, the off-center chin cleft—all familiar, and yet new.

"Maile," he said with quiet intensity. His expression turned into a stare of desire he could no longer control, and he bent to press his mouth to hers. She gave in as though anticipating the moment, welcoming it. He embraced her with passionate awkwardness, his cased instrument in one hand swinging at her back, the blanket hanging over his shoulders mashed between them.

She slid her arms around his heavy jacket to pull him tighter against her body. How long has it been, she wondered, how terribly long? Some forgotten bit of pleasure grabbed on the run in Manhattan, and nothing since then in this beautiful place except toiling through unfamiliar music, language, food. They kissed and kissed, their breath smoking as they snatched gulps of air, their cheeks and foreheads fever-hot. Under layers of clothing she sensed her bare skin, aroused, but here there was no soft evening breeze, no beach, no grassy yard.

She stepped back from him and felt a rush of cold air between them. "There's no place to go, is there?"

He stood motionless, delighted by the question, although he had only a lame reply. "A ladder. That's what men use in the countryside to get to a maiden's bedroom."

She pictured the vaudeville setup, the tiptoeing lover, the rung-by-rung climb ending in a headfirst disappearance through a second-floor window. His arms were still around her waist, more loosely. Her hands were at her sides. She exhaled with a little laugh of defeat. They walked on.

"There's one more event you can't miss," he said. "Stay awake for me. I'll be back at ten o'clock."

When Karl arrived hours later, Maile realized it was an unusual effort on the part of a born-and-raised Austrian. Just coming in by bus took an hour. Salzburgers were all at home. Meeting him downstairs, she was instantly reminded of their wild kiss, yet his expression and mood were calm. "What about your family?" she asked. "It's all right for you to be here?"

He smiled. "You're a guest in Salzburg. They understand that."

His reply recalled Kauai hospitality, unspoken rules no one questioned or had to explain. They walked down Getreidegasse through lightly sifting snow. Pairs and small groups of people joined them from side streets. All were silent. Elderly women in black scarves and shawls emerged from doorways, walking by themselves or arm in arm, until a small informal procession had formed, everyone headed in the same direction. On Dom Platz a fresh layer of snow covered the wide expanse of cobblestones. Every ground-floor window of every building displayed a tall lighted candle as thick as an organ pipe, capped by a dot of flame with a faint yellow halo.

The procession crossed the dim plaza to Sankt Peter's church, with its graceful curved onion spire. Next to it a high wall, the wrought iron gates in the center opened wide. One after another everybody passed through the gates into a cloud of light. Maile saw that they had entered a small enclosed cemetery open to the sky. Beside each tombstone or green marble mausoleum was a miniature pine tree covered with tiny lighted candles. A thousand flames illuminated the cemetery's winding paths and the people lining them. Specks of glinting snow fell into the light, onto the trees, the ground.

From the direction of the church came a low sound of chanting: *Venite, venite adoremus.* A monk in a hooded robe and holding a lighted taper led the way from the church into the cemetery. He was followed by five more monks with candles, only the tips of their beards visible, and their hands, the hands of old men. In a deep hypnotic tone they repeated the phrase: Come, let us adore. Slowly they circled through the cemetery as people stepped aside for them to pass, then the monks filed out, still chanting, *Do-mi-num.* The onlookers lingered in silence, then they too filed out, dispersing into the plaza and going their separate ways.

Maile and Karl walked back to Getreidegasse, where he took her hand, nodded in farewell, and went on down the street. She stood for a moment, still enveloped by the quietness; everything had been done in the briefest and simplest way, with light and music. Although what had really happened? The event wasn't on Advent schedules posted throughout Salzburg, was not part of the Midnight Masses held later in all twenty-seven churches. A little cemetery full of tiny lighted trees and visitors: for the ancestors, she realized, so they too shared in Christmas. It felt like a small, unexpected gift that didn't need to be fully understood. For now, that was enough.

SEVERAL TIMES A day Maile crossed the icy river bridge so hatted, scarved, coated, gloved, and booted that only her eyes were visible. She craved hot food. For lack of a place to go, sex remained at a distance, in a world of sun on skin that she could hardly recall. Classrooms were heated only enough to take the worst edge off the cold, which seemed to lurk just outside like the bears and wolves that Frau Metzger described coming down from the mountains before the war. Consulates were shuttered, their gardens heaped with snow.

Finally Jann assigned Maile arias to perform at recitals, but the joy she'd expected to feel was muted: same small concert hall, same piano accompaniment rather than orchestra, no costume or partner. From time to time she spotted the Rosenkavalier in the last row of the balcony, unnoticed by the audience below; now part of the city's background, simply a strange little figure. Then other singers began jealously saying she had the rare voice a dramatic soprano. This Maile from the Pacific would become a Konstanze, a Fiordiligi, a Donna Anna.

The nickname Super-Sopran spread through the Mozarteum and gave her new confidence. She longed for massive sound, drama, arias with blazing coloratura. Professor Jann considered Super-Sopran a clever but vulgar term, something out of the Vienna tabloids. He assigned her the Rose Aria from *The Marriage of Figaro*.

She practiced the piece over and over: *Dah—dee—dah* in a dragging andante with low notes she had to scrape from the bottom of her register. No matter how hard she worked, the aria's calm midrange gentleness eluded her.

Jann claimed it was an understated masterpiece of seduction, even though the soloist stood alone on a dark stage without the aid of props. "You must learn to understand simplicity," he said. "From an entire production, this aria is often the one thing an audience recalls. A servant girl is saying, 'Return to me, my love, and I shall crown you with roses.' But there is no begging. The character has the most beautiful soul in this opera."

Hour after hour Maile slaved on it. Two scant pages. No change in dynamics or rhythm from start to finish. No climactic high notes, no technical difficulties other than creating a single unwavering line. She imagined performances shimmering in theaters throughout Europe while she was forced to poke along with a piece based on simplicity. In revenge she found a room in the depths of the Mozarteum where Jann would not accidentally hear her. There she became Aida, Elvira, Violetta; flung herself at fate, tempted men and gods, suffered and died for the glorious sake of love. Singing was athletic, ecstatic. She would never work at a hated office job, with music as a hobby after the meals were made, the dishes washed, the laundry folded, the car insurance paid.

One afternoon the door to her secret practice room flew open and Jean-Paul marched in saying, "I cannot bearrr the sound of Bizet with yourr Frrrench." He pushed her away from the piano and stamped his cigarette underfoot.

His face had a drinker's brick-colored puffiness, and his clothes stank of rancid tobacco, but he was known as an excellent critic for any singer able to put up with his temperament. *"L'a—mour,"* he shouted, playing and singing along with Maile, then in speaking voice, *"Non, non!"* He turned to her with a wide-eyed stare of pain. "You use the coarse Piaf accent. Never for opera! *Répétez après moi."* She copied his r, no tongue flip at the back of the throat, and Jean-Paul let out a snarl of approval.

They worked through the aria five times until both of them were breathing hard. "You see, you see!" He jabbed the score. "To be vulgar in this role you must lose your natural vulgarity." He glanced up, no hint of humor or spice in his expression.

She wanted to bite him and kiss him at the same time, shove him into a shower with his clothes on and listen to him wail. "Out, you frog-swine. Is that vulgar enough?"

He rippled off a lovely Tschaikovsky cadenza. "I myself cannot play without exuding *élégance.* You are a mere Algerian, doomed to worship European culture. Men will always want your brown skin. I want a snow white Circassian."

"Who stinks like you? Who bathes once a week?" Maile struggled to recall a slur. *"Ule hawa 'oe!"* Filthy penis, the best Papakōlea insult. She snatched her score and hit him over the head with it.

Jean-Paul leaped up and vanished into the hall, saying he was going to see Brrrenda, the perrrfect Amerrrican, not a mongrrrel like yourrrself.

Maile kicked the door shut so hard one of her high heels spun off across the floor. She retrieved it, thinking he was headed for the dingy schnapps bar across the street. Brenda would fetch him before he made a scene and the police came. Brenda, who'd decided he was cute after she wore her high school cheerleader's sweater and he couldn't get enough of hearing her describe varsity sports. A baby mezzo with an unusually rich, deep voice. Her tremendous low A-flat could rattle the door of a practice room. Fooling around with Carmen, a prize mezzo role, was wasting time.

IN THE EARLY morning, when fresh snow blanketed the sloping fields and Karl went out to milk the cow and feed the pigs, the farm felt like a dream of peaceful beauty. But he learned that in Prague, two sprinters bound for the Mexico City Olympics next summer had been arrested for refusing to join the Party. The clandestine group in Salzburg could do nothing. He kept up a demanding schedule of practicing both horn and piano, the one instrument involving head, neck, hands, arms, torso and feet, with huge chords and multiple melody lines as intertwined as masses of wire; the other instrument based on a single melody line that vibrated his teeth, skull, shoulder and arm bones, and so dependent on breath that playing *forte* drained his lungs to the point of blacking out.

Prisoners of harsh weather, conservatory students gathered daily in the main corridor. It was their lounge, their bulletin board, an imaginary clubhouse without a trace of intimacy. Karl had no classes with Maile. Often he recalled her Christmas Eve question on a dark, snowy street: There's no place to go, is there? Being a European stuck in Austria felt like a nasty trick of fate. In American movies—and Hawaii was officially American—couples drove their cars to lovers' lanes or outdoor film screenings, or they went to motor lodges, or to spacious apartments where no godmother guarded the entrance. In Salzburg, the miserable economy and the Catholic stranglehold on morality made all that impossible. Spring, spring, he craved it.

During those shut-in months, Professor Jann followed developments in Czechoslovakia with increasing concern. The sheer size of the Soviet army unnerved him. Newspaper editorials from Salzburg to Berlin asked, "Safety in Diplomacy?" and "What Next: The Avalanche?" Instead of European politics, he discussed the American civil rights movement with his wife. He felt fortunate that Dora was educated, unlike most upper-class women of her generation, and she shared his interest in Negroes. If she was oddly reticent about the '36 Olympics and a famous handshake, Jann didn't press her for details. His own behavior during the Nazi years had been far from laudable.

One morning after Dora went out, a package arrived. Last week Jann had written a colleague in Vienna, an elderly tenor who owned a large collection of folk music records, everything from Irish penny-whistle tunes to Japanese ritual drumming. Had Maile Manoa made any recordings in Hawaii? It was just a guess. The quick response came as a surprise.

Jann opened the package with a spy's curiosity and wariness. For months he'd been puzzled by her ability to perform with ease at recitals, and progress so rapidly. Other voice teachers remarked that he didn't have to do much with such a natural talent. But all knew that natural talent stalled unless backed by work, work, work. He unfolded an enclosed note.

Greetings, Zander, and may you never encounter the gout that presently holds me captive indoors. Oh, the dietary restrictions, the humorless attitude of my physician. However, on to more pleasant themes: this time you gave me a difficult task tho' it is the sort of puzzle I enjoy. My collection grows ever more complete, and will be the subject of a lecture in the fall if I am ambulatory by then. The name you provided is not listed on any of these albums. That is often the case with folk music. As usual in the American manner, there are a number of photographs, so perhaps you will recognize a face. I did not include recordings of obviously male artists.

The first of six long-playing albums was entitled *Voices from the Reef.* The cover pictured four handsome, fat brown women in long red dresses and red flower necklaces. "All songs in English," he read. "Your favorites to the strains of native guitars. When the Lurline Sails, Your Moon and Mine . . . " The next two albums were by a trio of girls from a place named Hilo. Then a warm shock of recognition: on the fourth album Maile stood at the center of the Voices from the Reef, described only as the Polynesian Princess of the Airwaves. Lovely, no more than sixteen.

On the final two albums she appeared in front of the women, their featured singer, although still unnamed. Until she went to New York in 1967, he figured, she had been a local entertainer for most of her life. The staged photos and liner notes seemed as fraudulent as Alpine romances or marzipan portraits of Mozart.

He placed a record on the stereo and clicked the player arm. String instruments strummed a tinny introduction. A soprano voice floated in: "The surf is sighing, calling you, you, you . . . " He clicked forward to the next selection. "I stand—on the shore, My love—is no more..." Again he stopped the sound.

Maile's voice was a sweet, pure, crooning head tone, rehearsed but not trained, a limited, natural sound used to please tourists gathered for . . . what? Once more he studied the photographs. The "Banyan Courtyard" seemed to be a kind of daytime beach cabaret, like those in southern France, with people in swimwear seated at outdoor tables for a live radio broadcast. Singing for an audience with drinks in hand must have toughened her, he thought, but it had not made her coarse. She had no trace of a café singer's shallow vanity—desired by different men every night, giving favors to the owner and his friends to keep her job. The record albums did not suggest that sort of desperation. Even so, a woman on a stage of any size was forced to deal with the fascination she generated. Had a husband or a baby been left behind on a distant Pacific island? Musicians obeyed impulses the middle class could not understand.

He repacked the records, wondering with whom Maile slept, and how often. Any conservatory was a natural hotbed for affairs, an outlet for the furious joy and frustration of music. First in line would be Karl

Holzer, that spectacularly gifted young man. Jann's emotions flared at the thought of them as lovers. But music was cruel, and those destined to be soloists invariably became competitors, then love flew out the door.

MAILE'S CLASS IN nineteenth-century composition was cancelled, and she wandered outside. The softness of the April air crept over her like an assurance of life's underlying beauty. The trees and the ground, and the clothes and hats that people wore had changed from heavy to light, from black to green. Frau Metzger no longer barged into her room to tend the *Kachelofen*. Recital schedules no longer offered *Winterreise*. Her savings would stretch to July, at least to the start of the Festival.

In the Old City she passed the Silver Fawn and told herself that one day she would go there for a grand meal. She paused outside a café with a window box of miniature irises, delicately scented. Each slender green stem was topped by a dot of white, like a piece of popcorn on the tip of a straw. The display window held an array of pastries on a shelf covered with white linen. The polished glass formed a teasing barrier between Maile and a *Sachertorte* on a silver pedestal. One slice was missing from the small, thick wheel of dark chocolate, revealing thin strips of apricot jam seeping from between each layer. To the left stood an airy froth of cream cheese cake sprinkled with wisps of orange peel. On the right a porcelain plate held glistening wild strawberry tarts, bright red clusters of tiny fresh fruit, three, six, nine, a dozen of them. A bouquet of violets and a small watercolor portrait of Werner von Wehlen completed the arrangement.

UNSER DIRIGENT, a card under it read. Our Conductor. A few striking black brushstrokes on a pale blue wash formed a three-quarter profile dominated by a stare of authority. The opera performances Maile had attended were led by second-rank conductors. She thought that von Wehlen's fame was no doubt deserved. Once Karl had said he controlled the Berlin-Vienna-Salzburg axis of music. A weak interpreter of Mozart? She couldn't believe it. Even in a small watercolor, Maestro von Wehlen exuded artistic potency.

June came in swaths of pink and yellow wild flowers that filled the grassy hillsides on Mönchsberg and Reinberg and Nonntal, and the Kapuzinerberg meadows above the whores' street. Strawberries, apricots, and cherries appeared for sale in the open market. Three thousand Festival workers arrived to set up stages, sets, sound systems, and a complex government administration. Wealthy foreigners installed themselves in large villas where they stayed year after year, couples in Pucci silks and sleek suits who strolled along the banks of the Salzach and lounged on outdoor terraces. Shop owners selling luxury goods fetched chairs, coffee, water for lap dogs, a newspaper for *mein Herr* while *meine Dame* looked at antique clasps for capes. Consulates were aired out in preparation for the arrival of diplomats.

Frau Metzger couldn't understand why such a fuss was made about student riots in Paris when the Russki Bear was awakening from winter hibernation just north of Linz. She remembered Maile's consulate invitation and called in a favor to get a free Festival ticket for her tenant. The Rosenkavalier renewed his contacts with border police and customs officials, in case Soviet troop movements endangered the Festival and forced him to adjust his livelihood. Late one afternoon he put on his uniform and went out to Schloss Wasserstein to arrange with the greenhouse manager to receive his regular allotment of roses. Each year he looked forward to refreshing this obligation of the castle's owners, acquired years ago after he disposed of a cache of bones found in their garden maze; residue left by the SS.

The Mozarteum's summer session began and Maile plunged into the rigors of study. One morning she went downstairs to see that Frau Metzger's brass doorknob had been polished until it shone like a golden goose egg. The bell button also gleamed. Across the street, housewives washing windows chatted about a Sicilian mezzo. Girls pushed scrub brooms and glistening soapy water over the cobblestones. All along Getreidegasse, women at upper-floor windows set out boxes of geraniums with long strands of red and pink blossoms that hung down to the pavement. Café waiters arranged streamers of burgundy velvet over an entryway.

A group of men passed in front of Maile to go inside, each wearing a breast-pocket pass: FESTSPIELHAUS/WIENER PHILHARMONIK. Professionals, she thought with an envious thrill. The main window featured an oil painting of a man with a baton, and a card inscribed in delicate calligraphy: WERNER VON WEHLEN.

She walked on, aroused by the assurance that leading artists were filling the city. Tickets, however, were criminally expensive, and there were no student discounts or standing room. In a shop she saw a large photograph of von Wehlen, one arm outstretched in command over a section of violins. Briefly she admired it and continued down the street. He was in nearly every window, in formal poses or action shots with orchestra, dramatically profiled, baton raised. Always with a brooding scowl, never smiling.

The Beethoven look, she decided. He's overdoing it.

Within three short streets she counted fifteen more von Wehlens—in banks and government offices, staring at passersby from beside sewing machines and bolts of fabric, looming over rows of sausage. One man, again and again. Why so few pictures of sopranos, she wondered, pianists, violinists?

A book set on a stand under a small spotlight had the title, *Das Wunder von Wehlen.* The Von Wehlen Miracle. The cover showed the conductor emerging from a Formula One racing car in a crash helmet and asbestos jumpsuit. Such an obvious show of masculinity, of ego—of *mana*, Maile had to admit—offended her. It was Hollywood rather than concert hall. Still, his glamour could not be denied—an internationally famous musician in his mid-fifties, thick silver hair combed straight back, a dead-on gaze, strong brows, nose, and chin, firm mouth. No doubt a fascinating man. Would it be possible to meet him? Ha. Every woman in Salzburg wanted to meet him.

9

On the opening day of Salzburg Festival 1968, a drizzling rain kept everyone indoors through the morning and afternoon. Porters wearing oilskin capes ventured out to make deliveries, but people with money and leisure crowded into cafés. Horse-drawn carriages on Dom Platz stood idle. Awnings at the open market dribbled miniature waterfalls onto pyramids of tomatoes and plums. High above the city the castle remained hidden behind a mass of clouds, then shortly after five o'clock, the marshy atmosphere thinned into a rising mist. By six, the grayness of the day rolled away to reveal a deepening blue sky. Townsfolk joked that von Wehlen even had a grip on the weather.

At the Mozarteum Maile worked ten more minutes on the Countess' aria from *Figaro*. Professor Jann had again mentioned entering her in a summer music competition, although he would choose the piece she sang. She finished quickly, wanting dinner: bread, cold cuts, and fresh peaches, all waiting in her room on a natural-refrigerator windowsill never touched by sunlight. After that, back to the conservatory's radio room for the premiere broadcast of von Wehlen conducting Beethoven at the Grand Festival House, an event sold out since January. Six other performances elsewhere in the city had opening nights— solo recitals, chamber music, *Jedermann* staged on Dom Platz—all of which increased her sense of excitement even though she had no hope of attending.

Outside, she paused at the sight of people in evening clothes strolling toward the river promenade. A lady in a green chiffon gown glanced at her escort, her trailing sleeves swirling gently. Three women in daytime dirndls followed the couple like birds being fed cake crumbs. Eagerly Maile joined the crowd crossing Mozart Steg. Gentlemen in black tie trailed an aroma of citrus cologne. Ladies spoke French, Italian, Spanish, making Maile wish hopelessly that she'd been born von Regensburg, de la Givanche, di Marcosa. Soon she walked against the flow, feeling vaguely depressed. Miss Manoa from Hawaii was here simply to take a look, in a knee-length jersey dress of mustard yellow.

Behind her a male voice intoned, "Let us go see von Wehlen."

She started in surprise, and turned to see Karl eyeing her with a look of glee. "Are you his baton carrier?" she snapped. "You have front-row tickets?"

His cocky expression lost its edge. "No, but I can give you a close look."

She wanted to stalk off, but he held out the promise of something—not, she was sure, the slightest chance of getting into any of tonight's premieres, let alone the main one. "A close look? I want face to face."

"He will melt you, Maile."

They followed the crowds into the depths of the Old City, threading their way through short tunnels and unlighted streets. At a gilded Baroque building a sign in four languages announced a press conference; photographers outside waved their credentials. Performance schedules covered the exterior, the names of singers in large letters: Vladimiroff, Alcazar, Du Toit, Reichenhaller. Maile stared: Vladimiroff had been a guest at the Met.

In an adjacent room spiked with antennae, a technician adjusted dials on a bank of controls and asked in British-accented English, "Cape Town, Cape Town, do you receive? *Kapstadt,*" he repeated, *"bitte, melden Sie sich."* She imagined her name announced to a world audience, a live broadcast to thirty countries, her voice on the Grand Stage of the Grand Festival House, picked up by hidden microphones and sent instantly to radio transmitters on the tops of mountains.

Karl peered over her shoulder, and she sensed a sudden, eager tension in him. "You want this too, don't you?" she said. "Every bit of it."

Off to the left a church bell rang, low bass tones. "Hurry," he told her, "we only have about five minutes."

From a tunnel they emerged onto a wide street where townspeople stood five deep opposite the brilliantly lit entrance to the Grosses Festspielhaus. Along its front, floor-to-ceiling panels of glass were framed in bands of green Salzburg marble and bronze. Ticket holders in evening dress strolled into the foyer as ushers swept the doors open. Three men in Arab headdresses and white robes were motioned inside. A Rolls-Royce pulled up, followed by horse-drawn carriages garlanded with roses. A sleek blonde edged past Maile, her neck glittering with jewels, and remarked, *"De Ribes et sa scènes, c'est de trop."*

"Scusi," an elderly gentleman murmured to Maile.

She stepped aside for him and stared raptly at the crowd going in, so unlike theatergoers in Manhattan, where formal clothes had largely been replaced by bell-bottoms, Indian prints, sandals with socks. Here in Salzburg men and women of all ages were radiantly and unapologetically elegant, no bargain basement suits that sagged, no necklines slit to the waist, no leopardess makeup, the entire crowd like a magnificent school of reef fish gliding in a gentle current, the women in colors, the men in black and white. And what fun they were having! Bows, hand kisses, smiles of greeting, quiet laughter, as though they were on their way to a wonderful private party.

"Come on." Karl jerked his chin to the right. "The great one doesn't mingle. It's considered crude to get too close to him. Let's be crude."

She followed him to an empty alley behind the main theater. Everything seemed strangely neat and quiet; no arriving orchestra, none of the slam-bang activity that preceded a premiere. "Is this the stage entrance?" she asked.

Karl shook his head and led off to a high wrought-iron gate where a small group of men stood looking in. The grillwork had a lavish design of vines and gold knobs like the entrance to a consulate. On the other side was a small dark courtyard and a door. As Maile stepped up beside Karl, one of the waiting men gave her a look that became a rude stare. Karl spoke curtly to him in what sounded like dialect. The man faced away and muttered to his companions.

Confused, she was suddenly more intrigued by what he wore, what they all wore, five white-whiskered men so alike they could have been brothers, each with a green felt hat covered in enamel pilgrim's medals, suede vests embroidered in rich mossy shades and spanned by watch chains hung with silver coins. Filigreed silver buckles fastened their leather trousers below the knee. She eyed the men discreetly, thinking they must be from a village untouched by tourists, where people still did beautiful handiwork, raised sheep for wool. Karl's relatives! The ones who made wooden trumpets.

From the far end of the alley came the quiet sound of a motor. Everyone turned to look at a car entering slowly. The shiny black Mercedes had the broad grille, large round headlights, and curving fenders of a prewar model. A Festival official in a gray uniform walked alongside it. The Mercedes halted, and the official went up a tiny speaker affixed to the gate and said, *"Der Wagen."*

An overhead floodlight flashed on. Four men in dark suits stepped from the doorway into the courtyard. Light and shadow in a pattern of yellow streaks and black bars covered everybody watching outside. Maile felt as if a net had been thrown over them. The gate slid aside with an electronic hum. *"Nun, jetzt,"* the Festival official said, and motioned for the group of onlookers to stand back.

Everyone except Maile did so. The four men in suits came forward, and she stared from them to the official to the harsh shadows reaching toward the black car, and thought of soldiers chasing prisoners across a field lit by searchlights: years ago, an outdated newsreel at a Kauai movie theater, people fleeing, nearly naked. "Here's how the Nazis treat civilians," the newsreel reporter had said. Even as a child, she'd known that the people in the film were dead by the time it reached the other side of the world.

"Bitte," a man in a suit said, gripping her arm as the car approached. She pulled back and he let go. The Mercedes made a smooth turn past her into the courtyard, the front fender just a meter away, then the side door. A patch of light crept over a figure in the back seat, the now familiar hair and profile. "Von Wehlen!" she said, louder than intended. His head turned sharply as if tracking the sound of a shot, and there was an instant of eye contact. Maile felt like she'd been stabbed.

Karl stifled a laugh. "Guts," he murmured.

The car glided into place and the gate slid shut. The men in suits surrounded von Wehlen as he got out and disappeared into the theater.

The bearded men spoke among themselves, then all five turned to glare at her. One had a particularly hostile expression, nose wrinkled, lips drawn back as if about to spit.

"Samatta you," Maile hissed at him, "I owe you money, o wot?"

"*In hoc signo,*" he retorted. His right hand flew up, and he crossed himself. The others copied him.

"You fool," Karl blurted, "she's an artist, a soprano." He took Maile's hand, muttering, "Jesus Maria, are things still that bad?"

She let him lead off at a fast pace, her heart flipping as if on a fishing line inside her chest. Von Wehlen had looked her in the eyes, a fleeting, invisible assault. A frightening old newsreel. A stranger had nearly spit on her.

From the alley, Karl bypassed the crowds in front of the Festival House and went farther and farther from the center of the Old City. Finally he stopped on a quiet tree-lined street. "Those kinds of men," he said, "come out of the mountains maybe once in ten years, rustics who tap a hunchback's hump for luck or whip a Gypsy if they find one. Their lives run according to signs and omens."

"What did I do?" she asked. Then with a flash of insight, "Are those your relatives?"

For a moment he was silent, caught off guard. Yes, he admitted, although not exactly. They were from the same area, but wore their chamois-beard hat brushes higher than in his grandfather's village. "If they catch sight of a Jew, or a redhead or a witch, it's a curse worse than hunger or filth. They cross themselves to cancel the curse."

"Since I'm not a Jewess or a redhead, I'm a witch?" He grunted as though unwilling to confirm the insult. She decided that being a witch was outlandish enough to be comical, or weirdly glamorous. Maybe being an outsider in Austria wasn't all bad. Terrible things had happened in this country. People who once cheered *der Führer* were still calmly baking beautiful pastries.

Karl put an arm around her shoulders, but then he coughed artificially and clasped his hands at his back as if to erase his touch. "What did you tell those men? They're not easily frightened."

She winced at having lapsed into pidgin—in public!—and just because someone angered her. "Oh," she mumbled, "it's not translatable."

"Try."

He would keep asking, she knew, and he had delivered on his promise of von Wehlen up close, and revealed more about the poverty and ignorance of his relatives than she ever intended to tell him about her own family. Explaining you-looking-me-ugly-like-I-owe-you-money would make her sound like she also came from a remote village. Instead she said, "May sharks tear your stomach."

Karl grinned. "I've heard sharks have multiple sets of teeth."

"Continuous teeth."

"I should go back and tell them."

She smiled, warmed by the power of a good lie, of being able to inspire fear. After all, according to Professor Jann, a fully developed artist had to understand the entire range of life, good and bad, pure-hearted and wicked.

IT WAS PAST eleven when Maile returned to Getreidegasse after the Mozarteum's radio room broadcast of the Beethoven premiere. The kitchen light still burned on the ground floor and Frau Metzger called out, "*Ach*, Hawaii-Mädchen, I have a little surprise for you."

Her tone was so pleasant that Maile closed the front door with a feeling of mild suspicion. The landlady was usually in bed by nine. Frau Metzger strolled into the entry hall and from her apron she pulled out an oblong strip of green paper, teasingly and slowly, like a magician with a silk scarf. "A Festival ticket."

Maile recognized the color and shape from the voided samples on the window of the Festival box office. She reached for it.

Frau Metzger stepped back with an apologetic look. "I must confess, it is only for a dress rehearsal. However, you came to mind at once because the event is fully staged with singers."

Maile examined the ticket, tantalizingly out of reach. Small black letters spelled out RAPPRESENTAZIONE. An unpronounceable name. She had never heard of the work. Was it even opera?

"I must confess to something else." Frau Metzger fanned herself with the ticket. "What I love most are grand symphonies. As conducted by Herr Maestro von Wehlen. The mind is free to think of all sorts of things while listening. Fine thoughts. I used to see him playing as a boy, you know."

"How very interesting," Maile remarked.

In a hurt tone Frau Metzger said, "Salzburg diplomats receive tickets gratis. Because you made such an impression on your consul last fall, you will most certainly be attending performances."

Maile was stunned by the range and persistence of gossip in the city. She hadn't told Frau Metzger about meeting Mr. Casey nine months ago, nor had she heard about diplomats getting into the Festival for free. That was probably true. So this odd ticket wasn't a gift, just a trade, and the landlady wanted the better part of the bargain.

Frau Metzger's injured expression turned into a pout. "A young, important foreign artist like yourself has *entrée* in ways I do not. The cheapest von Wehlen concert costs five hundred schillings. For that sum I can have my kitchen painted."

Maile ached to see even a dress rehearsal but had no chance of repaying the favor. Being invited to a consular reception did not mean she was now part of Edwin Casey's social circle. Would he even remember her? Besides, if anyone gave her a von Wehlen ticket, she would go herself. Yet compared to Frau Metzger she did have *entrée*. She imitated the landlady's coy manner, tipping her head to one side with feigned consideration. "Herr Maestro does have a Wagner evening."

"Oh, yes!" Frau Metzger's cheeks bloomed pink. "Any performance with him would be wonderful. Even opera."

Maile smiled to seal the bargain. "You're so kind to think of me." She tucked the ticket into her purse, relishing the ease of making a promise with no hope of delivering. Another instance of Professor Jann giving her permission to explore all human emotions.

The next day passed in a veneer of studying over a core of excitement that lasted all the way to evening. Classes, food, nothing else mattered as much as being able to experience Salzburg Festspiele 1968. Maile wanted badly to wear a gown, but for a dress rehearsal she chose a smart black suit with a knee-length skirt and tiny rhinestone buttons on the jacket. Swooping her hair into a topknot, she completed the outfit with plain black high heels and a thin bracelet of black coral. Tonight she was not just a student listening to a radio broadcast. A live performance, in Mozart's city!

At the top of the stairs she listened for Frau Metzger, and hurried outside to avoid being stopped for inspection. The ticket gave only the name of a plaza. Maile paused at the dark end of Hofstallgasse, unsure which branching street to take, then went on, reasonably certain the plaza was not far beyond the wine cave. Soon nothing seemed familiar. Turning a corner, she found herself in the narrowest streets of the Old City.

A small figure glided from an unlit doorway. She saw the dull glow of a red bouquet, coils of silver braid on a jacket, the whites of the man's eyes as he approached her. *"Rosen, die Dame?"* he inquired.

He smelled of something chemical. Mothballs, an odor she had always hated. His discolored black eye sockets suggested some untreatable disease. *"Nein, danke,"* she replied. He murmured a courtesy and moved on with silent, waltzing steps.

She put a hand to her throat and strode off, wanting other people around, a crowd. He reminded her of childhood fears, a half-dead spirit creeping at night from a burial cave to steal souls. That was hysterical, unfair. North Shore stories, old folks talking. He couldn't help his looks. He was harmless, an elderly flower seller who once worked at a village operetta theater.

Ahead she saw a patch of light. Swiftly she walked toward it and stepped out onto a small plaza with a metal sign imbedded in a wall: KAPUZINER PLATZ. Men and women stood outside a large Baroque church with an inscription on white marble above the entrance: SKOLAREN KIRCHE, ANNO 1642, DEO GRACIAS. She looked at her ticket, thinking there must be a mistake—church and opera didn't mix—but the location was correct and all other buildings on the plaza were closed.

She got in line for an unreserved seat. Light rain sprinkled down on the crowd and people jostled forward through the wide doors. She followed them halfheartedly, sure that the evening would be a loss. Worst of all, Frau Metzger expected a von Wehlen ticket in return. The air inside the church was refreshing, cool but not chilly. Tall candles along the walls shed gentle light over the gathering audience and gave off the purifying scent of pine. Maile's eyes adjusted to the dimness. She sat down and felt drawn to look up. The vast arched ceiling of the church was covered with frescoes of clouds. From their center a flock of angels spilled down the walls, gracefully suspended in flight, their gazes directed on everyone below. Far to the right and left, at the end of each pew, statues stood every few yards all the way to the altar, figures carved so true to life that they seemed to move; robes, hair, and beards flowing as though blown by a phantom wind, men and women in courtly or heroic poses, yet with expressions of compassion.

Saints, Maile realized. Peter's head was tilted toward her in an attitude of kindly concern, one hand curved over his heart, the other extending a large key. She recalled Hawaii's austere Congregational churches, no statues or paintings, plain pews, plain pulpit, plain altar table. Here she was in a lavish European court of the Lord.

Streams of people came down the center aisle. Their increasing numbers surprised her, and about ten pews ahead she noticed Professor Jann. His presence seemed to imply that the performance would be worthwhile. Surely he wouldn't waste time attending a third-rate event.

A little girl sitting next to Maile was reminded by her mother not to applaud in a church. Of course, Maile thought, but it only added to her confusion about the performance. One-page programs were passed out. *Rappresentazione di Anima e di Corpo*, she read, and translated the rest. *A Representation of Body and Soul*, an allegory composed by Emilio de Cavalieri in 1603. Historically the first opera, preceding Claudio Monteverdi's *Orfeo* of 1607. Her mood sank.

Allegory meant prints of Virtue and Harmony in a freshman college text, the rigid image of Britannia in the Honolulu tax office. She recognized none of the soloists' names. The stage consisted of white planks constructed over the altar, with long staircases on either side. No scenery, no curtain. Dress rehearsal.

A brilliant fanfare came from an unseen orchestra and light flooded the stage, sending a current of expectation through the audience. Trumpets introduced a bishop who stepped out wearing a peaked mitre and gold brocade vestments. He raised his crozier and sang a stately description of the world, its glories and its snares. Slowly he swept his staff across the audience, then faded from view. The tempo changed from majestic to sprightly, and a glittering group of masked dancers paraded forward, each accompanied by a descriptive melody: a king, a knight, a courtesan, a beggar woman cradling a baby, a fat monk swigging a jug of wine. They formed a circle and danced out their stations in life, wielding a scepter, counting coins, drinking and laughing. The little girl beside Maile clasped her hands in delight.

High above the altar an archangel in a suit of armor appeared in a shaft of light. His broad wings expanded, and in the ringing tones of a tenor he proclaimed, "Behold the Wheel of Fortune." He gestured with his sword at the dancers below. A pocket was picked, an apple eaten, gems flashed. The beauty and liveliness of the scene filled Maile with increasing wonder; everything was new and yet old, theatrical yet spiritual. The tenor's voice soared: "Behold and beware!"

A thunder of timpani tore through the church, and the dancers ripped off their masks to reveal skulls; from the king to the beggar woman's baby, all were corpses standing rigidly in place. The entire audience seemed to hold its breath as the low sound of a dirge crept onto the stage and the dancers formed their own funeral march and drifted away into darkness.

Scene after scene unfolded in a panorama of life on earth contrasted with heaven's eternal rewards. Body, a young hunter, and Soul, an ethereal woman, pursued each other. Saints whose postures mirrored the statues lining the side aisles dismissed princes of the Church who accepted bribes, or lepers who abandoned hope. The little girl identified Theresa, Barbara, Cäcilia, and whispered the sacred names to her mother. The strangely archaic music switched from lyric to harsh and back, full of striking harmonies, an explosion of fantasy followed by a sense of grace. Maile's spirits hovered between heaven and earth.

All temptations ceased when a huge figure in black leaped onto the stage, snatched up a heap of rattling skeletons, and disappeared into a pit. Processions of victorious souls in golden robes singing hymns of praise ascended the staircases above the altar. A host of angels on a balcony were joined by massed choirs throughout the church exclaiming, "Gloria, Gloria, Gloria!" Violins, flutes, and trumpets blended in a crescendo that peaked at the same instant all light was extinguished. Only the glow of the candles along the walls remained as the final chord echoed into every curve of the vast ceiling, into each side chapel, through hundreds of listeners, and finally trailed off into stillness. A warm hush enclosed the audience.

In silence people finally stood up to move toward the aisles. The high front doors opened, and the cool evening air washed in. Maile made her way out onto the plaza, still tingling. Couples around her exchanged quiet comments. A man remarked that the production could become quite a success. All unknown singers, but excellent.

As the crowd moved into the damp night air, she watched for Professor Jann, eager to discover more about an opera that made allegory so gripping. Presently he came outside deep in conversation with an elderly lady. Maile recognized her from a Festival poster, hands poised over a piano keyboard, white hair swirled into a turban. It wouldn't be right to intrude, she knew, when they were talking artist to artist. Besides, tomorrow she had a voice lesson.

Maile walked off toward the Grand Festival House, where the audience was strolling away to dine. Beautifully dressed couples entered bright restaurants. She watched them absently, picturing the archangel with his gleaming sword, the hunter Body carrying a slain deer on his shoulders, the skull face on the beggar woman's infant—that incredible detail not spotlighted, just there. Most wonderful of all, the entire production reflected the lives of people in Salzburg, history as they knew it, stories passed down to the little girl seated beside her, who had seen familiar saints come to life.

A short distance away she saw a police officer stop a man in a tuxedo. Cursing drunkenly in Italian, the man fumbled in his jacket and dropped what looked like a passport. His tone turned belligerent. An argument erupted and another policeman joined them. Shouting now, the man was escorted off to a patrol car.

Maile gripped her evening purse and heard the things inside it click: lipstick case, key. The little bag seemed too empty. She dug through it but knew with dead certainty that she'd forgotten her precious ID. *At all times a foreigner must carry . . .*

She hurried toward Getreidegasse before a policeman stopped her for any reason at all. In the dark she rushed into a cloud of scent—irises in a café window box—but couldn't find the side street leading to Frau Metzger's. The possibility of arrest felt real, a disaster, then it was theatrical: Maile in handcuffs; Maile wronged; Maile suffering! A Mozarteum soprano would only get a scolding from a policeman as long as she charmed him and dropped the name of an aristocratic friend. She would invent one. La-la-la. This city with its hills and castle and costumed people was a constant opera, and not far away saints were putting aside their crowns and angels were folding their wings. All those beautiful feathers. Swan feathers, brushed with gold.

THE NEXT MORNING when Maile went downstairs, Frau Metzger held out a heavy ivory-colored envelope. "This just came," she said, her eyes wide. "A boy from Diplomats' Row." She handed it over and folded her arms.

On the back of the envelope Maile saw a United States seal stamped in gold, inside an engraved invitation with a handwritten message: *Dear Miss Manoa, It's been a while but I hope you're still willing and able to give us a tune or two on July 29th. Gershwin would be great. Yours sincerely, E. Casey.* This time the writing was legible. Gershwin? No problem. She smiled and left Frau Metzger seething for information.

At Professor Jann's studio Maile went through the formalities of greeting, then mentioned hearing the new Festival opera last night. "Oh, I'm pleased you managed to go," he said. "Wasn't it splendid? Unusual, of course. How did the performance strike you?"

Gratefully she took her mind back to it: the opening scene with the bishop, the dancers, the archangel high above the altar, and his declaration, "Behold the Wheel of Fortune." Then instead of a figure in gleaming armor, she recalled a knight in cardboard and tinfoil, years ago in Honolulu. Her memory locked. How proud she'd been of the costume, how deeply impressed by *The Magic Flute*—yet now she knew it had been nothing more than a pitiful attempt to imitate what Madame referred to as high art. Hawaii didn't have it. If people there tried to understand opera by producing one every ten years, they had no idea. She would never catch up with Europeans. In their bones and souls they understood that music was also history and refinement. She didn't even have the right to an opinion.

"It was beautiful," she said quietly.

Jann gave her a look of reproach. "Such a weak response? You must learn to be a critic. By that I do not mean tearing a work to shreds." He explained that *Rappresentazione* was a piece not performed for centuries, a typical stand-and-deliver series of arias interspersed with choruses. The visual monotony of this was overcome by the inspired use of mime dancers reflecting the rough medieval world as well as the aristocratic Enlightenment. Instruments borrowed from a Prague museum gave the orchestra its authentic sound.

Her sense of excitement returned as he spoke, a man eager to share what he admired. She offered comments and found that he was thrilled by the same moments in the performance. He complimented her grasp of drama and staging. She realized that she'd heard something unique, perhaps more important than a performance at the Grand Festival House. Half her lesson time slipped away. Jann glanced at his watch and said, "Conversation is good. However, I want to hear some simplicity from you."

She took her place at the grand piano and imagined rosebushes, waist-high. A dark stage. No props. Nothing except a melody about love, not tense, coiling seduction. Love. Be still. Open your heart.

He played the gentle introduction, its rhythm like a swaying hammock. She suppressed a sigh, and pictured a man close by, her one listener, her secret audience watching from shadows in the rose garden. "Belov-ed soul," she began in a calm tone, "hesitate no longer... " She sang to the night and the stars just appearing high above the garden. The piano received the phrase and carried it forward. She felt her lover listening. "My heart awaits . . . " A voice she hardly recognized as her own filled the room. "Come, my beloved . . . let me crown you with roses." The last notes of the accompaniment enveloped her, and receded to a light pulse merging into the air she and her audience shared. The conductor had lowered his baton. The singer stood motionless. Time and space and place were bound in a memory of love.

"Continue," Jann said softly. He turned a page. Leaves on the bushes outside his studio brushed against the window and a stray branch tapped on the glass. "Lights up!" he announced.

Figaro burst in with an outraged accusation, followed by the page-boy and the countess, Jann accompanying and singing all the roles except Maile's. In the fast recitatives he switched from one character to another, up, down, male, female. When she joined in as Suzanna, he changed from singing the Countess in falsetto to expertly singing Figaro or the Count, and he missed nothing on the piano. In the Act Four finale they sang their way furiously through secret love notes, a jump from a window, mistaken identities—a comedy that exploded in glorious music as characters came together in duets, trios, quintets. Jann acted as orchestra, cast, and conductor, a wild effort that had him and Maile helpless with laughter when he sang an inappropriate part or struggled to play fluttering tremolo octaves to imitate a surge of violins. They kept pace with each other to the end, a full-throated celebration of love, with aristocrats and servants united and resolved to adjourn in joy to a marriage feast. All hearts triumphed.

The final phrase left them panting for breath. They beamed at each other. "Aaah," he said, "you have the right spirit!"

She had never seen him so satisfied and happy. She wanted to throw her arms around him, but even in fun, Jann was still *der Herr Professor*. They would never address each other as *Du*. Never share gossip. Inwardly she withdrew to await his critique.

His smile relaxed. He closed the score, flexed his fingers and said, "The competition will be announced shortly, which is rather irritating because it takes place only two weeks hence. Teachers are in a hurry to submit candidates." He showed her a paper. Kazuo, Brenda, and Jean-Paul were listed along with Karl and other Austrians. "A small affair, although it offers good exposure." He took out a pen and added Maile's name to the list. "Over the next few years you will progress to more important contests. Enter with a Mozart piece, not the Rose Aria, because today you accomplished that beautifully. The only remaining test is whether or not you can sing it as well under the pressure of a live performance. Give yourself a different kind of challenge."

She hesitated, uncertain about competing against Salzburgers. In their city. With their Mozart. But a third of the participants were foreigners. Including Brenda!

"Choose a work that appeals to you," he said, "although not the Queen of the Night, please, or the Martyrs Aria from *Abduction*. I share your fascination for vocal pyrotechnics, but two weeks is not much time to prepare. This list will double with entrants from Spain, France, the East Bloc countries."

International competition. The phrase had weight and glamour.

He walked her to the door, sliding a hand under her left elbow in a refined gesture. "The winner performs at a prize concert with the student orchestra. That kind of recognition during the Festival is quite an honor. The government awards a thirty-thousand-schilling prize."

She wished him *auf Wiedersehen*, felt the warmth of his hand retreat as she went out, then in the hall she mentally divided thirty thousand by twenty-five: twelve hundred dollars. And the Rose Aria "beautifully accomplished!" All that work to arrive at a statement of something simple. Of love in all its subtlety.

10

MAILE NOTICED THAT Frau Metzger's attitude toward her was newly underlined by expectant smiles and small favors—dried mint for tea left outside her door, fresh rolls delivered one morning—although the ticket she owed her landlady was never mentioned. If Frau Metzger now had the upper hand, she also seemed aware of being dependent on her tenant's goodwill to repay. Their relationship developed a polite façade of hints given and ignored. Frau Metzger's new crossword puzzle magazine, conveniently displayed while saying good morning, had von Wehlen on the cover. When Maile passed in or out of the house, she heard quiet humming in the kitchen, always an easy Wagner piece like the Pilgrim's Chorus from *Tannhäuser*.

She considered trying to wheedle a von Wehlen ticket out of Casey's receptionist—and sneaking off to the performance without telling Frau Metzger. Which wouldn't work, of course, because of her landlady's uncanny knowledge of gossip.

On Friday a list of the Salzburg contestants was posted on the Mozarteum's front door and Kazuo withdrew into a robotic imitation of himself. Jean-Paul became even more maniacal. Brenda experimented with different poses: frightened little girl, conceited movie star. Karl entered and left the conservatory through the basement and was rarely seen.

Marlise ran a betting pool with odds that changed daily: Jean-Paul would win with his monumental Tschaikovsky concerto; or Kazuo, who had mastered half the entire violin repertoire, which spanned centuries, an achievement no other graduate student could match. Would Karl compete with piano or horn, Beethoven or Bach? The Super-Sopran might have an edge over all three men, but singing was riskier than playing an instrument, no key to press, no string to tune, all in the throat and the mind.

The halls developed a wordless intensity as contestants scrutinized each other for hidden faults that could mar a performance. Maile avoided the Mozarteum until she had chosen an aria. In her room she read through familiar and obscure Mozart roles: peasant girls, vengeful queens, women masquerading as boys. She imagined performing to a row of judges, a tiny audience with unsmiling faces and no colored cocktails to soften their responses. Kazuo and Jean-Paul worried her; both veterans of a half-dozen important contests who considered producing music under extreme pressure the true test of their abilities. If Professor Jann believed she was a born performer, fine. He would never know about her long apprenticeship at hotels singing two-minute songs that rhymed "hula skirt" with "aloha shirt."

Two weeks was barely enough time to memorize, get the breaths down, and live inside the character until the piece was hers. Should she be a sprightly maid, a seducible ingénue? Brenda was excellent in that genre and would flatten a soprano competitor. At times the itch of sex crept out of the piano like a lizard, snickering at Super-Sopran for singing about passion but living like a nun. Compared to New York, life in Salzburg was sexless. She considered going straight over to the conservatory basement, walking in on Karl while he was mid-phrase with Beethoven, and stripping off her blouse. He would be astonished, instantly erect! No, no, a terrible idea, something a thirteen-year-old did on a dare.

Maile turned to *Titus Andronicus*, rarely performed Mozart. Like *Rappresentazione*, the work had the grandeur and drama of past centuries. The arias were filled with rolling coloratura, wonderful for showing off, but she couldn't think her way into a Roman ruler's daughter who was also the rejected wife of a second Roman ruler in love with another daughter of another Roman nobleman. Perhaps she should sing a solo from one of the great masses: an angel who bestowed mercy. No, a contest was first of all about nerve. And an aria had to be based on a person, not a spiritual ideal—a baroness, a countess, a woman both vulnerable and strong.

She recalled racing through *Figaro* with Jann. The opera was saturated with love: *Liebe*, *Lee-beh*, solemn love, goofy love. She flipped through the comic scenes and looked for a kind of *Liebe* not tenderly symbolized by roses, but with passion and grief. A fierce decision to regain lost love. Countess Almaviva, Third Act.

Across the Old City the Dom bells struck the noon hour, signaling the end of apartment practicing for the morning. Silently Maile followed the black notes on the page: a slow melody beginning in a mood of distress, andantino, the tempo of longing, then a dramatic shift to allegro, and finally the conclusion: "My fidelity will triumph over his ungrateful heart!" She packed the score in her shoulder bag, uninterested in lunch or rumors about who had broken down and might drop out, needing only a practice room to see if she could really handle this piece. Technical hurdles. Emotional hurdles. Beauty all the way through. Mozart, the master of love's intricacies.

She headed downstairs feeling light enough to glide out the door and fly across the river. On the last step she heard a woman speaking clearly enunciated German. "But the sheets. Such a personal item." The voice came from the kitchen. "By the Catechism, I would not touch those sheets. She must buy her own linen."

"Oh, no," Frau Metzger replied with a nervous laugh.

"You are too modern, Josephina."

Sheets. Frau Metzger did the laundry, which was included in the rent, but Maile washed her own stockings and underwear, and always hung them on the washstand rather than at the window because the landlady made such a point of it.

The same woman remarked that her village church still refused burial to anyone connected with the theater. A third woman said such ostracism of the dead or the living was medieval. Musicians were chosen by God and deserved respect, although she drew the line at a dark-skinned foreigner entering her house. No Negress, even a diva or a diplomat's wife, would ever use her chairs or china. Not to mention the toilet.

Negerin.

"I must confess to examining the sheets," Frau Metzger said. "And I listen every day for water running in the shower. My Hawaii-Mädchen bathes more often than I do."

A cup clinked on a saucer. "Well, she has to, doesn't she? Do not complain when you must buy a new mattress along with sheets and towels. Everything she touches will have an odor you cannot be rid of.

I have often seen her talking to your godson. We know where that leads."

The third woman asked, "Have you heard men on the stairs at night? My Turkish cleaning girl starts wearing lipstick during the Festival. Of course, no wealthy visitor would actually marry one of them."

"Don't be unkind," Frau Metzger murmured, then said more firmly, "There has been no improper behavior in this house. Certainly not with Karl. My tenant is here to take our culture back to her people. Our American consul received her at once."

The other women agreed it was an important social connection but cautioned Frau Metzger that a sophisticated appearance was no guarantee of decency, that her tenant's manners had been acquired here and were not the result of a proper upbringing. In fact, her presence endangered Frau Metzger's reputation.

Maile stood frozen on the step. Her slightly brown skin was actually a layer of filth? Her dirty body was contaminating sheets and towels and Karl. She clamped her purse under one arm, about to brazen into the kitchen to ask how often they bathed or washed their braids—always shiny with grease—but a thorn of warning spiked through her anger. Never lose your sense of tact, Madame had said. Or was it Jann? Shouting at gray-haired women would fuel the worst kind of gossip: crude American, from the lowest class, trying to disguise herself as a diva.

Her fury collapsed. She crept back upstairs, too humiliated to look for a practice room to make herself into a countess. Salzburg's formality no longer seemed charming but a shrewd mask to hide centuries of vicious prejudice. Foreigners were sly and little better than prostitutes unless they achieved artistic status. Odor? At home in Honolulu the smell of so-called honest sweat was not appreciated. Even her country relatives swam or bathed every day and scented themselves with crushed ginger petals.

Ten minutes later, from her upstairs window, Maile watched Frau Metzger and the women leave the house with their market baskets. Her miserable mood had turned back into balled-fists, pacing-around-the-room anger. She wanted sympathy, and was afraid that if she didn't get it she would make a stupid, permanent mistake, squander her manners on a screaming fit. Proper behavior here was as valued as money. The only person she could complain to was Karl, but his family had no phone. Like most people, they got along without one and sent any message that couldn't wait by telegram. Teachers even rescheduled lessons via telegram, an inexpensive convenience within the city limits—another custom that no longer seemed charming but hopelessly old-fashioned. She couldn't imagine sending an idiotic plea: DEAR KARL FEELINGS WOUNDED STOP COME AT ONCE STOP MAILE.

She stalked downstairs to look for him. Halfway to the Mozarteum she realized that he might not be there. She'd have to take a bus out to Gaisberg, hike up a hillside she had never seen, asking all the way where the Holzer family lived. Even then he might not be home, and she would be trapped talking to his parents while they fed the chickens.

Closer to the conservatory she heard shouting, an unusual sound. Jean-Paul sat on the front steps with a younger French pianist, his page turner. Newspapers in several languages were draped over their knees. "The Sorbonne martyrs continue to inspire," Jean-Paul yelled at anyone entering or leaving. "The triumph carries over to Prague!" Some students went past with curious expressions. Others shrank from him.

In uneasy embarrassment Maile started up the far side of the steps. Raw emotion on the street belonged in Manhattan. Jean-Paul thrust a newspaper at her. She glanced at a photo of a crowd, and a caption: *Following the Vaculik manifesto, Prague Spring gains momentum.*

"You Americans know the underdog," he ranted. "Your Martin Luther King was shot dead, a Nobel laureate. You live with shame."

She stepped away. "I'm only American on my passport. What's so terrible about one more riot? In New York I got used to them."

His expression turned into a sneer. "You are just a low Tahitian."

"You stinking hypocrite! Aren't Tahitians French citizens?" She grabbed the newspaper and flung it aside. "Pick up your trash. Police can fine you a thousand schillings during the Festival, and it's a week in jail if you can't pay." A made-up threat, but it left him speechless, and she got into the conservatory before he came after her.

Algerian, Tahitian. If she didn't become a star here, she would be just another foreigner, like the Turks and Greeks who swept the railroad platform, men despised on sight because of their skin color.

Students in the main hall were crowded around the bulletin board. From the basement practice rooms came the bleeps, blaps, and booms of brass and percussion instruments, instant headache sounds. A French horn soared above the racket pouring up into the hallway.

Maile descended the stairs in a murderous mood and was assaulted by brawling thunder. Light bulbs in wire nets cast a feeble yellow glow on a stone corridor as forbidding as a catacomb. Kettledrums hit a *sforzato*, a blast of vibrations like sheets of metal crashing onto cement. She gritted her teeth, feeling stupid for prowling in the basement, and turned to escape. A melody swooped down on her—*dah, da, di-di-di-di da-da-da-da, DAH!* She chased it and banged on the door.

Karl jerked it open as if angry at being interrupted. His final tone still surrounded him. His forehead glistened. The veins in his hands stood out. "You look tense," he said dryly.

She barged in, bumping him out of the way. He lowered his horn in exasperation and shut the door. The room made her feel squashed, a low-ceilinged, whitewashed brick slot as chilly as a restaurant meat locker. He stepped over to a music stand and wiped his horn with a cloth. She wanted to throw herself on him and cry like a child. From adjoining rooms came the dulled roar of other instruments. She looked down at her hands, light tan. After two years away from the islands her color had faded and she thought furiously that tourists in Hawaii were obsessed with getting a tan but couldn't bear the idea of being born with one. Salzburgers didn't swim. The only locals with sun-browned skin were peasants. Her eyes stung, and a tear splashed onto her wrist.

"*Du*, Maile," he said. "You're crying."

"Am not." She killed off her feelings. "I've just got to talk to you."

"'*Ich muss,*'" he corrected her. "Or '*Ich möchte.*' In German, you don't say 'I've got—'"

"Shut up. Pack your horn."

He squinted in puzzled resentment, then slipped his instrument into its case. They left the basement through a back door. Outside on the street she couldn't bear to describe the conversation about sheets, odor, men on her stairs at night. Karl pried, coaxed. She couldn't open her heart to him, but refused to let him go.

The old bus they took from the center of Salzburg swayed onto a country road. Riders held baskets with plums, carrots, skinned rabbits with heads and feet still covered in fur. Karl tried to lift Maile's gloom with gossip and little jokes. When those had no effect, he put an arm around her. She still refused to talk. He peeled an orange for her. She ate it all before realizing that she hadn't shared a single bite.

"You're hungry," he said.

She looked out the window, thinking she was selfish, that's what. One stingy, greedy bugga, big-time. At home no one would have put up with dragging a man away from work, pushing her battered feelings on him as if he were to blame, then refusing to speak. By now Auntie Lani would have cornered her. "You, Maile-long-face, how come, how come?" Teasing and concern until she gave in. Laughs and a kiss when she finally smiled. She ached for someone to ask, "*E*, howzit," and ruffle her hair, the constant, sweet touching of relatives, their gentle attention to anyone sad, hurt, angry, or sick.

Passengers got off the bus until finally only Karl and Maile were left. Cabbage leaves and mashed strawberries littered the aisle. At the last stop they stepped down onto a road choked with weeds. He led her up a beaten path to a meadow above his family's farm, said he'd bring food, and hiked toward the house. She kicked off her shoes, relieved that she didn't have meet his family.

To the east the city was a violet-gray pool with the castle at the center. Above it spread a bright blue cloudless sky. Farther uphill a wooden fence wound into a forest. She sat down in a field of pink wildflowers. To the north stretched the dimples of steep meadows, with distant cows grazing in the deep grass as if floating through a placid sea of green. Below them an orchard sloped toward a pond partly hidden by tree branches trailing into the water. The landscape felt like a calm spirit telling her to let go, her miserable mood had gone on long enough. But if she explained everything, she would look bad no matter how she phrased it.

Soon Karl appeared, carrying a tray. He strode up to her announcing, *"Guten Appetit!"* and showed off an array of sliced cheese, smoked chicken, a heap of pickles, cherry jam, asparagus. Everything looked wonderfully homemade, right down to the crusty bread and soft butter. She snatched at a chicken leg.

"Oh, no!" He whisked the tray out of reach. "First you tell me what's gnawing your innards."

"Come on, Karl." She glowered. "I'm famished."

"You're an orange ahead of me." He balanced the tray with one hand, flipped a pickle into the air, and caught it between his teeth.

She could have strangled him. He tantalized her with lunges and retreats, his pale eyes glinting, two chips of ice. She grabbed and missed—grabbed again, missed again, both of them as stubborn as bullying children—until finally her story about sheets was traded for slices of chicken on buttered bread. She loathed him for dragging it out of her. Worst of all, he didn't seem upset, chewing hungrily and looking almost cheerful. "My godmother," he said, "is a reminder that we actually lead the world in two things. Culture and jealousy."

Maile gave him a sulky stare. "Don't start in on the Austrians."

He shrugged. "Glamour makes people here uncomfortable, that's all. Especially women whose finest entertainment is a weekly *Kaffeeklatsch*."

"Glamour?" She felt reduced to a word, but was also tired of being angry.

His eyes went shy. He examined a piece of cheese with a concentration that shut her out, ate the cheese, then lay back with his horn case propped under his head. "My liver has to relax after a big meal," he said. "Yours, too. Later we'll take a walk." He patted his solar plexus as though comforting his organs and closed his eyes.

She suppressed a groan. Frau Metzger also talked about her liver as if it were a temperamental friend who had to be coddled. Local students gravely mentioned weird illnesses: circulatory disturbance, egg poisoning, catarrh—all valid excuses to cancel a voice lesson. Karl breathed more and more slowly as his entire body gave in to the luxury of sleep.

At last Maile knew she had no more anger to spill, no energy left to criticize. Her hunger was satisfied, her story told, and she sat in the shade of a large tree on a pleasant afternoon.

Sometime later she felt a hand on her shoulder, rocking her awake. She opened her eyes, dazed, and saw Karl tucking his horn under one arm. The tray had disappeared. "Come," he said, sounding urgent. "We have to get there before twilight." He held out her purse.

She felt limp after falling into a dead sleep during the day. Across the meadows the low sun cast a blazing light. The orchard and the pond next to it were dense pockets of purple shadows. "What's the hurry?"

"It's a kind of pet. I promised my mother to release it tonight. She thinks it's evil, a shrunken devil." He pointed at Maile's high heels. "Can you walk without shoes?"

Barefoot on a reef, she thought, alert now. "I'll take off my stockings."

He didn't turn aside when she pulled up her skirt to unsnap her garters, but he stood watching, as she knew no American would, and his stare intensified as she slipped one nylon and then the other down over her knees, her ankles, then the moment she had her shoes and bag in hand, he headed off. She sprinted to catch up.

At a quick pace they went downhill into the shadowy light of the orchard. The perspiration of sleep dried quickly on Maile's face and neck, leaving her skin taut. Fallen apples in the grass gave off the musky smell of fermenting fruit. She trampled them deliberately so the pulp burst and oozed between her bare toes.

Beyond the last tree Karl said, "Be very quiet now." He put down his horn. She set her things alongside it. He crept toward the pond and a weather-beaten shed covered in moss. Under the eaves he poked at a crack and pulled out a smooth round stick resembling a perch from a bird cage. She eased up beside him. He put a finger to his lips, opened the shed door, leaned in, careful and silent, and drew back with something hanging from the stick.

"It's a girl bat," he whispered. "I think so, anyway. She's so young I can't quite tell."

Maile peered at a perfect fox face smaller than the tip of her forefinger, at shiny brown fur with a pale orange tint, at tiny folded black wings. The bat yawned and opened its eyes, revealing two dots of deep yellow and a bright pink throat. Its tongue rose with a barely visible flutter. Teeth no larger than grains of sand.

"She's thirsty," Karl murmured. He knelt at the edge of the pond and dribbled drops of water off a fingertip into the bat's mouth. It hung upside down, blinking and rustling its wings. He explained in an undertone that young bats didn't always know where to roost at night after feeding. If not under cover with their backs shaded, warmth from the morning sun stunned them. They dropped to the ground, where they died of thirst or were eaten by larger animals. As a boy he'd found a bat and learned how to care for it. Be sure it's not rabid, and even then don't touch it and leave your scent. Scoop it up in a piece of bark. Give it just enough water to recover. Hang it up like a miniature pair of trousers in a cool, dark place. Let it escape when it's ready.

The color of the little bat's fur was as delicate as the blush on an apricot. Maile wanted badly to stroke it but knew he was right; certain animals were wild things and could only exist apart from humans. Karl squinted at the setting sun. After a moment he said that the rays were probably no longer dangerous although it was best to wait a little.

The huge, glowing disc receded behind the Alps encircling the valley and left the distant city and its hills adrift in a lavender haze. The air around the pond cooled rapidly. The moss on the roof of the shed turned a deeper green and faded into a soft outline. Karl held the stick at arm's length, the bat suspended like a furled leaf. He inscribed a slow, wide arc left to right, then reversed direction, moving faster. The tiny wings sprang open. The bat let go to sail away over the pond with a chittering sound, dipped low toward the water, and glided upward and out of sight.

Maile watched the sky above them turn a glossy blue-black. Constellations appeared, none familiar, then the line of stars called *Nā Kao* slowly pierced the darkness, a school of stingrays with glimmering darts at the ends of their tails. On the horizon a wide curve of white eased its way higher, the upper rim of a large summer moon. It seemed to be escaping from a battlement of wooded mountains. At a smooth, stately pace it separated itself from the lower hills and slopes where clumps of ground fog lay motionless. Hina of the moon always looked around as she climbed and spread her reflection, overlaying all other light below with her own, silvering the grass, flowers and trees, the fences and slopes. Her brightness crept toward the dark ring of the pond where they stood. Something moved on its surface, a sudden white slash making ripples that widened into larger circles until absorbed by a fringe of foam at the edge. All was calm except for an occasional twitch on the water's skin; an insect, a fish, a spirit.

"On a night like this," Karl said, "gods went into the forests searching for a woman visible only by moonlight. They never found her." His voice was like a subtle current of air. He opened his instrument case. "For years my only goal was Bayreuth. *Siegfried* has a famous horn solo, performed flawlessly just three times since 1876. The names of those musicians are engraved on a marble plaque." He picked up the instrument and flexed his fingers over the brass key tabs. "I wanted my name etched on that stone, but as of tomorrow I'm concentrating on the piano. So farewell to the dragon slayer. I'll leave him in the forest."

Raising the horn, he took a deep breath and tensed his lips into a firm line. Lightly and decisively he began to play a hunter's call, buoyant staccato notes that ended on a sustained tone, *du, du-du-du, du-du-du, du-du-du-duuuuuu* . . . He kept his eyes on Maile and repeated the line in a hush. The melody sank to the bottom of the horn's register, a tone so low it had the faint rumbling of a heap of coals in an oven. She stepped closer to feel the sound. His posture stiffened, and again he played the hunter's call, a denser run woven with embellishments. Once more the last note dropped into pretended sleep, as if prey had been sighted and stealth was necessary. Slowly he woke the music, enticing it into a full, round tone that expanded like a balloon, rising to repeat the original melody. The notes came faster and faster, locked in a race, rushing toward capture and elation. He broke the final phrase to draw a ragged, gasping breath, but finished with a splendid blast at the top of the scale, a gigantic tone that leaped into the air and flew out across the night.

Maile stared ahead at a distant ridge, feeling the sound leave them, wanting to ride it up to the moon. She ran forward and heard a splash. Water, she felt water around her ankles. In confusion she raised her skirt, then pulled it off over her head, along with her blouse and brassiere. She stepped out of her panties, threw her clothing on the grass, and waded into the pond's silver sheen. Her hair unraveled, spilling down her back. Karl stripped off his clothes to wade in beside her. They stood thigh-deep, lapped by wavelets, staring and listening; Hina had taken the sound into her cool radiance. He stepped behind Maile, planted his hands on either side of her waist, and lifted her bodily onto his shoulders. She stretched out her arms and showed herself to the moon, intoxicated with bliss.

11

ALL MORNING AT the conservatory Karl and Maile spied on each other with a new hard edge of intimacy. He refused to say what work he had chosen for the competition but insisted she sing her contest aria for him: "I want a personal performance on a stage." She demanded he play his contest piece for her on a concert grand, his real instrument, so he claimed, or was she simply supposed to take it on faith that he was brilliant in two fields?

They came to no agreement. Neither mentioned last night. They had mated like swans in the water, then lain naked on the grass, combed their hair dry, and picked apples in the moonlight. He brought her back to the city on a borrowed moped but did not go upstairs. Now each wanted the other to reveal what went beyond sex: music, the ultimate form of nakedness, of confession.

Toward noon Maile tailed Karl to the Mozarteum's one-room library where scores were checked out over a Dutch door. He exchanged one slim volume for another, and disappeared down a hallway. She went after him. He jumped out from under a stairwell. The score slipped down over his stomach and she bent to read the title, Schubert, *Op. 15, Phantasie, Der Wanderer.*

"Aha!" she said.

"Let's go," he told her. "I gave the custodian twenty schillings to let me use the Bechstein."

"What's *Der Wanderer?* Another piece performed only three times without a mistake? Your name carved in marble?"

They looked at each other like gamblers raising their bets beyond the point of return, then walked off together. She understood his reluctance to compete on the French horn. Piano, voice, violin and cello, the instruments most favored by composers, had vast repertoires that attracted huge audiences. A superb contest performance on French horn was never enough to win against a fine pianist or singer headed for a soloist's career, not a seat in an orchestra.

The custodian let them into the concert hall and tapped his watch. "One hour," he said, and left. They bumped into each other on the staircase up to the stage. Karl flipped a schilling and won. He opened the grand piano's lid, adjusted the bench, and spread out his music. *"Allegro con fuoco, ma non troppo,"* he proclaimed. "Schubert warns me not to get carried away by fire." He shook out his wrists and assumed a tortured pose.

Maile laughed. "If you're doing a vaudeville act, I'm leaving."

"Test my memory," he ordered, handing her the score. "And the tone balance."

She had no idea what that meant but stepped off stage to sit ten rows back from the piano. "Ready."

Karl began in a driving tempo with broad romantic chords, immersing himself in the rich *Sturm und Drang* of Schubert's exiled wanderer, joyous playing that wiped out Maile's impulse to criticize. The score drooped in her hands. She fell into a trance, as if she too were a mythic wanderer, a nineteenth-century poet traveling Europe alone on horseback, in all seasons, in all weathers, in search of . . .

An off note made her madly turn a page. "G natural, not sharp," she called out.

Karl kept playing and called back, "Check the transition coming up."

From that moment she trusted him not to be rattled or make excuses. She followed the notations with a fingertip, black vertical clusters in fast horizontal motion, all of it memorized. He seemed to be rushing. *Ma non troppo,* she remembered, and almost shouted over the rolling music, but she understood nothing about piano repertoire. He might be using too much pedal, or playing in the style of Beethoven instead of Schubert, or imitating a famous artist's interpretation. One beautiful phrase after another swept over her—a piece rife with tricky variations, difficult runs no coloratura singer could match, opposing melodies as tightly woven as a tapestry. At the next transition he skipped five measures and continued on a dissonant ascending tremolo.

"Go back to C major," she said loudly.

He repeated the transition four times without mistakes, raised his hands from the keyboard and announced, "Madame Manoa, your turn."

They quibbled about who would be the accompanist. "I just chose this aria," she said. "I don't know it yet."

He shrugged. "So? I'll take you through it."

We've come this far, she thought, and he showed me his. "All right."

Karl played a cue chord and spoke the text of the first slow phrase. She sang in half voice: *"Where have they gone, those moments of tenderness. . ."* Light breath. As they moved on through the melody, he filled in notes or words, not pushing her, she felt, just dropping hints, but he wasn't a Juilliard coach or a substitute for Professor Jann; he didn't know the subtleties of her field either. She began using full voice. In small, exciting ways the aria started to feel right—the perfect choice, hers, out of so many.

"Size!" Karl declared. He jumped up to put his arms around her. "You can build a career on such womanly tone." She felt the warmth of his palms at the small of her back. "Scriabin slept under his piano," he whispered. "He believed it was alive and gave off secret tones and colors." They laughed. The deerhorn buttons on his trouser fly grazed the front of her skirt, and she pictured him naked in the moonlight, his body blue-white, muscled like a surfer's.

A side door clacked open. They sprang apart as the custodian bustled in saying the rector had returned early with a Festival artist to rehearse on the Bechstein. "Took a fat risk for you students, I want twenty more schillings."

Karl snatched up their scores and they hurried out into the corridor. Herr Rector came toward them around a corner, escorting the elderly lady Maile had seen with Professor Jann at *Rappresentazione*. The slender white-haired pianist wore only dove gray accented by rubies or emeralds, and only brooches, never bracelets or rings that might weigh on her marvelous hands.

"Kruzifix," Karl murmured as she passed them. "Wish we could hear her Bach. It's an inspiration."

The pair entered the recital hall and Maile caught hold of his arm. "What about listening backstage?" He didn't react. She tugged on his sleeve.

"That isn't done." He shook her off.

Man tut das nicht. Frau Metzger often used the same phrase to cordon off what did not constitute good manners. Maile's spirits revolted. "Maybe 'that' isn't done, but you took me for a close-up look at von Wehlen, even though it's . . . crass? I had no idea you were such a good little citizen."

"You have to be Austrian to understand."

"Nationality is not an excuse. It's unbearable, no Bach for us, not even listening to someone rehearse on the piano we just used. No tickets for students, ever. Tonight's *Othello* premiere is a world event in opera, and I'm stuck listening to it on a radio."

"All right, it's unfair. Am I supposed to conjure up tickets because I'm Austrian? Even we can't get in without a lot of money or contacts."

"What about sneaking in?"

"Body of Christ." He crossed himself backwards and upside down. "You would be caught in a minute."

"And turned over to police?"

"Exactly."

Twenty-four hours to leave the country, she thought. The kind of extreme penalty a foreigner could expect. "If sneaking in is too risky, what about passes? Press passes."

He snorted. Americans simply could not accept things as they were. People from the U.S. of A. were always sure they could change the impossible. "I have an errand in town," he added, and walked off.

She looked out a window at Mirabell Garten without noticing the yellow and white flower beds laid out in brilliant geometry. A waiter could get two hundred schillings simply for knowing who had Festival tickets to sell. Scalpers earned seven times the official price.

Downstairs she approached one student after another about alternatives to getting into the Grand Festival House tonight. Maxi said a journalist's backstage pass required a letter from a recognized newspaper or arts magazine. Marlise suggested finding a substitute orchestra member willing to turn over his Festival House ID, something she had never managed. Brenda said there must be a trick but hadn't found it.

Maile wandered outside, unwilling to admit that getting in was hopeless. Jean-Paul stood at the curb, about to cross the street to the schnapps bar, a private house where slumming tourists sought out local color. Off limits to any woman who valued her reputation. She eyed him with distaste. The nasty rat-goat-pig spent all day in the conservatory wrestling with Tschaikovsky until he couldn't take it any longer. His *Stammlokal* reminded her of a Waikiki dive where people did the kind of business not done in stores. Exactly.

"*Alors, mon monstre!*" she called out. Jean-Paul turned and she hip-walked over to him. "You are my last chance, *chéri,*" she said, smiling, exuding charm. "How can I get in to see *Othello?* One Moor must see another, *non?*"

He bit his tongue flirtatiously, a man relishing intrigue. "The premiere?"

"I can stand backstage. I'll make it worth your while. Just one ticket."

"I see." His expression changed to a concentrated stare as though shuffling through a mental list of shady connections. She stayed carefully silent, concealing her excitement. He pursed his lips, then gave off a sputtering sound, but couldn't hold it in, and he puffed out his cheeks in a choking laugh that exploded all over her: "Hah, hah, hah!" His head tipped back so far she saw rows of silver fillings.

She raised a hand to smack him on the chest but he darted off across the street, still laughing. As he reached the door of the bar, the Rosenkavalier materialized from behind a hedge. Briefly they spoke like old friends trading news, and went inside.

In a glum mood, Maile headed for Getreidegasse to shop for supper.

MINUTES BEFORE THE premiere began, students gathered in the Mozarteum's listening room. Rows of hard-backed chairs faced a brown plastic radio with a wood-grain pattern, a high-fidelity model donated by a local aristocrat. Marlise held forth to an audience. "My Viennese cousin is that city's leading stage carpenter . . . " This afternoon she had gotten inside the Grand Festival House with a temporary daytime pass. Maile listened in a fit of jealousy.

Of course, Marlise explained, singers were in their hotels resting for the premiere, but she had been led to the main stage, as high and wide as heaven itself. Racks, cables, and backdrop flies hung from the ceiling like pages in a huge book. Dozens of workers wore color-coded jumpsuits, designed by Maestro von Wehlen. Men in red descended in a metal cage to fasten a screen of gauzy clouds in place. Floor teams in orange positioned panels of painted waves. Maile recalled her glimpse of backstage at the Met; wisecracks and beer bellies, workers in T-shirts bearing their unofficial motto: FUCK OFF, I'M UNION.

From the radio came a trumpet fanfare and a broadcaster's voice speaking through it: *"Salzburger Festspiele 1968, Festival du Salzbourg 1968, Salzburg Festival . . . "* Maxi remarked that von Wehlen's color-coded workers should man the border to intimidate the Soviet soldiers. Karl rushed in late and bent over a German translation of Shakespeare's *Othello*. Maile sat down, prepared for inadequate sound from an outdated radio, not even stereo, nothing like von Wehlen's experiments with *Quadrophonie*.

"Our story begins in the year 1490," the announcer said.

Maile focused on the underlying dense hum of a packed theater, two thousand five hundred people. Row eleven, she thought, imagining herself in the middle, best seat in the house. Von Wehlen appeared in the pit, his head and then his torso visible as he approached the podium. Applause exploded down on him. He walked straight into it to shake hands with his concert master and turned his back on the audience to raise his baton. The frenzied clapping stopped so abruptly it left an echo that snapped through the air in final welcoming recognition. He swept the pit with an inclusive stare and slashed down. Sound leaped from the orchestra like a violent sheet of wind. She felt it as much as heard it, the powerful Vienna Philharmonic shaking everything in its path as Verdi's merciless storm lashed the coast of Venice.

૭૭   ૭૭   ૭૭

PROFESSOR JANN'S NOTE read, *Come see me at your first opportunity.* Maile wondered at the plain statement—a demand, in fact. Handwritten instead of a telegram. Initials instead of a full signature. She skipped breakfast and went straight to the Mozarteum although it was only eight o'clock.

When she entered his studio, Jann regarded her with a grave expression and said, "Close the door, if you please."

Yesterday afternoon, he explained, his wife returned home in a distressed mood; approached, she said, by that flower seller—you know to whom I refer, Fräulein Manoa—claiming that my highly regarded student was in a compromising situation: she had attempted to bribe her way into the *Othello* premiere. It would be best, the Rosenkavalier advised, to stop gossip before it caused regrettable complications with authorities.

Jann didn't mention that his wife had paid to have the rumor quashed, or that he'd slept fitfully, risen early, and given a neighbor boy a coin to deliver a message to Maile's address. Now she faced him with an inquisitive expression that told him she had no idea of the disaster she'd nearly brought down on herself.

He cleared his throat. "Bribes are common in Austria. So ordinary we call them Vitamin B. However, a foreigner who attempts bribery attracts the immediate attention of our *Kriminalpolizei.*" Anger overtook him. "Anything to do with them is a disgrace! They have never set foot inside the Mozarteum. A street officer occasionally tickets a student's Vespa, but that is the end of it."

"Bribes," Maile repeated, sounding baffled.

"Involvement with the police has severe consequences, such as your consul and myself having to approve your continued stay in Austria so your visa will not be revoked. You are supposed to sing Gershwin soon at the American consulate. That appearance came close to being cancelled."

"What are you talking about?"

"The *Othello* premiere."

She thought hard: speaking yesterday to half a dozen students about ways of getting into the Grand Festival House. But she hadn't offered anybody money. Except, she remembered saying, I'll make it worth your while. Algerian.

"Jean-Paul Gardes," she blurted, "the pianist! I only—"

"Do lower your voice." Jann held up a hand and took a long, slow breath to cool his emotions. "In a case like this, I am afraid that ignorance is no excuse."

Maile stared back, radiating an indignation that he felt suggested at least partial innocence. He sighed. "Each year the Festival consumes one fifth of our national budget. Designs for new productions are guarded like military secrets. And you wanted unauthorized entry to a premiere that attracts international attention." In a flat tone he described the thousands of Festival employees; painters, electricians, carpenters, boot makers, and dry cleaners; boom handlers, scrim spanners, mechanics, armorers, throat doctors, and sound engineers; contract experts on Eastern Bloc regulations; photographers, music scholars, reporters from more than twenty magazines and newspapers. "And above all this, Maestro von Wehlen stands at the peak of a personal empire. His theater security force works with Interpol, because a black-market tape—of say, the *Othello* premiere—is worth a million schillings in Japan, South Africa, South America."

"A tape?" Maile yelped. "I just wanted to hear a live performance."

"Stop defending yourself. Perhaps unwittingly, or foolishly, you nearly ruined your status here. Under no circumstances can you become the subject of low gossip."

She lowered her eyes, thinking that Jean-Paul was trying to get her expelled from the competition before it started. If she confronted the rat, he would simply lie, but now that made no difference. The absurdity of what Jann described had a logic she recognized as Austrian.

He continued mercilessly. Trying to gain illegal entry to a Festival premiere was hardly a minor offense. It challenged von Wehlen's code of perfection. And no matter what anyone thought of his past, he deserved his present status after decades of brutal self-discipline and tireless devotion to music.

"Sit down," Jann said finally.

The room had one fine chair upholstered in leather. Maile crept over to the piano bench, appalled at everything being blown out of proportion because it concerned von Wehlen. She longed to be excused but Jann's rigid posture indicated that he was not finished with her.

He remained standing and turned aside to deal with a mass of competing thoughts. Reprimanding his prize student had called forth a fatherly impulse to protect her. His anger had also aroused a decidedly non-fatherly attraction. Sensual desire—there from the beginning—surfaced to tempt him, vying with a powerful awareness of the mistakes he'd made at her age and the faults that still dogged him. She deserved to know some of that, he decided, bound as they were in pursuit of music.

"I know nothing about von Wehlen's private life," he said. "He presents himself as content with his family and his expensive hobbies. This is clever and necessary. The greater the career, the higher the personal cost." Jann walked over to a cabinet of inlaid rosewood and took out a cut-crystal glass and a bottle with a crumbling label. He held them up like pieces of evidence, his hard expression tinged by the ghost of an ironic smile.

Maile doubted that he was offering her a drink.

"One of my vices," he said. "I manage to keep it under control, although the struggle is constant. Two years ago I married my fourth wife. Every evening she replaces this glass, and every other evening she brings a new bottle. Cognac, by the way, not brandy. Dreadfully expensive." He put back the glass and the bottle, and closed the cabinet. She stared into her lap, ill with embarrassment, thinking that a *Kammersänger* didn't have such problems. Or if he did, he didn't talk about them to a student.

Jann's confession had steadied him and he walked over to sit beside Maile on the piano bench. "What I mean to make clear," he said, "is that being accused is sometimes the same as being guilty. No one at the top of the profession remains unscathed. Once you no longer have to fight for each contract, your worst battles are with yourself. The only way to survive is by having an inner conviction that never lets go. Talent and ego alone will fail you." Thoughtfully he poked a piano key and then shut the lid. The sound inside faded away.

Maile wanted to wail that she'd been betrayed by an envious racist. She turned to Jann, about to speak.

He motioned for her to be still. "In my youth," he went on quietly, "I had convictions. Mine were untested and thus worthless. When the war began, I was in my late twenties, not much older than you. I lied and hid to avoid being drafted. What terrified me more than the Fascists was the high chance of losing my legs or having half my jaw blown off. Coming home like that, you see. After Stalingrad the military hunted down any able-bodied man. I considered only myself, not my family, relatives, friends, not Jews, Gypsies, partisans. The French caught me shortly before the Armistice."

His face tightened all the way up to his hairline. "I spent a year in the ruins of a death camp. Survivors were replaced by Austrian prisoners of war. All former soldiers. They knew I had evaded military service, and tried to kill me so often I was put in an isolation pit for my own safety. A priest discovered I was a musician. The only daylight I saw was on Sunday when guards took me to a makeshift chapel to sing first for my captors, then for my countrymen. An hour later I was returned to the hole. A ghastly farce. Worse and stranger, I was dead to everyone until I came above ground and sang. Guards and prisoners alike were full of hate, forgiveness, indifference, pride, desire—the most terrifying audience I ever faced. Some in uniform, others starving. I came home weighing as much as you. I couldn't sing for three years, until my health returned. And I finally lost a bitterness and confusion that nearly drove me mad."

He put his hands on his knees and looked out across the room. Maile felt small enough to be flicked away like a crumb. No experience in her entire life came close to his. She hadn't even had the courage to tell him about singing for tourists in Waikiki. Had given him nothing more than the hard work a master teacher could expect from a graduate student.

"All right, now." Jann slapped his knees. "Let's have an answer from you."

Answer, she thought in fright. He'd spoken to her with spiritual resonance that required an honest response. When had she been similarly self-centered and been made to pay for it?

In a small voice she said, "Once I hid money from my family. Our roof leaked and there were medical bills, but I had this idea of saving to be a famous singer. They found out. In the end they gave it all back to me, and more."

Jann nodded as though mulling over an unexpected reply.

She sloughed off humiliating memories. Her visa was safe, her reputation unmarred. "All I did was ask how to get into the Festival House because I was wild to go, but I can see what you mean and I'll stay out of trouble."

In a decisive move Jann got to his feet and showed her his back. "I should think so, because if police are involved in some future incident, I will not come to your rescue." He let his words settle for the length of a heartbeat, turned around, and spoke with the full force of his personality. "Restraint! For God's sake, learn it!"

He stared her down and made her repeat the word "restraint" in German, English, Hawaiian. She struggled to recall *kāohi*—hold back, *e kāohi 'oe*, control yourself. He listened without a trace of sympathy and dismissed her, saying he expected the contest aria to be memorized at her next lesson.

In the hallway Maile leaned against a wall to feel something solid, her relief at escaping Jann's presence overshadowed by shame at having disappointed him. Yet she felt he must trust her deeply to reveal such personal details about himself: wartime cowardice, cognac, a fourth wife. And he understood that singing was work, work, work, as boring and solitary as punishment, a reminder of how far you had to go with a single aria, a role, a career. Every day the same routine for beginner and master alike: practice to the breaking point, then get up the next morning and do it all over again. Such drudgery tolerated because their souls were filled with visions of creating perfect music and failure was a form of death.

No matter what anyone thought of von Wehlen's past . . .

Did Jann mean affairs? Heroin? A Nazi scandal? More secrets. If Jann had fought neither for nor against Hitler, just tried to save his own skin, how many people knew about that? Buried alive, forced to sing, finding the will to survive. Then becoming an artist of such superiority that he received a knighthood.

Her own life seemed petty. Unlike Karl, she ignored the political struggles of others. She no longer contributed to her family, as he did. Beyond music, what did she value? The huge ego necessary for achievement as a singer seemed uncomfortably close to greed: me first and everybody else last.

AT MOZART STEG, Karl noticed a policeman watching pedestrians cross the river. Pickpockets were unknown in Salzburg. Local residents and wealthy visitors alike obeyed such strict codes of manners that all behaved unusually well in public. He headed for Getreidegasse to buy a block of preserving wax for his mother. More officers stood outside public buildings and in the marketplace. Two paced under the arch leading to the university.

This seemed more than just odd, and Karl spent his bus fare on a *Salzburger Nachrichten*. Another officer was posted next to the newspaper kiosk. A front-page photo showed books being burned in Prague, a bonfire on the main square. All stage productions and films from the West had been banned. Most theaters were closed.

Disturbing news, Karl thought, but it didn't explain the numbers of police stationed here in public. On the third page he found a small article: "Festival Protest: *Importierte Kulturrevolution*." Three Communist students had been arrested at last night's *Othello* premiere. They claimed to be planning more demonstrations funded by the Party in Vienna. Protesters had also disrupted the Bayreuth Festival in Germany, chanting, "Execute the financial beast of music!"

Quickly he scanned the rest of the paper for any mention of his Czech refugee group, which he sensed might have taken part in a protest without telling him. NATO leaders were holding a summit to discuss war games. Mao's *Little Red Book* had sold millions of copies worldwide. At Edelweiss-Kino, the Jewish comedienne Barbra Streisand in a new color film, *Funny Girl*.

Yet revolution, if only on a tiny scale, had at last arrived in Salzburg. He felt a mixture of pride and uneasiness: how deeply could he involve himself in what would surely become a dangerous situation? The Soviets were bent on extinguishing Prague Spring. Local police jailed local political activists for violating the country's neutrality. With daily protests in Prague, the refugee rescue network here was no doubt in full operation, but the group deemed Karl Holzer merely a musician. The others in the Action Plan for the Future were "border technicians," traveling back and forth to monitor obscure crossing points with binoculars.

He hated being shunted to the sidelines. Although an arrest for violating internal security would kill his career as a pianist. He was an amateur in politics with little hope of advancing beyond that. Until the contest was over, he had to put away Maile and moonlight and a shimmering pond so that nothing distracted him.

MAILE SLID HER hands into her silk gown so it glided down to settle on her shoulders with a shivery thrill. Black on black, the sleek fabric was covered with tiny beads in a geometric pattern that clung subtly to her breasts and hips and shifted gently as she moved; sleeveless, plain neck, the only point of style one long slit from knee to hem. She fluffed her hair into a ballerina chignon and left a teasing wisp at the nape of her neck. In the mirror she applied stealthy strokes of mascara, separated each lash with flicks of a toothpick, then put on deep red lipstick, and stood back.

Ha. People at home would look twice before recognizing her. "Makua's girl used to sing down Waikiki, teach school? *E*, Auntie Lani, you know her?" They would crowd around, pretend she was a stranger, a moo-vee star, ask the smallest children, "Who's 'at leddy, our Maile? Neva, not."

Tonight there were no Festival performances, a tradition that allowed Salzburg's consulates to host receptions, and Frau Metzger was on full alert. *"Fräulein Manoa, bitte sehr!"* she called out from below. Irked by the bossy tone, Maile went on assembling the contents of a little evening purse. No need to be reminded of the time, or how to get to her destination.

She descended the stairs into the wide-eyed gaze of the landlady and the grin of a United States Army officer so tall his medals were at Frau Metzger's eye level.

"Evening, ma'am," he said. "Mr. Casey sent me over."

Maile beamed in surprise: an escort, a gladiator, the kind of blond blue-eyed tourist who took surfing lessons at Waikiki and attracted a crowd of women onshore. She wanted to show him off to Brenda and Marlise.

Major Derek Wainwright excused himself for speaking no German, and Frau Metzger spoke no English, but she talked at him anyway: "It has been too, too long, *ach,* how many years since I had a man in uniform at my door!"

He offered Maile an arm.

Quickly she slipped outside with him to avoid doing the courteous thing and translating what the landlady had said. On the river promenade a scrim of dusk had already come down over the grassy banks. Formally dressed couples strolled under the dark trees like guests at a garden party on an estate, passing through circles of light from streetlamps outside the brightly lit villas with their identifying flags.

At the *Amerikanishes Konsulat* a jazzy piano riff reached down the front stairs and drew Maile inside. She and Major Wainwright stepped into the foyer, filled with men in tuxedoes and women in gowns, the same people, she knew, who entered the Festival House every night. The same delicate scents filled the air. Everybody spoke Italian or French, switching easily to German or English. And roses in deep yellow, stark white, and lush pink the color of flesh, were displayed in grand bouquets and woven into garlands of ferns.

The Honorable Edwin Casey came forward to greet Maile and take her arm. *"Ach, sie ist's,"* a nearby guest remarked, *"jene Sängerin aus Hawaii."* Casey introduced him to Miss Manoa, "A fellow citizen from the prettiest state in the Union." She felt *pili* leaping from throat to diaphragm, heart to liver.

Through more introductions they progressed outside to a lawn enclosed by a high hedge. Guests chatted around beds of pink tulips, in a white gazebo, and dallied on gravel paths. Others flocked to an outdoor bar, excited by the novelty of jiggers, shakers, glasses in various shapes and sizes, trays of garnishes. Men in crew cuts and steward's jackets waited on them, speaking American—"Yessir, yes'm,"—and rattled off drink suggestions: "Stinger, Spymaster, Moscow Mule."

Maile's giddiness settled into the familiar tension of being on stage. She circulated with Casey, translated for him, and pointed out prominent musicians. When full darkness had come and the garden lights flashed on, he asked, "How about a tune?" She smiled at the thought of the one piece she'd always been able to perform without a warm-up. Why of course, she told him, and went over to speak to the jazz pianist.

The bristle-headed lieutenant from Georgia by way of Berchtesgaden segued into Gershwin's chiming octaves. She leaned against the black grand like a club singer, one hip angled so her body formed a languid S curve. Focusing on the middle of the crowd in the garden, she let loose, high and wide: "Sum-mer—time . . . "

All heads turned her way with the sudden stillness of attraction, the net of her voice descending over a school of reef shrimp. Edwin Casey stood with guests fanned out behind him, his eyes narrowed in dreamy concentration. The melody slid from her throat in flowing phrases that rose into the evening air. She felt her voice holding the audience, directing their hopes and memories. At the end she took a deep swimmer's breath and her accompanist hesitated, alert for a final improvisation. Casey leaned forward. The heightened attention of both men made her want to reach for an invisible thread of music, a singer's risk. She looked up into the star-pierced sky and barely touched on a high B, an ecstatic sigh that held and floated out beyond the hedge enclosing the garden, then she let go of its bewitching sweetness and silence stretched on all sides, as if the entire city had paused and thousands had heard.

Applause rushed over her, calls of "Encore, encore!"

She was tempted to give them more, but years ago Danny O'Doyle had said, "Always leave them a little hungry," and he'd never been wrong about that.

With a bow, she rejoined Casey to make a round through the garden. Congratulations poured from guests delighted by such an American evening, *Das Jazz, Der Gershwin, Die Cocktails.* She sipped a glass of champagne, ate a tiny meatball on a toothpick, charmed people with a few phrases in her fledgling Italian.

Finally Casey asked, "One more favor? There's a fellow interested in Polynesian navigation, of all things." He led her over for an introduction to Baron Balthazar von Gref, the only man wearing a dark daytime suit.

"It is entirely my pleasure," the baron said, bending over Maile's hand. "Please excuse my fragile English."

A smile stalled on her lips. She had never met a titled person. His gold-rimmed glasses, bald head, and paunch made him resemble a retired professor. But according to local etiquette, after being properly introduced to a nobleman, she could greet him in public. At a place like Cafe Scimitar, which she'd never considered going into, with its customers who never looked at prices on a menu.

He exchanged a few words with Herr Konsul, and when their host went off to greet other guests, Baron von Gref adjusted his glasses and said in German, "I have heard only praise from Herr Kammersänger Jann for his new soprano. Tonight that was fully verified."

She nodded in thanks, delighted that he knew Professor Jann, although now the baron seemed be flirting, something a man of seventy or so could do very sweetly. "Have you traveled in the Pacific?" she asked.

"*Ach.*" A little laugh of regret. "Only in my imagination. Knowing that you study here creates a link between Hawaii and Salzburg, as marvelous as the magic carpet tales I loved as a child." He described his research on Polynesian navigators who covered vast distances in open canoes, their methods a mystery to modern scholars. "My particular misfortune," he added, "is being rather ignorant of music. May I introduce you to my nephew? He is quite knowledgeable about opera." The baron suppressed a smile. "However, his attempts to sing have thus far doomed him to disappointment."

They approached a young couple whom the baron introduced as Count Arnim von und zu Zala, and his fiancée, Sophia von Schönweilershof; both brunette and wolfhound slim, with blue eyes, dark lashes and eyebrows, refined noses, and small, neat mouths. Arnim's thin hair trailed over his tuxedo collar. Sophia's straight bob was pinned back by a diamond-encrusted butterfly. Her long dirndl of forest green brocade had sleeves with rows of jet buttons from elbow to wrist, set off by black lace gloves and a beaded purse on a chain.

Baron von Gref excused himself and the two stepped closer to Maile. "We have been aching to meet you," Armin said in a confidential tone. His eyes glittered with mischief. "You sang that aria magnificently, quite like a Negress."

Sophia gave her a softer look and whispered, "My mother is upset that Professor Jann's new soprano is American. Is that not outrageous?"

Maile mumbled a meaningless reply that went unnoticed as they traded rapid remarks in German, then Arnim remarked, his tone cozy with teasing, "There is a whiff of gossip that you attempted to tweak von Wehlen's Festival House security force and sneak into the *Othello* premiere. I hope it's true."

"Repeating a rumor is rude," Sophia told him. She nodded in the direction of the bar. "I want to try a cocktail, although have been warned that ice chips produce condensation on the glass." She pulled off her gloves and tucked them into her purse. Maile stared at a large pear-shaped diamond ring with a cluster of emerald leaves. Sophia fluttered her fingers playfully. "Yes, Arnim and I are engaged. Our families arranged it ten years ago when we were barely out of the nursery. However, we are emphatically not getting married."

"Quite right." Arnim straightened his back and clicked his heels with a sharp *pok!* "I do not intend to live with your collection of Hittite potsherds."

"Or I with your voice lessons. Verdi weeps." Sophia put a wrist to her forehead with an anguished look.

"Touché. But keep your guard up." They crossed forefingers like fencers, then turned to Maile, competing to tell her that since childhood they had bored each other to dust with their opposing tastes in everything from cars to books, from sports to rocky beaches versus sandy ones. "However," Arnim interjected, "we cannot survive a social season without escorts, so we go everywhere together under mutual agreement to act as advance scouts for ideal mates."

"I shall marry an archaeologist," Sophia said. "We have located four so far, all over the age of sixty. Arnim claims he has done his part, although to my mind, hardly." She gave him a severe look.

"Carbon-dating," he complained. "If archaeology meant unearthing gold cups rather than sifting layers of clay, it might do. I, on the other hand, seek a woman of fantasy who will demand I throw a leopard skin over my bare back and sing Radames."

His facetious tone didn't match the expression in his eyes, and Maile sensed a passionate music lover who would never get what he wanted.

"Our common problem," Sophia said, "is we must each find an appropriate spouse or neither of us will inherit a thing. We will end up beggars." She glanced past Arnim as though startled and said, "Over there on the stairs." She moved behind the slatted wall of the gazebo. He looked in the same direction, then quickly joined her. Maile regarded them with confusion.

"Your mother loathes Americans," he said to Sophia. "She only came to find us and go on about *Rienzi.*"

"You are right for once." Sophia leaned across him to speak to Maile. "At luncheon Mother insisted for an entire hour that when Wagner composed *Rienzi*, Meyerbeer had no influence on him. Spontini, yes. The details were paralyzing."

Maile could barely recall the opera, a youthful work with thumping martial choruses, a footnote to music history, a bore.

Arnim took Sophia's arm and announced, "We are immediately off to the Dutch reception, because of that tomb specialist you are straining to meet." He proposed escaping through the high hedge.

"*Liberum veto,*" Sophia said. "Have the Jaguar brought round back." She turned to Maile. "Do come with us, a trio is far more amusing than a duet."

Maile felt drawn to their world by a flood tide of I want, I want, I want.

With a quick detour to take leave of Mr. Casey, she caught up with them to exit the garden. The name *Rienzi* felt like a pebble in her shoe. Teachers agreed, she remembered, that the young Wagner had learned a lot from Meyerbeer. Spontini's influence, if any, was slight. But she also remembered that Meyerbeer had been a Jew. And *Rienzi* was Hitler's favorite opera.

THEY DID THE Dutch and the Thai consulates, and then the French and the Spanish, and at each Arnim and Sophia greeted schoolmates and relatives from their extended families, and presented Maile as their newest friend. Guests making the rounds recognized the exciting young diva from the American reception, a prize to be displayed.

Toward midnight, they surged away in Arnim's car to the outskirts of Salzburg, where the landscape had an ageless, velvety stillness. She was borne along in silence as they motored deep into the forested countryside at the base of Mount Untersberg, farther than she had ever been from the city. Soon she lost all sense of direction but would not ask like a child where they were going. In the light of a sickle moon, the surrounding alps were pale gray. Up there lived the mountain men. Where people stoned witches. Where Karl had gone as a boy.

The surrounding vastness shrank when the car entered a tunnel of oak trees. Arnim slowed to approach a white building tinted soft blue by the moonlight. The wide facade curved down like a giant bird with its wings spread, about to rise and take flight. The steps were scattered with purple flowers from bushes in stone urns.

They stepped into a main room larger than the Mozarteum recital hall. On a chandelier as wide as a carriage wheel, circles of candles reflected off crystal pendants like shards of trapped sunlight. Across the ceiling a naked goddess attended by plump cupids floated on clouds supported by muscular men. A sleepy servant in livery showed the three of them to an outdoor terrace, where they feasted undisturbed on the remains of a luxurious buffet.

When they finished Arnim gripped Maile's wrist. "Now," he said, affecting a villain's chuckle, "you shall be initiated into the waterworks."

"Stop frightening the poor dear." Sophia rapped his knuckles with a butter knife. "My archbishop ancestor," she told Maile, "built this as a pleasure retreat. He was an Aquarius with greater allegiance to the zodiac than the Vatican."

"There were indecencies in more recent times," Arnim added. "The SS used it as a retreat."

"Do hush." Sophia folded her napkin. "We already had *Rienzi* this evening." She stood to gaze at a large formal garden that spread out below the terrace.

To Maile it appeared to be a mass of hedges, a dark green tapestry with an elaborate design of hooked crescents and swirls. Beyond the maze rose a forest where the black crowns of pine trees formed a row of spikes. Two servants went into the garden and lit lanterns, making soft spots of yellow that bloomed like fireflies resting on the hedges and forming a pathway. When everything was ready, Maile followed her hosts down the terrace steps, then to her amazement saw that the garden was filled with intricate water displays; a miniature stage with animated figures; a fountain that sprayed mist over rotating stones; a brooklet coursing down little barricades to form transparent fans. "Constructed in 1662," Sophia said. "All the mechanics are hidden from view."

Maile stared, unable to conceal awe. "Made just for pleasure?"

Sophia let out a bored sigh. "The archbishop was a scientist. These are hydraulic experiments he had to keep secret from church leaders."

Arnim leaned across her and whispered to Maile, "Beware. The old satyr is centuries distant yet present among us." He plunged a hand into a pool and a statue shot up from the center, an entwined mermaid and merman turning lasciviously, their fish-scaled buttocks a buttery yellow in the lantern light. Maile laughed in delight.

"Some guests are quite offended," Arnim said. "Come, you must claim your reward." Sophia stepped back, smiling. He took a lantern and motioned to Maile. She followed him to the edge of the garden, then on into the pine forest where tall, densely packed trees shut out the moon. Heavy branches high above creaked and rustled. She stayed close behind Armin until they approached a wall of glass panes that glinted in the lantern light.

"The greenhouse," Arnim said, ushering her inside.

She walked past racks and tables of flowers in full bloom, a ravishing mass of color and scent; mouth-pink tulips, sun-yellow lilies, white narcissus. Lovely, lovely, she thought. Spectacular. In a corner she came to a can filled with cut roses. They seemed oddly familiar, of a peculiarly dark color, a strange hue, more intense than any variety of red wine, with rich undertones of purple and black. Arnim presented one to her with an operatic flourish, saying she had truly earned her reward.

All at once he raced out the door, lantern in hand, laughing. She was plunged into blackness. Dropping the rose, she stumbled outside after him but he had disappeared. In the distance a window at the Schloss formed a tiny yellow rectangle. Angry and confused, she retraced her way through the trees, afraid of falling, and reached the garden. *"Wo seid Ihr?"* she called out. No reply.

She stepped onto a flagstone that dipped under her weight. From the ground came a heavy metallic clanking as something leaped up, jagged and dripping. She gasped in terror. Inches from her face a mass of metal and fabric let out a watery sniggering. She lunged away. Her high heels threw her off balance, but she imagined a trip wire, a pit, and she ran crazily.

A short way ahead two figures emerged with a lantern. Maile staggered toward them, nearly weeping. "There was a thing," she cried out, "awful!" Arnim swallowed a whoop of glee. He linked arms with her and Sophia, and set off for the Schloss. "Family tradition," he explained gaily, "forbids warning new guests in advance. If you step on the stone again, His Nastiness disappears."

Sophia burst into giggles. "A Grand Prix driver once fainted dead away."

Arnim gave Maile a stare of mock gravity. "If that jester behaved like less than a gentleman, I will have him thrashed." She hated practical jokes but pretended this one had been great fun.

On the terrace they said good night in a mood of tired joviality. Maile was shown to a room with gilded furniture, where she undressed by candlelight, washed in a china basin, and fell into bed feeling that the evening had been one achievement after another; applauded by Salzburg's finest, including a baron; adopted by a chic aristocratic couple; guest at four other diplomatic receptions. Her name on so many lips, her singing in so many hearts.

The next morning when she opened her eyes, she noticed a fresh bouquet of summer flowers on the bedside table. The sheets had a caressing softness. The ceiling was covered with heaps of white clouds tinted gold against a pale blue sky. In the center a large swan with spread wings bent over a pink-nippled goddess lying on her back to receive him, hair and feathers and skin so vivid that the scene seemed to pulsate with life.

Somewhere close by a clock ticked. Somewhere outside quiet footsteps passed the door.

Maile recalled her audience last night, crowded up to the terrace at the consulate. Then swirling off into the night to a round of parties that ended at a castle on a lake. Arnim and Sophia were new friends. They would lead her upward into the social heart of the opera world. But there had also been *Rienzi*. And Arnim's late-night joking remark as they ate: SS troops had occupied this very building, so it wasn't quite the paradise it seemed. Although neither he nor Sophia were to blame for any of that. They were simply caught like a pair of dragonflies in the amber of their own history.

12

EVERY TUESDAY, THURSDAY, and Saturday afternoon during the Festival, the Rosenkavalier entered the kitchen at Schloss Wasserstein to fetch a new supply of fading flowers. Business had been brisk last evening once people left the consular receptions to gossip elsewhere over a final round of cognac. He found the old cook stripping thorns off his usual allotment. "The news here," she said, wrinkling her nose, "is our finest brought a guest at midnight, a brown one. That foreign student at the Mozarteum."

"*Ach,* a student." He shrugged with pretended indifference and glanced out at the vegetable garden. The sun shone down hard and bright. "Today we have kaiser weather," he remarked.

"God smiles on us." The cook bundled the flowers in newspaper and handed them over. "Seppl's taking the truck to town. You can catch him if you hurry."

The Rosenkavalier headed outside to the back road where deliveries were made, confident that his arrangement at the Schloss would continue unquestioned; the cook would go on providing him service without ever knowing why. Disposing of bones for the owners a quarter century ago had been a relief for them, a bargain for him.

On the ride into the city, he considered Fräulein Manoa: a student who was rising fast had certain value. Star performers were worth much more, although trying to sell the Vienna rag press details on Cara Alcazar's gambling had led to the Festival administration threatening him with a permanent ban from Salzburg. Potentially ruinous. He now concentrated on mid-level soloists desperate to conceal a mistress, a love child, a husband found inside the Dom clad only in women's underwear. Among students he traded small favors with no one except the French pianist and never approached the dangerously well-connected Yellow Peril violinist. The peasant Karl wasn't worth his time. The brown girl, however. At winter recitals he'd observed the keen attention her singing aroused in faculty members. Which paled in comparison to enjoying the favor of the American consul, capped off with a midnight meal as a guest at Schloss Wasserstein.

The truck driver lit another twist of Turkish tobacco, chain smoking, and the Rosenkavalier coughed and said, "Seppl, my friend, you must use a superior brand of cigarette. Only a *Gastarbeiter* has your taste." He fanned away the stinking blue haze.

"Who cares?" The driver took another puff. "These're cheap."

The Rosenkavalier stifled further complaint—a ride was better than taking a bus full of *Hausfrauen* bound for the market. At the traffic bridge, he climbed down from the truck and walked to the rear of the Silver Fawn to revive his roses in a bucket of water. His concerns moved ahead to the afternoon and evening; Frau Kammersänger Jann's monthly payment due today; a crate of schnapps brought over from the train station to pay off border guards. He stowed the bottles under his cot, checked his supply of Austrian currency to offer at his own exchange rate to foreigners, then his thoughts returned to Fräulein Manoa.

Her insult to the police while registering for a visa was old news, of no use now, but he'd capitalized on her attempt to attend a von Wehlen premiere by illegal means. The girl was reckless, with her eyes on a career that went straight to the top. Yet in a month Salzburg would again be a provincial town with only a third-rank operetta theater. Swift action was necessary to take advantage of her ambition.

BY THE TIME Maile got to the conservatory at noon, the only free piano was a twangy derelict with sprung strings that couldn't be properly tuned. She began with humming exercises, three low notes up and down. The tones sounded fuzzy after last night's food and wine. She recalled breakfast in bed on a tray, a note from Arnim and Sophia. They were indisposed; a chauffeur would drive her back to the city.

At last five tones slid from her throat well enough to add a leading consonant. *"Lah-lay-lee-loh . . . "* She paused, hearing a word: *lo-ko*. A Hawaiian word. She repeated the exercise. Once more her thoughts stopped at the same place.

She started over, concentrating on the buried sound within her, a living source that ran through wind and water, lived in trees, walls, and floors, waiting to be called on. No good. The hair on her arms stirred as if a ghostly presence had entered the room, and in her mind she heard, *Loko 'ino*. Evil lives here—her father's all-purpose warning if children got hold of the truck keys to play with the ignition, or found a razor blade in the medicine cabinet. Makua had never said it without reminding them that evil was a partner to good. One could not exist without the other. *Lōkahi*, the sacred balance that was the basis of life, his oldest lesson. Tūtū's as well.

Stubbornly Maile sang the opening notes of her contest aria, *"Wo-hin flo—en . . ."* Another o seemed to float above her like a bubble.

"Hele aku," she said. Go away!

Next to the keyboard she sensed a column of heat. Use this! she recalled Makua saying as he pushed his fist against his gut to emphasize that she'd missed a point. Everything had *mana*—a pebble, a hillside, a leg, a scrap of paper—and by itself a razor blade was not evil, so find the connection, the balance. *Loko 'ino*. Where was it in Salzburg, in how many places, in how many people?

A latch clicked and the door opened. *"Ach, wohl,"* Karl said, "at work after all."

She jumped up from the piano. He sauntered in, faked a bow, and continued in an affected whine, "I am calling on Mademoiselle Mah-no-ah to inquire about her diplomatic reception."

She gave him a startled look, then felt a prickling desire to fight. "You're just getting back at me for interrupting you in the basement. Weeks ago!"

He coasted past her to slouch against the wall. "Our tin aristocracy always flocks to a free meal, as long as it's on silver platters."

"You have two seconds to get out."

"Mademoiselle has no comments about last night?" He licked his lips and cupped his hands over his chest. "My own memory of past events is rather good. Did you ever memorize Goethe?" His eyes glittered with aggressive sensuality.

She scowled. Goethe. Standing naked in the moonlit pond, Karl's semen drying on her legs as he quoted from *Faust* and cradled her breasts, comparing them to ripe apples. Now his stare pressed on her as if an erection lurked in his trousers. Sex as revenge on diplomatic glamour. Come on, Maile, up against the piano. In a strange way that appealed to her, but if they fell into each other's arms, yanked off enough clothing to clear the way and did it hard and fast, he would end up picking her brain about everything last night. The magic would be ruined.

"If you will excuse me," she said in her best German, "I need to rehearse."

Karl folded his arms. "You were quite a success with the rich and mighty?"

He examined her so fixedly that she knew he wouldn't leave without a shoving match, and even then he might not leave unless he got at least tidbits of information about the reception. And not lies. They had been intimate in too many ways to deceive each other easily. "I did meet Baron von Gref."

"He sent my family cheese and medicine when things were lean after the war. A nice fellow. What else?"

Rienzi, she remembered. Sophia's mother who had to be avoided. Arnim's teasing hint about the SS being at Schloss Wasserstein. Karl watched her with an uncertain squint, his hair hanging over his eyebrows in a thick fringe.

"Are there still Nazis in Salzburg?" she asked.

He shoved his hair over his ears. "Mother of God, what happened last night?"

"Can't you give a straight reply?"

"I come up here with questions of my own and apples on my mind, and you're thinking about local Nazis." He let out a harsh laugh. She kept her eyes on him. "Morality aside," he said, "nobody is stupid enough to support Hitler in a recognizable way. Anyone caught running private 'study groups' can go to prison for up to twenty years and lose their house and land. That happened when I was a boy, mostly to war widows who couldn't believe the Reich was lost."

"What about the rich?"

"Oh ho!" His eyebrows rose with a crafty expression of discovery. "Last night some aristo bragged about art looted from Jews."

"Don't make things up." She stared harder, pinning him so he would keep talking.

"Ah, the fabled treasure hoards," he said. "Greek statuary was found in the salt mine twenty years ago. No doubt paintings and whatnot are still hidden. Amateur fortune hunters continue to poke around. Including you, in a slightly different vein." His tone became gleeful. "An American romantic combating evil right here under her nose. Like Leonore in *Fidelio*, who went into the dungeon and lived to sing about it. Although that rarely happens in opera. Think of all those dead heroines: Tosca, Marguerite, Aida."

"If I'm romantic, you're evasive. Suspiciously evasive."

"All right." His smile shrank to a look of cold amusement. "My father said our neighbors had crockery all done up in swastikas. They couldn't get rid of it fast enough in '45. To this day I'm sure attics all over Austria are full of similar rubbish. Maybe you've noticed this." He pointed to the inside of his upper arm. "SS men had a tattoo, a small letter in Gothic script, for blood type, in case of major combat injuries. Many survived the war and never went to prison. People protect each other."

She recalled the porter who'd carried her trunk, Frau Metzger's glare, the pulled-down sleeve. "The rich didn't lose much?"

"For a fascinating woman, you can be a real bore. Most noble families considered Hitler a street rat with a crude accent. But modern aristos hate being powerless. Among themselves they're likely trading fine paintings not seen in public since Paris fell." He leaned over Maile. "A woman from Ha-va-ee can go to sleep and dream of coral reefs. Not us. Our history has come down to art versus death camps. Mozart versus Adolf, born just hours away from this very building."

"You sound like an operatic martyr, and you don't even sing!"

"Sarcasm is cheap. You started this conversation."

They were at it again, she knew, competing and moving closer to cruelty because the contest started in only ten days. She refused to agree that she'd been cheap, or to apologize, and he refused to let go of his opinions, a man on home ground confronted by an outsider, the two of them standing almost nose to nose, heaping blame on each other.

Abruptly she said, "Take care of your hands. Keep your mind on music."

He hesitated, then a smile spread across his face, a genuine peacemaker's smile that she knew suggested a more forgiving nature than hers. In the air between them he conducted a miniature 4/4 bar.

"Music," he whispered. "It saves me every time."

His breath had the sweetness of freshly cut grass. He reached back for the door latch and stepped into the hall before she could tell him that he was wrong about coral reefs. Their bright beauty hid poisonous moray eels. Sea urchin spines could paralyze a hand or a foot. Even touching certain shells could be fatal. In her true world, innocence and death lived side by side and fed off each other.

FRAU METZGER SPREAD the kitchen table with her second-best cloth, starched and ironed this morning, and hid the darned spot under a vase filled with daisies picked at the cemetery. The coffee pot was in place. Lotte and Gerda arrived with their haul of final-opportunity vegetables from the open market. When they sat down, Josephina cut her fresh *Guglhopf* in anticipation of a comfortable chat about things more meaningful than church or politics.

After the coffee was poured and the cups were passed, Lotte ignored hers to stare at Gerda with blatant concern. Josephina handed out the plates of cake and then she eyed her guests; a hostess deserving an explanation.

Gerda's eyes were filled with tears. She whispered that she was worried, terribly worried. About a relative in Prague, a close relative. Josephina and Lotte traded looks of surprise, not ever having heard of a Czech family member in the fifty-five years the three women had known each other. With careless anguish Gerda admitted to having a grown son in Prague, a child never acknowledged, who to this day was a secret from her husband and her other children. For years she'd sent packages to the boy, and now feared the worst because he worked at a publishing house, and the government there was burning books.

Their coffee remained untouched, as did the cake so perfectly marbled with swirls of chocolate. The three of them had been best friends

since a school trip to Vienna in 1914 where they saw Emperor Franz
Josef pass by in a gilded coach on his way to review troops bound for
the war in Italy. Over the following decades Josephina, Lotte, and
Gerda had shared a treasury of emotion and suffering brought out
from time to time and examined from every angle: weddings that
should not have taken place, fatal tumors, disappointing children, the
general beastliness of men. Each week's gossip was reviewed for potential scandal. Frau Metzger could hardly imagine they had any secrets
left. But a child out of wedlock. Worse—a Czech! Certainly not as bad
as a Jew or a Gypsy, still frightfully shaming.

Lotte finally picked up her fork and attacked her cake, muttering
that the Rosenkavalier could have solved Gerda's problem years ago
when he still did that kind of work. Gerda burst into sobs. Frau Metzger knew that Lotte was right, yet her heart went out to Gerda. She
smacked the tabletop and invoked the Infant of Prague to curse all
Communists for murdering Holy Russia, bloody Cossacks who would
bomb our churches and Mozart's birth house with his sweet little violin.

Gerda accepted the comforting gift of a lace-trimmed handkerchief. At this Lotte put down her fork, her cake demolished but uneat-
en. An insult of such magnitude left Josephina speechless. When a
telegram boy came to the door, her guests departed without asking to
whom the message was addressed.

Frau Metzger set it against a toothpick holder. Their lack of interest
in such a fertile seed for gossip seemed like a bitter omen signaling the
end of their sisterly trio. She doubted they would ever sit down together again. It was all the fault of the Soviet swine across the border.
Filthy miscarriages, every one of them. In a fit of impatience she waited for her tenant, then gave up and trudged upstairs, left the telegram
for Maile, and went out to shop.

MANY MANY THANKS STOP, the message read, YOU WERE TERRIFIC
STOP MADE MY EVENING STOP CASEY. Maile set the telegram on the
music stand, hoping that he had another event in mind, perhaps a
formal dinner. Although she had to admit that Casey was connected

through twists and turns to people who talked casually about the SS, which led directly—no getting around it—to *loko 'ino*. The conversation with Karl came back to her, and she thought what a child she was. What a fool! Evil would follow her until she faced it, an ageless force that would always exist to balance good.

She opened the piano and rippled off Hilo-style hula chords, crish-crash all over the keyboard. Garantee hunnerd percent, Auntie Lani was still performing comic routines at third-rate hotels, driving the surplus Army jeep Maile had bought for her, painted purple with Voices from the Reef on the hood. Before and after work Auntie cooked, sat with the sick, and organized the clan to pick flowers in the mountains for a wedding luau. Got drunk once a month on the front *lanai* with her old lady friends.

Impatiently Maile unwrapped a packet of cold cuts: sausage speckled with large bits of fat and chunks of gristle; a soft slice of cheese concealing a heap of leathery end pieces substituted behind the counter if a customer wasn't looking. She threw out half and arranged the rest on a plate like a *Jauseplatte* she had seen served on the terrace of Cafe Scimitar. Hers was a poor imitation. She imagined hot food on a real plate, not her snack-size saucer bought at the market along with a pretty wineglass gathering dust on a shelf. In frustration she went downstairs for a walk.

At the river promenade a workman slathered a kiosk with glue. He smoothed on new performance schedules, one reading, MOZARTEUM PREIS-KONZERT, 21.AUGUST.1968. The sight of it gave Maile a violent desire to win. Unlike the contest, a closed event for judges and teachers, the winner's concert four days later was a student's only chance to perform with full orchestra for fellow students, agents, the press. A Hawaiian soprano who triumphed in Europe would get her picture on the front page of the *Honolulu Morning Bulletin*, Maile Manoa in the lower right-hand corner reserved for beauty queens, sports stars, marlin fishermen. No local singer had ever made it to the Top Forty on the mainland pop charts, and she would beat them all by way of opera rather than a cute tune about making eyes at a girl. News worth a long-distance call: register at the *Postundtelegraphenamt*, wait hours for an open phone line to Munich-Paris-London-NewYork-Chicago-

LosAngeles-Honolulu, a terrible expense but worth every cent to hear Makua's voice. He would shout her name and be engulfed by aunties, brothers, little ones, everybody grabbing for the phone as if the lost daughter had returned from the dead.

But each would ask the same question: So, now you come home arready?

All she had yet to attain pressed down on her like stagnant clouds that would not release the rain they held, and would not lift. She longed to be elsewhere, doing something easy and familiar that didn't require a grand personality. Her old routine, chores at home in Papakōlea. Changing the strings on a guitar, washing sand from a pile of seaweed, picking mangoes. Ironing in the living room before anyone else was awake. Open the wooden board that always gave off the same one-note creak, run a hand over the sheet nailed to the top as tightly as skin, let the iron warm up, sprinkle cool water on starched clothes fresh from the line in the yard. Lick one finger to test the hot metal for just the right sizzle, then swing the heavy iron over a rumpled *muʻumuʻu* and breathe in steam that smelled like Auntie Lani's ginger lei from the day before.

I'm not coming home, she thought. *ʻAʻole. Nein.* No language could disguise the truth of her reply to her family. She had made a choice to trade the ancient values—what few were left—for a new soul of music, but so far that didn't exist except as a goal, with no more substance than a handful of air.

Feeling empty and useless, Maile wandered into the Old City and came to Skolaren Kirche. A small group of men and women stood outside. They wore traditional suits and dirndls in conservative greens and browns, ordinary citizens dressed for a special occasion. Once a week, she knew, the cast of *Rappresentazione* had a day off and the church was used for local events.

The people held candles, short and thin, with small flames. Several women fingered rosaries. A priest in a long black robe came out and motioned to them. As they entered the church, Maile had a powerful desire to relive the spectacular performance she had seen. She waited briefly so she wouldn't interrupt whatever service was about to take place, then followed them inside.

The only light came from the candles as the group slowly moved toward the altar. Far ahead, someone lit two more candles, spots of flame that made tiny white circles. The dark rows of statues looming beside the pews resembled twisted tree trunks. The walls were chilly sheets of black. No lovely angels cascaded from heaven with messages of joy. Maile stumbled against a prayer bench and held on to its railing.

From somewhere behind her came a harsh musical sound, like pebbles pinging into a brass bowl. She turned to see an altar boy at the entrance with a lighted taper that illuminated only his face. He led a small procession, more people holding candles no bigger than sticks of chalk. In the vast darkness they appeared disembodied, like heads gliding forward on an invisible raft borne along by an unseen river. She stepped aside for them. A young couple passed, weeping quietly, followed by four somber children and a gray-haired woman carrying a small painted casket the length of her forearm. On top of the casket, a cluster of baby's breath tied with a white ribbon. Everyone filed down to the altar. Above them, in the accumulating light of candles, the bottom of a huge crucifix slowly emerged from the shadows, revealing the feet of Christ pierced by a large nail.

The priest blessed the casket and the mourners. He chanted in a rapid undertone, the chimes sounded again, the people knelt and rose and murmured responses, and then the candles on the altar were extinguished. The priest and the boy left through a side door. The procession re-formed and passed Maile again with a dry clicking of heels and the dull shuffling of children's feet. The girls' braids ended in knots of string rather than ribbons. Sweat stains ringed the men's hats. A poor family, she realized. For them no staged fantasy about the journey of Body and Soul, no splendid singing to open the gates to paradise. They lived outside of Salzburg's wealth. In their suffering they seemed close enough to touch, but they gave off a stark sense of privacy, refusing even a glance from a stranger.

The mourners filed outside, taking all light with them. The glory Maile had seen here dissolved into the surrounding blackness.

ॐ   ॐ   ॐ

THE CONTEST WAS just five days away. Intermediate students at the conservatory were asked to give up their lesson times so that participants could have extra instruction. The recital hall was in constant use for rehearsing. Occasional arguments and bursts of crying were heard behind the doors of teaching studios.

In her room Maile struggled to capture the feeling of love betrayed that was at the heart of her aria. She had completed the technical work: breaths for each phrase, tone placement, quality, volume. All that, she knew, only amounted to Step One. A superior singer, particularly in competition, had to also show sincerity and nuanced expression.

Silently she repeated the recitative: three tempi, three different emotions. Her thoughts wandered to an old woman carrying a coffin small enough for a baby just a few days old. None of her sisters or aunts had lost a child. She reminded herself that only rich opera singers could afford the luxury of creating their own families.

At the garderobe mirror she practiced casting her eyes down, and slumped her shoulders, but just a little, because a countess did not slouch. *"Einst—ge-liebt...,"* she sang, Once loved... and she stretched the tones into a cry of pain.

Her expressions looked snooty, she decided, or overly dramatic: cramped forehead, a groan of agony calculated to occur exactly at the quarter rest.

With every repetition her face grew tenser, her jaw stiffer. Too much *e nei*, she imagined Auntie Lani saying, her standard phrase when they'd been working hard on a new show. *Pau* for now. Go beach. You head too full.

On impulse Maile slipped into a blue linen dress with a tight waist and narrow skirt that made her feel sleek. A single idea occurred to her: frivolity. I want to be waited on, to enjoy myself without worrying about the cost. She tucked twenty schillings into her purse.

Downstairs she stepped outside into a refreshing breeze. The coolness made her hungry for a delicacy she had never tasted, like *Doboschtorte* laced with West Indian rum, in a place she had never been to, like Café Scimitar. The former home of a noble family had a reputation for excellent service, steep prices, small portions, and pastries no chef in Austria could match.

She took a shortcut to the river. On the opposite shore stood the café with its white marble terrace. As she crossed the footbridge, there was a flicker of lightning, a blast of thunder, the sharp scent of ozone. A downpour swept toward her.

Thrilled, she dashed into Café Scimitar. Dozens of people at little Art Deco tables sat in chairs with water lilies curving up the backs. Waiters in black suits moved neatly past each other to a counter filled with pastries on porcelain stands. They offered magazines to ladies and gentlemen.

Maile joined hopeful customers behind a velvet rope. At the front of the line the headwaiter surveyed the room, a man as coldly handsome as a model for Parisian formal wear, except for a hairy mole on his neck. The waiting people watched him with pretended indifference but she sensed their suppressed tension. According to Frau Metzger, being seated at the Scimitar was never a matter of arriving first. Status, fame, past tips, and favors owed were all equally important. One could wait an hour and be told with a little smile to try again tomorrow.

Minutes passed as rain streaked the tall French windows. People in line glanced at wristwatches. No one got up to leave even after empty plates were cleared away. Then the headwaiter's gaze skimmed over those waiting as politely as petitioners at the archbishop's palace. He unlatched the rope and said, *"Frau Manoa aus Honolulu."*

A man in front of Maile whispered to another, *"Wer, denn?"* Who's that?

She stepped forward to follow the headwaiter, concealing jittery curiosity. The room seemed huge, the path between the tables long and winding. *"Sopranistin,"* she heard as she passed seated customers, "Gershwin."

At a broad table with a crest, Baron von Gref rose from an upholstered chair. Sophia sat beside him with a welcoming smile. *"Gnädige Frau,"* he said to Maile, gracious lady, making the old-fashioned greeting sound natural. She felt at the center of the city, under its spotlight, guided here by her three souls.

"What may I order for you?" the baron asked as she sat down.

Food had lost all importance. "Just coffee," she murmured. "Thank you."

He expressed pleasure at unexpectedly seeing her again. The beauty of her singing at the consulate was still with him. Sophia looked alert, as if eager to chat but politely deferring to Arnim's uncle because of his age. She wore a navy cloche that curved over one ear and ended in a slim feather accenting the graceful line of her chin.

"I have never lost a boyish delight in people from faraway places," the baron said. "A vanity, I admit." He paused as Maile's coffee was set down. She picked up tongs to ease a cube of sugar over the edge of the cup, missed his next remarks, then heard him say, "You have my best wishes for the music competition. A shame that the judging is not a public event. However, I always attend the prizewinner's concert."

"Competition?" Sophia asked.

The baron explained and turned again to Maile. "If you will allow," he said, "I would like to ground our acquaintance with a small gift." He smiled. "Another vanity of mine. My nephew has pointed out that singers must of necessity travel a good deal, and cannot be burdened with large or overly delicate possessions." His librarian's glasses slid down his nose. "Do visit me at Am Waldsee and choose a memento which will travel well."

Maile envisioned another Schloss Wasserstein. She could have thrown her arms around him. "You're very kind."

"Artists deserve kindness. Their lives are often difficult." He slipped a watch from his vest pocket and sighed. "*Ach wohl*, how unfortunate." His face took on a sweet look of apology. "I am in the old *commedia dell'arte* position of having to excuse myself for excusing myself, although cocktails with your consul will be a pleasure. I leave you a lovely partner for conversation." He kissed Sophia on both cheeks and shook Maile's hand.

The headwaiter led the way to the entrance, opened the door, and unfurled an umbrella. Baron von Gref angled it like a lance and marched straight into the downpour. Maile felt like applauding.

"Gifts," Sophia remarked. "Arnim is giving me gifts again. He does that when seriously attracted to another woman."

"How nice for you," Maile joked, but felt on uncertain ground.

Sophia opened a tortoiseshell case and took out a long brown cigarette. For a moment their eyes locked dangerously. "I hope as a singer you do not mind the odor of tobacco."

Maile did. "Oh, no, not at all."

"Arnim loves to play the romantic adventurer, although it never works." A hand with a lighted match descended between them. Sophia tilted her cigarette at it, inhaled, gave the headwaiter a nod, and once more eyed Maile. "You and Arnim would make a fabulous couple. Physically, of course. Also because of your mutual devotion to music. But he is like a nineteenth-century suitor who adores the pain of infatuation with types he cannot possibly marry."

Her tone had no bitchiness. Maile still waited for the ax to fall.

Sophia leaned forward, her expression lively and confiding. "His most recent disaster was von Wehlen's laundress, a Turkish girl as beautiful as a prize harem slave." She sipped on her cigarette. "One night Arnim arranged for horses so they could flee. He had costumes, a turban for himself, but he's a terrible rider, much too high-strung. He was thrown into a pond of sleeping swans. The birds attacked him. Bottles of wine trampled, saddles drenched. The most terrible racket. His mother and I had everything hushed up."

They put their heads together to share a delicious little laugh at Arnim's expense. Maile loved the idea of a real-life philandering Count Almaviva, straight out of *Figaro*, racing off at night on horseback, never mind if it was a spectacular flop.

The headwaiter brought a porcelain tray with an envelope, and told Sophia that her driver was waiting in the Italian courtyard. She read a note. "Heavens," she said to Maile, "I have left a dozen relatives dangling. We must continue our conversation. I enjoyed it immensely." She left, dropping her cigarette into an urn filled with sand.

Her driver. For some women, Maile thought, social engagements were the same as a job that involved actual work. Sophia von Schönweilershof had servants who sewed on buttons, mailed letters, ironed skirts, did the shopping, the cooking, the dishes. But none ever sat with her in this café.

The headwaiter returned to offer more coffee. "Just the check, please," Maile said. He looked away as if busy with something else.

Anyone at the baron's table, she realized, was a guest. Although a tip was no doubt expected. Having only a twenty-schilling note, she slipped it under her saucer.

Like her host, she was also escorted to the entrance and given an umbrella. No deposit required, she thought in nervous satisfaction, no niggling reminder that the umbrella must be returned. Her huge tip had been worth it. And Arnim with von Wehlen's laundress! That was a fortune in gossip.

Outside, the rain had turned into a heavy fog that rolled up from the river in slow swirls, obscured the promenade, and coiled around tree trunks. Familiar sights appeared as vague, rounded shapes. Pale yellow clouds tumbled from the overcast sky, clung to rooftops, and crept down the sides of buildings. Maile crossed the footbridge feeling as if the city were afloat. Soon it belonged to her alone, and she walked on aimlessly, filled with a strange, unnamable desire.

In streets still deserted after the storm, water in its most secret form had come to visit; trickling under bushes, droplets plinking onto the base of a statue, a faint sound like breath as fog brushed against a wall. Moisture clicked into cracks and window frames. In a courtyard a random scarf of mist dipped and enclosed her. She inhaled its cool dampness, then held the umbrella at arm's length and swept it in a circle.

Sunlight spread around her as the fog rose. She had wandered into the Old City's maze of crooked back streets. A dog shook its wet fur and a hail of water drops rattled against a wall; butcher boys sprinkled sawdust on wet steps. She furled the umbrella, and the concerns of daily life plodded back: contest aria, grocery shopping.

A short way ahead of her, the Rosenkavalier stepped out of a hidden stairway. He cradled his flowers on one arm so he could doff his cap to her. She regarded him with distaste. Deep wrinkles furrowed his scalp, three vertical lines on flour-white skin, as if the skull beneath had shrunk.

"Ach, Fräulein Manoa," he said, "the lady I have been seeking." Ten minutes ago he had learned by way of a Scimitar sub-waiter that Professor Jann's student had sat at Baron von Gref's table. "I have a most

interesting proposal. My calling card," he added with mild humor, and offered her a rose.

She didn't take it. His teeth were the color of granite. His chemical scent spread around them. She broke eye contact.

He withdrew the rose, saying, "My services are available at any hour: money changing, locating a doctor, a chauffeur. My many contacts also include Festival House personnel at the highest level."

"And so?"

She spoke in a haughty tone, but he saw curiosity in her expression. Carefully he drew her in with an outline of what he could arrange: a message to a certain Festival House secretary, relayed to the daily schedule manager, passed on to a conductor's assistant, who—in the midst of rehearsals, performances, and social events—would inform the most famous *Dirigent* in the world that the few auditions granted during the very busy Festival should include a certain young singer. If she were fortunate enough to win the upcoming contest, that did not guarantee being granted such an audition. First the path had to be smoothed, and before Festival professionals departed for the year. Should Fräulein Manoa not win the contest, of course there would be no audition. If she auditioned and was not successful, the process the Rosenkavalier had initiated would cost her nothing.

"I see," she said. She edged around him to walk on.

He bowed as she passed. What he'd described was not entirely a fantasy—the upper reaches of the music world had many backdoors. In his string calendar he made a knot to mark the conversation.

Reluctantly Maile returned the Scimitar's fine umbrella, and went on to the Mozarteum to continue the work she had abandoned. Her practicing felt automatic, lifeless. Nothing more than lost time, but she stuck to it out of a sense of duty. She revised her opinion of the Rosenkavalier from creepy little busybody to someone who could be useful. It made excellent sense to get an audition when Europe's greatest musicians were in Salzburg. Her savings were nearly gone and soon she would dip into money put aside for the trip home. Although if she won the contest, Professor Jann would not approve of an audition that he didn't arrange himself. Would he really refuse to let her sing for the world's most famous *Dirigent?* He might. No, he wouldn't allow it.

On the way back to Getreidegasse Twenty-Five, Maile shopped for soup cubes and toilet paper. She hated the idea of another year of struggling for recognition, eating gristly sausage, singing in student recitals, grateful to be someone's guest.

The instant she stepped inside the house, Frau Metzger rushed out of her kitchen. "Dangerous news has reached my ears," the landlady exclaimed. "Come with me."

Maile was used to her dramatic announcements. "Sorry, I have to study."

"Your reputation is at risk!" The landlady put hands on hips and leaned forward. "You were seen speaking to a certain disreputable person, after your so recent triumph among diplomats. Have your standards descended to the gutter?"

Against her will Maile followed her into the kitchen, thinking sourly that she had spoken to the Rosenkavalier just an hour ago, that the quick spread of gossip should no longer be a surprise.

They sat facing each other. "It pains me deeply to explain certain things," Frau Metzger said, "but you will see I have your best interests at heart." She wiped her brow with a handkerchief and launched into a recitation.

Originally, the Rosenkavalier came from far out in the valley, a section so poor that a family with glass windows was considered rich. Decades ago, peasants dealt with illegitimate or deformed babies by a method they called "making angels." He was *der Engelmacher*. Frau Metzger shuddered so violently that her cheeks wobbled. He never had a real name, she continued, people just knew to ask around. At night a new mother took an infant to him, and he had it baptized, then left it in a secret place where animals couldn't reach it and people couldn't hear it crying. Within days the baby starved or froze. The *Engelmacher* buried it and received his payment.

Frau Metzger paused to pour herself a tot of schnapps from a bottle she whisked off a low shelf. "In my youth I once saw him with a newborn," she confided. "My own eyes." She drank, coughed, and leaned over the table to whisper, "During the Reich you could be executed for making angels, but after the war it was common again when Occupation soldiers, especially Negroes, fathered children all over the countryside." But that job didn't last, she went on, and about fifteen years ago he began selling flowers to Festival visitors, roses stolen from graves. Now he wore a clean uniform and supposedly supported himself through currency exchange, but in fact by trading in scandals, especially among prominent musicians.

"So," Frau Metzger concluded, "you are warned. Your reputation is so precious. Promise me you will not again go near him."

Maile stared past her. She had been flattered that the Rosenkavalier knew about Super-Sopran. The possibility of an audition as he'd outlined it seemed part and parcel of the way things were done here—nothing wrong with taking advantage of that. Although in spite of music, the city's real industry seemed to be secrets: fresh gossip, gossip thirty years old, diplomatic gossip in fourteen consulates on levels she couldn't imagine. What Frau Metzger described had a powerful ring of truth: poor, ignorant people dominated by church laws. Allowing a baptized infant to starve was evidently preferable to the sin of abortion. The clan would never believe such a tradition had existed anywhere in the world, much less in the name of God. They would not understand how she could stay one more day in this country.

At last she said, "I thought he was a former concentration camp guard."

"Oh no," Frau Metzger exclaimed, "that would have been much better than his true occupations."

13

THE NEXT MORNING Maile came downstairs to see a news vendor whipping papers off a stack as customers tossed coins into a tobacco tin. Most Salzburgers read free copies in a café to save a schilling for a roll to go with coffee. Politics, she thought, vaguely worried. The Red Army.

She bought the *Nachrichten*, headlined, TAUSENDE TSCHECHEN FLIEHEN IHRE HEIMAT. *Thousands of Czechs Flee Their Homeland.* Soviet leaders had declared an end to Prague Spring. Mass arrests were taking place throughout the country. An Austrian journalist was quoted: "Citizens shouted, 'Go west before the Russians come!'" A map showed the movement toward Prague of over a million Warsaw Pact troops.

People around Maile made grim jokes: Germany is west, France is west, Salzburg is dead south—we'll get tanks instead of refugees. *Niemals,* others disagreed, we are protected by the diplomats here. That's reasonable, she told herself. Armies don't advance on a whim. There's no reason to attack a city full of musicians.

A Festival House press release took the rest of the front page: von Wehlen's eight-track recording of *Othello* would be filmed next month in Italy. The storm scene required hundreds of extras on Piazza San Marco; a Medici bedroom was on loan for the scenes of love and murder. Maile went on to the conservatory and found the main hall jammed with singers, from beginners to advanced, all speculating about highly paid film work. Before the first class started, contestants from across Europe began arriving.

Two hours later, fourteen had checked in with the registrar. Those from Western Europe quickly made contact with local students, but competitors from Iron Curtain countries rebuffed any attempt to draw them into conversation. Word spread that a singer and a violinist from Prague had been delayed. By the next day their arrival seemed doubtful.

The only Soviet entrant, a pianist, was accompanied everywhere by two chaperones who waited at the door when he used the WC. His stylish suits outshone the shoddy clothes and shoes of competitors from Dresden and Bucharest, who were housed in the drab youth hostel under the watchful eye of a local Communist matron. The three Russians had a suite at Salzburg's best hotel. Austrian students shrugged off such inequalities among supposed comrades.

Maile constantly saw Karl at the conservatory—after breakfast, before lunch, after lunch, before dinner—but they never spoke, their past relationship discarded to engage in mental combat. When they met on the way to separate practice sessions, they traded stares, wordless challenges. According to recent gossip, he had made an important emotional breakthrough with interpreting Schubert. A red stripe on his right wrist, it was said, showed where a sickle had sheared off a patch of hair and skin. She finally solved the riddle of her aria: it was the hope of love rather than love itself that animated her character.

NO DINNER THE night before, no breakfast. For lunch a seedless roll washed down with tea and honey. Maile felt properly hungry and lean, nothing to block the nimble movement of her diaphragm or obstruct the flow of her spirits between throat and gut.

The world would begin at three o'clock. The archbishop of Salzburg had donated the use of his palace for the afternoon. Contestants had drawn lots. Karl was number six, she number seven. Any piece longer than eight minutes had been condensed. Pauses were built into the schedule to allow for the tolling of the Dom bells, a sound that by law could not be silenced.

Maile knew that seeing Karl before he stepped out to perform would be unbearable. To keep her nerves from fraying, in her room she worked on an Italian crossword puzzle. At three-twenty she did only a basic vocal warm-up, on Jann's advice. She arranged her chignon higher and fuller than usual, as befitted a modern-day countess. At three-forty, when she estimated that the first four performers must have finished, she went downstairs.

The usual crowds of leisurely afternoon shoppers irked her—people blandly unaware that her life would change before nightfall. A series of slow booms from the cathedral's bell tower announced the three-quarter hour with vibrations that pierced her hollow stomach. She climbed the palace stairway slowly to prevent a racing heartbeat, a dry throat, a twisted ankle.

On the top step the Soviet pianist was smoking a black cigarette with a gold filter tip while his minders used pocketknives to clean their nails. He looked through her, and she stifled a nip of fear. Last night's gossip had awarded him first place: no one else could match the brilliant arrogance of his playing, which gave him the crucial edge, the extra five percent that marked a winner. The Czech contestants had not arrived, two fewer competitors to worry about. Mozart, she recalled, was never allowed inside the palace, never considered more than a servant.

She entered and felt reduced to a speck.

Columns of green and black marble rose two stories to a network of gilded vines that twined across a distant vaulted ceiling. Ahead stretched a white marble floor that looked as long as Getreidegasse, with a carpet running down the center like a river of purples, blues, and reds. She walked past massive oil paintings, tapestries of Crusaders battling Turks, and came to the archbishop's receiving chamber.

The tall door stood open. People were clustered outside, relatives of local contestants. The interior resembled a gigantic jewelry box lined with burgundy brocade. Four men and two women sat in ornate chairs, their backs to the door; in front of them a black concert grand piano on a low platform. The registrar stood to the right beside a screened gallery where professors were seated, unseen by performers or judges.

Workmen rolled a gleaming harp onto the platform, set a stool in place, and stepped out of sight. A slender Parisian with a long brown braid entered alongside her accompanist, announced a Ravel scherzo, sat down, placed her hands over the strings. A shower of sixteenth notes sprang into the air. The piano answered and the room filled with fresh, exotic melodies.

Enviously Maile imagined a French painting—pastel ponds, bridges, picnics, ladies strolling in weather that was always summer. Her own Mozart aria offered nothing new. This much more modern music had the allure of scented mist. A countess in a Baroque opera was as familiar as the rye bread people ate every day. Even shop signs here were Baroque. Old hat, boring.

The last tinkling notes of Ravel drifted away. Maile walked off to a side room reserved for contestants, and from the Dom came a rumble of bells, four strokes to mark the hour. They faded, followed by the registrar saying, *"Nummer sechs, bitte."* Karl had just missed getting her own number, seven, lucky number seven.

As he stepped out on stage, she eased in front of contestants standing in the wings. *Pili* crept out from between her ribs, eager to explore. "Go back!" she whispered, and clapped a hand to her side.

Karl flexed his wrists, announced composer, opus, title, sat down and adjusted the bench. He extended his hands over the keyboard but didn't touch it—a pause to invoke the instrument so it would not refuse him. His posture was taut: head, neck, back, arms, legs. He lowered his fingers and the insistent beat of the opening chords filled the room: double forte, crescendo, arpeggio. He repeated the driving melody a step higher, and the dynamics unfurled, intensifying and racing up the scale.

His notes spattered Maile's face like sharp raindrops. Tone, he'd once said, had to be drawn out of an instrument, and he was doing that beautifully. She gave in to the sweep of his sound as the lead phrase climbed again and again and ended with a smartly accented *peng!*

At the first transition he went through a run at almost double tempo—a tiny one-measure mistake she was certain no one else heard. He glossed over it and returned to the Wanderer's restless theme. She listened hard for the emotional breakthrough the others had talked about: it was there. After laying the groundwork, he plunged into phrases without hesitation, throwing himself into the splendor of wandering freely. Emotion literally flowed from him, the piano an extension of his body, his innermost beliefs, his soul. She longed to be a pianist and make music in the same way, to have joyous physical contact with an instrument, to be a hero of Romanticism, in search of love and truth—

A climbing line of chords broke off. In her mind Maile filled in the missing notes, but a white gap opened up in the room, as distracting as a burst of light: three seconds' worth of silence.

Karl continued with the descending run and recaptured the theme. The save was smooth. She breathed in. He had kept perfect pace. Neither timing nor tonality was marred, and he finished with a flawless display of verve that celebrated the driven, solitary artist—yet as he struck the final majestic chords and they expanded around him, against all logic the short, awkward silence hung in the air. She saw it and felt it, and knew that the judges did too.

He got to his feet and stared at the keyboard, a terrible hesitation, as if to accept that all the beauty he had created was not enough. Close, very close, but his efforts had fallen short, were no more than a pile of damp ashes. She wanted to shout that a minor defect meant nothing, that no one deserved to fail for a three-second memory lapse. But music was made, not discussed and defended, and contestants had no power except what they demonstrated on stage, under pressure, naked.

Karl faced the judges, bowed, and stepped off the platform. As he approached the contestants waiting backstage, Jean-Paul lunged to one side. Others gave way like ghosts. From somewhere far off Maile heard the registrar ask for entry number seven. *Pili* set her lungs on fire. The platform ahead looked twenty feet tall. She took a long breath. Heat rose around her like a suffocating tide of sand. Wings, she thought, wings, wings, and imagined them with such obsession that she felt feathers caressing her neck.

A SPANISH HELDENTENOR sang with great conviction. Brenda performed well for a mezzo whose immature voice would take another decade to develop fully. Jean-Paul tore a fingernail on Tschaikovsky and had to drop out. The Soviet pianist proved to be an ice-cold technician, note-perfect and no warmth. Kazuo stunned everyone with his fluid bowing style, emotional range, and tasteful touches of humor, yet at six that evening the registrar announced, "A unanimous decision for first prize: Miss Maile Manoa, United States of America."

She swam forward through applause, the judges a blur of shapes, and she shook hands with each one. Nothing felt real until she turned to acknowledge the clapping of her fellow musicians. Her people. Nobody else understood what they all went through for the sake of a single piece of music, working alone hour after hour, spending years building nerve, never certain it would hold for the few minutes of a performance that decided one's future.

The applause continued and her dizziness turned to clarity. Some participants looked bitter. Others clapped in dutiful slack-wristed relief that weeks of tension had finally ended. She bowed at the crucial moment before the applause started to shrink. When she straightened up, a hot silence flowed over her, a current of desire from the audience, a powerful longing she had often felt, but now everything was reversed. They wanted to stand where she stood, to be the one different from all the rest of them. They wanted her magic, the only thing that could not be taught.

She stepped off the stage, a queen joining her court, and the Mozarteum contestants surrounded her, demanding her autograph. "Beer at the Red Horse," Brenda yelled. "Winner pays!"

East Bloc competitors were hustled away by the Communist matron and the Soviet chaperones. A Spanish student shouted condolences at them in fractured German. Teachers came from behind the screened-off gallery, their expressions ranging from casual to grim. Maile scribbled her magic name on sheet music, posed for photos with the French harpist and a Dutch baritone, traded addresses and promises to write with a half dozen others, everybody breathless, colliding in a sea of emotions, speaking in phrases and thick accents no one understood, reverting to their own languages.

She jumped when Kazuo touched her on the shoulder. One of her long hairpins pinged down onto the floor, and he retrieved it and said with careful formality, "You brought great honor to my family." He blushed violent pink. "Do forgive me, your family."

Professor Jann walked over to announce with theatrical gravity, "I assert a privilege." He raised an eyebrow, assumed an exaggerated operetta stance, and offered Maile an arm. "You may claim Miss Manoa in an hour," he told the others. "However, celebration begins with champagne at the Silver Fawn." To her he said, "I admit to reserving a table on the advice of a withered Gypsy in the marketplace."

The restaurant of her dreams! Maile almost shouted in delight, but played her part and curtsied in her daytime dress, knees poking sideways like a clumsy servant girl's. "Why, of course, sir, the Fawn before the Horse."

The students laughed wildly, still unwinding. She promised to join them later and pay the bill. The circle around her dissolved as they picked up instruments, grabbed scores, looked for a misplaced cap, then hurried away in a pack. Teachers, judges and relatives headed for the door.

Maile took Jann's arm, curling her fingers over his jacket sleeve. A secret erotic charge went through at being allowed to touch him. Workmen pushed the grand piano off the platform. They brought in the archbishop's reception throne, and a priest covered it with a velvet cloth. She looked around at the burgundy brocade walls, feeling her triumph still filling the room.

Jann guided her out into the entry hall. "After the prize concert," he said, serious now, "you will have all the trimmings. Flowers, photographers, press reviews. If you perform as well as you did today, your life will become a lot more complicated. I do not intend to lose you to that kind of attention."

"Of course not," she murmured, thinking, *Erster Preis. Mit Einstimmigkeit, My-lee Ma-no-ah.*

"Enough about the future," Jann said, chiding himself. He tucked her arm tighter against his side. "My dear, how wonderfully you sang of love. Love lost, the hope of regaining it." They continued out on the purple-blue-red carpet as he described being a young man in love for the first time, hearing the same aria sung to perfection by the immortal Delia Grazia, what a lasting impression it made. Certain singular performances had the power to sustain joy and enrich the spirit. Such memories were cherished for a lifetime.

Outside at the top of the staircase, the world was dark and cool. A breeze from the river drifted across the empty cathedral plaza, drawing them toward it in an agreeable silence. As they descended the steps, Maile saw what looked like an abandoned heap of clothing at the bottom. Karl sat hunched with his knees drawn up, his jacket slung over his back. One shirt cuff was sloppily rolled, the other hung loose.

"Excuse me a moment," she said to Jann. He nodded and walked off to wait by a streetlamp on the plaza.

Karl didn't stir. His posture made Maile want to weep, or embrace him, but she also despised him for being in such an obvious place, and making such an obvious bid for sympathy. Worse, they had never talked about what would happen to them if he or she won. If they'd both lost, at least they would share something. Now her victory separated them.

Gently she touched his shoulder. He glanced up, muttered, "Congratulations," and stared again at the cobblestones.

"Thanks," she said, relieved to hear him speak. "Your performance was beautiful. Schubert just decided to hide from you for a second."

He shoved her hand away and kept his eyes on the ground. "I wanted to be the Wanderer, the one who leaves everything behind. Like you, I admit. Coming here from the Pacific. Risk, right? For art, right? Well, I failed."

"One blank measure is not failure."

"I had it every time I rehearsed." He pounded his knees, still not looking at her. "That passage was never a problem."

"And it won't be in the future. You put wonderful feeling into the entire piece, that's undeniable. You were the Wanderer, from the very first phrase. Everyone felt it. When you finished, I saw you standing on a cliff like a hero."

"Christ, don't be such a fool. Perfection is all that counts until you're famous. Then you can have a bad day and it's chalked up to deep insight."

"Would you rather be some robot who delivers every last note and bores the audience to death?"

"Go sing for von Wehlen. He weighs each tone on a jeweler's scale."

The last was said with such hostility that she felt afraid for him. Instead of concealing self-pity, she sensed that his words exposed something more dangerous—doubt that he possessed the crucial degree of nerve, that he could take the next risk, that he loved music enough to go on no matter what.

She reached for his hand, knowing there was little chance he would accept anything from her, but they had yearned for the same things. He had given her comfort, advice, the wine cave when she was still a stranger in the city, the bat on a moonlit night.

"Come have something to eat," she coaxed. "Let's drink brandy til dawn."

He leaned away from her with the weariness of an old man. "I'm quitting the Mozarteum," he mumbled, then in a sudden explosion of energy, he grabbed his jacket and scrambled to his feet, saying, "I'll catch you yet." He strode away into the black shadows along the palace wall.

Soon she couldn't hear his footsteps. She rejoined Jann on the plaza. He walked beside her, hands clasped at his back.

She wondered miserably if musicians could ever truly love each other. Maybe they only had surges of passion that fed their own music. Maybe Karl was on his way to an old sweetheart, some neighbor girl who'd showed him her ripe apples one fine day when both of them were fourteen. They'd have a farmhouse full of babies, a happy life of love and work and growing old together. Maile loathed him, and loathed the girl, an ordinary sort who could offer a man relief instead of rivalry, cotton socks instead of sleek nylons. He would spend the rest of his life sinking between her thighs, taking revenge on Miss Maile Manoa from Honolulu for being the Wanderer.

A heavy mist spilled down from the castle into the dark streets and obscured spots of light farther on. The Dom bells tolled to mark the passing of another hour. In silence Maile approached the Silver Fawn beside Jann. The maître d' swept open the door and greeted him with, *"Ja, der Herr Kammersänger Doktor Professor,"* as though reading a row of medals on his chest.

She stifled a nervous laugh and stepped forward.

Inside, Jann looked around with the calm of a veteran musician who had experienced countless celebrations in his honor. The restaurant's one large room was decorated with vases of roses and Biedermeier cabinets that gave it the exclusivity of a private home. Waiters in mauve silk jackets and britches angled around a silver sculpture in the center that depicted Bacchus with grapes in one hand and a fawn in the other. Slim ladies ate melon for dessert. Men smoked pencil-thin cigarillos. Maile felt starved and brimming with excitement, and knew that she had to conceal both.

As they were seated, the maître d' nodded across the room to a wine steward, who brought a bucket of iced champagne to Jann's table, popped the cork, and filled two glasses with the smooth precision of a bird gliding into their orbit and out again.

"Countess Almaviva." Jann raised his glass. "To your continued success."

Maile touched her glass to his, feeling blessed. Delicately she took a moistening sip of champagne. He gave her a subtle look of amusement. She put down the glass and sat back in a more relaxed frame of mind.

"A close contest," he said. "I had it down to three possibilities. The tension among the teachers in that shut-off gallery was agony. Worse, I believe, than when we were still active on stage."

With the generosity of victors, they discussed Kazuo's performance, the harpist's dainty appeal, the tenor doomed by his comically mispronounced German. They sympathized with competitors from the East Bloc, never allowed out at night unless they won top honors. Karl's rendition of Schubert was not mentioned, but Maile felt it on the edge of the conversation, his frightening loss a reminder of how fragile they all were. Every performer, from student to world-famous professional, dreaded an onstage memory lapse. A few seconds of paralyzing fear could shatter years of work.

People began leaving for Festival performances and Jann said, "I dare not keep you from your friends." From his jacket he took a brown leather box, nicked and scuffed with age. It fit into the palm of his hand and had been polished so often that the lid had the high gloss of lacquer. "Your monetary award comes from Vienna and will not arrive for a few days. Tonight a winner deserves more than mere handshakes."

He opened the box to show her a wooden locket carved in the shape of a miniature book. A black velvet ribbon was threaded through a tiny gold circle embedded in the wood. "Years ago a teacher gave this to me after I sang my first Giovanni. It had been passed down to her from a nineteenth-century singer, and so on back to where it cannot be traced." He clicked open the little book, took out a tiny piece of paper, and unfolded it. "This has no value as such—it has never been proven—but my teacher believed, and I believe, that these notations are from the hand of Mozart. He had a peculiar way of flagging an eighth note. You see, here . . . "

The oval scrap, smaller than a postage stamp, was covered in a fine network of wrinkles. On the left, the curl of a treble clef; in the middle, two notes, one dotted, one flagged. Jann explained each pen stroke, then refolded the paper, returned the book to the case, and held it out to her. "You must pass this on to someone else when you are my age."

She couldn't speak. He didn't seem to mind.

"Now, put it in a safe place," he said, "and let me offer a final toast."

AT THE RED Horse, Maile descended the cellar stairs into a din of clanking plates and arguments over soccer scores. She felt light-headed from the champagne, twice as hungry as before, and she hurried down to throw herself into the rest of the evening.

The basement was as wide as a meadow. Hundreds of Austrians filled rows of heavy trestle tables. At their feet dogs gnawed on ham bones tossed to them by their owners. Stocky waitresses in tightly laced dirndls fetched beer from chest-high kegs lining the walls. Students from the contest sat at a center table drinking from liter mugs.

They spotted Maile working her way toward them, and stood up to cheer and shout that their credit was about to run out. She arranged for a tab payable at the end of the week, then ordered another round and a dozen roasted chickens. Minutes later everything arrived at once: waitresses with dripping steins, men hefting a wooden plank with a row of crisp-skinned birds topped by slabs of bread. Contestants pulled off legs and wings, yelling jokes and congratulations from both ends of the table.

When the scraps were cleared away and more steins arrived, no one was allowed to touch them until kisses were exchanged across the table. The French harpist obliged with Jean-Paul. Brenda pecked the Dutch baritone on his nose. Kazuo leaned forward to give Maile a drunken smack on the lips and asked, "Where is Karl, the bah-stahd?" She scooped a glob of foam off her beer and smeared his cheeks as everyone hooted and beat their fists on the table.

"Karl 'n' Maile're getting married," Brenda yelled at Jean-Paul. "Where's my ring, cheapskate?"

He stiff-armed his stein and intoned, "To Herr Three-Seconds!"

Others knocked their steins against his, sloshing beer onto the table, into their laps, shouting, "The execution of Schubert!"

They savaged Karl and competed to tell their own stories about a single mistake that had ruined a performance and haunted them for months, years! So Maile, winner, don't feel bad for him, just hope he doesn't get a memory lapse in bed: ha, ha! She tried to be a good sport, for his sake, grinning until her jaw ached.

Finally they left to prowl through the heart of the Old City. Everyone waded into the archbishop's fountain, splashing and shrieking until policemen ordered them out under threat of arrest. Jean-Paul was carried off by two friends so drunk that they kept dropping him. Brenda broke a high heel and flung it into the river. Kazuo insisted she take his shoes, which fit, and he walked off in his socks whistling the Toreador's aria.

Long after midnight Maile climbed the stairs to her door. Her key went into the lock without a struggle. In the dark room she slipped out of her clothes and underwear, pulled apart her chignon, shook her head, and stood naked with her hair flowing over her shoulders and back. She lit the candles on the music stand. Between them she set the leather box Jann had given her, and took out the wooden locket on its velvet ribbon.

Had she really deserved to win? All the contestants, she knew, had attended special music schools or taken private lessons since childhood. It didn't seem possible that she had outstripped them after studying for less than three years. Winning one small yet important contest might have been sheer luck, and nothing was more fickle. Luck could desert her next time. Success was just seconds away from failure.

Carefully she opened the little book. The bit of paper inside slipped out as if it had a life of its own and fluttered to the floor. In the darkness at her feet it looked like a snowflake that could melt in an instant.

14

CAFÉ SCIMITAR WAS again full, but not overcrowded as on the day of the storm, and Baron von Gref sat by himself. When Maile was brought to his table, he repeated apologies made in his telegram: due to a pressing business trip, he had to rescind the invitation to visit his home. "Of course," he added, "I would not leave without speaking to you in person."

The pleasure she felt at seeing him again was familiar now, the thin monk's fringe, the glasses, the paunch, all agreeably professorial except for his beautiful dark blue suit. With a mischievous look he said, "I shall not be tedious about my hobby, just one map." He opened a nautical chart of Captain Cook's voyages through the Pacific. "This explorer commanded the finest technology of his day, fully equipped ships riding ten meters above sea level. Your navigators traveled thousands of kilometers in open canoes."

The mention of this came as a sudden and painful reminder of her lost life with Tūtū. "Yes." Maile spoke quietly, hoping to deflect questions about ancient Hawaii.

"Their methods remain a mystery to modern scientists," the baron remarked, and pointed to various islands and routes, then sighed and slid the map aside to reveal a newspaper clipping faded to the color of tea. "This has to do with a more important topic than my hobby." She looked at a photo of the Festival House decorated with dozens of Nazi banners: streamers from roofline to sidewalk, rectangles draped over the entrance, bouquets of miniature flags at eye level. The display was so florid she thought it bordered on satire but the caption was dated 1938.

"After the facade was primped in this manner," von Gref explained, "Toscanini refused to set foot inside. I thanked him, although to this day—thirty years later, mind—many here will not mention his name." He gave her an examining look. "If Hawaii had nothing to do with such matters, in Salzburg you will face them. Especially as a prize winner."

"I see," she said uncertainly.

"That is a brave response. However, a foreigner come to us from a great distance, is not able to 'see.' Allow me one example of a well-known detail Austrians never discuss. In 1945 Salzburg's honored son Werner von Wehlen fled ahead of the Allied advance. He had been a National Socialist for more than a decade. American soldiers found him hiding on a farm in Italy and sent him back across the border, a trip of several days standing up in a truck with twenty other prisoners. No doubt an unforgettable experience."

She pictured the glamorous conductor covered in road dust, hair lank, clothes filthy—a captured Nazi. She tried to feel surprise, to assume a shocked expression, but it was no use pretending. Last fall, soon after arriving here, in the wine cave Karl had suggested such a background.

"Forgive me if your teacher has already mentioned such this," von Gref said.

Jann's words, she thought: *Despite what anyone may think about von Wehlen's past . . .*

That put the conductor in a positive light.

"Now you must select your gift." The baron pulled over a small tray covered with a piece of linen. "Arnim has reserved tickets for your concert. I hope you will be our guest afterwards."

He raised the cloth and Maile saw a little silver figure of Orpheus holding a lyre, an enameled brooch of a harpsichord, a tiny gold flute. She picked up a small lace square embroidered white on white with a cluster of angels, their faces and hair emerging from a background of clouds like visible spirits embedded in the threads. "This," she said.

"Ah." Von Gref smiled. "Made by my great-aunt. She wrote frightful poetry in Vienna and founded the Salon for the Unmasking of Words, because corruption at court disgusted her. She had no artistic gift, just a keen suspicion that art could disguise evil." His gaze lingered on Maile, inviting comment, but she looked down again at the angels and thanked him.

✥ ✥ ✥

"WHAT A SULTAN'S ransom!" Professor Jann said. "Seventeen arias."

Opera scores were arranged on his piano desk, the lid, on music stands, on a bookcase. Maile joined him in scanning library copies with yellowed pages and pencil marks that showed decades of use: Mozart's most glorious roles for women. Today Jann would choose what she performed at the prizewinner's concert. Something conservative, she was sure, but agents would be in the audience, and she was determined to impress them with fire: Donna Elvira's passionate rage from *Don Giovanni*. As with *Carmen* and other forbidden fruit, she knew that aria only from practicing with Jean-Paul in the basement.

"I have given this piece the most consideration." Jann picked up a *Figaro* score. In silence they studied the countess's first aria, a plea to Amor: *Be attentive, O god of love* . . .

"Beautiful," she said. "Not very dramatic."

He laughed lightly. "Your usual complaint. For a prize concert I admit a need to impress—"

"With explosive coloratura!"

"Certainly not." He warned that singing with an orchestra for the first time would be humbling. A soloist had to fight off a sense of chaos produced by the massed sound of instruments. Arias from *Giovanni* or *Cosi* were dangerously heavy.

They argued their way through *Idomeneo* and *Titus*. After half an hour had come full circle to *Figaro*, and Maile felt on the losing end of the decision. "Donna Elvira," she said. "I have it memorized."

Jann gave her a suspicious look. "A little practicing on your own?"

"Can't I experiment? You once encouraged that." He didn't reply. She admitted being coached on the piece by Jean-Paul in exchange for a carton of cigarettes.

Brusquely Jann cleared his piano desk and paged to the aria. "Skip the recitative. Stand over there in the corner."

She took up her position and pictured herself as a Spanish noblewoman in Renaissance Madrid: white ruff, black gown, string of pearls. Bedded by Don Giovanni, cast aside, tortured by the memory of love.

"Well?" Jann played an introductory chord.

She inhaled so deeply it left her dazed, and she sang in accusing tones, "He betrayed me before heaven and earth . . . "

Jann fastened onto the melody, the pacing perilously swift. "Hold the tempo."

She tipped up her chin, cheeks prickling. He cued her next entrance with the stab of a forefinger. She hurled the phrase at him: "Shamed me and left me to mourn!"

"Six beats," he said, "not five and a half."

His fingers raced up the keys, playing the interlude with such intensity that it stole her concentration, and she didn't get a full breath as he passed the coloratura line to her, and she attacked it on instinct: "Though cast down . . . abandoned . . ."

Her response slipped perfectly into place, and their melodies entwined and caught fire. Jann's notes swarmed over her. She took them in as if gulping red wine.

"Draw back now," he shouted over the onward rush of the music.

In a logical corner of her mind she knew that he wasn't leading or bullying, they were simply entangled. She eased into the lyrical core of the piece, the rage for vengeance overcome by love.

"Forgive him and keep going," Jann cried out.

They recaptured the furious pace of the beginning, unleashed emotion held in check by human pity. "Forgives," she concluded. "Love forgives . . ."

Jann didn't bother to play the final phrase. "Quite so!" he exclaimed.

Maile breathed heavily, coming down, thinking that they had crawled into each other to make music. In ecstasy. No coddling. *Can you sing this or not? I can.*

"This really is a beastly aria," he said in a more critical tone. "The student orchestra will give it an adequate although not brilliant rendition, which is fine." With a pencil he made rapid notes on the score. "By the way, yesterday I turned down an agent who wanted you for Wagner this fall. An ambitious little theater on the Danish border. Good Lord. Certain death. Voices like yours make agents greedy."

She almost howled in disappointment. The Rosenkavalier claimed he could get her a Festival House audition, but true or not, that had to remain a secret. She dared to scowl. "When will I get my chance? It doesn't have to be Wagner."

Jann pointed to photos on the piano of himself in *Tosca, Don Carlo*. "In these works, the brass sections—not to mention the timpani—are so powerful a lead singer can lose ten pounds during a three-hour performance. Constant diaphragm pressure forces the liver four inches out of place. The stomach is compressed until it resembles a mashed orange."

She put a hand over her midriff. "You're scaring me."

"Good. Agents or conductors may approach you directly. I expect to be informed. Perhaps something can be worked out. I doubt it. Contracts are notoriously final."

Conductors, contracts. The words had sexual appeal.

"Another consideration: a tour of South Africa is very lucrative, but most artists have an unspoken agreement not to go there."

"Isn't a Hawaiian soprano too tan for Cape Town audiences?" She grinned. He didn't react. She turned on him in protest. "You're taking over my life!"

His expression remained unperturbed. "At twenty-eight I sang *Mephisto* against my teacher's advice. It took my voice six months to recover. Then I rushed from London to Hamburg to perform Boris four times in one week. Ego, ego. Critics ridiculed my exhausted czar." He picked up a small black-and-white photo. "I keep this as a reminder of my greatest mistake. You must live with yourself after your performing days are over."

A picture of two men in street clothes. After a moment she recognized a young Alexander Jann and an equally youthful Werner von Wehlen.

"Americans have their own mentality about culture," he said. "In Europe, artists were and still are held to a moral standard. Yes, such a position is old-fashioned and romantic and too often a farce, but for me it is reality."

"The two of you were friends?"

His eyes lit with a hard gleam as though dragging a memory into the present. "Von Wehlen conducted the victory concert when Paris fell to German troops. After the Allied victory, he evaded trial for war crimes and was put to work salvaging the Salzburg Festival. Briefly I sang under his baton." Jann replaced the photo with neat finality. "If you are offered a role in next year's *Rappresentazione*, I will do my all to see that you get it. In return, promise me you will not audition anywhere without consulting me. Then let's get back to work."

She imagined herself as Soul in the midst of angels and demons, swirling though life with them, climbing the stairs to paradise. The possibility of auditioning at the Festival House faded away.

"I promise."

THE AUGUST HEAT felt unnatural, tropical, the air moist enough to scoop up in handfuls. Thankfully, Jann thought, Salzburg suffered such temperatures only a few days a year. At home he changed into linen trousers, a cotton shirt, sandals, then threw open the front room windows in the hope of attracting a breeze off the river. Outside in the garden the flowers drooped in the late-day heat.

Dora peered in from the kitchen asking, *"Fisch oder Fleisch, Zander?"* Fish, please, he replied, and she said their *Jause* would be ready in five minutes. He heard the insistent rhythm of chopping. From a mail tray he picked up two telegrams that had just arrived: the first announced auditions for Bach concerts with Konsort Wien, the second for a leading role in *Rappresentazione*. Each, he felt, a perfect opportunity for Maile. He hated the thought of telling her because it signaled a further step in letting her go.

He couldn't wait until he had the house to himself, and chose the first number that occurred to him: nine. From the kitchen came a light sizzling sound. He shut it out and opened Plato's *Apologia*. The presence of his wife persisted.

Dora, who stayed slim for him, who assembled elegant little meals, who was intelligent and schooled, and to whom he now owed everything because he was no longer rich or famous enough to attract a fifth wife. Last night she'd distressed him with a confession. For months she had been giving money to the Rosenkavalier. Jann knew about years of similar payments to a certain Sondergeist, for his silence concerning her decade of sexual slavery. Even the idea of going through such degradation aroused Jann's deepest sympathy, but he'd never been able to rid himself of feeling that his own masculinity had been compromised—a stupid, deplorable attitude, he knew. He and Dora hadn't even met until years after the war. Before going to bed, they agreed that her only choice was to continue making discreet "legacy" payments; exposure would be ruinous to their lives in Salzburg.

Stubbornly Jann paged through *Apologia*, looking, as first intended, for the wisdom of Socrates on teaching and students. His work as a music professor continually inspired bursts of internal and external emotion, which was expected, but the harder edge of physical desire had been growing for months. It began, he now admitted, after Maile finally sang a perfect Suzanna and crowned him with roses, then it intensified at the contest when she so exquisitely expressed the hope of love while he sat behind the screen in the archbishop's chamber. An hour ago that same desire had become nearly unbearable with Elvira's aggressive eroticism as she begged Don Giovanni to resolve her passion.

Socrates on the role of the teacher: Jann studied a page, his Greek rusty. Nine lines were too many to translate. With difficulty he put together a single sentence: *Truth must be relentlessly pursed, not discovered like a lucky coincidence.* A poor version of the original, he thought, although the gist was there. Yes, yes, the true teacher lit a blaze in a student, including the flames of love, but directed those to the subject being taught. Seducing a student was easy, low, a pathetic form of self-love. His second wife had been a student, and he'd fed her need for his approval. A teacher had to bring all the glories of sex into play, then instead of crossing the physical line, focus on what was beyond sensuality: the creative soul. Socrates would view sex with a student as a betrayal, a sterile act, impotent.

Jann closed *Apologia*, feeling outmaneuvered. He didn't need to struggle with a language he'd studied fifty years ago to discover a truth. He didn't need a book, any book. He knew life's rules, and love's rules, and was confounded by his blithe willingness to trample them. To recapture, even briefly, the splendor of being young? To inhabit the great roles again, the rulers and rogues that had made him famous? The control of an overwhelming attraction should be ancient history for a man of his age.

"Komm, Zander," Dora called gently, *"fertig ist's."*

Nine was null and void. He would have to start over later.

Putting *Apologia* aside, he went join his wife. They conversed pleasantly but throughout the meal he plotted with the silent finesse of a Shakespeare villain. On what pretext could he get Maile to come here? Yes, the sauce was excellent. When would the house next be safely his for several hours? Indeed, the heat should lift by evening.

THE NEXT MORNING Maile entered the recital hall with two minutes to spare. Her thoughts vacillated between the exhilaration of me, me, me, up there in front of the orchestra, and the panic of being one voice pitted against so many instruments. Violinists and cellists called out jokes: they would play only Russian repertoire after the Soviets invaded Austria, the conservatory would be renamed the Stalinareum.

As she mounted the stage, the musicians fell silent. She walked into what felt like a cloud of respect and envy, all those eyes, everyone thinking, Prove yourself, we're just part of the background. She faced away from the orchestra to stand between the conductor's podium and the first violinist. Her audience of three sat in the middle of the hall: Professor Jann, the registrar, the head of the conducting department.

"*So, meine Herrschaften,*" the registrar announced. "*Elvira aus* Don Giovanni.*"

The first chord was so loud she clenched her fists in surprise. No friendly piano to start her off. The student conductor had a florid style with a looping beat she could hardly follow. The string players just behind her gave off astonishing vibrations that struck her back like a collapsing wave. Every *fortissimo* shook the wooden floorboards underfoot. Worse was the massed sound Jann had described: a whirl of violins, violas, and cellos, the orchestra's workhorses, which she was supposed to count on, and did, but only for a few measures until flutes and clarinets joined in to create a flood of wailing sonorities.

She sang in desperate search of rhythmic or tonal cues; melodies parallel to hers were embedded in different instruments, no easy echo from an oboe, no matching harpsichord line. The conducting professor ignored her to constantly stop his protégé: "Repeat measure fifteen! The initial trills are impossibly muddy."

Vibrations continued to slam into her horizontally and vertically, a weird, stunning effect, like being trapped by opposing waves and tides. And with an orchestra of only twenty-five! Not the sixty and more instruments required for *Aida*. For twenty minutes she barely hung on. Jann sat rigid and expressionless, by tradition not allowed to comment. The student conductor gave her no attention as he wrestled with the greater task of holding so many musicians together. Finally there was a runthrough. Maile got a flying upbeat and sang, "Hell has opened to swallow the betrayer!" Cellos growled out earthquake sounds, predicting Don Giovanni's doom. "God's mercy will not stay the arm of justice!" The orchestral answer came with an unexpected, perfect force that nearly lifted her off the trembling floor as her projecting voice and the accumulated instruments fused in a violent expression of hatred and love.

Wow, she thought, and missed her next entrance.

Ten minutes later, Jann led her out to the corridor. She still shivered with excitement and could have sung on and on for the sheer joy of it. He walked slowly and heavily, as if he had just run a marathon.

"Not bad," he said. He gave her a honey lozenge. For the dress rehearsal, he told her to follow the first violin for tempo and cues. "Watch just the tip of the bow. Your peripheral vision must take in the conductor to your left and reality to your right. Often the concert master is the true leader."

She nodded, proud to receive insider's advice. First violin. Tip of the bow.

"Go rest. You must let all your muscles ease. Jaw, neck, back. Off with you."

Outside the conservatory she felt ecstatic and huge for having survived. "Not bad" meant excellent. Meant superb. Meant marvelous, my dear. Every hedge and tree glowed at her with an intense green. The sky throbbed blue. She walked down Schwarzstrasse, feeling the entire orchestra trailing behind her, an immense, invisible cape of sound.

      √   √   √

A DAY LATER at the registrar's office, Maile got a free ticket to the prizewinner's concert for Frau Metzger in the hope of paying off her old debt for *Body and Soul*. She was also given two telegrams and an envelope, which aroused her curiosity so much that she opened them in the hall as students walked around her.

Her prize money would arrive at the conservatory tomorrow. In cash! *"Please present your passport as identification."* The second telegram, from Professor Jann, invited Maile to visit his home at 2:00 p.m. She couldn't quite take in such a break in the traditional student-teacher relationship, but of course she would go.

The third message was handwritten in English: *At noon today you are scheduled for a five-minute interview with Herr Maestro Werner von Wehlen at the Festival House. Be prompt. Signed, A.E.G., Secretary.*

She bit her lips and went outside before someone she knew asked what was so exciting.

In her mind she heard a voice from the past: Cool head, main thing. This afternoon at Jann's house there would be tea, served formally by his wife—a huge compliment. But before that, there would be von Wehlen, who wanted to speak to the contest winner. Was the Rosenkavalier responsible for this chain of contacts that led to the top? It made no difference. A five-minute interview wasn't time enough to sing anything. Talking to von Wehlen would be harmless; no chance of being offered a job. The Festival still had three weeks to run, and ill performers, even in minor roles, were always replaced by experienced singers flown in from Berlin, Rome, London.

All the way back to her room Maile practiced an imaginary conversation. Every sentence, she decided, had to begin with Herr Maestro to avoid accidentally addressing him as *Du*. Upstairs she waited in a knot of impatience for the approach of noon. Walking to the Festival House would take only ten minutes. Less. Finally the Dom bells struck the three-quarter hour.

Frau Metzger called out from below, "A gentleman of quality to see Frau Manoa!" Maile grabbed her purse, then hesitated. "Quality" was the landlady's word for any man in a good suit, and there was no need for von Wehlen's secretary to come here. Unless to cancel the interview.

She crept down to the front door as if moving quietly could ward off bad luck.

Arnim peered in with a coy smile. "News from the Scimitar's highest level reached my ears," he said. "Champagne is a wonderful betrayer of Festival House secrets."

The sight of him startled her. "Has something gone wrong?" She stepped outside.

"Not unless a Soviet tank division is rolling down the autobahn and no one has informed me." He gave her a mock salute. "I've come to escort you. I promise to watch the time."

At a brisk pace they went through courtyards and alleyways to Furtwängler Garten. The sunny little park was deserted except for an elderly woman dozing on a bench with a dachshund puppy curled in her lap. "Twelve minutes remaining," Arnim said. "I congratulate you on your contest triumph." He bowed over Maile's hands and kissed one, then the other, his black hair falling forward. Her wrists tingled at his touch.

He straightened up. "Someday I shall prove myself worthy of the marvelous soprano from the Pacific who would have thrilled Wolfgang himself, however, at the moment I can only bristle with envy. For years I have struggled to gain a Festival audition." He stepped toward the old woman, flung out an arm, and sang, *"Mein lieee-ber Schwaaan..."*

His thin voice was a tuneless screech. The dachshund tumbled to the ground, barking frantically, and its owner snapped awake. Arnim sang another line to her, proclaiming himself Protector of Brabant. The woman gave him a baffled stare, gathered up the puppy, and hurried away.

"Ach," Arnim sighed. "My audience."

Maile looked at him in shock, an idiotic amateur who wailed in public at the first available stranger. He flicked at the bench with a silk handkerchief and gestured for her to sit. She perched on the edge like a nervous bus passenger. "Come with me tonight to the lakes," he whispered. "I am your Siegfried. There is a ravine, a waterfall, raw nature—"

She pulled away.

"My dear diva," he declared, "I beg pardon. Of course you have other concerns at present." He checked his watch. "I am told that being alone with Herr Maestro, even briefly, has a strange effect on people."

Hand in hand they skirted an open market. From an ironmonger's shop came the sound of hammering, the sizzle of metal plunged into water. A man stepped outside and something at his back flashed in the sunlight. Maile shaded her eyes against the glare, then stopped dead at the sight of Karl. He carried a scythe. His shirt had been washed so often the armpits were shredded. Karl looked from Maile to the dark-haired stranger holding her hand, dressed in the latest gentlemen's casual wear from Milan, and he said, "By the five wounds of Christ."

Arnim gave him an annoyed glance, as if he hadn't quite heard and couldn't be bothered. "If you do not mind," he murmured, taking Maile's elbow.

Karl stepped in front of them. A scruffy three-day beard covered his cheeks.

"See here," Arnim said with polite insistance.

"New friend, Maile?" Karl asked.

"Meet my…" she said, struggling to sound indifferent. "This is …"

Karl smirked and extended his right hand. Arnim made no move to take it. Maile stared down at a mass of blisters healing into calluses, the palm tough and scored with brown cracks, then Karl looked down as well, withdrew his hand as if concealing evidence, and walked off.

"Come back to the Mozarteum," she said. He kept going, the blade glinting, mocking her. "Schubert!" she shouted.

Arnim tugged her toward the Festival House. "How," he asked with irritable emphasis, "do you know such a son of the land?"

"He's a pianist," she insisted.

"With those hands? Pardon my skepticism."

"He played beautifully at the competition."

They crossed Hofstallgasse, Arnim scolding, "Slowly, now. You must not rush in like a tardy office worker. And do choose your friends with more care. One who uses a scythe does not enhance an artistic image."

"He's a musician, not some amateur." She went ahead to speak to a Festival House guard and stepped inside.

VON WEHLEN'S WAITING room had the same intimidating elegance as the archbishop's palace except that everything was modern: black-and-white domino carpet, black leather chairs, chrome lamps, black abstract sculpture on a white marble table. Maile's hands were damp and her pulse was racing. Five minutes seemed like barely enough time for introductions. She looked at an onyx wall clock and watched the dying seconds of the minute now passing.

The fame of conductors no longer mystified her, their immense salaries, the exaggerated respect they commanded. If singers joked about the silent baton—What does it sound like?—a soprano couldn't lead a Beethoven overture past the first measure. One page of an orchestral score had up to sixty instruments on twenty staff lines with a half dozen clefs. A conductor had to grasp what amounted to a complex math problem, and use tempo, cues, and volume to create art. Werner von Wehlen knew dozens of scores by heart. He dominated all the artists around him, building a vast, ordered tapestry of sound while he remained mute, a figure of immense power and sensuality.

She glanced around the anteroom, searching for any touch of color. A flat glass box on a wall had a display in yellowish brown. She got up to examine it: rows and rows of small pointed objects, perhaps a hundred, similar to arrowheads, vaguely animal-like. Not quite art, not quite natural history. Bird's beaks, she realized. Neatly detached from the skulls and arranged in horizontal lines. Songbirds? Extinct birds?

From an overhead speaker she heard a man's voice, *"Frau Manoa, bitte sehr."*

An inner door opened with a soft rush of air. She entered a larger black-and-white room. Von Wehlen sat behind a desk of burnished steel. He wore a soft black turtleneck sweater. No watch or ring. His thick silver hair was combed straight back. His skin had the taut sheen of a swimmer's. A potently attractive man, coolly aware of it.

He motioned her to sit, and in the same moment the sound of a soprano filled the room, accompanied by piano. *"Wo-hin floh—en..."*

Maile sat forward, shocked to hear her own voice. Her singing, a tape from the contest, she realized, although recording anything had been forbidden. Von Wehlen braced his elbows on the desk and conducted to himself with light movements of one hand. Making a tape on the sly no longer mattered, she was terrified of mistakes he might hear. She wanted to be anywhere except in his private office as he quietly absorbed her best effort.

When the *andantino* section concluded, he signaled with a wave. The tape stopped. "Only two other sopranos have mastered those initial phrases," he murmured to himself. "A delicate agony of love in doubt. The listener is elated." He raised a forefinger. She heard a soft whirr, then the *andantino* section replayed. He listened, signaled, and the sound cut off. "The transition to *allegro* fails," he said. She shriveled into her chair.

He put the tips of his fingers together and focused on her. "Your gift is a combination of raw talent and naiveté, which will fade quickly, and high intelligence, which can be formed, and appearance, which is not to be underrated. I like young musicians for all those reasons. In your rendition, I hear an important emotion: the ability to hate. This interests me. You?"

Everything about him stunned her. She didn't like the question but knew it was a test. Cautiously she replied, "All emotion interests me, Herr Maestro."

"Why hate in particular?"

She clenched her toes inside her shoes. "It's a mirror."

"What kind of mirror?"

"A reflection of transforming love. Denial is another form of recognition." She cringed to hear herself straining to speak like a philosopher.

"You are pretending, although it is rather successful." He seemed tempted to smile. She wasn't sure if he had praised her or condemned her. "Anyone," he said, "who relinquishes her country to travel a great distance for the sake of music possesses admirable fanaticism. That trait is more important than talent. Beautiful music is luxurious trivia. Its secret resides in the arousal of fear." He paused with deliberate drama. "Turmoil in the East Bloc makes listeners twice as sensitive. Have you noticed?"

"No, Herr Maestro."

"Good. Only a student trying to impress me would agree. Musicians from alien cultures like the Pacific exist only to validate European culture. We must move with the times even if our composers never intended singers to be Africans or Asiatics. Your skin color is light enough to be acceptable. One aria on tape proves nothing. You must audition for me. This will take place before your Mozarteum concert."

From an overhead speaker, a male voice: *"Herr Maestro, bitte sehr. Studio Eins."*

Von Wehlen rose and gave her a final examining stare. He walked toward a back door that slid aside as he approached it.

She felt as if he'd slapped her: validate our culture, Mozart never intended, light enough to be acceptable. Yet, despite all that—an audition.

15

SHORTLY BEFORE TWO o'clock Maile found her way to Kreuzritter-weg. The tree lined street of Baroque-style homes had display gardens laid out in perfect symmetry. She kept recalling Herr Maestro's words and picturing his office, the steel desk, the sound system. He reminded her of no one. A great artist with such a demanding schedule literally did not have a minute to spare, yet he had asked questions and listened carefully to her replies. Had not invited her to audition, he'd demanded it. Which meant that he and Jann must be in contact with each other, she thought, about her. She had won the contest for Jann and could now present him with the gift of more success, a von Wehlen audition. Perhaps something can be worked out. Jann's exact words.

Number Eight was an impressive stone villa. Her thoughts reversed and she approached the door in fear that Jann would tear into her for going to the Festival House. If he knew, and he might not know. Not yet. He and Baron von Gref were old friends and no doubt both considered von Wehlen hopelessly compromised. Soul of a Nazi, even today.

Jann heard the door knocker drop, brass on brass, a sharp *tak*. He gave the mirror in the foyer a final critical glance. He wore his hair in the current fashion, much longer than the styles of ten years ago. Appropriate for a man in his sixties? He ran a hand over his jaw; too much cologne? Maile had only seen him in a suit and tie, never an open-necked shirt and summer slacks.

She greeted him with a look of nervous uncertainty. That was expected, he felt, from someone who was still officially a student. Smoothly he invited her in, a spider disguised as a gentleman at leisure—this meeting so calculated, the invitations from Konsort Wien and *Rappresentazione* waiting, Dora at the veterinarian with her schnauzer. He reminded himself that seduction was an art, not a crime against nature.

Maile paused to look around the front room. Her impression was of a beautiful stage set made to be lived in: long magenta silk curtains, walls lined with books, a dark green armchair and hassock, watercolors of costumes for *Boris Godunov*, an antique ivory chess set, warriors with scimitars, the queen veiled. She had never been inside such a home, not in Hawaii or New York. Gradually she realized that no one else had come in to be introduced. No sounds came from other rooms. Only the two of them were here.

He gave her time to enter his private world, filled with mementos of his finest roles and fiercest battles. She seemed appreciative but edgy. "My dear," he asked, "would you care for tea?" In the kitchen, water simmered on the stove, a tray of dainties stood waiting. "Sherry, or perhaps a glass of wine?"

She turned to him with an expression of longing, of needing to speak, or perhaps of agitation—he wasn't sure, but it was a vulnerability that delivered her to him. He put both hands on her shoulders and said, "At your orchestral rehearsal I heard a certain maturity. A sharp reminder that our relationship will end soon."

She regarded him with surprise. "I only remember being terrified."

"You have reached a certain plateau." He heard his tone intensify, and he struggled to hold back. "You will never again be as dependent on me." She stared up at him, slipping under the spell of his praise. He overflowed with emotion that had haunted him all week, all month, since last fall, when she had arrived to belie every cliché: no Pacific Island pleasure girl, no exotic servant eager to please, no pampered beauty expecting easy assignments, no gifted student throwing prima donna fits before she had the right. The urge no man could control came over him with its familiar heat. He pulled her against him, and felt her breasts pressed to his chest, his groin at her waist. He wanted to swoop her into his arms and bear her like a gift to the little side room with the vase of roses from his own garden. In dizzying elation he waited for her to raise her arms to embrace him, to consent with her eyes to a kiss.

Maile was electrified by the invisible shift from professor to lover, in his home among the things he treasured. She wanted whole worlds from him. At the Mozarteum, for a long, long time, she knew now, the tension of passion had hovered between them. Fulfilling it would be natural, like the final phrase in an aria. She had idealized Herr Kammersänger from her first sight of him in his studio. From that day onward he'd offered her slivers of his soul. Now he would show himself to her in his bedroom. They would undress. The pleasure and assurance of mutual seduction filled her. She pictured white chest hair. The thought of it pushed her forward into reality, and memories of everything that had happened today; a collision of messages, possibilities, the certainty of again being summoned to the Festival House.

Her arms did not rise to embrace him. He waited an instant, still hoping, but whether in surprise at his touch or in courteous rejection, she didn't move at all. With an inward shudder of humiliation, he released her and stepped back, a small motion that felt as painful as a violent break. "Of course we are not finished yet as student and teacher," he said. "Sit down, I have news for you."

They eyed each other awkwardly, still retreating from the edge of sexual intimacy. He seated her at a small table and brought a tray with pastries, sherry, tiny glasses, and two telegrams. Konsort Wien. *Rappresentazione.* He promised to keep her informed.

Maile sipped her sherry, didn't like the taste, and took a bite of *Doboschtorte.* "Delicious," she murmured. Jann nodded, his expression neutral. He doesn't know, she thought. No idea where I went before coming here. Her stomach stirred, sick with dread. It was impossible to have things both ways.

She forced herself to say the only thing that mattered. "Today at noon I had an interview at the Festival House with Maestro von Wehlen. He asked me to audition."

Jann lowered his chin and adjusted his gaze as if taking aim at a target. "Soon?"

"Tomorrow or the day after, when he has time. Before Friday."

Silently Jann went to a cabinet, poured himself a glass of cognac, and drank it off. Maile gripped the arms of the chair, rigid with embarrassment. He glared and set the glass down, his neck stiff. "You should not see me like this," he said. "Not because of drunkenness. You cannot possibly understand, you are too young. Does nothing occur to you?"

228

She shook her head dumbly.

"If you audition well and he hires you for even a single concert, you will join the elite circle of international soloists. At your prize concert you will appear as von Wehlen's soprano. Naturally," he added, "you fear betraying me." He pursed his lips in bitter amusement. "Perhaps I am being taught my own lesson: no teacher, however advanced, can possess a student, however advanced. I can no longer dictate important decisions to you. These you must make yourself."

He walked over to the front door, opened it, and gestured for her to leave.

Outside on Kreuzritterweg, her head felt full of waves that surged and broke, surged and broke. If von Wehlen hired her, there would be no slow climb through the lower ranks of mediocre theaters. A voice teacher could never give a singer the opportunities that a conductor had at his fingertips. Yes, the difference between the two men was much more than that, but was she responsible for other people's history? How much did their wars matter to her? In Tūtū's day, ninety percent of Hawaiians had been wiped out by foreign diseases, the survivors doomed to poverty. Should Austrians feel sympathy for Polynesians?

THE ROSENKAVALIER FINISHED his afternoon café rounds and crossed the river to the Mozarteum. Once a year, by prearrangement, he went to a rarely used delivery door. On his way to the back of the building, he always paused to look up and recall the unforgettable sight of three hanged men. Not at the front of the conservatory, which would have been too public; instead the bodies tucked away but still easily accessible for viewing. How clever to have them executed here, a testament to the power of *der Führer,* who loved the arts but tolerated no deviation from his laws. Life had never regained that high standard.

With a sense of nostalgic disappointment, the Rosenkavalier lowered his gaze and knocked on the prescribed door at the prescribed time. The registrar's assistant passed him an envelope containing fifty tickets to the Mozarteum prizewinner's concert. Sales had been brisk. Seats at twenty schillings allowed every pensioner and shopgirl to attend. The Rosenkavalier disliked dealing in such small change, although soon the concert's soloist would audition at the Festival House. Arranged without his assistance, but such a significant invitation didn't mean witch shit unless a contract was signed. Then the Mooress could be approached with a claim that he had laid the groundwork. She wouldn't dare make inquiries and risk revealing a connection to him— yet he'd only be paid if she auditioned successfully. Singers were pissy, as breakable as glass figurines at a summer carnival. They failed all the time.

"Eh!" The Rosenkavalier snorted in disgust. He pocketed the tickets and walked off toward Maxglan to deliver a payment to the mother of a tenor's baby, provided by the tenor himself after drawn-out negotiations. By the time that was done, the second seating of café customers would be in place.

OUT WHERE THE bus line ended and the green hay fields rose steeply from the road, Karl paused to wipe sweat from his forehead. He gripped the scythe again, swung in perfect, angry rhythm, and a row of stalks fell with a whish that ended in a clang. He scowled.

Every time the blade struck a concealed rock, the cutting edge lost a fraction of its bite. He used to file it automatically at the end of each row, regardless of how many stones he hit or whether he sensed a drag on his swing. Now he inspected the new blade after each clang. From his shirt pocket he took a magnifying glass, clamped it to the scythe, and began removing the gouge. His father said that only a man who needed to cut an abscess out of a cow's eye spent that much time honing metal.

The quiet zeet-zeet of his file gave Karl an obsessive kind of satisfaction. He was just taking a little vacation from music. Of course Maile was right that his career wasn't over because of one contest— dear Schubert, damn Schubert.

He returned to slashing at the ripe hay and thought about Prague. The volatile situation both inspired and depressed him. The university students' Action Plan for the Future had been accelerated. He was assigned to keep track of expenses: train tickets to border towns; food for refugees in hiding; soap and razors for those who fled with only their clothes. Being so close to important events and yet locked out rekindled his anger. He attacked the field into mid and late afternoon, scouring stalks off the slope, the neat pattern of arches left in the stubble giving him no pleasure.

Finally he dragged the hay into rolls he could get his arms around. Down the slope he glimpsed movement in the tall weeds. He hadn't heard the bus arrive, not listening for it; someone walking uphill past the trees. Her small figure grew larger: the victor, the one person he wanted to see, couldn't bear to see. With the tip of the scythe he hooked another heap of hay.

Maile continued to the end of the path but Karl ignored her and kept working. She sat down to wait him out. After leaving Jann's house, she had walked aimlessly along the river. The heavy placidness of the water did not still the phantom waves that pursued her. In her room she put on flat shoes, and then took the bus to the countryside without knowing what to say when she found Karl.

At last, sullenly silent, he joined her. They sat side by side in the darkening meadow below the pond where he had played his horn on a night she could hardly recall. Felled clover and wildflowers lay around them in damp heaps. His arms were crisscrossed with grass cuts and bumpy from insect bites. His beard had grown in more and hid the off-center cleft in his chin. Now that it couldn't be seen she missed it, a small, odd feature she hadn't thought about for weeks, months— how long since the night they met and he compared her to Gauguin?

All at once Karl started talking in an angry flow of words that excluded her. After a lecture about the dynamics of musical memory, he lit into Arnim, and ripped up shorn clumps of clover like a fussy gardener dissatisfied with his work. "That limp cucumber, that pathetic photo-model boy." He leaned at her, giving off a rank odor of sweat.

She sat back, controlling her temper. "He's just an opera fan."

"Oh, Blood of Christ. He sees you as Tannhäuser's naked Venus."

"Stop acting like I've slept with him."

"You'll never marry an aristo, you know."

"My ancestors were ruling chiefs."

"Hawaiian ancestors?" Karl sniffed, affecting the droopy-eyed expression of a cartoon marquis. "Here that's the equivalent of Gypsy royalty, nowhere near noble enough. Besides, you're a racial mixture. No aristo will stand for that in a wife."

No peasant either, she realized. Not in a country where people believed that skin color ruined bed sheets. "Shut up about marriage."

In an abrupt shift of mood he said, "My family is killing me. Years ago they only agreed to music studies so I wouldn't take a job in Africa working on irrigation." He paused with a pained expression that cramped his face. "You should see them at a recital. Whether I play a Beethoven funeral march or a Mozart minuet, they have the same embalmed expressions. Respect, respect, and afterwards the same comment, 'How nice.' " He yanked at a loose shoelace, his lips drawn back, ugly with anger. The leather strip snapped and he tossed it into the grass. "When my sister listens to a concerto she's just relieved to sit for an hour instead of milking the goats. I can't imagine your family. Hawaii. Jesus." Suddenly gentle, he said, "Tell me. Please."

Again he was the man she had known. She told him about her mother, a cook for the army, dead at forty-two; her father, a bus driver; her eight brothers and sisters, most with children before they were out of high school; her ten years of singing at a hotel.

Karl listened without interrupting, squinting out at the dusky sky. "At first I was sure you were rich. Perhaps we're more alike than anyone could guess. Except—" He coughed, an artificial, stunted sound. "In Salzburg, one decent but not excellent pianist makes no difference to anybody."

Mentally she filled in what he had not said: Except for giving up.

He gripped his knees. "There's a lot more at stake in the real world. Last week four editors escaped from Prague. My university network got them here, but mental patients and criminals are also being shoved into Austria. We have to hide artists when they cross or our police arrest them as 'undesirables.' "

She let out a dry laugh. "Are you going to cut barbed wire on the border? Sneak past land mines? You're wasting yourself on dreams. Where's your other kind of nerve?"

He sat motionless, then said in a quiet, considered tone, "You took your great risk to come here. Americans can do that. Austrians are strangled by history, tradition, the weight of it. I'm not complaining. You're just freer than I ever was, or can be."

The sun had gone down behind the mountains. In the darkness his face was barely visible, but she sensed a chance for honesty between them that would slip away unless she grabbed it. "Von Wehlen wants me to audition," she said. "Jann told me I have to make my own decision." She started to mention standing in his front room, his embrace, his unmistakable attraction. It would sound like trashy gossip.

"Why do they hate each other?" she asked.

Karl groaned and lay back on the ground. A swarm of midges hovered over his face. He batted them away and described the country after the war, occupied by foreign armies, the Festival almost dead, but Jann was its leading bass and people were hungry for music. When von Wehlen was allowed back in Salzburg, he forbade mention of his Reich years, even though everyone knew he had conducted birthday concerts for Hitler. Jann asked him to make a public statement about the civic role of a conductor, the traditional moral responsibility to music's purity—in other words, to show some regret. Von Wehlen refused. Jann came to his own *Don Giovanni* dress rehearsal in street clothes, handed envelopes to the soloists, and left. In each envelope was a page with one word on it. Together they made up a sentence: A WAR WAS JUST FOUGHT TO DEFEAT FASCISTS.

"But goes back before the war," Karl said.

In the distance Maile saw a bright yellow flash, the headlights of the last bus from the city. Soon the driver would turn around below at the end of the route and rest briefly before making his final return trip.

Karl sat up. "Von Wehlen's orchestra always had Gestapo informers, but he held onto his best Jewish musicians. Then in '45, when things were falling apart, he handed over three violinists. They escaped, got arrested here, and were hanged behind the Mozarteum. My father says the bodies were there for a week. He saw them. Everybody did."

She recoiled as if punched in the stomach. "Why haven't I heard about this? The way you talk it's common knowledge."

"It is. Von Wehlen's past is an embarrassment to a lot of people. Including me."

A breeze brought the faint mechanical sounds of the bus. She patted the dark ground in search of her purse.

Karl passed it to her, and with sudden athletic grace he swung himself onto his knees and loomed over her. "We're stuck. I have to get Czechs across the border, you dream of singing Desdemona at the Festival, and Jann has an ethical streak running through him like the Salzach at full flood." He covered her mouth with a rough kiss tasting of sweat and salt. "Luck to both of us."

VON WEHLEN'S SECRETARY informed Maile by telegram that auditions took place between eleven and one. Several hours in advance she would be notified. Until then she was not to contact the Festival House. If she canceled for any reason, the audition would not be rescheduled.

She stayed in her room. The leather case with the Mozart locket was gathering dust and she slid it into a drawer. On her desk the embroidered angels from Baron von Gref were in danger of picking up ink stains. She wrapped the little cloth in tissue paper and put it away with the locket.

At ten o'clock she received a hand-delivered message asking if she could sing for the conductor of *Rappresentazione* at noon. Her memory of the production had faded, and the risk of conflict with von Wehlen's unknown schedule was too great. She declined with thanks, then had to justify the decision to herself: Herr Maestro's violinists were likely not betrayed by him but by an informant. Or maybe, when the Gestapo came, he had given in to avoid a greater catastrophe.

By twelve-thirty it was clear that her audition had to take place tomorrow, and no later than one o'clock because her prize concert was that same night. What if von Wehlen's secretary forgot to notify her? He dealt with dozens of international stars and ongoing Festival events. Taking a walk or going outside for the rest of the day had no appeal. She washed her hair and sat with the wet strands over the back of a chair. Unconsciously she listened for the soft rush of surf against shore, the rise and break and fall of waves that went on and on and made the world whole. She cleaned her shoes, did sit-ups with her feet hooked under the bed frame. Afternoon melted into evening. She recalled that von Wehlen admired her fanaticism. The secret of music had to do with fear. Hatred interested him. She couldn't nap, study, eat.

At nine-forty-five, she heard Frau Metzger's heavy tread on the stairs. A white envelope was slipped under the door. The bell at the entrance hadn't rung, and Maile couldn't imagine who wanted to contact her. *"Herr Maestro is unavailable tomorrow,"* she read. *"Please be ready to audition at 10:30 p.m."*

She dropped the note. One hour's notice at this time of night was outrageous, unfair! She could have been at a movie, or having a glass of wine with friends. Or asleep, and not even found the envelope until tomorrow morning.

Her voice had lost its edge. Even a brief warm-up in her room would have neighbors knocking on their walls with broomsticks. She piled up her hair and took the required three scores. Minutes later she was headed toward the Mozarteum. Waiters dawdled outside the Silver Fawn as busboys laid fresh linens for the next round of diners. She hurried through deserted streets, crossed the empty footbridge. At the conservatory she got into the basement through an unlocked door, vocalized in the dark, and went back out.

Twenty minutes after receiving the telegram Maile arrived at the Festival House, breathless from so much fast walking. A guard led her into the foyer. A rumble of Berlioz came from the main hall. Tonight's concert was being conducted by a von Wehlen protégé, and she figured that as soon as it concluded and the audience left, it would be her turn on the Grand Stage. That seemed unusual, even strange, but Herr Maestro made his own rules.

A woman in a blazer and short skirt motioned to her. They went up a flight of stairs to an ordinary corridor. As they walked, the sound of the orchestra grew fainter until it seemed to be coming from a distant radio. Neither the guard nor the woman had spoken. Maile wondered if they knew who she was.

"Mein Vorsingen?" she asked.

"Natürlich." The woman stopped to open a door and gave her a pat on the shoulder. *"Bitte sehr, Frau Manoa. Der Herr Maestro kommt."*

She left and Maile stepped into a huge room with scenery flats piled against the opposite wall. A cluster of dark spotlights hung from a bare beam. Far to the left was a small platform about twelve feet high; next to it, a scuffed grand piano. No windows, no chairs. A large clock face showed the time, ten-fifteen. Instead of the Grand Stage, she had been assigned to a room used for work and storage. The world's most famous conductor would hear her sing in a warehouse.

A short, fat man with brilliant blue eyes and kinky blond hair came in and introduced himself as her accompanist, Egon Janowitz. At the piano they did a blitz review of *tempi* and *rubato*. He promised to pay attention to her breath marks. She sang a quick scale to test the room's acoustics. Her voice seemed to be sucked into a hole that gave nothing back. She tried again, heard the same effect, and turned to Egon with a stare of panic.

"Sing away from the flats," he said. "When they're stacked up like that, the area in front of them is a dead zone. Project toward the door."

Von Wehlen entered promptly. From fifteen meters away, Maile saw only a silver head of hair moving to the center of the room. His secretary called out for her to step onto the platform. Wooden blocks at the back formed steep stairs with no railing. She bent forward for balance, teetered up in her high heels, then positioned herself on a plank rectangle no larger than her mattress.

Egon conferred briefly with Herr Maestro, returned to the piano and said, "Elvira."

The piece she'd managed to get Jann to approve for her concert, she thought, a dizzying transfer of allegiance. She nodded down to Egon who now sat four meters below.

"Moment," von Wehlen called out. He stood *sportlich-elegant* in a gray sweater and trousers. On a side wall his secretary flipped a row of switches, plunging the room into blackness, instantly replaced by a blue-tinted spot that enclosed Maile in a narrow column of light. She swayed and clamped her legs together to steady herself.

"Also jetzt," von Wehlen said.

She felt on the edge of the pit that doomed Don Giovanni. Egon played the opening chord.

"What monstrous excess!" she sang.

The piano replied with a heavy, beating rhythm that mapped out a chase through twisting streets. She imagined a horse, a ghost horse behind her as she fled down alleys in the Old City.

"What terrible love . . . " Her mind leaped ahead, a woman who could outrun man or beast. Beyond the spotlight von Wehlen's shadowy outline paced in the cavernous interior. She accused her betrayer as he bore down, a horse that filled her with exalted vengeance and terror. The aria ended in a cry of forgiveness. She heard her final note echo and knew that her voice had not landed in the dead zone. Spain, horse. What horse? Why a horse?

She blinked as the spot was switched off and the overhead lights came on. Her face and neck were wet with perspiration. In the distance she saw von Wehlen fold his arms, movements that made him appear to undulate like a mirage. Then he spoke firmly, but she caught only the final word: office. He walked toward the door with his secretary.

It was over. He was leaving.

The door to the hall swung open, and four men in dark suits entered. Von Wehlen paused with a startled tilt of his head, then he joined the men and all went out.

"That is odd," Egon said. He rose and shuffled her scores into a stack.

Maile crept down off the platform. Egon kept staring at the open door. "Personal security never escorts Herr Maestro inside the house," he added. Dully she took the scores from him.

He walked with her toward the door, saying, "Congratulations. The key phrase is 'Make an appointment with my office.' Not 'my scholarship foundation,' which has thousands of applicants every year for two openings. Go first thing tomorrow morning. Now excuse me, I'm going to find out what sort of little crisis is brewing."

"Does 'office' mean a contract?"

"That has always been the case."

Büro, office, she thought. *Vertrag*, contract. Make an appointment. *Melden Sie sich in meinem Büro.* A beginner's contract for next year.

She found her way back to the main entrance, feeling drained and yet wildly excited.

The departing Berlioz audience was streaming outside in a warm cloud of pleasure. They exclaimed over the freshness of the evening air, perfect for *saumon mousse en croute*, in honor of all things French. She slipped into their midst, wanting to take hold of glittering strangers and shout, *A toast a toast a toast to von Wehlen's new soprano!*

16

AT THREE IN the morning, a whore passing behind the Silver Fawn told the Rosenkavalier about a rumor she'd heard from two different customers in the last hour. He hurried across the city to the train station and rapped on the watchman's window, telling him to turn on his radio, *Jetzt, wichtig ist's!* A dozing cabdriver yawned and got out to see what was worth a fuss at this hour. The men listened until the announcer repeated the bulletin, then the Rosenkavalier took five cartons of Turkish cigarettes on credit and slipped away. The few night workers who heard the news rushed home to rouse relatives, but in most of the city word spread slowly until dawn: a radio clicked on just long enough to confirm the worst, then shut off as if silence could erase what had just been broadcast into a bedroom, a kitchen. .

While theatergoers slept heavily after rich food and cognac at midnight, ordinary people with jobs awakened to the accumulating staccato of announcements in the same voice, coming from buildings along Getreidegasse, on both sides of the river, and all the way to the outskirts of Salzburg where the last houses stood. Men and women cursed under their breath and crossed themselves. As time passed, they raised their voices. On the Old City's streets they asked each other, Who will help us? A jittery porter at an elite hotel refused to fetch luggage belonging to a wealthy couple and walked away shouting like a town crier, "The pigs're leaving, fend for yourselves! They're leaving!"

The shouting porter passed under Maile's window. She woke and wondered groggily why pigs were leaving. He walked on, his meaningless words fading, overlaid by the peculiar sound of dozens of radios, a tense drone that reminded her of tidal wave warnings, the same announcement coming through the window and the walls to the left and right. " . . . received official notice that trains may no longer enter or exit. All flights over the country are being rerouted. River traffic on the Danube east of Vienna has been halted at the frontier." She sat up, fully awake. Radios announced in unison, "Repeat. Repeat. The Soviet aggression was launched at two this morning. Repeat, repeat. Prague is now fully occupied."

In the entry hall below, the front door was wrenched open so hard that the latch banged against the inside wall. Maile threw on a bathrobe, ran to the landing, and saw Frau Metzger stagger in, a market basket in each hand crammed with bags of sugar, flour, salt. A net of apples hung from one shoulder, and another net slung around her neck bulged with bread and jars of honey. The landlady looked up, panting. "Buy what you can," she gasped. "Vienna will fall by noon!"

Office, Maile remembered. Contract. First thing in the morning! She washed and dressed in less than a minute, and got downstairs.

Radios all along Getreidegasse broadcast at full volume. Prague was on the lips of every announcer and passerby. She headed toward Sigmundsplatz and a side street that led to the Festival House and von Wehlen's *Büro*. People shoved past her onto the main street, one man's jacket misbuttoned, a woman's braids flopping on her shoulders. Everyone carried string bags and baskets. Invasion, they said, Russkis. Tanks. Maile recalled old Life magazine photos of Soviet tanks invading Hungary, tight little streets full of civilians, soldiers shooting teenagers armed with rocks—cobblestones, she now realized, the same as the ones under her own feet. Tank cannons destroying whole buildings. Frau Metzger's house would crumble like sand.

A wire grate screeched up at a tobacconist's shop and men and women fought to get inside. Maile dodged them to run toward the Festival House. No guard stood out front. No workmen hung up new posters. She tried the door to the administration wing: locked, along with all other doors. *"Bitte, aufmachen!"* she called out.

At a second-floor window a curtain shifted but no one peered down. She went toward the back of the theater to find von Wehlen's parking space, the gate for his car. A sawhorse manned by a police officer blocked the entrance to the alley. He lit a cigarette and turned up a transistor radio on the barricade. *"Eintritt verboten,"* he said. *"Los, Nigger."*

She sucked in her breath as if he'd slashed her with a knife—not *Negerin*, not even *Moor*. The other word had made its way to an alley behind a theater in a small city in the middle of Europe. She wanted to claw his face with both hands, but fought down her hate. With the cold discipline of a performer she said, "I auditioned for Maestro von Wehlen. I have to sign a contract."

The name evoked a startled blink of respect. The officer pinched off his cigarette and immediately took Maile to a backstage entrance. From there, without further difficulties, a security guard led her through a maze of corridors to the administration wing. She barely recognized the place where she'd gone for an interview on a quiet afternoon. Office workers crisscrossed the hallway, talking loudly over ringing telephones that went unanswered. The door to von Wehlen's waiting room stood open. His secretary was surrounded by staff clamoring for attention.

Maile caught his eye and called out, "Excuse me!" The secretary glanced over with a frown. "Elvira," she said.

People kept talking to him and over each other. After a moment he replied in English, "I beg your pardon, Miss Manoa. Please wait outside."

A harried assistant asked if she would like a coffee, and showed her to an alcove with tables. He brought *eine kleine Braune* with a Kaiser roll on a porcelain tray. She could have eaten three omelettes. More staff streamed past complaining that international phone calls could not be made, telegrams could not be sent. The Rumanian baritone scheduled for tonight's *Don Carlo* had checked out of his hotel. American warplanes from Berchtesgaden were on alert, trolley barricades had gone up in Vienna, a Dutch mezzo could be hired to replace . . .

Maile tried to believe that only the waiting-to-sign-a-contract part of this mad scene was happening; to forget that Jann would never speak to her again; to deny that the Festival House would be abandoned if the Russians crossed the Danube.

An hour later she was taken back to von Wehlen's waiting room, where office workers still surrounded his secretary. *"Bitte, meine Herrschaften,"* he said. They stepped aside for her. He unlocked a file cabinet, pulled out a small orange card, wrote on it, stamped it, and handed it to Maile, saying, "Tomorrow morning, nine o'clock." She saw *Solistin* at the top and her name at the bottom, partly covered by the Festival House seal. Valid for one day only.

From an overhead speaker came a low voice: *"Bühne."* Everyone emptied into the hall. Maile followed them past a sign with an arrow pointing to the stage. Where, she was sure, he waited. Where she did not yet belong.

Staff crowded past her talking about rearranged performances, cast lists, costumes, sets, props. She tucked the card away, frightened by the thought of what could happen between now and nine o'clock tomorrow morning. Until the contract was signed she was no one's soprano, no longer Jann's, and not yet von Wehlen's.

She went back to the Old City's narrow streets where Salzburgers going in both directions bumped into each other. Their arms were loaded with toilet tissue as well as fine chocolates. A British couple argued about selling their Festival tickets for half price, and debated the best route to the German border. Maile worried that buying bread would somehow bring on disaster. A radio at a magazine kiosk blared local updates: Nonntaler hospital on alert, police petitioning to carry guns, veterans on twenty-four-hour river watch.

"Fräulein Manoa!"

A short way ahead she saw the young son of the fruit grocer carrying a wooden flat of peaches, weaving to avoid an old man grabbing at them. The boy shouted that he had a message for her under this load just in from Gaisberg, thank the saints he'd seen her so he didn't have to deliver it. She yanked out a protruding piece of brown paper before the boy disappeared into the crowd, the old man at his heels.

The note in pencil read: *Come stay with us. The countryside is safest at a time like this. You have my love. Karl.*

The plain words flooded her with guilt. Since leaving the meadow last night, she hadn't given him a single thought, let alone written a note or figured out how to send it. He had been slipping away from her ever since the contest, and she'd let it happen. Compared to him, she was a beast of selfishness. She hurried off to find the nearest bus stop. Maybe Karl had been waiting for her to come since early morning. He regretted their last argument. He was no longer flaunting some grand sense of justice. He loved her.

The crowds thinned as she left the center of the Old City. The river promenade was empty and she crossed the footbridge alone. The water under it flowed on unchanged but ominous now, a route for invasion, boats of armed men, rafts with artillery. On the opposite side no cars drove past, no porters delivered handcarts of groceries. The bus schedule inside a glass case bolted to a pole was covered by a notice: PUBLIC TRANSPORT IS SUSPENDED UNTIL FURTHER NOTICE, 21.VIII.68.

She slapped the pole in frustration. The metal rang dully. Her palm stung. She felt suddenly hungry, then not, then had a fierce urge to smoke a cigarette. To jump into the Salzach, swim hard, and get to Karl that way.

Down the street at the Mozarteum, a piece of white paper on the front door fluttered in the breeze. She suspected it was a notice that classes were also suspended, but she wanted to read it anyway. As she started to cross Schwarzstrasse, a man in gardener's clothes emerged from a villa farther on. He dragged two large suitcases out to the sidewalk. Kazuo followed him, clutching a violin case to his chest.

"Miss Manoa," he shouted, "my plane! It is the last one!"

"What?" she shouted back, but had heard clearly.

The gardener hauled the luggage across the street and vanished among the thick trees outside Mirabell Garten. "May we meet in better times," Kazuo shouted, bowing down and up like a marionette.

"Wait," she said as he too disappeared among the trees. Stubbornly she repeated it, louder, knowing he would not stop to hear about her audition. He was leaving, like the others, and would go all the way to Japan, in the Pacific Ocean. Her ocean.

Once more the street was quiet. She lingered on the steps of the Mozarteum. The entire building seemed to be empty. The notice on the door read, CLOSED, PRIZEWINNER'S CONCERT CANCELLED. Karl and Kazuo and Jean-Paul and Brenda and Marlise and Maxi and Frau Metzger would not sit in the audience tonight, along with agents and theater scouts. The student conductor's shivery downbeat would not worry her. There would be no huge bouquet of roses at the end, no review in tomorrow's paper: *Frau Maile Manoa, Mozart aus Hawaii.*

JANN HAD TO make the decision every time he entered his front room, or visited a friend who had a similar cabinet with his favorite cognac.

So far this morning he had resisted taking a drink because of vanity: when the city was evacuated, he would not be a wobbling drunk, dependent on his wife. Staying spit-eye sober was a matter of safety, yet his thoughts were so chaotic and trivial he wondered if unawares he had consumed an entire bottle of alcohol. Would the Russians breach the border or stop on the Hungarian side, as in '56? Could he still get money from the bank? If he and Dora fled, was taking her beloved schnauzer an unacceptable risk? If he boarded up the house, would his framed Rilke manuscript be stolen by marauders?

His gut told him that this time the Russians would overrun Austria. Twelve years ago, Soviet troops massed in Bratislava had seen the flat Danube lands ahead, virtually undefended because of Austrian neutrality. Now again they were so close, and taking Vienna would be too tempting to pass up. Or orders within the Red Army could be misinterpreted. Whole regiments might spill over the frontiers before mistakes were even noticed.

As soon as he convinced himself that life as he knew it was over, his thoughts swung in the opposite direction: the Soviets wouldn't dare chance a war with NATO. Austria was, quite frankly, a poor country and not a battle trophy. A third of it was too mountainous to be conquered.

Most nerve-wracking of all, beyond politics, facts, speculation, his daily routines had been disrupted to the point where he had no idea what to do with himself. He repeatedly went to his closet to straighten a row of jackets, spacing each one with care. Halfway through breakfast an imaginary scene staggered through his mind: pulling off Dora's clothes to mount her like a crazed soldier-invader deaf to her screams. From his front window he could see a public nuisance ignored by rubbish collectors: a split keg—honey or syrup—lying on a sidewalk and attracting an ever-larger cloud of flies.

Worst of all, Maile was a stone in his heart. Why had he done the inexcusable? Giving in to his overwhelming attraction and "declaring himself," as used to be said, although that poetic term hardly applied to his crude approach. The futility, the stupidity! Comedy all the way back to the Greeks featured a decrepit suitor pursuing a beauty decades younger. He still relived the encounter—their bodies pressed together by the force of his embrace, the scent of her hair—and he pictured himself lifting her in his arms and carrying her into his bedroom. These fantasies had to stop. Yesterday afternoon, before all their lives were thrown to the winds, Balthazar von Gref had come by and offered to be Maile's patron for the next year. Then, long after dark, word of her successful audition at the Festival House came in the form of a note delivered at an unacceptably late hour by that loathsome little man in the green uniform who lived off rumors, yet had to be paid because his facts were never wrong.

"SOCIALISM WITH A face?" Karl's father bent over a lamb that lay on the ground in front of him. "What a bag of witch shit." He spread the lamb's hind legs with a wooden bar and reached for a coil of rope.

"A human face," Karl said. The argument was hours old but he still felt defensive. At dawn the entire family had driven their animals to the highest pastures to conceal them from Russian army scouts coming to seize anything edible. The weather was now uncomfortably humid. His mother, sister, and several cousins were back down at the farm, while he and his father stopped to kill the lamb. It bleated pathetically, one foreleg crushed by a fall onto rocks. Too injured to save.

"You said new-style Communism would work. You even said it would triumph. Talking like some poet." The lamb struggled as its legs were tied. "Jesus Christ," Karl's father muttered, "I'm doing this backwards." He loosened the rope, turned the lamb on its side, knelt on its thighs, and pulled a knife from his belt.

Karl picked up a chipped enamel bowl. His note to Maile had left in the predawn darkness with their usual load of summer peaches trucked into the city. The driver brought news of an impending invasion, then waited for Karl to run to the house for paper and pencil. Now he wondered if she would come up the path any minute and see him holding a bowl of blood. The idea was humiliating. Could she even find her way this far up the mountain? He had never imagined a Soviet military takeover of Austria, a Warsaw Pact ally.

The blade slid into the lamb's neck. Its mouth dropped open as if in surprise, but it made no sound. Karl watched a dark streak run down over the dirty wool and pushed the bowl in place. *"Agnus Dei,"* he said.

"Hold still," his father mumbled. "Don't blaspheme."

Karl stifled a smirk. As the lamb lay quietly bleeding to death, he sucked in a breath, bothered more by the harsh, rusty smell of blood than by the sight of it. He picked out bits of fluff as the bowl filled, each time pausing to wipe his sticky fingers on his trousers. The red smears merged with other stains on his lederhosen. His father didn't think there was much chance of seeing soldiers today in Gaisberg. The real danger, he insisted, would come after the army had settled in and needed to be fed. Squads would scour the countryside to strip farms of everything that could be carried off, including tools and women—which made frightening sense to Karl. He felt a sudden desire to be far away, in some clean place where he could curl his entire body around Maile and protect her from perils seen and unseen.

WHEN NIGHT FELL, Prague was reported "under control," with a million Soviet troops advancing outward in all directions. Since early morning Frau Metzger had listened to the radio in the hope that some great saving event would occur, but in midafternoon she took off her daytime dirndl, always laced up as tight as a corset. Clad only in a nightgown—shocking, like a real *Schlampe*—she went on cooking and pickling and salting down pork butts as she had done in 1956. By evening her breathing was labored. Worse, cancer had invaded her left knee, making it weaker and weaker. Each time it bumped against her right knee, she feared that the cancer would spread. She sat at her kitchen table and tearfully massaged both knees. When she stopped to wipe her eyes, she felt the cancer jump off the ends of her fingertips and slip into her skull.

Upstairs, Maile sat on the floor with her back against the piano. A disease seemed to have spread through the city, an unpredictable epidemic that distorted everything. The room darkened around her. She wanted to hold on to the light, to stop time and return to the safety of Professor Jann's teaching, his pride in her, so hard won month by month, but she had erased all that for the sake of an orange card. The

Mozarteum's concert hall stage was empty when it should have been filled with musicians dressed in black, responding to the concert master's tone that signaled them to tune up. Only an idiot would believe that the world was still in order, that the Festival House would open tomorrow morning so she could sign her contract and workers could continue mending costumes and arranging the curls on wigs.

She pulled the blanket off her bed and wrapped it tightly around her shoulders. Death seemed to be bearing down on the city, a red mass moving with the terrible, deliberate force of a lava flow: the Soviet army, only as far away as the hour's drive from Honolulu to the North Shore.

Frau Metzger's voice shot up the stairs. *"Komm schon 'runter!"*

Maile jumped to her feet, shedding the blanket.

The kitchen was dark, the back door open. The landlady waited outside with a finger to her lips. Two skinny gray braids snaked down the front of her rumpled nightdress. She stood on a small cobblestone square that resembled a miniature prison yard surrounded by the blind walls of three neighboring buildings. "You have money," she whispered. "I know it came from Vienna." In one hand she clutched a small metal box. "I make a hole out here. It's safe, I did this before."

Maile had hidden her prize winner's cash in the piano upstairs. Banks were shut down. With Russian troops approaching the Danube in tanks, she knew that Austria's tiny peacekeeping force wouldn't last two minutes if Soviet generals gave orders to invade. But burying currency under cobblestones was like a bad joke in an operetta.

"My money is safe," she said.

"Well! Then be of use and guard the front door. Do not answer the bell."

Maile felt a twitch of curiosity about what was in Frau Metzger's box—a deed, garnet jewelry, a saint's bone? "All right, all right," she said.

At the kitchen window, in the last gloomy light she watched the landlady pry up cobblestones with a crowbar. On the kitchen counter, news trickled from the radio, turned down low: border traffic to the west backed up ten kilometers, waiting time twenty hours; seventy Czech refugees at Mariahilf Youth Hostel.

Frau Metzger dug out the oily dirt, put the box in a hole the size of a cheese loaf, replaced the stones in order, tamped the dirt around them, made the sign of the cross, and kissed the rosary now hung around her neck. The sight of such diligence filled Maile with anxiety that she was not doing enough. Was in fact doing nothing. Within hours looters could storm the house, set it on fire, burn her piano before she could save the cash. A money belt! She had to make a money belt to strap on next to her skin.

The doorbell rang, its metallic rattle piercing her like a rifle shot. Frau Metzger rushed into the kitchen, ordering, "Don't open! Ask first."

Maile went to the entrance and demanded, *"Wer ist da?"* A vaguely familiar voice replied, something about the Festival House. She cracked open the door. A man pressed a paper roll into her hands and reconfirmed her appointment tomorrow morning.

"Welcome," he added with a deep nod. She recognized the assistant who had brought her coffee this morning. "Excuse my haste," he said, "but I must get back for tonight's performance." He stepped away out of sight.

Frau Metzger came from behind with a flashlight, and reached past Maile to yank the door shut and slam the bolt in place. *"Sag',"* she hissed, *"wer war's?"*

The roll of paper was thick and soft, like a large sheet of handmade stationery. Inside lay a single rose of a strangely dark color, a deep crimson more intense than any variety of red wine, with rich undertones of purple and black. Maile stroked it with a fingertip. Tied to the stem was a small white card engraved in black letters: Werner von Wehlen. Under his name, written in stark black script: *"Grüsse,"* and his signature.

Frau Metzger aimed the flashlight at the card. "Him?" she sputtered. "On the street, in person?"

Maile took the rose upstairs to savor it alone. One flower and the briefest message felt like a bridge of hope into tomorrow, something solid to counter the relentless news of the world falling apart. Minutes later Frau Metzger knocked and asked to see the signature again. Maile showed her the card, and the landlady admired the handwritten name at length, then left. No sooner had Frau Metzger reached the entrance hall than she toiled back up the stairs and blurted that bombers were droning over the city, just like years ago, the same sound. Together they listened hard until it was clear that the low hum was a washing machine in the building next door.

The landlady returned to her kitchen. A quarter of an hour later she climbed the steps once more to call out the latest local bulletin: *The Festival will proceed. Herr Maestro von Wehlen emphasizes there is to be no interruption* . . . She had put on a fresh dirndl, arranged her braids, and insisted her tenant join her for supper. Famished, Maile obliged and went downstairs. The moment they faced each across the kitchen table, Frau Metzger recited the cost of bread, sausage, fresh pork, sugar, all the things Maile hadn't bought and were now gone from the stores, or twice as expensive as this afternoon and sure to be three times more tomorrow.

They ate carelessly, greedily, and drank a bottle of wine without getting tipsy. The landlady described fleeing the city with her husband and son when Hungary was invaded twelve years ago, the three of them pedaling toward the Swiss border with a ham and cooking pots and goose-down quilts tied onto their bicycles. News so scant in those days that they didn't find out for weeks if Austria had fallen or not.

A memory nagged Maile, of von Wehlen's bodyguards coming for him after her late-night audition. She realized that his organization must have received advance notice that Soviet troops were no longer playing war games. His connections were as good as the prime minister's. No matter what happened, she would be safe with Herr Maestro. The rose meant she belonged to his charmed circle. The Festival would continue. Or maybe that announcement had been a ruse. The staff might be gone by morning.

At eleven o'clock when performances ended, Frau Metzger refused to budge from her kitchen. Maile walked over to the Festival House, eager to reassure herself that the schedule would not be interrupted but equally afraid of seeing one more notice: DUE TO UNFORESEEN CIRCUMSTANCES WE REGRET . . .

The elegantly dressed audience streamed outside, fewer now. No onlookers stood opposite the theater, no open carriages or luxury cars were lined up at the entrance. An idle valet told her that the horses had been taken to the countryside and gasoline would be rationed starting tomorrow. Everyone smoked cigarettes, although just yesterday a woman who lit up on the street was signaling her profession. A man complained loudly that two soloists listed as "indisposed" had actually fled to France. They were cowards. Traitors, in fact.

Maile heard the same complaint twice more: singers leaving, breaking their contracts. This morning, she remembered, von Wehlen's staff had been frantically rescheduling soloists. An ecstatic thought came to her: She would be asked to perform! She knew forty-one arias by heart, and thirty-seven duets, trios, and quartets. The possibility of being on stage boiled over in her mind until she had to admit that a role was not made up of bits and scraps. She could not have sung the part of a single opera character from beginning to end without a score in hand.

At the Silver Fawn she saw ladies and gentlemen clustered outside, exclaiming that other fine restaurants were closed. Such a thing had never happened. They crowded forward, noisily calling out their titles to the maître d', who stood with teeth clenched in a rigid smile, the tables behind him full. She went on to a wine bar so packed that customers were drinking on the street and telling anyone who would listen, It's artillery first, then tanks. Civilians will mount machine guns on rooftops, plant mines in window boxes.

"Das Licht," one man said. He pointed toward the Fortress. Conversations stopped.

Maile looked up in time to see the remaining Festival pennants on the guard towers disappear from sight, not illuminated as usual through the night. Hohensalzburg still loomed grandly, its walls awash in pale blue floodlights. She felt a burst of love for the city, which had endured for centuries despite armies bent on destroying it, then one after another, swaths of light dissolved into darkness, taking with them the towers, the high stone gates, the vast walls, and the sky was lowered like a curtain.

ço   ço   ço

EVERY ESTABLISHMENT THAT sold liquor stayed open all night. The street below Maile's room echoed with drunken yells. Someone wept uncontrollably. She slept in snatches, alert for news from the radios playing nearby. Shortly after dawn the first bulletins came: the Soviet embassy in Vienna had been fire-bombed by Austrian students; Russian tanks lined the border north of the capital and thrill seekers were swarming out to get a look; thousands of citizens had fled westward. Troops were coming, she decided. No, they weren't. Yes, they were on the way. The broadcast was interrupted by loud static. She heard no more for three hours, then: *All communications are now under government control. Citizens are advised that our country's constitutional pacifism will be respected. Daily routines should not be interrupted.* Nothing about the Salzburg Festival.

At a quarter to nine, Maile tucked her fountain pen in her purse and went out into crowds once again shopping furiously. A gray sky hung over the city with a promise of drizzling rain or summer humidity. In the now empty marketplace, boys played at shooting imaginary rifles—ack-ack—clutching their chests and falling. At the Festival House, men strung a long banner across the front: SONDERKONZERT, ACHT UHR. She stared at the banner as she showed her soloist's pass to a guard. A special concert, eight tomorrow evening.

Inside, a man introduced himself as a conducting assistant and said that Fräulein Manoa was scheduled immediately on the Grand Stage.

"I just came to sign a contract," she said, "not to sing."

"A warm-up will suffice," he replied.

No one sat in the huge auditorium. The chairs in the orchestra pit were empty. In frightened docility she went up side stairs and stepped out onto the wide, swallowing stage. Workers behind her continued adjusting scenery. She started with a vocal exercise, a low "nuuuu." She felt the sound project, and continued, but struggled against the oddness of what she was doing. The assistant walked from left to right among the hundreds of seats fanning out below her. She made her tones strong and even, going down from midrange and up to fuller strength, calculating the reach of her voice in a space larger than she had ever attempted.

"Step down, if you please," he interrupted. "This way."

She followed him, fingering the pen in her purse, agonizing over what a warm-up might mean. Or not. For the next hour she worked in a studio with Egon Janowitz, who replied to her surprised greeting with a businesslike nod. He took her through nine standard duets she knew by heart, tediously redefining the dynamics of each phrase. Twice he left. The second time he returned to say they would concentrate on the *Don Giovanni* duettino, a safe piece because it was short, a midrange soprano role with only one tempo change.

"Is this for the special concert?" she asked.

Egon moved closer, although no one else was present. "Two soloists left by private plane after commercial flights from Salzburg ceased. This bit of news will appear in tomorrow's *Nachrichten*. You are to replace the soprano. Do not discuss so-called missing singers with anybody."

She nodded and felt a rush of dizziness; her dream was coming true minute by minute but nothing was as she'd imagined. A blocking coach arrived to take her through the duet step by step. After fifteen repetitions she stopped counting. *La ci darem la mano*, the lovely peasant and the irresistible rake, two and a half minutes of music repeated until every note and gesture was imprinted. At noon she went back to the Grand Stage, where a dozen prominent singers conversed with a quiet sense of shared anxiety. None introduced themselves. A stage director sent her to wait in the wings. On the opposite side she saw a man with a Vandyke beard: her seducer. Step forward, she thought. Wait two beats.

Othello and the other stars mimed arias to recordings of their voices that played offstage. Instead of singing they concentrated on entering and exiting smoothly. Technicians above them on the racks labored with silent intensity to adjust lights and abbreviated scenery. At last Don Giovanni pretended to sing while his voice and that of his missing partner poured from speakers. Maile mouthed her text and traded glances with him. He whispered as he moved and gestured: watch here for Herr Maestro's upbeat, turn to me slowly, lean back now, not one note sooner.

At two o'clock everyone was dismissed with an announcement of more rehearsals tomorrow. Maile went to Publicity for head shots, to

Solo Costumes on the third floor, then back down to the administration offices. Von Wehlen's secretary was still besieged by staff with questions about unions, no-show clauses, canceled block tickets. On a cluttered table Maile signed her contract. The secretary thanked her for contributing to the special concert and gave her a free ticket.

"The eyes of the world are upon us," he said.

"I understand," she told him.

She hadn't read the two pages of tiny print, or seen von Wehlen since her audition, but he would be in the pit tomorrow night, conducting her and Don Giovanni in a performance meant to defy the tanks poised to crush Austria.

IN THE OLD City, news continued to blare from radios at open windows, in shops, on courtyard balconies. Maile was brought to a halt behind a couple who stopped suddenly in the middle of a throng to listen to a bulletin: . . . *hundreds of Viennese eyewitnesses sighted Soviet aircraft, although a swift denial* . . . The man and woman stared up at the afternoon sky. Maile also strained to see death approaching. Only a few scattered clouds hung motionless under the late-summer sun, and soon the pair tittered in embarrassment and walked on.

Mindlessly she followed them, needing the crowd, at the same time infuriated by the bumping and shoving. Marlise Stäbler eased out of a greengrocer's shop, carrying a box heaped with vegetables. Their eyes met in sudden recognition, but Marlise hurried off, swallowed by a wave of people before Maile could shout a greeting.

From inside the shop came a chatter of sound: *This order takes effect immediately. All foreign residents of Austria, without fail, must report to their consulates.*

Maile felt the dull movement of things beyond her control. She came to a newsstand that displayed a copy of *Figaro* and attracted the attention of passersby. The front page photo showed a young Czech inserting a carnation into the muzzle of a rifle pointed at his chest. Three more guns were aimed at him. He was smiling, the soldiers were not. She glanced around, wanting to hear someone say the picture was insane, brave, ridiculous.

"Beg pardon," a man said and leaned past her. He snatched up the *London Times*, excusing himself; he had to get to his consulate. Others buying French and Italian papers excused themselves to Maile in the same way and for the same reason. More obvious foreigners walked toward the river.

She followed them, feeling dutiful but ready to argue with Mr. Casey over her rights as an American if he insisted she go anywhere except back to her room. So far nothing had happened! No planes with red stars flying over the city. No explosions, no tanks.

The upriver footbridge was blocked by protestors waving Austrian and Czech flags and chanting in English, "Freedom NOW, Free-dom!" A policeman shouted at them to move on or be arrested. Half the group clambered up onto the railings, slashing their flags through the air, chanting louder. Students, Maile realized. She looked for Karl, afraid to see him among them. He wasn't there. Other foreigners clustered behind her speaking a mixture of languages.

"Fussgänger, weiter!" The policeman ordered pedestrians to use the traffic bridge a quarter mile away.

She joined a crowd that increased at each side street leading out of the Old City, everybody moving faster and faster. At the main bridge more police blew whistles and directed vehicles clogging the lanes in both directions. Truck drivers honked and cursed, headed north with Tuscan oil and olives, and south with German steel bars. Small private cars were crammed full of passengers, luggage and cardboard boxes strapped onto the roofs. A man on a loaded bicycle wove past the pedestrians surging across the bridge. At the far end, the crowd dispersed to the Italian Viceconsulate, the Royal Swedish, Danish, Belgian and Greek consulates, the Swiss Consular Agency.

A man in military uniform waved at Maile. She couldn't remember his name, her escort on a lost evening that no longer mattered. "Mr. Casey sent me," Major Wainwright called out. Quickly he walked her toward the villa with the American flag. "You're going home, Miss Manoa," he said. "Hawaii, you're real lucky."

She turned on him. "You have no idea! I can't go home!"

He urged her up the stairs into the consulate. The rooms were packed with gray-haired couples speaking American English, and dressed in pastel skirts and blouses, plaid slacks, short-sleeved shirts, sport shoes. She had never seen them in Salzburg.

"Who are these people?"

"Army retirees from the lake area." He edged her to the front of the crowd. "They got notice to leave, and they're going."

Edwin Casey came out of his office, flipped a pink tablet into his mouth, and tugged at his tie. Everybody fell silent. His short hair was twisted into odd tufts, his eyes like holes burned in an old gray towel. He held up a sheet of paper. "I have here a directive that originated in Washington and came through our embassy in Vienna. This consulate will close as of five p.m. All U.S. residents within the district of Salzburg are strongly advised by the State Department to leave the country at once." The page fluttered. "This is not an order, but it is in your best interests. When leaving, do not aggravate local police. Stay calm and get moving. I'll answer questions in my office until three o'clock."

He caught sight of Maile and said gruffly, "C'mere a minute." She stepped up to him, and he went on in a low monotone, "Soon as we close, my sec's taking the BMW to Berchtesgaden, so pack some stuff and come back here. We'll get you on a stateside flight from the base."

She pictured the route as a dotted line on a map: crossing the Austrian-German border with a small suitcase, getting on a plane, landing back in New York. Then what, call Madame Renska from the airport?

"I have a contract with Maestro von Wehlen! There's a special concert! The Russians won't—"

"Get. Out. Now." Casey aimed a thumb over his shoulder. "The BMW's making one trip." He waved a couple into his office.

Maile went outside, then wanted to go back in and tell Casey thanks, thanks anyway, so she wasn't cut off from him, but sections of her life were falling away faster than she could follow. As if to prove a point, Brenda rushed out of the consulate onto the promenade and yelled, "Over here, J-P!"

Jean-Paul ran to her from a neighboring villa, and they embraced and spun around. "Hey, Maile," Brenda shouted, "we're hitching to his mom's house, but we gotta go through Switzerland! Wanna come?" She stuck out a thumb. Jean-Paul grabbed her hand, and they raced toward the traffic bridge, dodging long lines of people outside other villas.

Maile walked off in the opposite direction, past the bus stop, the Mozarteum, the entrance to Mirabell Garten. The remainder of Schwarzstrasse was empty. She continued along a side street leading to the train station, then realized that she had nowhere to go except back to her room.

In the middle of the street stood a marble fountain with life-sized figures in robes, below them a date, ANNO 1702. She remembered arriving in the city by taxi and being thrilled by the statue, so old, so European. Three people sat at its base, their heads together. Two of them got to their feet and left, tucking loose cigarettes into their pockets. The Rosenkavalier bent to close a canvas bag at his feet, sat up, and tapped the vacated space beside him.

"*Frau Solistin,*" he said, "*setzen Sie sich.*"

Her new title, she thought, Soloist, was less than a day old but it came effortlessly from his lips. Posters for the music contest had announced the first place award of thirty thousand schillings. She had auditioned at the Festival House and signed a contract. But she would not sit down with him.

He pulled a cluster of strings from his jacket and looked up at her. "How long," he asked, "do you think foreigners will be allowed to remain in Austria? Such a small country, you see, where Americans can be found within days and put in camps not run by the International Red Cross. Soviet camps." He smiled with polite insinuation and fingered the knots. "Every last foreigner will be loaded onto trains bound for Novgorod, because Russians never throw anything away. Thriftiest people on earth. However, a soprano from Honolulu is now under the protection of Herr Maestro. His soloists have no reason to fear. For that you have me to thank."

Smooth as cream, she thought. He should be on stage. "You had nothing to do with my audition. That was my success, mine alone!"

He got to his feet and tipped his head back with the confidence of a loan shark reminding a customer of a debt that was dangerously overdue. "I do not expect a lady to walk about with fifteen thousand schillings in her purse. Tomorrow evening, after the special concert, I will find you."

Fifteen thousand schillings! She turned away from the sight of him, afraid of his evil *mana*. At her back she heard a brittle snigger. She felt trapped, then trapped only by money. Herr Maestro von Wehlen would protect her, but staying in Salzburg was a risk. If things got any worse, it could be a life-and-death risk.

She walked off into the stillness of Schwarzstrasse. Her high heels made loud clicks on the pavement as if announcing her exact location to officials looking for foreigners. She concentrated on tomorrow's rehearsal at the Festival House, on her picture taken this afternoon at Publicity, her costume, her signature on the contract. Her world was still in order. At Mirabell Garten the long beds of marigolds formed disturbing carpets of yellow-orange flames. She could pay the outrageous amount in cash, but it would go to the *Engelmacher*, who had taken babies at night to the back of a church to be baptized so their souls wouldn't be lost, and then put them where their cries could not be heard and animals couldn't get at them—a cave, a box with air holes? A man who did that, then played dominoes or ate dinner or read a newspaper, and checked on a baby until it died and he could bury it and collect his fee. How many babies?

On the door of the Mozarteum the cancellation notice still hung in place. She walked along the side of the conservatory, past the teaching studios and the rehearsal stage, all the way to the dense clumps of ornamental bushes at the end of the property. From there she turned to look back, expecting to see beams that jutted from the building below the eaves, or a heavy iron railing across a bricked-up balcony, or a tall old tree with branches that could bear the weight of men.

There was only a blank wall about forty feet high, the exterior of the concert hall. At the top, black and distinct against the yellowing sky, large hooks as thick as her forearm were attached to beams bolted to the roof. For hauling pianos to upper floors. Frau Metzger and her husband and everyone they knew must have come to stare. Had students continued classes as usual? Had someone practicing an aria glanced outside from time to time and accidentally glimpsed what no one wanted to admit was there? All over the city, people who had seen the bodies were still alive, still going about their business and buying fresh rolls for breakfast. With butter, please.

AT CAFÉ SCIMITAR there was no waiting line. The velvet rope drooped in a corner. A haze of tobacco smoke hung over tables crowded with people talking at each other in noisy anxiety. Maile looked around for Baron von Gref or Sophia, but doubted they were here. Across the room a man swayed to his feet and his chair banged to the floor with a crack as loud as a rifle shot. Everyone fell silent, then just as suddenly conversations flared again. The headwaiter walked up to her saying, "Frau Solistin, we regret there is no pastry." Cigarette ash dusted his lapels. "Cognac is gratis." He motioned at the baron's table.

She saw Arnim standing beside it holding an empty balloon glass. He angled toward her through the smoke, his tie loose, jacket unbuttoned. "Maile, my treasure." He bent to kiss her hand. "I can protect... nay, shield you from harm. Come away with me."

No one, she realized, was forcing her to stay here. "Where?"

He glanced at the baron's empty chair. "Uncle Baltha left for Vienna at dawn. Petrol shortages and roadblocks will be his least obstacles."

"He's in danger?"

Arnim shrugged. "Viennese are less hysterical. These provincials are operatic, although not in an amusing fashion." He held up a car key. She followed him outside, not caring where he was headed.

Soon after driving off, Arnim took a detour to avoid the traffic bridge and sped away toward the rural end of the valley. Within minutes they were alone on the road, no other cars, no trucks. No one on foot or riding bicycles. The emptiness made her uneasy. Had people gone into hiding?

"Dear diva," Arnim said, "I have been remiss. Congratulations on your audition." Without warning he trod on the brake, jolting them in their seats. "Will you look? Imbeciles!"

At a farmhouse beside the road, men nailed plywood over windows and hammered boards across doors. Women piled bedding into a handcart. Children prodded geese across a meadow toward higher ground, a waddling flock that joined a line of people and cows and horses stretching ahead, all moving up a zigzag path that became a scratch against Untersberg in the distance. Maile imagined Karl and his family doing the same. She said, "The Soviet army is just over those mountains."

"Cossacks, you mean." Arnim tittered. "However, I have a plan."

He accelerated with a squeal of tires, careened around one corner, another, then swerved off the highway onto a dirt road through a wheat field. Ripe stalks lashed the hood as the Jaguar plowed over potholes, jerking him and Maile side to side. He came to a halt, turned off the motor, and faced her. Dots of sweat fringed his upper lip. Spots of red colored his jaw. In a frantic whisper he said, "This could be our last moment on earth. Missiles. A fireball sucks the river dry." He unbuttoned his trousers. "Half the Schloss left this morning for Rome. Now you and I are also going by private plane."

Horses and geese, she thought. Von Gref and von Wehlen. Rehearsal tomorrow morning, concert tomorrow night. Private plane. Arnim with his trousers half open. "I'm not going anywhere!"

He leaned toward her. "For love?"

She loathed him for demanding payment to save her, and take her into a world she already belonged to, as an artist. "Not for love, definitely not for love."

Abruptly he restarted the car. Soon the rough road gave way to pavement and the tall wheat was replaced by vegetable gardens. Farther on the Jaguar passed under a marble archway to enter a courtyard with rows of stables. Beyond it the upper story of Schloss Wasserstein was visible over the tops of trees.

As Arnim pulled in beside an antique sleigh, a sharp rapping of high heels sounded in the courtyard. "Where have you been," a woman demanded. "Why make me come out here?" Sophia walked up to his side of the car.

Arnim motioned at Maile, saying, "She's coming with us."

Sophia gave him a look of disbelief, her glance going from his face, then to his lap, the loosened belt, his open fly. "Grow up," she said. "The plane is so full, half the luggage must be sent by land. Moreover, cook died while you were out racing around, and we have to deal with the coroner before leaving, which is . . ." She looked at a tiny diamond wristwatch. "In fifty-two minutes."

Arnim got out, buttoning up, and stood with his head bowed like a reprimanded boy. Maile got out as well, wondering how she would find her way back to Salzburg. Sophia shot her a brief, examining stare, then said in the tone of a lady dismissing a maid, "I shall see to it you have a ride into town." She and Arnim walked off discussing family matters, mentioning names Maile didn't recognize, people whose affairs did not concern her. She was simply a singer naive enough to have believed her gifts and personality could lead to friendship. In fact she had been merely an amusement. An entertainer.

Minutes later a truck heaped with suitcases and steamer trunks stopped at the marble archway. The driver shouted at her that he'd been told somebody needed a lift. Maile realized she had to accept this offer, and sit next to him like another piece of luggage, or spend hours walking back to the city. Soviet troops could spill over the border before the sun went down. The driver spat loudly and gunned the engine. She approached the truck, certain of being watched from the Schloss by a countess who stood looking down at her from a high window.

17

DARKNESS MADE EVERYTHING worse: the explosive flush of a toilet next door, an odd color in the night sky. Maile walked from the wash-stand to the music stand and picked at hardened drips of wax on the candleholders. She had run out of things to wash or mend and was too nervous to read. Doubts filled her mind and crushed her spirits. Maybe Jann had released her because he felt guilty about wanting her in bed. But if Jann still hated von Wehlen for conducting at a Festival House decorated with swastikas, such things meant a great deal more to an Austrian than to Miss Manoa. Perhaps von Wehlen had accepted her only as revenge on Jann, and she hadn't really earned a contract. She might be just another bird's beak to put under glass.

Below in the entry hall Frau Metzger exclaimed, *"Saperlot, Frau Manoa, kommen Sie sofort 'runter!"* Maile went out to the landing. The landlady glared and pointed at the front door. "That miscarriage, who I once clasped to my bosom, just now made demands on me to speak to you in this very entryway. Madame Soloist or not, if you believe I will allow his foot to cross my threshold, you are vastly mistaken!"

"It's Karl," a voice shouted. "Come outside, then."

"But he's your relative," Maile told Frau Metzger.

"Not by blood. My hope is he will yet return to the Church. I have always guarded your reputation, and you will thank me one day."

Maile went downstairs, shocked by her vehemence, and wondered how she could continue to live in this country.

Getreidegasse was dimly lit and deserted except for Karl. He had on the dark suit he'd worn at the archbishop's palace. His hair and beard were trimmed.

She regarded him with surprise. "Where are you going?"

He shrugged. "I just wanted to check on you."

Not dressed like that, she thought. "You sent a note. I couldn't come, the buses were canceled. How did you get here?"

"Walk with me." He glanced at the door as it eased open to reveal a shadowy figure and the glint of an eye. "Salzburg is safe, at least for now. A pirate radio station reported no movement on the border." He took Maile's arm.

She fell in step with him, nervous about what he had in mind. They went through dark streets where low fog had left wet patches on cobblestones that shone slick and black. The few people they passed spoke in hushed voices, as if deals were being made. She looked for the marble wall with the flood line etched on it, the iron ring on the door to the wine cave, but Karl took a route with no reminders of their past.

They approached the river promenade and he said, "The university students need help from your consulate."

That's why the suit, she thought. "It's closed. We were told to leave, just hours ago."

"The consul is your friend." Karl explained that the network had to get two Czech writers across the border, a couple in their fifties who otherwise faced certain death for defying censorship.

"It's no use," she interrupted. "Mr. Casey offered to get me out in his own car. I refused."

"You're so eager to stay?" It wasn't quite a question and she felt that Karl knew how her life had changed since they last spoke. "If not the Americans," he said, now seeming distracted, "the Dutch are as good. Maybe better."

He walked on. She kept pace with him, worried that he would accuse her. Beyond Mozart Steg he stopped to study the opposite shore. Streetlamps along the promenade formed an orderly series of yellow spots, but in the villas upriver only a few lights burned. "You're right," he said, "the Americans are shut tight." A moment later, "The Dutchmen are still awake."

She sensed something pulling at him with such force that she knew he would go on, with or without her. They started across the footbridge where students had chanted and waved flags. His penciled message sent on that same day came to mind: You have my love. It seemed like a very long time ago. She hadn't said to him, I love you, and wanted to say it now.

When they reached the end of the bridge, Karl stopped under a streetlamp and faced her with an expression of stark intent. "The entire city knows you sang for von Wehlen," he said.

In the stillness of the summer night she could almost hear the dry, splintering sound of them breaking apart. Only a short time ago they had lived in a world dedicated to Mozart, Schubert, bound to each other by the mysteries and splendors of music. They had survived the misunderstandings that went with their crazily different backgrounds. Now the only thing they shared was truth, or nothing. He had found a higher goal than being on stage and would never perform again. She would, if the world held together for another twenty-four hours.

"Tomorrow I have a rehearsal at the Festival House," she said, "for a special concert on the Grand Stage."

Karl's eyes took on a liquid sheen of anger. "I did not believe you would audition. Now you are surely under contract. What was your excuse? Music is power is beauty? Like some slogan von Wehlen borrowed from the Reich?" He bit off each word. "The first time we talked, in the wine cave, and the last . . . Just because I do not go on about his past does not mean I tolerate it. I loved you, and I wanted success for you, but not like this."

She looked away, cut. "For you love is some perfect legend."

"Jann loved you too."

"You're just making up reasons to hurt me." Again she fastened her eyes on Karl.

Unexpectedly his expression softened, with memory, she thought, or longing, or mourning, and he leaned down to kiss her. Her wash of anger vanished at the touch of his lips. The kiss was full and strong, and she closed her eyes to make it last longer, but all at once he drew back so quickly she felt cool air on her tongue. His attitude was now hesitant, as if wanting something but unwilling to ask for it. He would go up to the border, she knew, unless she changed things for them, unless she said, *I love you, don't take that risk, think of your family, and of me.* Unless she said, *You're right, I can't work for von Wehlen, let's go back, start over.*

He turned away from her and the light cast by the streetlamp. She stepped toward him, still unable to speak. How far back did they have to go? Before the contest? Before Prague was invaded?

Indecision paralyzed her, and Karl continued walking down the empty promenade toward the one consulate with a window illuminated in yellow. Soon his black suit made him invisible except for the muted glow of his hair, the faint outlines of his hands. Farther along the riverbank he passed under another streetlamp, and another beyond that, each forming smaller and smaller circles of light until the last sign of him merged into the darkness. He was a spirit now, gone from this world, and she could not save him.

ON THE GRAND Stage, the exiled princess Aida sang of her lost homeland with passionate intensity, *O patria mia, mai piu, mai piu* . . . Offstage in the dark Maile listened for a gasped breath or a stretched note that could make beautiful feeling slide off pitch—the tiny slip that every singer feared, an omen of disaster for herself. The Italian text flowed easily through her mind, then it snagged on another scene that frightened her: years ago, a teacher setting a needle to a record for a classroom full of outer-island children who wanted to know why that lady was screaming.

But that was then, and now her peasant bride costume was laced tight, an embroidered bodice with a wide skirt and layers of petticoats, set off by a bridal crown of silver filigree. All she needed was double luck, triple. Behind her the blocking coach murmured that he would assist from the wings with hand signals. "Sshh!" she hissed. He backed away into the darkness.

The soprano's final phrases expanded, pouring from her in grief for the country she would never see again, *O blue skies, soft breezes, O perfumed shores* . . . The last note ended with a heart-stopping sense of urgency that gripped Maile. The audience was utterly silent. Backstage technicians stood motionless as the orchestra's closing chords spread outward in a benign wave of grandeur that bound every listener— music, the greatest expression of love.

Applause swept toward the stage with the hard sounds of a summer rainstorm pelting the river. Raucous shouts punctuated the ovation: *Ja, ja! Fantastisch!* The soprano exited, the curtain descended, and workers rolled hedges onstage for the duet from Don Giovanni.

Maile's partner stepped up beside her, a tall, warm presence in silk and brocade. "This audience is coarser than usual," he whispered. "Because of the current situation." He pulled a small gold crucifix from the neck of his doublet, kissed it, and tucked it back next to his skin.

She coveted each motion, wanting a similar amulet, the one she dared not wear, a small wooden locket on a velvet ribbon. But her pulse beat up and down her arms, tense with what she knew was the right kind of tension. After so many rehearsals of a safe piece, no one and nothing could steal her strength.

Applause shrank to random coughs, the faint rustle of programs as people tried to read in the dark. My name, she thought, mine mine mine.

The *Bühnenmeister* signaled with his flashlight. Don Giovanni led the way to the dark center stage and slipped behind a hedge. Maile positioned herself in front of it, feeling equally liable to float up from the floor in exaltation or crumple in terror, certain that she would triumph or die, or both. The curtain rose with a silent swoop. The auditorium looked as huge as a sports stadium. Lights burned down on her. Heat rolled up from the orchestra pit. The air felt horribly alive, two thousand five hundred people waiting, staring, demanding. On all sides of her gaped a silence that could only be brought to life by music.

From somewhere outside came a muffled thud, very loud—past the foyer, on the street, a large interfering sound that did not belong, like a loaded truck dropping from the sky, or a tank, or artillery. Maile didn't trust her ears. Every stage was full of spirits and invisible lights and noises no one else heard. In the last row she saw a tiny figure get up and step into the aisle. Two people seated in the center craned their necks to look back at the foyer, then they also got to their feet. An usher hurried toward them as they bumped their way to the end of the row, but they pushed past him and headed for a side exit. Other ushers rushed out to the foyer.

Maile now saw a half dozen people struggling toward the aisles in a spreading panic.

Behind her Don Giovanni said, "It's come."

Von Wehlen stood with his back to the audience, his baton at waist level. In the pit the timpanist on the top riser motioned urgently to him. Herr Maestro turned around. Ushers strode back into the auditorium from the foyer and exits, gesturing palms down at the audience: Sit, sit, nothing's wrong. Clusters of people continued shoving toward the aisles and the doors, elbowing each other, holding on to their hats, their voices rising.

"*Halt!*" von Wehlen shouted.

Heads jerked in his direction. The ushers and the audience froze. He crossed his arms, his baton erect in his right fist, and he stared out until silence had reclaimed the auditorium. With a faint nod he turned to face his orchestra once more.

People filed back to their seats. The ushers retreated up the aisles to their posts. Maile breathed out and felt her lungs deflate, her jaw clenched tight. In her mind she saw through the walls to the street, where a Soviet tank cannon was aimed at the glass entrance doors, and thirty feet ahead she saw the white line of a baton glide into a downbeat. The instruments responded with a prolonged sigh of melody.

"*La— ci da-rem...*" Don Giovanni sang, thin and shaky. Yet the tempo was exactly as rehearsed, and it grounded her, and by the end of the phrase his proposal was sweetly tempting: *Give me your hand.* She concentrated on a point inside her mouth—just back of the nose, upper palate, the place where all tone began—and eased in with her reply: *In truth, fine sir . . .*

From the first note she realized that she could actually perform while a conductor quietly stirred the music so it wound into her heart. Soprano and baritone passed the melody back and forth, pacing the seduction, creating a world of emotion for the delight of the audience. On cue she turned to her seducer. He toyed with the ribbons on her bridal crown. She leaned against his shoulder. They sang the lovely phrases that brought two people closer: *Will you?* and *Oh, yes,* then together, *Come, let us seek happiness.* Hand in hand they faced each other as the orchestra played out the trills that sealed their choice to be lovers.

As the last tones trailed off, the lights on both sides of Maile seemed to bulge and swirl. She couldn't feel her legs or feet. A searing wave of applause nearly knocked her backwards. She moved forward through glinting dust motes as thick as snow, gulped a breath, and her nose trembled with a sneeze. She puffed out her cheeks to suppress it and found herself on the edge of the orchestra pit beside her partner. The curtain came down behind them with a heavy draft that shivered her skirts. The clapping went on and on, peppered by rowdy cries that reminded her of the Red Horse. She noticed Don Giovanni acknowledging her, one arm extended in a courtier's gesture, giving her a full share of their success. Below in the pit she caught sight of von Wehlen, smiling, warm and indulgent. He motioned for her to curtsy.

She took hold of her skirt, right hand and left. The audience in the front rows became individual faces, and she looked from one to the next feeling helplessly grateful: her people, a mix of aristocrats and grocers and butchers. She strained to find Frau Metzger in the middle of the eleventh row, proud possessor of a von Wehlen ticket, what she'd held out for, a lifetime dream fulfilled. Two, four, six, eight, Maile counted, and in row nine saw a tall white-haired man, his expression anguished. She completed the bow but her energy collapsed into the memory of curtsying for him after the contest, joking and going off to drink champagne. Countess Almaviva, Countess Manoa. She bent forward in another deep bow, and the Grand Stage at the Grand Festival House closed around her, a dark cell with only the awful beating of her heart.

OFFSTAGE, MAILE COULDN'T reply to a security guard who asked where to find her for the final curtain. She let him lead her down a hall into a side room with comfortable chairs, where a woman served tea and the on-call doctor was summoned. After a few tactful questions they left her alone. She sat still, assailed by melodies cycling in her brain: *Sweet Leila—ni, Pa—nis ange-li-cus*, a sonorous cello solo.

Sometime later the guard returned to take her back for the last bow, the performers joining hands in a line to parade forward into a crushing atmosphere of heat, lights, and wild applause. Maile gestured to the audience like the others, right arm out in thanks or straight up in an Olympian's salute. She smiled with radiant generosity, as they did, and accepted a bouquet from assistants who came out bearing bundles of red roses. The cloud of fragrance made her even dizzier.

Backstage again, she plunged into a crowded hallway, thrust the roses at a wardrobe worker, and pushed on through union men and rehearsal coaches, secretaries, bodyguards, all exclaiming about Herr Maestro's victory. Panic could not stop him! What was that thud? *Ein kleines Boomlein.* Who cares?

A smiling, bright-cheeked dresser waited for Maile. She sent the woman away and yanked at the bodice lacings. Her pulse knocked against her ribs, one-two, one-two. She shook off the costume. The sound of her heartbeat changed, becoming fuller and deeper: *tok-tok.* She clamped both hands over her breasts as if the tones might escape into the room, the hall, the theater, an unnamed secret whispering itself to the world. A mirror reflected her image head to foot, naked except for a glittering bridal crown. She pulled it off and the sounds shivered down through her diaphragm into her hipbones, where they throbbed like a second heartbeat: *tok-tok, tok-tok.*

She turned on the shower and stepped under a steaming mist of liquid hot needles. Gasping, she drenched herself, shut off the taps and pulled on a robe. She answered knocks on the door, handing out costume pieces to workers from the headdress, garment, and shoe departments. Another knock and she grabbed up the heap of petticoats, flung them out, and slammed the door. Her wild pulse slowed. The only clothes left in the room belonged to her.

From a drawer she took out an evening purse with a long shoulder chain. The sound of a hand striking a gourd seemed to be waiting within her, a spirit ready to leap out like the dead calling to the living, a law without hope of appeal. Madame Renska had said, "You know nothing about European conductors." She recalled seeing von Wehlen for the first time in his grand car, a black-and-white newsreel racing through her mind, his stare meeting hers.

She slipped on her black beaded gown and sat down to arrange her hair. From the hallway came the thump of costumes being loaded onto rolling racks. Hangers zinged on the metal bars. D-sharp, she thought automatically, then doubted it, and the note swam away. Somewhere outside workers chanted, *"Hoch, hoch."* Lift, lift, the pitch as definite as if written on a score, low B-flat—but that wasn't right either. She tried to label every sound she heard, but each seemed higher or lower in a wavering world where nothing familiar made sense. A handful of hair-pins spilled to the floor with a pinging clatter of more notes she couldn't name. She kicked the pins aside and shoved open the window.

The warmth in the dressing room flowed into the night in a stream that felt strong enough to pull her out into the endless current of the sky. Everything was higher or lower than something else: the warehouse below, dressing rooms above; Professor Jann in the audience, she above him on the stage; the conductor above the orchestra and below the singers, controlling all the performers and listeners. In every great opera, passion fought with honor, and souls were lost or won. Yet life offstage was never that clear. Her purse held a roll of fifteen one-thousand-schilling notes. I will find you, he'd said. Somewhere in private, she was sure, because he valued discretion, and knew that she couldn't risk refusing to pay him.

From the dressing rooms Maile found her way to a private elevator that went down to the artists' reception on the main floor. The world changed again when she walked into the brilliantly lit foyer. Guests were lined up to speak with Othello, Aida, Don Giovanni. Waiters served trays of champagne flutes that glowed with a chilly golden blush. Bouquets of roses stood on pedestals. Everyone spoke rapidly in a mixture of congratulations and relief. She thought the lovely clothes, the jewelry, and the charm on display were like a visual reply to a long-ago question from a German teacher who had asked why students in Hawaii wanted to study his language and culture. Because it belonged to poets and philosophers, because it was elegant and uplifting.

Maile took her place last in the receiving line. The majority of the audience was outside, townspeople in their evening best, staring in through the floor-to-ceiling glass doors. No tanks behind them on the street, no frightened expressions.

"Fine work, Frau Manoa," an elderly man said to her in English, "most particularly for one who comes to us from so far away." She warmed with pleasure and shook his hand. He introduced her to somebody else, and one after another more guests came down the line to bestow their compliments: her singing was a model of Mozartian refinement; her stage presence revealed a beguiling manner. Their accumulating praise felt earned. Only six weeks ago, on opening night, she had been an onlooker in street clothes. Now she was not only inside but at home among the world's finest musicians, to whom a phrase in a duet mattered more than a car, house insurance, taxes, whatever concerned most other people most of the time.

A rustle of clapping spread from the head of the receiving line. Everyone faced the main hall, saying, *"Er ist's,"* and *"Jetzt kommt er."* Ladies and gentlemen plucked fresh champagne flutes from the trays of passing waiters.

Von Wehlen entered the foyer, his hands at his sides, his expression elated, regal. Guests raised their glasses in a cheer. The people outside pressed against the glass doors, shouting, *"Maestro, Herr Maestro!"* He glanced around slowly as the sound grew until it quivered against the ceiling, then he raised a hand in a precise motion that produced instant silence.

"Please," he said, "no toasts in my name. This success belongs to you, my supporters, and to my orchestra, although above all . . . to my singers."

He stepped over to the receiving line. His admirers receded in a flushed, respectful mood as he shook hands with the first soloist. Maile faced the guests so she wouldn't stare at him. Her thoughts focused on old questions: Who was Werner von Wehlen, apart from the Festival, apart from performances in Berlin and Vienna, apart from recordings and films? Why should it matter to someone from Honolulu?

He took his time with each performer. A particularly fine tribute was repeated softly by ladies and gentlemen in front, and passed on to those farther back. Maile watched him from the corner of an eye and felt the energy he emanated moving closer and closer. She tucked her purse under one arm, the other, then hung it from her left shoulder by its chain. He was three singers away. She kept her back straight, her eyes lowered. Two more singers. She saw only the motion of arms and hands, then just one pair of hands, his hands, and she understood that his *mana* was not in his head, mind, or heart, but in his conductor's hands. If she touched them, she would belong to him, and work with fabulous musicians in fabulous productions for the next thirty years. For the sake of music she would never speak of how the world's most famous conductor had climbed through the ranks, or the secret of his continuing wealth, or the silence maintained by an entire nation over so many years. She would never speak of her own past: Jann, Karl, Madame Renska, Makua, Auntie Lani. Evil was necessary in life, and good would come around again. Her choice was about *lōkahi*, balance.

Von Wehlen stepped in front of her. "Ah, my protégée," he said. She raised her head, and he extended his hand. "You proved yourself. I have a role for you this fall in Venice."

In her mind Maile heard another voice, from the realm of ancestors, Tūtū asking, "You still have three souls, or none?"

Inwardly she shivered and sensed a sickening blankness where her souls should have been. After coming so far, living so lean and working to exhaustion, the accusing question had caught up with her. It mattered all the way back to childhood, when the world was in balance from the highest level in the sky to the deepest place in the ocean, from the eastern to the western horizon. She could not simply respond to von Wehlen with a rank insult—Nazi, filthy penis—the man who had only given her what she craved. Around her the room went black. The heat of so many people was suffocating.

She kept her hands at her sides. "Herr Maestro, I cannot accept your offer." He tilted his head slightly, as if perplexed. The guests behind him fell silent. His expression didn't change. For a moment Maile thought she'd accidentally spoken to him in English, although he was fluent in four languages, including English. "Or your contract," she added.

He tucked his outstretched hand into his vest, gave her a demolishing glance, and stared at a point above her head. "Leave."

Guests peered around him. A trickle of whispering among those who were closest quickly intensified. Maile felt the air surge and stepped behind the receiving line, wild to get away, close to fainting.

"A toast to music," Don Giovanni called out. "A toast!" Someone handed him a glass and he raised it. "To music, to music!" the crowd repeated, but their words didn't cover the ferment of gossip as her name passed up the row of singers, the outrage confirmed by guests and murmured among waiters. By the time she got outside, people on the street said to each other, "That's her." Some gawked, most deliberately turned their backs. She had done the unthinkable, the inexcusable.

Her knees trembled and she sat down on the rim of a fountain. The stone was like a block of ice. It sent a jolt up her back and she clenched her fists to stop shaking. A couple in peasant clothes walked past, pointing at her. She wanted to cry, to sink into the water. The frigid marble made her thighs ache.

She strode off in a rush of humiliation, watched by remnants of the audience, Festival House guards, ushers and box office staff on their way home, townspeople, a rubbish collector. Gossip swept her into the streets of the Old City—*"Herr Maestro…"* "That woman…"—and moved ahead of her like mist blown by wind. The doorman at an elite hotel frowned when she stopped in front of it, breathless. Move along, no unescorted women allowed here.

With no sense of direction she went on until she saw nobody and nothing except the high sides of unlit buildings. Curving cobblestone paths warped away into darkness. At last she caught her breath, but still felt smothered. Above the rooftops the Fortress was a faint black mound against the dead, moonless sky. The height of it fascinated her, a place with fresh air.

She headed deeper into the dark city, walking hard, looking for the narrow road that led up to the castle though stone gateways that were always open. Outside Skolaren Kirche, something detached itself from a pillar, a glinting shadow. The Rosenkavalier danced toward her with mocking little steps, flipping his hands as if shooing flies. "Pariah, fool," he crowed. "You murdered your career!"

The sight of him numbed her. From his jacket he pulled out a key and waved it, imitating a baton. "This opens the door to the cathedral tower, my Mooress. Go on up. The leap from there will be quick and painless." The silver braid on his sleeve sketched a wild pattern in the dark.

All she wanted was her hands around his skinny neck. He leered and minced just out of reach. She dug into her souls for the worst curse she knew, and stood with her legs spread wide, and splayed her fingers. In a hideous quaver she chanted, *"O . . . 'oe . . . ka'u."* You . . . are . . . mine.

He lowered the key and stepped back. She swung her arms side to side and repeated, *"O . . . 'oe . . . ka'u,"* chopping each syllable. His expression changed from startled to confused to fearful. He raised a hand to cross himself, but his arm stiffened and stopped at his forehead. She laughed—the *Engelmacher* asking for God's help—and she clawed at him and arched her spine like a lizard goddess, claiming him piece by piece. *"O 'oe ka'u!"*

His shoulders trembled, his head, his torso. He leaped away from her, and his hat spun off and skidded over the cobblestones. He bent to snatch it up but fell on all fours, slipping, scrambling, pursued by fiends, a frantic figure that scrabbled off along a wall and vanished around a corner.

Once more she stood alone in a dark, deserted part of the city. The silence made her feel hollow, her curse nothing more than a fit of mindless rage. It hadn't changed anything. Only she had changed, beyond hope of forgiveness; she had given in to the wrong kind of enchantment, all for the sake of some grand ideal that was rotten at its core. Turning down von Wehlen didn't feel good or brave, just obvious and disappointing, like a child caught lying and having no way out except to admit, I did it. Now she had no future whatsoever. Nothing more to do tomorrow except pack—and then leave. His final word.

She retraced her steps, looking for landmarks that led back to Getreidegasse. Her chignon shifted and threatened to uncoil into tangled loops. Her beaded gown covered a heap of ashes in the shape of a woman who would dissolve with the slightest breeze. The lump of money in her purse was only a reminder of how close she'd come to being wrong for the rest of her life. Newspapers littered the street in front of a kiosk. She stepped over photos of tanks along the Danube and wondered if it was still possible to get across the border. The thought of leaving Salzburg felt like a wound opening up. Had the lie begun with staring at the von Wehlen posters before the Festival started? Seeing him in the flesh for the first time? Going to the interview? Pinning it down no longer seemed important. An hour ago she had sung perfectly. The greater soul of music that should have grown within her was not there.

At Getreidegasse Twenty-five she pushed her key into the lock. A man stepped from an adjacent passageway, reading a score in the light from a shop window. Professor Jann. Turn the key, she told herself, slip inside, shut the door—fast, clean, gone.

He offered her the score, his expression neutral. "The solos are difficult," he remarked. "The pay is negligible."

She never expected to hear his voice again. The buildings around her wavered as if the entire street had slid underwater. She took the score, an old library copy of Mozart's *C-minor Mass*. The title on the cover dissolved. She couldn't feel her breath or the movement of her lips, tongue, cheeks, palate, throat—her voice! The only thing she had left. Her eyes filled with tears.

"Betrayal does not have to be final," he said. "Betrayal also goes both ways."

She gripped the score and leaned into him, her forehead pressed to his chest, and she cried without understanding or caring, because there was nothing left of what they once shared and argued over and fought for. Nothing left of anyone else at the conservatory.

He remained silent, holding her lightly in his arms.

"I'm dead," she mumbled.

"My dear young woman." He lowered his hands. "You gave up a great deal, and it probably does not seem worth it. Not even philosophers have resolved the dilemma you encountered."

"I've ruined everything."

He regarded her with a look of pained consideration. "In one sense that is true. Gossip dies out in time, although as long as von Wehlen is alive, he will never allow you to sing at the Festival. Not under another conductor, and not as a substitute, however badly needed."

She held her breath in the awful realization that she had sacrificed far more than ever intended. Would she be allowed to perform in houses where von Wehlen did not conduct? Would she ever be invited to sing at the Met?

"No one owns music," Jann said. "This is glorious. Don't you see?"

She didn't. Why had she ever admired Mozart? Taken a single voice lesson? Gone so far to end up with nothing?

Jann took the score from her, paged through it, and handed it back.

She looked at notes that unfolded in a familiar pattern, a melody line and supporting clusters of chords. *Et incarnatus est.* And the divine became human. The ageless gift, the spiritual resonance of music based on selfless love. In the past when life offered only misery, this same piece had spoken to her spirits with such grace and purity that it went beyond church or opera toward some higher goal. For the first time she knew what it was: the quality of mercy, the promise of forgiveness.

About the author

Originally from Hawaii, Waimea Williams spent a decade in Austria and Germany as an opera singer and has received fiction awards from Glimmer Train, The Lorian Hemmingway Competition, and *Salamander Review*. She has enjoyed the honor of a writing residency at the Ragdale Foundation, and her short story "Vienna Quartet with Dog" received First Prize from the *Chariton Review* in 2012. She currently lives near Honolulu.